Titles by LaVyrle Spencer

Years

LaVyrle Spencer

B

BERKLEY BOOKS, NEW YORK

THE BERKLEY PUBLISHING GROUP
Published by the Penguin Group
Penguin Group (USA) LLC
375 Hudson Street, New York, New York 10014

USA • Canada • UK • Ireland • Australia • New Zealand • India • South Africa • China

penguin.com

A Penguin Random House Company

Copyright © 1986 by LaVyrle Spencer.
Penguin supports copyright. Copyright fuels creativity, encourages diverse voices,
promotes free speech, and creates a vibrant culture. Thank you for buying an authorized
edition of this book and for complying with copyright laws by not reproducing, scanning,
or distributing any part of it in any form without permission. You are supporting writers
and allowing Penguin to continue to publish books for every reader.

BERKLEY® is a registered trademark of Penguin Group (USA) LLC.
The "B" design is a trademark of Penguin Group (USA) LLC.

Berkley trade paperback ISBN: 978-0-425-26314-3

PUBLISHING HISTORY
Jove mass-market edition / March 1986
First Berkley trade paperback edition / August 2003
Second Berkley trade paperback edition / December 2013

PRINTED IN THE UNITED STATES OF AMERICA

10   9   8   7   6   5   4   3   2   1

Cover art by Jim Griffin.
Cover design by Diana Kolsky.

*This book is dedicated with love
to all my readers,
to the many I've met
and the many more I haven't,
but especially to those
whose faithful letters
just keep coming.*

*A special thank-you to
Arvid Gafkjen and Meredith Sogard Gafkjen,
whose memories of Alamo, North Dakota,
inspired this book.*

Years

1917

LINNEA BRANDONBERG WAS neither asleep nor awake, but in a whimsical state of fantasy, induced—this time—by the rhythmic clatter rising through the floor of the train. Her feet rested primly together and often she glanced down to admire the most beautiful shoes she'd ever seen—congress shoes, they were called—with shiny, pointed patent leather toes giving way to smooth black kid uppers that hugged not only her foot but a good six inches of ankle as well. Miraculously, they had no buttons or ties, but slipped on tightly with a deep gusset of stiff elastic running from mid-shin to below the ankle bone on either side. But best of all they were the first shoes she'd ever owned with high heels. Though the heels added scarcely an inch to her height, they added years to her maturity.

She hoped.

He would be there at the station when she arrived, a dashing superintendent of schools who drove a fancy Stanhope carriage for two, drawn by a glossy blood-bay trotter. . . .

"Miss Brandonberg?" His voice was rich and cultured, and a dazzling smile broke upon his handsome face as he removed a beaver top hat, revealing hair the color of rye at sunset.

"Mr. Dahl?"

"*At your service. We're all so delighted you're here at last. Oh, please allow me—I'll take that valise!*" As he stowed the suitcase in the boot of the carriage she noticed the sleek fit of his black suit coat across nicely shaped shoulders, and when he turned to help her into the buggy, she noted the fact that his celluloid collar was brand new, stiff and tight for the occasion. "*Careful now.*" He had marvelous hands, with long pale fingers that solicitously closed over her own as he handed her up.

A reed-thin whip clicked above the trotter's head, and they sped away, with his elbow lightly bumping hers.

"*Miss Brandonberg, to your left you'll note the opera house, our newest establishment, and at the first opportunity I hope we can attend a performance together.*"

"*An opera house!*" she gasped in ladylike surprise while delicately steepling five fingers over her heart. "*Why, I didn't expect an opera house!*"

"*A young lady with your looks will put the actresses to shame.*" His smile seemed to dim the sun as he approvingly scanned her narrow shoes, her new wool serge suit, and the first hat she'd ever owned without a childish wide brim. "*I hope you won't think me too bold if I say that you have a definite flair for clothes, Miss Brandonberg. . . .*"

"Miss Brandonberg?" The voice in her fantasy faded as she was roused by the conductor, who was leaning across the empty aisle seat to touch her shoulder. "Next stop Alamo, North Dakota." She straightened and offered the older man a smile.

"Oh, thank you!"

He touched the brim of his blue cap and nodded before moving away.

Outside, the prairie rolled by, flat and endless. She peered out the window but saw no sign of the town. The train lost speed as its whistle sounded, then sighed into silence, leaving only the *clackety-clack* of the wheels upon shifting steel seams.

Her heart thumped expectantly, and this time, when she placed a hand over it, there was no pretending. She would see it soon, the place that had been only a word on the map; she would meet them soon, the people who would become part of her daily life as students, friends, perhaps even confidantes. Each new face she'd meet would be that of a total stranger, and for the hundredth time she wished she knew just one person in Alamo. Just one.

There's nothing to be frightened of. It's only last-minute nervousness.

She ran a hand up the back of her neck, checking the hairstyle she wasn't yet adept at forming. Within the crescent-shaped coil around her head, the rat seemed to have slipped loose. With shaky fingers she tightened several hairpins, then checked her hatpin, smoothed her skirt, and glanced at her shoes for a last dose of confidence just as the train huffed out a final weary breath and shuddered to a halt.

Dear me, where is the town?

Lugging her suitcase down the aisle, she glanced through the windows, but all she could see was the standard small-town depot—a wood-frame building painted the color of a rutabaga with six-over-six windows flanking a center door that faced a waiting platform whose roof was held up by four square posts.

She eyed it again as she emerged from the dusky depths of the passenger car into the bright September sun, the metal steps chiming beneath her smart new heels.

She glanced around for someone who might look like a superintendent of schools and quelled her dismay upon discovering only one person in sight, a man standing in the shade of the depot porch. But judging from his mode of dress, he was not the man she sought. Still, he might turn out to be a parent of one of her students: she flashed him a quick smile. But he remained as before, with his hands inside the bib of his striped overalls and a sweat-stained straw hat shielding his eyes.

Forcing a confident air, she crossed the platform and went inside, but found only the ticket agent, busily clicking the telegraph behind his caged window.

"Excuse me, sir?"

He turned, pushed a green celluloid visor higher on his head, and smiled. "Yes, miss?"

"I am to meet Mr. Frederic Dahl here. Do you know him?"

"Know who he is. Haven't seen him around here. But have a seat—he'll probably show up soon."

Her stomach began to tighten. *What shall I do now?*

Too nervous to sit still, she decided to wait outside. She took up her station on the opposite side of the veranda from the farmer, set her valise down, and waited.

Minutes passed and no one came. She glanced at the stranger, caught him studying her, then self-consciously snapped her attention to the train. It huffed and hissed, spit out funnels of steam with each breath, but seemed to be taking an inordinate amount of time to be on its way again.

She chanced a peek at the man again, but the moment her eyes turned his way, his quickly darted toward the door of the train.

Theodore Westgaard studied the train steps, waiting for the new teacher to emerge, but a full three minutes ticked by and the only person to alight was the thin young girl playing grown-up in her mother's hat and shoes. His eyes were drawn to her a second time, but again she looked his way and self-consciously he shifted his attention toward the door of the train.

Come on, Brandonberg, let's get going. I've got harvesting to do.

From a pocket on his bib he withdrew a watch, checked the time, and shifted his feet impatiently. The girl glanced his way again, but their eyes barely met before her attention skittered down the train track as she crossed her wrists beneath a folded coat she was holding.

He studied her covertly.

Sixteen or so, he'd guess, scared of her own shadow and hoping nobody could tell. A cute little thing, though that hat with the bird wings looked ridiculous and she should still be in pigtails and flat-heeled shoes.

To Westgaard's surprise, before anyone else got off the train, the conductor picked up his portable step, stowed it inside the car, and waved an arm at the engineer. The couplings started clanging down the length of the train and it slowly groaned to life, then rumbled away, leaving a magnified silence broken only by the buzzing of a fly about the girl's nose.

She flapped a hand at it and pretended Westgaard wasn't there while he grew irascible at having made the trip to town for nothing. He took off his hat, scratched his head, then settled the brim low over his eyes while cursing silently.

City boy. Got no idea how a wheat man values every hour of daylight this time of year.

Angrily he stomped inside.

"Cleavon, if that young whelp comes in on the next train, tell him . . . aw, hell, forget it. I guess I'll just have to wait for it myself." Alamo offered no livery stable, no horses to rent. How else would the new teacher get out to the farm when he finally got here?

When Theodore clomped out the door again the girl was facing him with stiff shoulders and a frightened expression on her face. Her hands still clutched the coat, and she opened her mouth as if to speak, then closed it again, swallowed, and turned away.

Though he wasn't one to speak to strange girls, she looked all bird-eyed and about to break into tears, so he stopped and inquired, "Somebody supposed to meet you?"

She turned back to him almost desperately. "Yes, but it seems he's been detained."

"Ya, same with the fellow I was here to meet, name of L.I. Brandonberg."

"Oh, thank heavens," she breathed, her face suddenly rekindling a smile. "I'm Miss Brandonberg."

"You!" Her smile was met with a scowl. "But you can't be! L.I. Brandonberg is a man!"

"He is not . . . I mean, *I* am not." She laughed nervously, then remembered her manners and extended a hand. "My name is Linnea Irene Brandonberg, and as you can see, I most certainly am a woman."

At that his eyes made a quick pass over her hat and hair, and he gave a disdainful snort.

She felt the blood rush to her face, but stubbornly kept her hand extended, inquiring, "And whom do I have the pleasure of addressing?"

He ignored her hand and answered rudely, "The name's Westgaard and I ain't havin' no . . . *woman* livin' in my house! Our school board hired L.I. Brandonberg, thinkin' he was a man."

So this was Theodore Westgaard, at whose home she was to board and room. Disheartened, she dropped the hand he still ignored. "I'm sorry you were under that impression, Mr.

Westgaard, but I assure you I didn't mean to deceive you."

"Hmph! What kind of female goes around callin' herself L.I.!"

"Is there a law against women using their initials as part of their legal signature?" she asked crisply.

"No, but there should be! Little city girl like you, probably guessed the school board would rather have a man and set out to deliberately hoodwink them."

"I did nothing of the kind! I sign all—"

But he cut her off rudely. "Teaching school out here's more than just scratchin' numbers on a slate, missy! It's a mile's walk, and buildin' fires and shovelin' snow. And the winters out here are tough! I don't have time to hitch up no team and haul a little hothouse pansy to school when it's thirty below and the snow's howlin' out of the northwest!"

"I won't ask you to!" She was enraged now, her face sour with dislike. How dare they send a garrulous old man like this to greet her! "And I'm not a hothouse pansy!"

"Oh, you ain't, huh?"

He eyed her assessingly, wondering how long a little thing like her would last when an Alaskan northwesterly smacked her in the face and the snow stung so hard you couldn't tell cold from hot on your own forehead. "Wall"—he drew the word out in a gruff note of disapproval—"the fact remains: I don't want no *woman* livin' at my house."

He could say the word *woman* the way a cowpoke said *sidewinder*.

"Then I'll board with someone else."

"And just who might that be?"

"I . . . I don't know, but I'll speak to Mr. Dahl about it."

He gave a grumpy, disdainful *hmph* that made her want to poke sticks up his nose. "Ain't nobody else. We've always had the teachers livin' with us. That's just the way it is— cause we're closest to school. Only one closer's my brother John, and he's a bachelor, so his place is out."

"And so what do you propose to do with me, Mr. Westgaard? Leave me standing on the depot steps?"

His mouth pinched up like a dried berry and his brows furrowed in stern reproof as he stared at her from beneath the brim of his straw hat.

"I ain't havin' no woman livin' under my roof," he vowed again, crossing his arms stubbornly.

"Perhaps not, but if not yours, you'd best transport me to someone less bigoted than yourself under whose roof I will be more than happy to reside, unless you want a lawsuit brought upon you." Now, where in the world had that come from? She wouldn't know the first thing about bringing a lawsuit upon anybody, but she had to think of some way to put this uncouth ox in his place!

"A lawsuit!" Westgaard's arms came uncrossed. He hadn't missed the word *bigoted*, but the little snip was throwing threats and names out so fast he had to address them one at a time.

Linnea squared her shoulders and tried to make him think she was worldly and bold. "I have a contract, Mr. Westgaard, and in it is stated that room and board are included as part of my annual salary. Furthermore, my father is an attorney in Fargo, thus my legal fees would be extraordinarily reasonable should I decide to sue the Alamo school board for breach of contract, and name you as a—"

"All right, all right!" He held up two big, horny palms in the air. "You can stop yappin', missy. I'll dump you on Oscar Knutson and he can do what he wants to with y'. He wants to be head of the school board, so let 'im earn his money!"

"My name is Miss Brandonberg, not *missy!*" She gave her skirt a little flip in exasperation.

"Yeah, a fine time to tell me." He turned away toward a waiting horse and wagon, leaving her to grouse silently. *Dump me on Oscar Knutson, indeed!*

Reality continued to make a mockery of her romanticized daydreams. There was no fancy-rigged Stanhope carriage, no glossy blood-bay trotter. Instead, Westgaard led her to a double-box farm wagon hitched behind a pair of thick-muscled horses of questionable ancestry, and he clambered up without offering a hand, leaving her little choice but to stow her grip in the back by herself, then lift her skirts and struggle to the shoulder-high leaf-sprung seat unaided.

And as for gentlemen in beaver hats—ha! This rude oaf wouldn't know what to do with a beaver top hat if it jumped up and bit him on his oversized sunburned nose! The nerve of the man to treat her as if she were . . . as if she were . . .

dispensable! She, with a hard-earned teacher's certificate from the Fargo Normal School! She, a woman of high education while he could scarcely put one word before another without sounding like an uneducated jackass!

Linnea's disillusionment continued as he flicked the reins and ordered, "Giddap." The cumbersome-looking horses took them through one of the saddest little bergs she'd ever seen in her life. Opera house? Had she really fantasized about an opera house? It appeared the most cultural establishment in town was the general store/post office, which undoubtedly brought *culture* to Alamo by means of the Sears Roebuck catalogue.

The most impressive buildings in town were the grain elevators beside the railroad tracks. The others were all false-fronted little cubicles, and there were few of them at that. She counted two implement dealers, two bars, one restaurant, the general store, a hotel, a bank, and a combination drug and barber shop.

Her heart sank.

Westgaard glared straight ahead, holding the reins in hands whose fingers were the size of Polish sausages, with skin that looked like that of an old Indian—so different from the long, pale fingers of her imagination.

He didn't look at her, and she didn't look at him.

But she saw those tough brown hands.

And he saw her high-heeled shoes.

And she sensed how he hunched forward and glared from under that horrible-looking hat.

And he sensed how she sat like a pikestaff and stared all persnickitylike from under those ridiculous bird wings.

And she thought it was too bad that when people got old they had to get so crotchety.

And he thought how silly people were when they were young—always trying their best to make themselves look older.

And neither of them said a word.

They drove several miles west, then turned south, and the land looked all the same: flat, gold, and waving. Except where the threshers had already been. There it was flat, gold, and still.

When they'd been traveling for half an hour, Westgaard

pulled into a farmyard that looked identical to every other one they'd passed—weather-beaten clapboard house with a cottonwood windbreak on the west, the trees only half-grown and tipping slightly south by southwest; a barn looking better kept than the house; rectangular granaries; hexagonal silos; and the only friendly looking feature reigning over all: the slow-whirling, softly sighing windmill.

A woman came to the door, tucking a strand of hair into the bun at the back of her head. She raised one hand in greeting and smiled broadly.

"Theodore!" she called, coming down two wooden steps and crossing the patch of grass that looked as golden as the fields surrounding them. "Hello! Who do you have here? I thought you had gone to town to get the new schoolteacher."

"This is him, Hilda. And he's wearin' high-heeled shoes and a hat with bird wings on it."

Linnea bristled. How dare he make fun of her clothes!

Hilda stopped beside the wagon and frowned up at Westgaard, then at Linnea. "This is him?" She shaded her eyes with one hand and took a second look. Then she flapped both palms, pulled her chin back, and smiled as if with scolding humor. "Oh, Theodore, you play a joke on us, huh?"

Westgaard jabbed a thumb at his passenger. "No, she's the one who played a joke on us. She's L.I. Brandonberg."

Before Hilda Knutson could respond, Linnea leaned over and extended a hand, incensed afresh by Westgaard's rudeness in failing to introduce her properly. "How do you do. I'm Linnea Irene Brandonberg."

The woman took her hand as if not actually realizing what she was doing. "A woman," she said, awestruck. "Oscar hired us a woman."

Beside her Westgaard made a throaty sound of ridicule. "I think what Oscar hired us is a girl dressed up in her mother's clothes, pretending to be a woman. And she ain't stayin' at my house."

Hilda's face sobered. "Why, Theodore, you always kept the teachers. Who else is gonna keep her?"

"I don't know, but it ain't gonna be me. That's what I come to talk to Oscar about. Where is he?" Westgaard's eyes scanned the horizon.

"I don't know exactly. He started with the west rye this mornin', but it's hard to tell where he is by now. You might see him from the road if you head on out that way though."

"I'll do that, but I'm leavin' her here. She ain't comin' to my house, so she might's well stay here with you till you find someplace else for her."

"Here!" Hilda pressed both hands to her chest. "But I got no spare rooms, you know that. Wouldn't be right stuffing the teacher in with the kids. You take her, Theodore."

"Nosirree, Hilda. I ain't havin' no woman in my house."

Linnea was incensed. The nerve of them, treating her as if she were the chamber pot nobody wanted to carry out back.

"Stop!" she shouted, closing her eyes while lifting both palms like a corner policeman. "Take me back to town. If I'm not wanted here, I'll be more than happy to take the next tr—"

"I can't do that!"

"Now see what you've done, Theodore. You've hurt her feelings."

"Me! Oscar hired her! Oscar's the one who told us she was a man!"

"Well, then go talk to Oscar!" She threw up her hands in disgust, then, belatedly remembering her manners, shook hands with Linnea again and patted the girl's knuckles. "Don't pay no attention to Theodore here. He'll find a place for you. He's just upset cause he's wastin' time out of the fields when all that wheat is ripe out there. Now, Theodore," she ordered, turning toward the house, "you take care of this young one like you agreed to!"

And with that she hustled back inside.

Defeated, Westgaard could only set out in search of Oscar with his unwanted charge beside him.

Like most Dakota farms, Knutson's was immense. Traveling down the gravel road, they scanned the horizon over his wheat, oat, and rye fields, but there was no sign of his team and mower crossing and recrossing the fields. Westgaard sat straight, frowning across the ocean of gold, peering intently for some sign of movement on the faraway brow of the earth, but the only thing moving was the grain itself and a flock of yapping blackbirds that flew overhead in ever-changing patterns before landing somewhere in the oats to glut themselves. The wagon came abreast of a shorn field, its yield lying in heavy plaits stretching as far as the eye could see. Drying in the sun, the grain gave up its sweet redolence to the sparkling air. With a subtle shift of the reins, Westgaard turned the horses off the gravel road along a rough grassy track leading between the cut field and another on their right whose grain was still straight and high. The track was bumpy, created chiefly for access to the fields. When the wagon suddenly lurched, Linnea grabbed her towering hat as it threatened to topple from its perch.

Westgaard angled her a silent glance, and for a moment one corner of his mouth tipped up. But her chin was lowered as she busily reset the hatpin to hold the infernal nuisance on.

They rocked and bumped their way up the track to a slight rise in the land. Reaching it, Westgaard intoned, "Whoa."

Obediently, the horses stopped, leaving the riders to sit staring at an eternity of Oscar Knutson's cut rye, with no Oscar in sight.

Westgaard held the reins in one hand, removed his hat and scratched his head with the other, mumbled something under his breath, then settled the hat back on with a disgruntled tug.

This time it was Linnea's turn to smile. *Good enough for him, the rude thing! He agreed to keep me, now he can put up with me, whether he likes it or not.*

"You'll have to come to my place till I can get this straightened out," Westgaard lamented, flicking the reins and turning the horses in the rye stubble.

"So I shall."

He gave her a sharp, quelling glance, but she sat stiff and prim on the wagon seat, looking straight ahead.

But her ridiculous hat was slightly crooked.

Theodore smiled to himself.

They set off again, heading south, then west. Everywhere was the sound of the dry, sibilant grain. The heavy heads of each stalk lifted toward the heavens only momentarily before bending low beneath their own weight.

Linnea and Theodore spoke only three times. They had been

traveling for nearly an hour when Linnea asked, "How far from Alamo do you live, Mr. Westgaard?"

"Twelve miles," he answered.

Then all was still but for the birds and grain and the steady beat of the horses' hooves. Three times they saw mowing machines crawling along in the distance, pulled by horses who appeared minuscule from so far away, their heads nodding as they leaned into their labor.

She broke the silence again when a small once-white building with a belfry appeared on their right. Her eager eyes took in as many details as she could—the long narrow windows, the concrete steps, the flat yard with a grove of cottonwoods at its edge, the pump. But Westgaard kept the team moving with the same unbroken walk, and she gripped the side of the wagon seat and craned around as the building receded too fast for her to take in all that she wanted to. She whirled to face him, demanding, "Is that the schoolhouse?"

Without turning his eyes from the horses' ears, he grunted, "Yeah."

Ornery, pig-headed cuss! She bunched her fists in her lap and seethed.

"Well, you could have told me!"

He rolled his eyes in her direction. His mouth twisted in a sardonic smirk as he drawled, "I ain't no tour guide."

Anger boiled close to eruption, but she clapped her mouth shut and kept her rebuffs to herself.

They rode on a little farther down the road, and as they passed a nondescript farm on their left, Theodore decided to rankle her just a little more. "This here's my brother John's place."

"How wonderful," she replied sarcastically, then refused to look at it.

Less than ten minutes from the school building they entered a long, curving driveway of what she supposed was Westgaard's place—not that he bothered to verify it. It was sheltered on its north side by a long windbreak of box elder trees and a parallel row of thick caragana bushes that formed an unbroken wall of green. As they rounded the windbreak, the farmyard came into view. The house sat to the left in the loop of the driveway. All the outbuildings were to the right, with a windmill and water tank situated between a huge weather-beaten barn and a cluster of other buildings she took to be granaries and chicken coops.

The wood-frame house was two stories high, and absolutely unadorned, like all they'd passed on their way from town. It appeared to have been painted white at one time, but was now the color of ashes, with only a flake of white appearing here and there as a reminder of better days. It had no porch or lean-to to relieve its boxlike appearance, and no overhanging eave to shade its windows from the prairie sun. The center door was flanked by long narrow windows giving it the symmetrical appearance of a face gaping at the vast fields of wheat surrounding it.

"Well, this is it," Westgaard announced in his own good time, leaning forward to tie the reins around the brake handle of the wagon. Bracing his hands on the seat and footboard, he vaulted over the side and would have left her to do the same, but at that moment an imperious voice shouted from the door of the house, "Teddy! Where are your manners! You help that young woman down!"

Teddy? thought Linnea, amused. *Teddy?*

A miniature whirlwind of a woman came hustling down the footpath from the kitchen door, her frizzy gray hair knotted at her nape, a pair of oval wire-rimmed glasses hooked behind her ears. She shook a finger scoldingly.

Theodore Westgaard made a dutiful about-face in the middle of the path and returned to the wagon to reach up a helping hand, but the expression on his face was martyred.

Placing her hand in his and leaping down, Linnea couldn't resist mocking sweetly, "Oh, thank you, Mr. Westgaard, you're too kind."

He dropped her hand immediately as they were joined by the bustling woman who made Linnea—only a little over five feet tall—feel like a giant. She had a nose no bigger than a thimble, faded brown eyes that seemed to miss nothing, and lips as straight and narrow as a willow leaf. She walked with her fuzzy knob of a chin thrust forward, arms swinging almost forcefully. Though her back was slightly bowed, she still managed to give the appearance of one leaning into each step with great urgency. What the woman lacked in stature, she made up for in energy. The minute she opened her mouth, Linnea realized she wasn't one to mince words. "So this is the new schoolteacher. Don't look like no man to me!" She took Linnea by both arms, held her in place while giving her a thorough inspection from hem to hat, and nodded once. "She'll do." The woman spun on Westgaard, demanding, "What happened to the fella?"

"She's him," Westgaard answered tersely.

The woman let out a squawk of laughter and concluded, "Well, I'll be switched." Then sobering abruptly, she thrust out her hand and pumped Linnea's. "Just what this place needs. Never mind that son of mine I should've taught more manners. Since he didn't bother to introduce us, I'm his ma, Mrs. Westgaard. You can call me Nissa."

Her hand was all bones, but strong. "I'm Linnea Brandonberg. You can call me Linnea."

"So, *Lin-nay-uh.*" She gave it an old country sound. "A good Norwegian name."

They smiled at each other, but not for long. It was becoming apparent Nissa Westgaard never did anything for long. She moved like a sparrow, each new action abrupt and economical. "Come on in." She bustled up the path, yelping at her son, "Well, don't just stand there, Teddy, get her things!"

"She ain't stayin'."

Linnea rolled her eyes toward heaven and thought, here we go again! But she was in for a surprise. Nissa Westgaard spun around and cuffed her son on the side of the neck with amazing force. "What you mean, she ain't stayin'? She's stayin' all right, so you can just get them ideas out of your head. I know what you're thinkin', but this little gal is the new schoolteacher, and you better start watchin' your manners around her or you'll be cookin' your own meals and washin' your own duds around here! I can always go and live with John, you know!"

Linnea covered her mouth with a hand to hide the smile. It was like watching a banty rooster take on a bear. The top of Nissa's head reached no higher than her son's armpit, but when she lambasted him, he didn't talk back. His face turned beet red and his jaw bulged. But before Linnea was allowed to watch any more of his discomfiture, the banty whirled around, grabbed her by an arm, and pulled her up the path. "Bullheaded, ornery thing!" she mumbled. "Lived too long without havin' no woman around. Made him unfit for human company."

It came to Linnea to say, "I couldn't agree more," but she wisely bit her tongue. It also occurred to Linnea that Nissa was a woman. But obviously, in these parts having a "woman" in the house did not mean living with your mother.

Nissa pushed Linnea through the open back door into a kitchen that smelled of vinegar. "It ain't much, but it's warm and dry, and with only three of us Westgaards livin' here, you'll have a room of your own, which is more than you'd have anyplace else around here."

Linnea turned in surprise. "Three of you?"

"Didn't he tell you about Kristian?"

Feeling a little disoriented from the woman's ceaseless speed and authoritative tone, Linnea only shook her head.

"What's the matter with that man! Kristian's his boy, my grandson. He's off cutting wheat. He'll be in at suppertime."

Linnea looked around for the missing link—the wife, the mother—but it appeared there was none. It also appeared she was not going to be told why.

"This here's the kitchen. You've got to excuse the mess. I been puttin' up watermelon pickles." On a huge round oak pedestal table fruit jars stood in rank and file, but Linnea scarcely had a chance to glimpse them before Nissa moved on through the room to another. "This is the front room. I sleep there." She pointed to one doorway leading off it. "And that's Teddy's room. You and Kristian are upstairs."

She led the way into the kitchen, and as they breezed through it to the doorway leading up, Linnea caught a glimpse of Theodore coming in with her suitcase. She turned her back on him and followed Nissa up a steep, narrow stairwell to the second floor. At the top was a cramped landing with matched double-cross doors leading both left and right. Her room was the one on the right.

Nissa opened the door and led the way inside.

It was the crudest room Linnea had ever seen. Nothing was pushed flush against the wall, for there were no walls, only the sharply pitched roof angling from its center ridgepole to the outer edges of the room. From underneath, the joists and beams and sub-roof were plainly visible, for the ceiling was neither plastered nor wainscoted. The only upright walls were the two triangular ones at either end of the room. But they, like the ceiling, were unfinished. Opposite the door, facing east, was a small four-paned window with white lace curtains tied back to the raw wood frame. Now, in late afternoon, the light coming through the panes was negligible, but from across the tiny landing the afternoon sun streamed through a matching window, warming Linnea's room slightly.

The floor was covered with linoleum bearing a design of large pink cabbage roses on a dark-green background. It did not quite reach the edges of the room, leaving a border of wide, unfinished floor planks exposed. To the right of the door, crowded beneath the roof-angle, was a single bed with a white-painted iron frame, covered with a chenille bedspread of bright rose. Across its foot lay a folded patchwork quilt and on the linoleum beside it a homemade rag rug tied with green warp. Beside the bed, on a square table with turned legs, a kerosene lantern was centered upon a white crocheted doily. Pushed against the opposite roof-angle was a chest-high dresser draped with an embroidered dresser scarf of snowy white cotton edged with crocheted lace. In the corner left of the door, the wide black stovepipe came up from the kitchen below and continued out to the roof. Across the way, beside the window, was a low stand holding a pitcher and bowl, with a door underneath that undoubtedly concealed the "nighttime facilities." On the wall beside the washstand hung a mirror in a tin frame with an attached bar holding a length of white huck toweling. Next to the tiny window was an enormous oak rocker with green and pink calico cushions on its seat and back.

Linnea's eyes moved from it to the rugged beams overhead, and she stifled her disappointment. Her own room at home was decorated with floral wallpaper and had two large windows facing two different directions. Every other spring her daddy gave the woodwork a fresh coat of ivory paint, and the oak floorboards were kept varnished until they shone. At home a large grate blew a steady stream of heat from the coal furnace, and down the hall was a newly installed bathroom with running water.

She looked at this raw-beamed, dark attic and searched for some comparison that would find it desirable. She glanced at the snowy-white dresser scarf and doily that were obviously starched and ironed with great meticulousness, at the hand-loomed and tied rug, at the linoleum that looked as if it had just been added for the new teacher, while beside her Nissa waited for some sign of approval.

"It's . . . it's so big!"

"Ya, big all right, but you'll be bumpin' your head on these rafters anyway."

"It's far bigger than my room at home, and I had to share that with my two sisters." *If ever you wanted to be an actress, Linnea, this is the time.* Disguising her disappointment, she crossed the room, looking back over her shoulder. "Do you mind if I try this out?" Nissa crossed her hands over her stomach and looked pleased as Linnea sat on the padded chair and rocked widely, throwing her feet in the air. For added effect, she gave a little laugh, massaged the curved arms of the chair, and said truthfully enough, "At home, with three of us in one room, there wasn't any space left over for rocking chairs." She tilted her chin up to look back at the miniature window, as if overjoyed. "I won't know what to do with all this privacy!" And she flung her arms wide.

By the time they headed downstairs again, Nissa was beaming with pride.

The kitchen was empty, but Theodore had left her suitcase by the door. Glancing at it, Linnea felt disappointment well afresh. He hadn't even the courtesy to offer to take it upstairs for her, as any gentleman would.

Nissa thoughtfully offered, but Linnea felt suddenly deflated by her dubious welcome into this home.

"Nissa, I don't want to cause friction between you and your son. It might be better if—"

"Nonsense, girl! You leave my son to me!" And she would have taken the bag upstairs herself if Linnea hadn't quickly done so.

Alone for the first time in the room under the rafters, she set the suitcase on the rag rug and dropped disconsolately onto the bed. Her throat constricted and her eyes suddenly stung.

He's only one man. Only one crabby, bitter old man. I'm

*a qualified teacher, and an entire school board has approved
me. Shouldn't that mean more than his bigoted opinion?*

But it hurt.

She'd had such dreams of how it would be when she got
here: the open smiles, the welcoming handshakes, the respect—
ah, that she wanted most, for at age eighteen she felt she had
truly earned the right to be honored not only as a teacher but
as an adult. Now here she sat, blubbering like an idiot because
the welcome she'd received hadn't matched her expectations.
Well, that's what you get for letting yourself be carried away
with all your silly imagining. Tears blurred the outline of her
suitcase and the cabbage roses and the homemade rag rug.

You had to spoil it, didn't you, Theodore Westgaard?

But I'll show you.

I'll show you!

2

THE LITTLE MISSY was still upstairs when Theodore stalked out of the house and headed back for the fields. Women! he thought. The only thing worse than having one of them around was having a pair. And what a pair he had now!

He was infuriated by the way his mother had treated him in front of the girl, but what choice did he have except to stand there and take it? And how much longer would he have to put up with her bossing him around? His face burned yet with embarrassment.

She didn't have no right to humiliate him that way! He was a full-grown man, thirty-four years old. And as for her old threat about moving in with John—he wished to high heaven she would!

But at John's house there'd be nobody to butt heads with, and she knew it.

Still disgruntled, Theodore reached the place where two figures, guiding two teams, could be seen in the distance, mowing wheat. He paused and waited at the end of a windrow. There was a measure of ease to be found in watching John and Kristian change the profile of the field. The whirling blades of the sickles sliced away at the thick stand of grain, which appeared burnished gold on top, tarnished along its hewn edge. They cut parallel swaths, with John's rig slightly in the lead,

Kristian's close behind, forming a steplike pattern on the edge of the grain as they crept along at a steady, relentless pace.

In time the pair became dots on the horizon, then swung about, returning in Theodore's direction, growing more distinct with each strenuous step the horses made. As they drew closer, he could hear the soft clatter of the wooden sickle bars as they met the bed knife. He watched the stalks topple, and inhaled— nothing sweeter than sweet wheat drying in the sun.

Sweet, too, was the price it would bring this fall. With the war on in Europe, each grain was pure gold in more than just color. Standing in the molten sunlight, watching the reapers bring it down, Theodore thought it a sacrilege that something so beautiful should end up in something so ugly as war. They said the day would come when that wheat might feed Yankee soldiers, but not the way things were going. Though American training camps bulged with restless recruits, word had it they had neither uniforms nor guns. Instead they drilled in civilian clothes armed with broomsticks. And with people all over the country singing songs like "I Didn't Raise My Boy to Be a Soldier," it seemed the only war Theodore had to worry about was the one between himself and that young whippersnapper of a teacher.

He was still pondering the thought when his brother drew up.

John reined in and called, "Whoa, girls," then ponderously stepped down from the iron seat. The horses shook their heads, filling the still afternoon with the jingle of the harness.

"You're back," John said, sliding off his straw hat and wiping his receding hairline with a forearm.

"Yeah, I'm back."

"Did you get him then?"

"Yeah."

John nodded his head in his customary accepting way. He was a content man, not particularly bright, and not particularly minding. Thirty-eight years old, a little thicker than Theodore at the shoulder, thinner at the pate, and much slower at every- thing: from finishing chores to angering. He was built big and sturdy and moved with a singular lack of haste at once awk- ward and graceful. His frame was well-suited to bib overalls, dome-toed boots, and a thick flannel shirt. On the hottest of days he kept his shirt buttoned to the throat and wrist, never complaining about the heat as he never complained about anything, ever. His interests ranged only as far as the edges of the fields, and in them he earned his daily bread at his own unhurried pace. As long as he was able to do that, he asked little more of life. "Mowin's goin' good," he observed now. "The three of us oughta nearly finish this section before nightfall." John hunkered down, balancing on the balls of his feet, letting his eyes range over the field while he chewed a stem of wheat.

As always, it perplexed Theodore that his brother lacked curiosity about the goings-on around him. Yet he did. His contentment was such that it did not occur to him to question or defy. Perhaps it was because of this vagueness that Theodore loved him unquestionably and felt protective toward him.

What goes on in that mind of yours, John, when you hunker all motionless and gaze at the horizon?

"*He* turned out to be a *she*," Theodore informed his older brother.

John raised uncomprehending eyes but didn't say a word.

"She's a woman," Theodore explained.

"Who's a woman?" The question came from Kristian who'd drawn abreast and was jumping down from the seat of his machine with a quickness totally opposite that of his uncle. Like the other two men, he was dressed in striped overalls, but beneath them his back was bare and on his head he wore no hat. He had wiry brown arms with dips at the biceps that had only become defined during the past half-year. The sudden spurt of growth had left his neck with a gangly appearance, for his Adam's apple had developed faster than the musculature around it. His face was long and angular, becoming handsomer as each day added flesh to the lengthened bone and brought him closer to maturity. He had his father's brown eyes, though they lacked the cynicism that often stole into Theodore's, and his mother's sensual lower lip, slightly fuller than the upper. When he spoke, his English pronunciation held the slight distortion of a Norwegian who has grown up speaking bilingually.

"The new schoolteacher," his father answered with an even more pronounced accent. Theodore paused and considered before adding, "Well, not exactly a woman. More like a girl pretendin' to be one. She don't look much older than you."

Kristian's eyes widened. "She don't?" He swallowed, glanced in the direction of the house, and asked, "She stayin'?" He understood, without ever having been told in so many words, that his father had an antipathy toward women. He'd heard the old folks talking about it many times when they didn't think "little ears" were around.

"Your grandma took her upstairs and showed her her room, as if she was."

Again Kristian clearly understood—if Grandma said she was staying . . . she was staying!

"What's she like?"

Theodore's chin flattened in disapproval. "Wet behind the ears and sassy as a jaybird."

Kristian grinned. "What's she look like?"

Theodore scowled. "What do you care what she looks like?"

Kristian colored slightly. "I was just askin', that's all."

Theodore's scowl deepened. "She looks puny and mousy," he answered cantankerously, "just like you'd expect a teacher to look. Now let's get back to work."

Supper started late during harvest, for the men stayed out in the fields till the last ray of sunlight disappeared, stopping in the late afternoon to do the milking and eat sandwiches to tide them over until they came in for good.

Though Linnea had politely offered to lend a hand with the suppertime preparations, Nissa wouldn't hear of it, brushing her off with a terse declaration: "Teacher rooms *and boards* here. It's part of your pay, ain't it?"

So Linnea decided to explore the place, though there wasn't much to see. Tucked behind the L formed by two granaries she found a pig pen not visible from the house. The chicken coop, tool shed, corncribs, and silo offered little attraction, and it wasn't until she entered the barn that she found anything remotely interesting. It was not the immense, cavernous main body of the building that arrested her, but the tack room. Not even at the livery stable in Fargo had she seen so much leather! There seemed enough to supply a cavalry regiment. But for all the hundreds of loops and lines strung upon the walls, sawhorses, and benches, it had an orderliness and functionalism to rival that of a spider's web.

The tack room was glorious!

It had character. And redolence. And a fettle that made her wonder about the man who kept it so religiously neat. Not a single rein was draped over a narrow metal nail on which it might crimp or crack in time. Instead, they were hung fastidiously on thick wooden pegs with no loose ends allowed to touch the concrete floor. Smaller individual leather lines without hardware were coiled as neatly as lariats—no tangles or snags in sight. An assortment of oval collars trimmed one wall while a pair of saddles straddled a sawhorse wrapped with a thick swath of sheepskin to protect their undersides. A rough bench held tins of liniment and oil and saddle soap arranged as neatly as a druggist's shelf. Hoof trimmers, shears, and curry combs were hung upon their designated nails with fanatic neatness. Near a small west window sat an old scarred chair, stained almost black, with spooled back and arms. There were two paler spots worn in the concave seat, and its legs had been reinforced long ago with strong, twisted wire. Over one of its arms hung a soiled rag, folded precisely in half and draped as neatly as a woman drapes a dish towel over a towel bar.

Punctilious person, she deduced. All work and no play, she imagined.

Somehow it was irritating to find perfection in such an irascible man. Waiting for him and his son to return from the fields, her stomach growling with hunger, Linnea imagined how she'd put him in his place some day.

With that thought in mind, she went to her room to wash up and recomb her hair before supper. Holding the brush in her hand, she leaned close to the oval mirror in the painted tin frame and whispered as if to more than just her reflection.

"You treat your horses better than you treat women. As a matter of fact, you treat your horses' harnesses better than you treat women!"

Linnea looked indignant at the imagined reply, then she cocked a wrist and touched her fingertips to her heart. *"I'll have you know, Mr. Westgaard, that I have been courted by an actor from the London stage and by a British aviator. I've turned down seven . . . or was it eight . . . "* For a moment her forehead puckered, then she flipped the brush back saucily and flashed a gainsome smile over her shoulder. *"Oh well,"* she finished airily. *"What difference does one little proposal make?"* She laughed in a breathy whisper and went on brushing the hair that fell to her shoulder blades.

"The British aviator took me dancing to the palace, at the special invitation of the queen, on the night before he flew away to bomb a German zeppelin shed in Düsseldorf." She hooked her skirt up high and swayed while tipping her head aside. A dreamy look came over her face. *"Ah, what a night that was."* Her eyes closed and she dipped left, then right, her reflection flashing past the small oval mirror. *"At the end of the evening we rode home in a carriage he'd assigned especially for the occasion."* She sobered and dropped her skirt. *"Alas, he lost his life in the service of his country. It was ever so sad."*

She mourned him a moment, then brightened heroically, adding, *"But at least I have the memory of swirling in his arms to the strain of a Vienna waltz."* She stretched her neck like a swan while lissomely stroking the hair back from her face. *"But then, you wouldn't know about things like that. And anyway, a lady doesn't kiss and tell."* She dropped the brush, picked up a comb, and parted her hair down the middle.

"And then there was Lawrence." Suddenly she spun, bringing her hips to the edge of the commode stand and leaning back provocatively. *"Have I ever told you about Lawrence?"*

The crash of splintering china brought Linnea out of her fantasy with chilling abruptness. The commode stand teetered in its angled place; the pitcher and bowl were no longer in sight.

From downstairs Nissa yelled, "What was that? Are you all right up there?" Footsteps sounded on the stairs.

Horrified, Linnea covered her mouth with both hands and bent over the commode. When Nissa reached the door she found the girl peering into the corner at the pieces of pottery that had been a pitcher and bowl only seconds before.

"What happened?"

Linnea whirled to face the doorway with a stricken expression on her face. "Oh, Mrs. Westgaard, I'm terribly sorry! I . . . I've broken the pitcher and bowl."

Nissa bustled in. "How in tarnation'd it get back there?"

"I . . . I accidentally bumped the stand. I'll pay for it out of my first month's salary." For only a second she wondered how much a pitcher and bowl cost.

"Lawsy, if that ain't a mess. You all right?"

Linnea lifted her skirts and looked down at the wet hem. "A little wet is all."

Nissa began pulling the commode out, but Linnea immediately took over. "Here, I'll clean it up!" When the piece of furniture was turned aside, she saw the shattered pottery and the water running underneath the linoleum, wetting its soft underside. "Oh, my . . . " she wailed, covering her mouth again while tears of embarrassment burned her eyes. "How could I have been so clumsy? I've probably ruined the linoleum, too."

Nissa was already heading downstairs. "I'll get a pail and rag." While she was gone Linnea heard voices outside and glanced through the window to see the men had arrived while she'd been daydreaming. Frantic, she fell to her knees, gathering broken pieces into a pile, stacking them, then using the side of her hand to press the water away from the edge of the linoleum. But the puddle had already made its way underneath, so she lifted the corner . . . which proved to be a mistake. Water sailed down the curve of the linoleum, wetting the skirt over her knees.

"Here, let me do that!" Nissa ordered from the doorway. "Drop them pieces in the pail."

Linnea set the broken pottery in the bottom of the pail with great care, as if gentle handling would somehow improve matters. She swallowed back the tears and felt clumsy and burdensome and disgusted with herself for letting childish whimsy carry her away again and get her into trouble, as it so often did.

When all the pieces had been picked up and Nissa sat back on her heels, Linnea reached to touch the woman's forearm with a woeful expression on her face.

"I . . . I'm so sorry," Linnea whispered. "It was stupid and—"

"Course you're sorry. Nobody likes to look like a fool when they're new to a place. But pitchers are—why, you've cut yourself!" Linnea jerked back her hand to find she'd left blood on Nissa's sleeve.

"Oh, now I've soiled your dress! Can't I do anything right?"

"Don't fret so. It'll wash out. But it looks like that hand is bound to bleed for a spell. I'd best get something to wrap it." She jumped to her feet and disappeared down the stairs. A moment later Linnea heard voices from the kitchen and her mortification redoubled as she realized Nissa was probably telling the men what had just happened.

But the old woman returned without a word of criticism, and wrapped the hand in a clean strip of torn sheet, tying it securely before heading for the steps again. "Fix up your hair now, and be downstairs in five minutes. The boys don't like to be kept waiting."

Unfortunately, Linnea was inexpert at arranging her hair in the new backswept style with *two* good hands; with one bandaged, she was inept. She did her best but was still fussing when Nissa called that supper was ready. Hands still frantically adjusting and ramming hairpins against her skull, Linnea glanced at her skirt—wet knees, wet hem, and no time to change. A peek in the mirror showed that the rat upon which she'd wrapped her hair was off-center. Blast it! She gave it a good yank to the left that only messed it further, and hurriedly reinserted three pins.

"Miss Brandonberg! Supper!"

The boys don't like to be kept waiting.

Giving up, Linnea headed for the stairs, hoping her clattering footsteps sounded jaunty.

When she came into the kitchen from the shadows of the stairwell, she was surprised to find *three* tall, strapping men turning to gawk at her.

The boys?

Theodore, of course, she'd already had the misfortune of meeting. He took one look at her red face, disobedient hair, and wet skirt, and a ghost of a smile tipped up one corner of his mouth. Dismissing him as an uncouth lout, she turned her attention to the others.

"You must be Kristian." He was half a head taller than herself and extremely handsome, with a far kinder and prettier mouth than his father, but with the same deep-brown eyes. His hair was wet and freshly combed, a rich golden brown that would probably dry to near blond. His face shone from a fresh washing, and of the three, he was the only one without a shirt or white line across the top half of his forehead. She extended a hand. "Hello. I'm Miss Brandonberg."

Kristian Westgaard gawked at the face of the new teacher. *Mousy and puny?* Cripes, what had the old man been thinking? He felt the color rush up his bare chest. His heart went *kawhump,* and his hands started sweating.

Linnea watched him turn the color of ripe raspberries as he nervously wiped both palms on his thighs. His Adam's apple bobbed like a cork on a wave. At last he clasped her hand loosely, briefly. "Wow," he breathed. "You mean *you're* gonna be our new teacher?"

Nissa passed by on her way to the table with a bowl of meat, and admonished, "Watch your manners, young man!" at which Kristian's blush rekindled.

Linnea laughed. "I'm afraid so."

Nissa interposed, "And this here's my son John. Lives just across the field over there but eats all his meals with us." She nodded east and moved back to the stove.

Linnea looked up into a face much like Theodore's, though slightly older and with a receding hairline. Shy, hazel eyes; straight, attractive nose, and full lips—nothing at all like Nissa's thin slash of a mouth. He seemed unable to meet her gaze directly or to keep from nervously shifting his feet. His face brightened to poppy red above the hat line, sienna-brown below. His timid eyes flickered everywhere but to her own. At their introduction, he nodded jerkily, decided to extend a hand, got it halfway out, and retracted it in favor of two more nods. By this time, Linnea's hand hung between them. At last he took it in a giant raw-boned paw and pumped once.

"Hello, John," she said simply.

He nodded diffidently, looking at his boots. "Miss." His voice rumbled soft and gruff and very, very bass, like thunder from the next county.

His face was shiny, fresh-scrubbed for supper, and his receding brown hair combed in a fresh peak down the center. He wore faded black pants and red suspenders. The collar of his red plaid shirt was buttoned clear up to the throat, giving him a rather sad, childish look for so big a man. Something warm

and protective touched her heart the instant his enormous hand
swallowed up her own.

The only one who hadn't spoken to her was Theodore. But
she sensed him watching guardedly and decided not to let him
off that easily. If he thought manners became inessential when
a person aged, she'd show him that one was never too old to
be polite.

"And hello again, Mr. Westgaard." She turned and confronted him directly, giving him no alternative but to recognize
her.

"Yeah," was all he said, his arms crossed over a blue chambray shirt and black suspenders.

To vex him further, she smiled sweetly and added, "Your
mother showed me my room and got me settled in. It'll do
very nicely."

With the others looking on, he was forced to bite back a
sharp retort. Instead he grumbled, "Well, we gonna stand here
yammerin' all night, or we gonna have some supper?"

"It's ready. Let's sit," Nissa put in, moving to place one last
bowl on the round oak pedestal table covered with snowy linen.
"This'll be your chair." Nissa indicated one positioned between
hers and John's, perhaps hoping a little distance between Linnea
and Theodore might buffer his antagonism. Unfortunately it put
them directly across from each other, and even before Linnea
sat she felt his eyes rake her once with palpable displeasure.

When they were all seated, Theodore said, "Let's pray,"
and clasped his hands, rested his elbows beside his plate, and
dropped his forehead to his knuckles. Everyone followed suit,
as did Linnea, but when Theodore's deep voice began intoning
the prayer, she opened her eyes and peeked around her knuckles in surprise. The prayer was being recited in Norwegian.

She pressed her thumbs against her forehead, watching the
corners of his lips move behind his folded hands. To her
dismay, he peeked back at her! Their eyes met for only a
second, but even in that brief moment there was time for
self-consciousness before his glance moved to her bandaged
hand. Guiltily she slammed her eyes shut.

She added her amen to the others, and before she could
even move her elbows off the tablecloth the most amazing
action broke out. As if the end of the prayer signaled the

beginning of a race, four sets of hands lashed out to capture four bowls; four serving spoons clattered against four plates— *whack, whack, whack, whack!* Then, like a precision drill, the bowls were passed to the left while each of the Westgaards took the one arriving from their right. Linnea sat agape. Apparently her delay in taking the bowl of corn from John threw a crimp into the works, for suddenly all eyes were on her as she sat empty-handed while John balanced two bowls in his big hands. Silently he nudged her shoulder with the corn bowl, and as she took it Theodore's eyes took in the bandaged hand again.

"What happened to her?" he asked Nissa.

Nissa clapped a mound of potatoes on her plate. "She broke the pitcher and bowl upstairs and cut her hand cleanin' it up."

How dare he talk around me as if I can't answer for myself! Linnea colored as four sets of eyes turned her way and perused the bandaged left hand holding the bowl of corn. The circus picked up again, bowls and spoons passing under her nose until finally it ended as abruptly as it had begun: four pairs of hands clunked down four bowls; four heads bent over four plates; four intense Norwegians started eating with an absorption so exceedingly rude that Linnea could only stare.

She was the last one holding a bowl, and felt as conspicuous as a clown at a wake. Well, manners were manners! She would display those that had been drilled into her all her life and see if a good example would faze these four.

She finished filling her plate and sat properly straight, eating at a sedate pace, using her fork and knife on the delicious beaten beefsteaks that were cooked in rich brown gravy and seasoned with allspice. When her knife wasn't in use, it lay properly across the edge of her plate. Potatoes, corn, coleslaw, bread, butter, and a bevy of relishes rounded out the meal.

The entire Westgaard family gobbled it with their napes up!

And the sounds were horrendous.

Nobody said a word, just dug in and kept digging until the plates began emptying and one by one they asked to have bowls passed to them again. But they did it with the manners of cavemen!

"Spuds!" Theodore commanded, and Linnea watched in disgust as the "spuds" were passed by John, who scarcely looked up while mopping up gravy with a slice of bread, then stuffing it into his mouth with his fingers.

A moment later Kristian followed suit. "Meat!"

His grandmother shoved the meat bowl across the table. Nobody but Linnea saw anything amiss. Minutes passed with more grunts and slurps.

"Corn!"

Linnea was unaware of the stalled action until the sudden silence made her lift her eyes from her plate. Everyone was staring at her.

"I said corn," Kristian repeated.

"Oh, corn!" She grabbed the bowl and shot it across the table to him, too disconcerted to take up the subject of manners on this first night in her new home.

Good lord, did they eat like this all the time?

They fell to their second helpings, giving her time to study them individually.

Nissa, with her little oval spectacles and gray pug head bent over her plate, too. As a mother she had been remiss in teaching manners, but she had indubitable control over her "boys" just the same. Had it been Nissa instead of Theodore who'd decided Linnea was not welcome, she wouldn't be sitting at the supper table now, Linnea was sure.

John. Sitting beside him she felt like a dwarf. His red plaid sleeve rested on the table and his broad shoulders bowed forward like a yoke. She recalled his hesitancy to shake her hand, the red flooding his face as he politely called her "Miss." She would never have to fear John.

Kristian. She had not missed his furtive glances throughout the meal. He'd been sneaking them at her ever since they sat down. He was so big! So grown-up! How awkward it would feel to be his teacher when he towered over her by half a head and had shoulders as wide as a plow horse. Nissa had referred to him as "Theodore's boy," but he was no more boy than his father or his uncle, and it was obvious Kristian had been instantly smitten with her. She'd have to be careful not to encourage him in any way.

Theodore. What made a man so cantankerous and hard to get along with? She'd be a liar to deny she was afraid of this one. But he'd never know it, not if she lived in his house for five years and had to fight him tooth and nail all that time. Inside every hard person hid a softer one; find him and you might, too, find his soul. With Theodore that would undoubtedly be a difficult task, but she aimed to try.

Unexpectedly, he looked up, straight into her eyes, and she was startled to discover that Theodore was no old man. His brown eyes were clear and unlined except for a single white squint line at each corner. In those eyes she saw intelligence and pugnaciousness enough for two, and wondered what it would take to nourish the one and subdue the other. His hair was not the color of sunset over waving ripe rye, as she'd fantasized, but brown and thick, drying now after being slicked back with water, rebelliously springing toward his forehead in willful curls. And neither had he an oversized sunburned nose. It was straight and attractive and tan, like the rest of his face up to within an inch of the hairline where a band of white identified him as the farmer that he was. Unlike John, he wore his collar open. Inside it his neck was sturdy; above it no jowls drooped. When he stubbornly refused to break eye contact with her, she self-consciously dropped her gaze to his arms. Unlike John's, they were exposed to mid-forearm. His wrists were narrow, making both hands and arms appear the more mighty as they swelled above and below. Was he forty? Not yet. Thirty? Most certainly. He had to be to have a son Kristian's age.

Then,.with a silent sigh Linnea decided she'd been right after all: somewhere between thirty and forty was very old indeed.

She peeked up again and found him bent low, eating, but still with his gaze pinning her. Flustered, she glanced around the table to find Kristian had been watching the two of them. She flashed him a quick smile and said the first thing that came to mind. "So you're going to be one of my students, Kristian."

Everyone at the table stopped forking and chewing while an immense silence fell. They all looked at her as if she'd sprouted fangs. She felt herself blush, but didn't know why. "Have I said something wrong?"

The pause lengthened, but finally Kristian replied, "Yes. I mean, no, you ain't said nothin' wrong and yes, you're gonna be my teacher."

They all fell to eating again, dropping their eyes to their plates while Linnea puzzled over the silence. Again she broke it.

"What grade are you in, Kristian?"

Once again everyone paused, startled by her interruption. Kristian glanced furtively around the table and answered, "Eighth."

"Eighth?" He had to be at least sixteen years old. "Did you miss some school—I mean, were you ill or anything?"

His eyes were wide and unblinking as he stared at her and the color spread slowly up his chin. "No. Didn't miss no years."

"Any years."

"Beg pardon?"

"I didn't miss any years," she corrected.

For a moment he looked puzzled, then his eyes brightened and he said, "Oh! Well, me neither."

She could feel them all looking at her but couldn't figure out what it was they were so surprised about. She was only making polite supper conversation. But none of them had the grace to pick up the conversational ball she'd thrown out. Instead, they all clammed up and continued to stuff their gullets, the only sounds those of ostentatious eating.

Theodore spoke once, when his plate was cleared. He sat back, expanding his chest. "What's for dessert, Ma?"

Nissa brought bread pudding. Stupefied, Linnea watched everybody silently wait for their serving, then return to eating with reintensified interest. Glancing around, studying them, it finally dawned on her: eating was serious business around here. Nobody profaned the sacrosanct gobbling with idle chitchat!

Never in her life had she been treated so rudely at a table. When the meal was over, she was surrounded by a chorus of belches before they all sat back and picked their teeth over cups of coffee.

Not one of them said excuse me! Not even Nissa!

Linnea wondered how Nissa would react if she requested a tray in her room from now on. Most certainly she was disinclined to join them at this table and listen to them all carrying on like pigs at a trough.

But now, it seemed, the inviolable rite was done. Theodore pushed back and spoke directly to Linnea.

"You'll want to see the school building tomorrow."

What she really wanted to see tomorrow was the inside of a train taking her back home to Fargo. She hid her disillusionment and answered with as much enthusiasm as she could muster, "Yes, I'd like to see what books I'll have to work with, and what supplies I'll have to order."

"We milk at five and have breakfast right after. Be ready to go soon as breakfast is done. I can't waste time comin' in from the fields in the middle of the mornin' to haul you down there and give you no tour."

"I'll gladly walk. I *know* where the school building is."

He sipped his coffee, swallowed loudly, and said, "It's part of what they pay me for, showin' the new teacher the school building and telling him what his duties are soon as he gets here."

She felt the damnable blush creeping up, no matter how she tried to stop it. And though she knew it would have been better to ignore his jibe, she couldn't.

"He?" she repeated pointedly.

"Oh . . . " Theodore's eyes made an insolent tour of her lopsided hairstyle. "She. I forgot."

"Does this mean I'm staying? Or do you still intend to *dump me off* on Oscar Knutson when you manage to run him down?"

He sat back lazily, an ankle crossing a knee, and wielded the toothpick in a way that pulled his upper lip askew, all the while studying her without smiling.

At last he said, "Oscar don't have no room for you."

"*Doesn't* have *any* room for me." It was out before she could control the urge to set him down a notch.

He slowly pulled the toothpick from his mouth, and his lip fell into place, but it thinned in anger, and she saw with satisfaction the blush begin to creep up his face, too. Though she knew he fully understood he was having his speech corrected, she couldn't resist adding insult to injury. "Don't and no are double negatives, thus it's incorrect to say Oscar don't have no room. Oscar *doesn't* have any room for me."

The white stripe near his hairline turned brilliant red and he lunged to his feet, the chair scraping back on the bare wood floor as he pointed a long, thick finger at her nose. "He sure as hell don't, so I'm stuck with you! But stay out of my way, missy, you understand!"

"Theodore!" his mother yelped, but he was already slamming out the door. When he was gone, the silence around the table became deadly and Linnea felt tears of mortification sting her eyes. She glanced at the faces around her. Kristian's and John's were beet red. Nissa's was white with anger as she stared at the door.

"That boy don't know no manners atall, talking to you like that!" his mother ranted.

"I . . . I'm sorry. I shouldn't have goaded him. It was my fault."

"Naw, it was not," Nissa declared, rising and beginning to clear away the dishes with angry motions. "He just got ugly inside when—" She stopped abruptly, glanced at Kristian, who was staring at the tablecloth. "Aw, it's no use tryin' to straighten him out," she finished, turning away.

To Linnea's surprise, John made the one gesture of conciliation. He began to reach for her arm as if to lay a comforting hand on it, drew back just in time, but offered in his deep, slow voice, "Aw, he don't mean nothing by it, Miss."

She looked up into friendly, shy eyes and somehow realized that John's brief reassurance had been tantamount to an oration, for him. She reached out to touch his arm lightly. "I'll try to remember that the next time I cross swords with him. Thank you, John."

His gaze dropped to her fingers, and he flushed brilliant red. Immediately she withdrew her hand and turned to Kristian. "Would you mind taking me to the school tomorrow, Kristian? That way I won't have to bother your father."

His lips opened, but nothing came out. He flashed a quick glance at his uncle, found no help for whatever was bothering him, and finally swallowed and smiled broadly, growing pink in the cheeks yet again. "Yes, ma'am."

Relieved, she released a breath she hadn't realized she'd been holding. "Thank you, Kristian. I'll be ready directly after breakfast."

He nodded, watching her rise to pick up a handful of dishes. "Well, I'd better lend Nissa a hand with cleaning up."

But even before she'd gotten to her feet, she was being excused.

"Teachers don't clean up!" Nissa informed her. "Evenin's are your own. You'll need 'em for correctin' papers and such."

"But I have no papers to correct yet."

"G'won!" Nissa flapped a hand as if shooing away a fly. "Git out from underfoot. I'll tend to the cleanin' up. I always have."

Linnea paused uncertainly. "You're sure?"

Nissa peered up at her from behind her oval lenses while reaching for the empty cups and saucers. "Do I strike you as a person who ain't never sure of things?"

That made Linnea smile again. "Very well, I promised my mother I'd write to her immediately after I arrived and let her know I'd made it without mishap."

"Fine! Fine! You go do that."

Upstairs she lit the kerosene lantern and studied her room again, but it was as disappointing as ever. Nissa had replaced the pitcher and bowl with a blue-speckled washbasin. The sight of it brought back Linnea's disappointment not only in the room and the Westgaard family but in herself. She wanted so badly to act mature, had promised herself time and again that she'd give up those childish flights of whimsy that forever got her into trouble. But she hadn't been here thirty minutes and look what she'd done. She swallowed back tears.

From her first thirty dollars a month she'd have to pay the price of a new pitcher and bowl. But worse, she'd made a fool of herself. That was hard enough to face without having to confront Theodore's antagonism at every turn.

The man was truly despicable!

Forget him. Everyone told you becoming an adult wasn't going to be easy, and you're finding out they were right.

To put Theodore from her mind, she took up a wooden stationery box and sat on her bed.

Dear Mother and Father, Carrie and Pudge,
    I have arrived in Alamo all safe and sound. The train ride was long and uneventful. When I arrived I searched the horizon for a town, but found to my dismay only three elevators and a handful of sorry buildings I would scarcely

classify as a "town." Yes, Daddy, you warned me it would be small. But I hadn't expected this!

I was met at the station by Mr. Westgaard, who escorted me to his farm, which appears to be of immense proportions like all the others out here, so big we tried to find one of his neighbors working in the field, but could not. Mr. Westgaard—Theodore is his first name—lives here with his mother, Nissa (a little bandy-legged spitfire whom I loved immediately), and his son, Kristian (who will be my eighth-grade student, but is half a head taller than I), and Theodore's brother, John (who comes here at mealtimes but the rest of the time lives at his own farm, which is the next one up the road to the east).

We had a delicious first supper of steak and gravy, potatoes, corn, bread and butter and bread pudding and more relishes than I've ever seen on a table in my life, after which Nissa would not allow me to lift a finger to help her clean up—Carrie and Pudge, I know you're green with envy because I don't have to do dishes anymore! And now I'm settled into my very own private room with nobody to tell me to put out the light when I'd rather read a little longer. Imagine that, a room of my own for the first time in my life.

But then she glanced around that room, at the bare rafters overhead, the minuscule window, the commode where the new blue washbasin stood. She remembered the untarnished optimism she'd felt while riding toward her new home on the train, and her immediate disillusionment from the moment Theodore Westgaard had opened his mouth and declared, "I ain't havin' no woman in my house!" She glanced at the letter from which she had carefully winnowed all the disappointments and misgivings of her first six hours as the "the new teacher," and suddenly the world seemed to topple in on her.

She curled into a ball and wept miserably.

Oh, Mother and Daddy, I miss you so much. I wish I was back home with all of you, where suppertime was filled with gaiety and talk and loving smiles. I wish I could pick up the dish towel and complain loudly about having to help Carrie and Pudge before I was excused from the kitchen. I wish all three of us girls were back together, crowded into our pretty little flowered bedroom with the two of you siding against me when I wanted to leave the lights on just a little longer.

What am I doing out here in the middle of this godforsaken prairie, with this strange family, so filled with anger and reticence and a total disdain for manners?

I wish I had listened to you, Daddy, when you said I should stay closer to home my first year, until I knew how I liked independence. If I were there, I'd be sharing all this with you and Mother right now, instead of burying the hurts inside and sobbing out my sorrow in this sad little attic bedroom.

But she loved her family too much to tell them the truth and give them the burden of worrying about her when there was nothing they could do to comfort her.

And so, much later, when she discovered her tears had fallen upon the ink and left two blue puddles, she resolutely dried her eyes and started the letter again.

3

By TRADITION, THE school year officially began on the first Monday of September. Linnea had arrived on the Friday preceding it. Saturday hadn't quite dawned, when some faraway sound awakened her and she groggily checked her surroundings in the muted lavender light of the loft.

For a moment she was disoriented. Overhead were the unfinished beams of a roof. She groaned and rolled over. Oh yes . . . her new home in Alamo. She had slept poorly in the strange bed. She was tempted to drop off for a few more precious winks, but just then she heard activity below, and remembered the events of yesterday.

Well, Miss Brandonberg, drag your bones out of here and show 'em what you're made of.

The water in the basin was cold, and she wondered if she'd run into Theodore or Kristian if she sneaked down to warm it. Maybe nobody'd lit a fire yet: a glance at the window told her it was very early. She eyed the stovepipe, scurried out of bed, and touched it. Ah, someone had been up a while. She drew on her blue flannel wrapper, buttoned it to the throat, tied it at the waist, and took her speckled washbasin downstairs.

She tried to be very quiet, but the stairs creaked.

Nissa's head popped around the doorway. Her hair was already in its tight little bun, and she wore a starched white

38

ankle-length apron over a no-nonsense dress of faded gray and red flowered muslin.

"You up already?"

"I . . . I don't want to keep anybody waiting this time."

"Breakfast won't be for a good hour yet. The boys got ten cows to milk."

"Are they . . . " She glanced above Nissa's head and pressed the basin tighter against her hip. "Outside already?"

"Coast is clear. Come on down." Nissa dropped her eyes to the bare toes curled over the edge of the step. "Ain't you got no slippers for them bare feet?"

Linnea straightened her toes and looked down. "I'm afraid not." She didn't want to mention that at home she'd only had to slip down the hall to reach the lavatory.

"Well, appears I better get out my knitting needles first chance I get. Come on down 'fore you fall off your perch. Water's hot in the reservoir."

In spite of Nissa's brusque, autocratic ways, Linnea liked her. The kitchen, with her in it, became inviting. She whirled around in her usual fashion, reminding Linnea of the erratic flight of a goldfinch—darting this way and that with such abrupt turns that it seemed she wasn't done with one task before heading for the next.

She lifted a lid from the gargantuan cast-iron stove that dominated the room, tossed in a shovelful of coal from a hod sitting alongside, rammed the lid back in place, and spun toward the pantry all in a single motion. Watching her, Linnea almost became dizzy.

In a moment Nissa breezed back, pointing to a water pail sitting on a long table against one wall. "There! Use the dipper! Take what you need! I draw the line when it comes to givin' the teacher a bath!"

Linnea laughed and thought if she had to put up with some nettlesome tempers around here, Nissa would more than make up for it. Upstairs again, all washed, with the bandage removed from her hand and her hair done in a perfect, flawless coil around the back of her head, Linnea felt optimistic once more.

She owned five outfits: her traveling suit of charcoal-gray wool serge with its shirtwaist of garnet-colored silk, a brown skirt of Manchester cloth bound at the hem with velvet and a contrasting white-yoked shirtwaist, a forest-green skirt of twilled Oxford with three inverted plaits down the back and a Black Watch plaid shirtwaist to match, a navy-blue middy dress with white piping around the collar, and an ordinary gray broadcloth skirt and plain white shirtwaist with no frills except a pair of narrow ruffles dropping at an inward angle from each shoulder toward her waist.

The suit was strictly for Sundays. The middy made her look childish. The Manchester cloth would be too warm yet, stiffened as it was with percaline. And she was saving the new green skirt for the first day of school because it had been a gift from her parents and was the most adult of all her outfits. So she chose the utilitarian gray skirt and plain white blouse. When she was dressed, she eyed herself critically.

Her hair was perfect. Her skirt was dry. Her bandage gone. Her clothing sensible, sober, even matronly. What could he possibly find to fault her for?

Suddenly she realized what she was thinking, and her chin took on a stubborn thrust. Why should I have to worry about pleasing an old grouch like Theodore? He's my *land*lord, not my lord!

She returned downstairs to find breakfast cooking, the table set, but the men still absent.

"Well, look at you! Now don't you look pretty!"

"Do I?" Linnea smoothed the front of her white shirtwaist and looked at Nissa uncertainly. "Do I look old enough?"

Nissa hid a smile and gave the girl a thorough inspection over the tops of her wire-rimmed spectacles. "Oh, you look old, all right. Why, I'd say you look at least . . . oh . . . nineteen, anyway."

"Do I really!"

Nissa had all she could do to keep from chuckling at the girl's pleased expression, then Linnea's tone lowered confidentially. "I'll tell you something, Nissa. Ever since I saw Kristian I've been awfully worried about looking younger than some of my students."

"Aw, go on," Nissa growled, pulling her chin low. "You might even look twenty in that crisp little skirt. Turn around here. Let me get a gander at the back." Linnea turned a slow circle while Nissa rubbed her chin studiously. "Yup! Twenty for sure!" she lied.

Again Linnea beamed, but the smile was followed by another sober expression as her hands pressed her waistband and she looked as if she were about to admit to a horrible crime. "I sometimes have . . . well, a little trouble, you might say. Acting grown up, I mean. My father used to scold me for being daydreamy and forgetting what I was about. But since I've been to Normal School I've been trying really hard to look mature and remember that I'm a lady. I thought the skirt helped."

Nissa's heart warmed toward the youngster. There she stood, all dressed in grown-up clothes, trying to act like she was ready to face the world, when she was scared out of her britches.

"I reckon you're going to miss your family. We're a strange bunch here, lots of new things to get used to."

"Why, no! I mean . . . well, yes, I'm sure I'll miss them, but—"

"You just remember," Nissa interrupted. "Ain't nothing stubborner nor bullheadeder than a bunch of hardheaded Norwegians. And that's about all there is around here. But you're the schoolteacher! You got a certificate says you're smarter than all the rest of 'em, so when they start givin' you sass, you just stand up square and spit in their eye. They'll respect *that!*"

Giving me sass? Linnea silently quailed. Were they all going to be like Theodore?

As if the thought materialized him, Theodore stepped through the door, followed by Kristian.

Catching sight of her, Theodore paused a moment before moving to the pail and washbasin. Kristian stopped in his tracks and openly stared.

"Good morning, Kristian."

"G . . . good morning, Miss Brandonberg."

"Goodness, you *do* get up early."

Kristian felt like he'd swallowed a cotton wad. Not a word came out while he stood rooted, admiring his teacher's fresh young face and pretty brown hair, all slicked up spruce and neat above a skirt and blouse that made her waist look thin as a willow whip.

"Breakfast is ready," Nissa advised, moving around him. "Quit your dawdling."

At the basin Theodore soaped his hands and face, rinsed, and turned around with the towel in his hands to find his son standing like a fencepost, gawking at the little missy who looked about thirteen years old again this morning. She even stood like a girl, her prim little shoes planted side by side. Her hair wasn't bad though, all hoisted up into a clever female puff that made her neck look long and graceful.

Theodore put a tight clamp on the thought and said, "The basin's yours, Kristian," then turned his back on the teacher again.

"Good morning, Theodore," she said, somehow managing to make him feel like a fool for not having said it first. He turned back to her.

"Morning. I see you're ready in time."

"Most certainly. Punctuality is the politeness of kings," she offered, and turned toward the table.

Punk-what? he thought, feeling ignorant and rightfully put in his place as he watched her take her chair.

"Didn't John help you this morning?" she asked, forcing him to talk to her when he didn't want to. He plunked himself down with a surly expression on his face, at the same chair he'd taken last night.

"John's got his own livestock to tend to. Kristian and me milk our cows, he milks his."

"I thought he ate all his meals here."

"He'll be along in a minute."

Nissa brought a platter of fresh bacon, another of toast, and five bowls containing something that looked like hot school paste. While Theodore said the prayer—again in Norwegian—Linnea stared down into her bowl and wondered what it was. It had no smell, no color, and no attraction. But when the prayer ended, she watched the others to see what she was supposed to do with the glutinous mess. They slathered theirs with pure cream and sugar, then decorated it with butter, so she followed suit and cautiously took a taste.

It was delicious! It tasted like vanilla pudding.

John came in shortly after the meal had begun. Though they all exchanged good mornings, Linnea's was the only one that included a pause in her eating and the addition of a smile. He blushed immediately and fumbled to his chair without risking another glance at her.

Like last night, the meal was accompanied by serious smacking and no conversation. Testing her theory, Linnea said, loud and clear, "This is very good."

Everybody tensed and stopped with their spoons halfway to their mouths. Nobody muttered a word. When their jaws started working again, she asked the table at large, "What is it?"

They all looked at her as if she were a dolt. Theodore chortled and took another mouthful.

"What do you mean, what is it?" Nissa retorted. "It's *romograut*."

Linnea tipped her head to one side and peered at Nissa. "It's what?"

This time Theodore answered. "*Romograut*." He gestured toward her bowl with his spoon. "Don't you know what *romograut* is?"

"If I did, would I have asked?"

"No Norwegian has to ask what *romograut* is."

"Well, I'm asking. And I'm only half Norwegian—my father's half. Since my mother was the cook, we ate a lot of Swedish foods."

"Swedish!" three people denounced at once. If there was a Norwegian born who didn't think himself one step better than any Swede on earth, he wasn't in this room.

"It's flour cereal," Linnea was informed.

They were in a hurry to get on with the day's work, so she was spared the burping session at the end of the meal. As soon as the bowls and platter were empty, Theodore pushed his chair back and announced peremptorily, "I'll take you to school now. Get your bird wings if you need 'em."

Her temper went up like a March kite. What was it about the man that gave him such pleasure in persecuting her? Happily, this time she had an answer she was more than elated to give.

"You won't have to bother. I've asked Kristian to take me."

Theodore's eyebrows lifted speculatively and his glance shifted between the two. "Kristian, huh?"

Kristian's face lit up like a beacon and he shuffled his feet. "It won't take long, and I'll hurry back to the field soon as I get her there."

"You do that. It'll save me the trouble." And without another word, he left the house. Linnea's glare followed him out the door, and when she turned, she found Nissa watching her shrewdly. But all Nissa said was, "You'll need cleaning supplies and a ladder to reach them windows, and I packed you a lunch. I'll get it."

Kristian drove her to school in the same wagon she'd ridden in before. They hadn't gone twenty feet down the road before Linnea totally forgot about Theodore. It was a heavenly morning. The sun was up a finger's width above the horizon, peering from behind a narrow strip of purple that dissected it like a bright ribbon, making it appear all the more orange as its golden rays radiated above and below. Its oblique angle lit the tops of the grain fields to a lustrous gold, making the wheat appear a solid mass, unmoving now in the windlessness of early day. The air was fragrant with the smell of it. And all was still—so still. The call of a meadowlark came lilting to them with clarion precision and the horses perked up their ears, but moved on as before, their rhythm never changing. In a field on the left several sunflowers lifted their golden heads.

"Oh look!" She pointed. "Sunflowers. Aren't they beautiful?"

Kristian eyed her askance. For a schoolteacher, she didn't know much about sunflowers. "My pa cusses 'em."

She turned to him, startled. "Whatever for? Look at them, taller than all the rest, lifting their faces to the sun."

"They're pests around here. Get 'em in a wheat field, and you'll never get rid of 'em."

"Oh."

They rode on. After a minute she said, "I guess I have a lot to learn about farms and such. I may have to rely on you to teach me."

"Me!" He turned amazed brown eyes on her.

"Well, would you mind?"

"But you're the teacher."

"In school. Out of school, I guess there's a lot I can learn from you. What's that?"

"Russian thistle," he answered, following the path of her finger to a patch of pale-greenish blossoms.

"Ah." She digested that a moment before adding, "Don't tell me. Theodore cusses it too, right?"

"It's more of a pest than sunflowers," he verified.

Her eyes strayed behind, lingering on the blossoms as the wagon passed. "But there's beauty to be found in many things, even when they're pests. We just have to take a second look. Perhaps I'll have the children paint pictures of Russian thistle before winter comes."

He didn't quite know what to make of a girl—a woman?—who thought Russian thistle was pretty. He'd heard it damned all his life. Oddly enough, he found himself craning to look back at it. When she caught him, she smiled brightly and he felt confused. "That there's John's place," he offered as they passed it.

"So I've been told."

"I got aunts and uncles and cousins scattered all over around here," he volunteered, surprising himself because he'd always been tongue-tied around girls before. But he found he enjoyed talking to her. "About twenty of 'em or so, not counting the greats."

"The greats?"

"Great aunts and uncles. Got a few of them, too."

"Crimany!" she exclaimed. "Twenty?"

His head snapped around in surprise and he smiled wide. He hadn't imagined a schoolteacher saying *crimany* that way.

Realizing what she'd said, she clapped a hand over her mouth. Realizing she'd clapped a hand over her mouth, she dropped it, looked at her lap, and nervously smoothed her skirt. "I guess I have to watch myself, don't I? Sometimes I forget I'm the teacher now."

And for the moment, Kristian forgot, too. She was only a girl he wanted to help down from a wagon when they drew up in the schoolyard. But he'd never done it before and wasn't certain how a man went about these things. Did he tell her to stay put while he hustled around to her side? What if she laughed? Some girls he knew would have laughed at him—

girls laughed at the strangest things. The idea of taking Miss Brandonberg's hand made him feel all flustered and queer in the stomach.

In the end he deliberated too long and she leaped to the ground with a sprightly bounce, promising herself she'd do something about the manners of the Westgaard men if it was her only accomplishment here.

From the back of the wagon Kristian grabbed the ladder and followed her across the school grounds while she carried a bucket and rags.

At the door she spun to face him. "Oh, we forgot the key!"

He looked at her in amazement. "The door ain't locked. Nobody locks their doors around here." He leaned over and placed the ladder next to the foundation.

"They don't?" She glanced back at the door. In the city, doors were locked.

"Naw. It's open. You can go right in."

As she reached for the doorknob her heart lifted expectantly. She had waited for this moment for years. She'd known since she was eight years old that she wanted to be a teacher. And not in a city school. In a school just like this one, a building all her own, where she and she alone had responsibility for the education of her charges.

She opened the door and stepped into a cloakroom—a shallow room running the width of the building, with an unfinished wooden floor and a single window on each end. Straight ahead was a pair of closed doors. To the left and right of them were scarred wooden benches and above them metal hooks for coats and jackets. In the far left corner stood a square table painted pale blue upon which stood an inverted pottery jar with a red wing design baked into its side and a wooden spigot, much like a wine cask. The floor beneath the spigot was gray from years and years of drips.

She glanced to her right. In the corner leaned a broom, and from a nail above hung a big brush by its wooden handle. She glanced up. Above her head the bell rope hung from the cupola, the huge knot at its end looped over a nail beside the wide white double doors leading straight ahead to the main body of the school.

Slowly she set down her pail.

Just as slowly she opened the doors, then stood a moment, rapt. It was totally silent, totally ordinary. But it smelled of chalk dust and challenge, and if Linnea Brandonberg thought as a girl regarding many things, she embraced this challenge with all the responsibility of a full adult.

"Oh, Kristian, look . . ."

He had seen the schoolroom a thousand times before. What he looked at was the new teacher as her wide, eager eyes scanned the room.

The sun streamed in through the long narrow windows, lighting the rows of desks bolted to their wooden runners. Wall lanterns with tin reflectors hung between the windows. Dead center was a two-burner cast-iron stove, its stack new and glossy, heading up through the tin wainscot ceiling. At the front of the room was a raised platform that, to her disappointment, held no desk, but a large rectangular table holding nothing more than a single kerosene lantern. There was a wooden chair and behind it a tiny bookshelf filled with volumes whose spines had faded into pastel shades of rose, blue, and green. There was a globe, a retractable map—tightly rolled—and blackboards on the front wall, with recitation benches on either side.

Her heart tripped in excitement. It was no different from a thousand others like it in a thousand other similar country settings. But it was hers!

Miss Brandonberg.

The thought made her giddy, and she moved across the length of the room, her skirts lifting a fine layer of dust. Her footsteps startled a mouse that came running toward her, then darted quickly in the opposite direction.

She halted in surprise and sucked in a quick breath. "Oh look! It seems we have company."

Kristian had never before seen a girl who didn't yelp in fright at the sight of a mouse.

"I'll get a trap from home and set it for you."

"Thank you, Kristian. I'm afraid if we don't, he'll eat up the books and papers—if he hasn't already."

At random she chose a book from the shelf. She let it fall open where it would. Petroleum, it said. She forgot about the mouse hole chewed at the edge of the pages and faced

Kristian while reading aloud, "The observation that Horace Greeley made that 'the man who makes two blades of grass grow where only one grew before is a benefactor to his race' finds an analogy in the assertion that he who practically adds to the space of man's life by increasing the number of hours wherein he can labor or enjoy himself is also a benefactor. The nineteenth century marked its course by a greater number of inventions, discoveries, and improvements, promotive of human civilization and happiness, than any like period that preceded it, and perhaps no feature of its record was more significant or beneficent than the improved methods of lighting our dwellings brought into use largely through the instrumentality of the great light bearer—petroleum."

She slapped the book closed and the sound reverberated through the room while she inhaled deeply, standing straight as a nail. He stared at her, wondering how a person could possibly learn to read such words, much less understand what they meant. He thought he had never known a smarter or prettier girl in his life, and welcomed the queer, light-bellied feeling that she inspired.

"I am going to love it here," she said with quiet intensity, pinning Kristian with a beaming blue-eyed look of great resolve.

"Yes, ma'am," Kristian answered, unable to think of anything else to say. "I'll show you the rest, then I got to get back to the fields."

"The rest?"

"Outside. Come on." He turned and led the way through the door.

"Kristian." At his name he stopped and turned.

"It's never too early to begin teaching each other, is it?"

"No, Miss Brandonberg, I guess not."

"Then let's begin with the oldest rule of all. Ladies first."

He blushed the color of a wild rose, hung a thumb from the rear pocket of his overalls, and backed up, waiting for her to pass before him. As she did, she said politely, "Thank you, Kristian. You may leave the door open behind us. It's stuffy in here."

Outside he showed her the pump and the empty coal shed, little more than a lean-to against the west wall of the building.

The wheat fields crowded the edge of the school property to the north and east. To the west stood a tall row of cottonwoods, beneath which were the wooden privies with lattice walls guarding their entrances. The playground had two rope swings supported by a thick wooden spar, and a teeter-totter, also homemade of a rough plank. On the east side of the building was a flat grassy stretch that looked like it was used as a ball diamond.

When they'd explored the entire schoolyard, Linnea lifted her eyes to the tip of the cupola and said impulsively, "Let's ring the bell, Kristian, just to see what it sounds like."

"I wouldn't do that, Miss Brandonberg. Ring it and you'll have every farmer off his rig and running to help."

"Oh. It's a distress signal?"

"Yes, ma'am. Same as the church bell, but that's three miles in the other direction." He thumbed toward the west.

She felt childish once again for having made the suggestion. "I'll just have to wait until Monday then. How many students will I have?"

"Oh, that's hard to say. A dozen. Fourteen maybe. Most of 'em's my cousins."

"Your life's been a lot different than mine, growing up with so much family so close around. All of my grandparents are dead, and there are no aunts and uncles in this part of the country, so mostly it's been my parents and my two sisters and me."

"You got sisters?" he asked, surprised. He felt honored at being told something so personal.

"Two of them. One is your age—Carrie. The other one is four years younger. Her real name is Pauline, but she's at that age—you know—when girls sometimes get rather round and roly-poly." Suddenly she struck a pose, bulging out her cheeks with a big puff of breath until her lips almost disappeared and she waddled and pretended to hold a fat belly. "So we call her Pudge."

He laughed, and she did the same.

No, he really didn't know much at all about how girls changed. He'd never paid any attention to them before. Except to avoid them at every turn.

Until now.

Miss Brandonberg sobered and went on. "She doesn't like it when we tease her, and I suppose sometimes we do it too much, but both Carrie and I went through the same stage and had to put up with teasing, and it didn't hurt either of us."

It was hard for him to imagine her pudgy. She was thin and small-boned, one of the most perfect females he'd ever seen.

"Aw, you was never pudgy."

"*Were* never pudgy," she corrected automatically, then added, "Oh, yes I was. I'm glad you didn't see me then!"

Suddenly he realized how long he'd been here dawdling away the time with her. He glanced toward the fields, hooked his thumbs in his back pockets, and swallowed. "Well, if there's nothing else you need, I . . . I got to get back to help Pa and Uncle John."

She spun around quickly and motioned him away. "Oh, of course, Kristian. I can get along just fine now. I have plenty to do to keep me busy. Thank you for bringing me down and showing me around."

When Kristian was gone she went back inside and eagerly set to work. She spent the morning sweeping and scrubbing the floor, dusting the desks, and washing windows. At midday she took a break and sat on the front steps to dig into the lunch Nissa had packed for her in a small tin molasses pail. Munching a delicious sandwich made with some mysterious meat she'd never tasted before, Linnea relaxed in the sun and dreamed about Monday and how exciting it would be when she faced her first group of children. She imagined some would be eager, receptive, while others would be timid and needing encouragement, and still others would be bold and needing restraining.

The thought brought to mind John and Theodore, so different from one another. *Don't ruin your day with thoughts of Theodore,* she scolded herself. But when she had wandered down to the pump to get a drink of cold water to wash down her sandwich, she found herself gazing west. All the fields for as far as she could see belonged to the two of them. Somewhere out there they were cutting wheat, Kristian along with them.

The land out here was so vast, treeless for the most part. To some it would seem desolate, but Linnea, gazing at the clear blue sky and munificent plains, saw only bounty and beauty.

Her mother always told her she had the gift for finding the good in anything. Perhaps it had something to do with her imagination. In the worst of times she always had an escape ready at hand. Lately, her mother had agreed with her father that it was time to give up such child's play. But fantasy was magic. It took her places she'd never see any other way. It gave her feelings she'd never experienced any other way. And it made her happy.

She wiped the cool water from her lips with the back of a hand and did a dance step across the schoolyard. She leaped onto a swing, sending it into motion, then leaning back and pumping, let herself glide into her own magical world again.

"Well, hello, Lawrence. I hadn't expected to see you so soon again."

Lawrence was dressed like a real dandy today, in a spiffy straw hat, a red and white striped shirt, and bright scarlet sleevebands. He had a way of standing with all his weight on one leg, one hip jutting, that often provoked her to flutter her eyelashes.

"I came to take you on a picnic."

"Oh, don't be silly—I can't frolic off across a field to have a picnic with you. I have school to teach, and besides, the last time you left me with the mess to explain. I was very displeased with you." She pouted as prettily as possible.

Lawrence stepped behind the swing and stopped it, putting his hands on her waist as if to make her step down off the wooden seat.

"I know a place where nobody will find us," he said in a low, encouraging invitation.

She clung to the ropes and laughed teasingly, the sound lilting across the meadow. . . .

Superintendent of schools, Frederic Dahl, guided his horse and buggy into the driveway of Public School 28 and found a most arresting sight waiting to greet him. A lissome young girl dressed in a full gray skirt and white shirtwaist clung to the rope of a swing high above her head, twisting it like a pretzel, first left, then right.

Across the grass he thought he heard a laugh, but a quick check of the surrounding area told him nobody else was in sight. The swing came unwound. She dipped her knees and set it in motion, then let her head hang back.

She was talking to someone—but to whom?

He halted the horse, secured the reins, and stepped from the carriage. As he approached, he could see that the girl was older than he thought, for with her arms upraised, he detected the shape of her breasts.

"Hello!" he called.

Linnea jerked upright and looked over her shoulder. *Crimany, caught again!*

She leaped down, brushed at her skirts, and blushed.

"I'm looking for Mister Brandonberg."

"Yes, it seems like everybody is, but you'll have to settle for me. I'm *Miss* Brandonberg."

His face registered surprise, but no displeasure. "And I'm Superintendent Dahl. My mistake for not clarifying the point in our correspondence. Well, this is a pleasant surprise!"

Superintendent Dahl! Her face grew hotter and she immediately began rolling down the sleeves of her shirtwaist. "Oh, Superintendent Dahl, I'm sorry. I didn't realize it was you!"

"I've come to bring your supplies and make sure you're settled in all right."

"Oh, yes, of course. Come inside. I . . . " She laughed nervously and gestured at her rather soiled skirt. "I was cleaning, so excuse the way I look."

Cleaning? he thought, glancing back over his shoulder as they moved toward the building. But still he found nobody else about. Inside, a ladder leaned against the wall, and the raw wood floor was still damp. She whirled to face him, clasping her hands and exclaiming, "I love it! My first school, and I'm so excited! I want to thank you for recommending me to the school board here."

"You've earned your certificate. Don't thank me. Are you satisfied with your lodging at the Westgaards?"

"I . . . I . . . " She didn't want him to think he'd hired a complainer. "Yes, they're fine. Just fine!"

"Very well. I'm required to make an annual inspection of the property each year at this time, so you go about your work and I'll join you when I've finished."

She watched him walk away, smiling at the real Mr. Dahl, who was nothing at all like the dashing swain she'd imagined.

He was scarcely more than five feet tall, about as big around as a rain barrel, and had balded so perfectly his head appeared tonsured. The circlet of hair he hadn't lost was bright rust colored and stuck out like a May Day wreath above his ears.

When he'd gone outside, she rested an arm across her stomach, covered her smile with one hand, and chuckled softly.

Some knights in shining armor you dream up, Miss Brandonberg. First Theodore Westgaard and now this.

He inspected the outside of the building, the coal shed, even the privies, before he returned inside to do the same. When he was finished, he asked, "Has Mr. Westgaard mentioned the coal?"

"Coal?" she asked blankly.

"Since the Blizzard of '88, when some schools were caught unprepared, there's been a law that there must be enough wood or coal on hand before the first of October to see you through till spring."

She hadn't an inkling about the coal. "I'm sorry, I didn't know. Does Mr. Westgaard supply the coal?"

"He always has in the past. That's got to do with an arrangement between him and the school board. They can pay whoever they want to bring in the coal, but it's my job to see that the arrangements are made."

"Mr. Westgaard is working somewhere in the fields. You might be able to find him and ask him."

He made a notation in a ledger he carried, and replied, "No, that's not necessary. I'll be making my circuit again within two weeks, and I'll make a note here to remind myself to check on it then. In the meantime, I'd appreciate it if you'd remind him about it."

She really didn't want to have to remind Theodore Westgaard about anything, but she nodded and assured Mr. Dahl she'd see to the matter.

He had brought her supplies: chalk, ink, and a brand-new teacher's grade book. She held it reverently, running a palm over its hard red cover. As he watched, he saw beyond the frivolous child who'd been daydreaming on the swing when he drove up. He had a feeling about this one: she'd be dedicated.

"As you know, Miss Brandonberg, school is in session from nine in the morning until four in the afternoon, and your duties include building the fire early enough to have the building warm when the children arrive, keeping it clean at all times, doing the necessary shoveling, and becoming an integral part of the community life around you so that you get to know the families whose children you teach. The last you'll find easiest of all. These are good people. Honest, hardworking. I believe you'll find them cooperative and helpful. If you're ever in need of something and can't reach me fast enough, ask them. I think you'll find nobody gets as much respect around here as the local teacher."

As long as he's a man, she thought. But, of course, she didn't say it. They wished each other good-bye, and she watched Mr. Dahl walk back toward his buggy. But before he reached it, she shaded her eyes with one hand and called, "Oh, Mr. Dahl?"

"Yes?" He paused and turned.

"What happened to those teachers and students who ran out of fuel during the Blizzard of '88?"

He gazed at her steadily while the warm September sun beat down upon them benevolently. "Why, don't you know? Many of them froze to death before help could get to them."

A shiver went through her, and she remembered Theodore's admonition as they'd confronted each other at the train depot. "Teaching school is more than just scratching numbers on a slate, missy! It's a mile's walk, and the winters out here are tough!"

So he hadn't been just trying to scare her off. His warning held merit. She gazed out across the waving wheat, trying to imagine the high plains denuded of all but snow, the arctic wind whistling out of the northwest, and fourteen children depending upon her for their very lives while they waited for help to come.

There'd be no solace to be found in fantasy then. She would need to keep her wits sharp and her head calm when and if that ever happened.

But it was hard to imagine, standing on the steps with the sun warming her hair and the striped gophers playing hide-and-seek in their holes and the meadowlarks singing and the finches feeding on thistle seeds and the grain waving slowly.

Still, she decided, she'd speak to Theodore immediately about the coal, and to Nissa about storing some emergency rations at the schoolhouse . . . just in case.

4

THERE WERE TIMES when Linnea remembered there was a war, but these were chiefly spawned by irritation or romanticized fantasy. Irritation when she had to do without the things she liked best such as sugar, bread, and roast beef, and romantic fantasy whenever it happened to beckon: soldiers kissing sweethearts good-bye as the train pulled from the station . . . those sweethearts receiving soiled, wrinkled letters filled with crowded words of undying love . . . nurses with red crosses on their scarves sitting at bedsides holding wounded hands . . .

Walking home from school that day she thought of the conflict going on in Europe. President Wilson had beseeched Americans to go "wheatless and meatless" one day each week to help keep supplies flowing to France. Glancing around at the endless miles of wheat and the large herds of cows in the distance, she thought, "How silly, when we'll never run out!"

As always, even such a brief reflection on war was too distressing, so she put it from her head in favor of more pleasant thoughts.

The gophers and prairie dogs were hard at play, their antics delightful to watch as they scurried and chattered among the brown-eyed Susans. Stepping along at a sprightly pace, Linnea considered her new class list, which she'd found inside the teacher's grade book. Kristian hadn't been exaggerating when he said most of them were his cousins. Of the fourteen names on the list, eight of them were Westgaards! She couldn't wait to ask Nissa about each of them, and hurried along, eager to get home.

But before she was halfway, she realized her new congress shoes were far less practical than they were dapper. It seemed she could feel every pebble of the gravel road through her soles, and the elevated heels only served to make her ankles wobble when she stepped on rocks.

By the time she was trudging up the driveway, her feet not only hurt but the left one had developed a blister where the tight elastic joined the leather and rubbed her ankle bone. Nissa saw her hobble up and came to the kitchen door. "The walk a little longer than you 'spected?"

"It's just these new shoes. They're still rubbing in spots."

Nissa eyed them speculatively as Linnea climbed the steps and entered the kitchen. "Purty's fine, but sturdy's better out here."

"I'm beginning to see that," Linnea agreed, dropping to a kitchen chair with a sigh of relief. She lifted her ankle over her knee and winced.

Nissa stood with hands akimbo, shaking her head. "Got a blister, have ya?" Linnea looked up and nodded sheepishly. "Well, git 'em off and I'll take a look."

It took some doing to get them off. They were tighter than new cowboy boots, fitting securely well above the ankle. By the time Linnea had tugged and squirmed out of them, Nissa was chortling in amusement. "Don't know what you'd do if you had to get out of them things fast. You got others?"

Linnea's expression turned woeful. "I'm afraid not."

"Well, 'pears we better get you some straight up." She hustled off toward her bedroom and returned with a pair of heavy knit slippers of black wool and a Sears Roebuck and Company catalogue.

"Now, let's see that there blister."

To Linnea's chagrin, it was while Nissa was off fetching some gauze and salve to put on the blister that the men returned to do the milking. She was sitting with her bare foot pulled high up onto her lap, tenderly exploring the fat, bubbled blister when she felt somebody watching her.

She looked up to find Theodore standing in the door, one corner of his mouth hinting at amusement. She dropped her foot so fast it became tangled in her long skirts and she heard stitches pop. Color flooded her face as she covered one foot with the other and gazed up at him defiantly.

"Came for the milk pails," was all he said before moving into the kitchen and crossing to the pantry. Nissa arrived from her bedroom with a tin of ointment and went down on one knee before Linnea. Theodore stepped out of the pantry and asked, "What's wrong with her?"

"She got—"

"I have a blister from my new shoes!" Linnea retorted, suddenly not caring that her face was blazing red as she glared at Theodore. "And I've also got a Teacher's Certificate from the Fargo Normal School that says I'm quite capable of interpreting questions and answering them for myself, in case you're interested!" Angrily she grabbed the ointment and gauze out of Nissa's hands. "I can do that myself, Nissa, thank you." With an irritated twist she took the cover off the tin, wedged her foot sole up, and disregarded her audience while applying the unguent.

Theodore and Nissa exchanged surprised glances. Then Nissa pushed herself to her feet, handed over a needle, and advised dryly, "While you're at it, better bust that thing before you cover it up."

Linnea accepted the needle, raising her eyes no farther than Nissa's hand before tending to the unpalatable task. Nissa looked at her son and found him watching Linnea with an amused crook at the corner of his mouth. When he glanced up, his eyes met Nissa's and he shook his head—hopeless case, his expression said—then left the house with the milk pails swinging at his sides.

When he was gone, Linnea's heel hit the floor with an exasperated *klunk* and she glared at the door. "*That* man can make me so angry!" Suddenly realizing she was speaking to Theodore's mother, she mellowed slightly. "I'm sorry, Nissa, I probably shouldn't have said that, but he's . . . he's so exasperating sometimes! I could just . . . just . . ."

"You ain't hurtin' my feelings. Speak your piece."

"He makes me feel like I'm still in pinafores!" She threw her arms wide in annoyance. "Ever since he picked me up at the station and stood there almost laughing at my hat and shoes. I could see he thought I was little more than a child dressed up in grown-up clothing. Well, I'm not!"

"Course you're not. This here's just a misfortune, that's all. Why, anybody can get a blister. Don't pay no attention to Teddy. Remember what I told you about bullheaded Norwegians and how you got to treat 'em? Well, you just done it. Teddy needs that."

"But why is he so . . . so cross all the time?"

"It goes a long way back. Got nothin' to do with you atall. It's just his way. Now you best get that padding on and let me go get some sandwiches made for them two. When they come in they don't want to waste no time."

While Nissa made sandwiches, Linnea told her all about Superintendent Dahl's visit, then read the list of names from her red book while Nissa filled her in on each one.

The first name on the list was Kristian Westgaard, age sixteen.

"Kristian I already know," Linnea said. "How about the next one—Raymond Westgaard, sixteen?"

"He's my oldest son Ulmer's boy. Him and Kristian've always been close. You'll meet Ulmer and his wife, Helen, and all the rest at church tomorrow. They live the next township road over."

Linnea read the next two names. "Patricia and Paul Lommen, age fifteen."

"Them's the Lommen twins. They live just the other side of Ulmer's place. Sharp as whips, them two. Always fierce competition between 'em, which is natural, being twins and all. Patricia won the country spelling bee last year."

Linnea noted it beside the name before reading on. "Anton Westgaard, age fourteen."

"That's little Tony. He belongs to Ulmer and Helen, too. He's shy like his uncle John, but got a heart the size of all outdoors. Tony had rheumatic fever when he was younger, and it left him a little weak, but he's got a good head on his shoulders nevertheless."

Linnea noted his nickname, and a reminder about his health.

"Allen Severt, fifteen."

"Allen's the son of our local minister. Look out for that one. He's a troublemaker."

Linnea glanced up, frowning. "Troublemaker?"

"I sometimes think he knows he can get by with it because there's only one person gets more respect around here than the schoolteacher, and that's the minister. If the teachers we had in years past had taken him to task like they should've, and told Reverend Severt some of the monkey business Allen's been up to, he might not be such a handful."

"What sort of monkey business?"

"Oh, pushing the younger ones around, teasing the girls in ways that aren't always funny—nothing that could ever be called serious. When it comes to the serious stuff, he's crafty enough to cover his tracks so nothing can be pinned on him. But you watch him. He's mouthy and bold. Never cared for him much myself, but you form your own opinion when you meet him."

Promising to do just that, Linnea went on to the next name. "Libby Severt, age eleven."

"That's Allen's sister. She pretty much gets ignored, cause Allen sees to it he gets all the attention in that family. She seems to be a nice enough child."

"Frances Westgaard, age ten."

"She's Ulmer and Helen's again. She's got a special place in my heart. Guess it's because she's slower than the rest. But you never saw a more willing or loving child in your life. You wait till Christmas time. She'll be the first to give you a present, and it'll have plenty of thought behind it."

Linnea smiled, and sketched a flower behind the name. "Norna Westgaard, age ten."

"Norna belongs to my son Lars and his wife Evie. She's the oldest of five, and she's forever mothering the younger ones. Farther down your list there you'll find Skipp and Roseanne. They're Norna's younger sister and brother."

Nissa became thoughtful for a moment before going on as if answering some silent question. "Least I think Roseanne is starting school this year. They're good kids, all of 'em. Lars and Evie brought 'em up right, just like all my kids brought their own up right."

Linnea smiled at the grandmotherly bias, lowering her face so Nissa couldn't see. The next name on her list was Skipp's, and she bracketed his name with those of his siblings while noting that besides Skipp there were two other eight-year-olds on her list—third grade would be her biggest. "Bent Linder and Jeannette Knutson."

"Bent belongs to my daughter Clara. She's my baby. Married to a fine fellow named Trigg Linder and they got two little ones. Expectin' their third in February." A faraway look came into Nissa's eyes, and her hands fell idle for a moment. "Lord, where does the time go? Seems like just yesterday Clara was going off to school herself." She sighed. "Ah, well. Who's next?"

"Jeannette Knutson."

"She's Oscar and Hilda's—you know? The chairman of the school board?"

"Oh, of course. And I have two seven-year-olds. Roseanne and Sonny Westgaard."

"Cousins. Roseanne I already told you belongs to Evie, and Sonny is Ulmer's. He's named after his pa, but he's always gone by 'Sonny.' "

Linnea's notes were growing confused, just as she was. Her face showed it.

Nissa laughed, set a plate of sandwiches on the table, and returned to the stove, wiping her hands on her apron. "You'll keep 'em straight once you meet 'em all. You'll be callin' 'em by their first names in no time, and know which family they come from. Everybody knows everybody else around here, and you will, too."

"So many of them are your grandchildren," Linnea said with a touch of awe in her voice.

"Thirteen. Be fourteen when Clara has her next one. I always wondered how many more I'd have if John had got married and if Melinda hadn't . . . "

But just then the men clumped in and Nissa's mouth clapped shut. She threw a wary look across the room at Theodore, then abruptly hustled into the pantry to put away a butcher knife.

Who is Melinda, Linnea wondered. Theodore's wife? Kristian's mother?

If Melinda hadn't what?

Linnea covertly studied the father and son as they entered. She tried to picture Theodore with a wife. What would she have been like? Blond, which would account for Kristian's bright hair. And pretty, she decided, noting, too, the young man's attractive features. Was Kristian's shapely mouth and full lower lip inherited from his mother? More than likely so, for Theodore's mouth was shaped differently—wide, crisply defined, but not as bowed. Hard to imagine it ever smiling, for she'd never seen it do so.

From her seat at the table she watched him cross to the water pail, watched his head tilt back as he drank from the dipper. Suddenly he turned and caught Linnea studying him. Their eyes met as he slowly replaced the dipper in the pail, then even more slowly backhanded his lower lip. And something odd happened in her chest. A brief catch, a tightening that caused her to drop her gaze to the list of names in the open book on the kitchen table.

"Came for the sandwiches," he said to no one in particular. Momentarily he appeared beside her, picked up the stack of fat sandwiches, and handed two to Kristian. "Let's go."

"See you at supper," Kristian offered from the door, and she looked up to return his smile.

"Yes, see you at supper."

But Theodore bid no word of farewell, only followed his son out while Linnea wondered what it was that had just struck her. Embarrassment, she supposed, for somehow the man possessed the power to rattle her nearly every time the two of them were within speaking distance.

Nissa returned, set the coffeepot to the hottest part of the stove, and shifted a look to the doorway through which Theodore had just exited.

Linnea drew a deep breath for courage before asking, "Who is Melinda?"

"You want to order them shoes or not?" Nissa nodded toward the catalogue on the table.

"In a minute . . . " Linnea paused before repeating, quietly, "Who is Melinda?"

"She was Teddy's wife, but he don't like to talk about her."

"Why?"

Nissa took off her glasses, held them by the nosepiece, and dampened them with her breath. She lifted the skirt of her apron and paid great attention to their careful polishing while answering. "B'cause she run off and left him with a one-year-old baby and we never seen her in these parts again."

It took an effort for Linnea to withhold her gasp. "W . . . with a one-year-old baby?"

"That's what I said, ain't it?"

"You mean Kristian?"

"Don't see any other babies o' Teddy's 'round here, do you?"

"You mean she . . . she just . . . deserted them?" Something twisted inside Linnea, a twinge of pity, a compulsion to know more.

Nissa sat down, riffled the thick pages with one thumb, searching. The catalogue fell open. She licked a finger and with two flicks found the correct page. "These ones here . . ." She stretched her neck to peer at the row of black-and-white drawings through the polished lenses. "These ladies' storm boots. Good sensible lace-up ones. These'd be good for you." She tapped the page with a forefinger. The finger had skin the texture of jerky and wouldn't quite straighten anymore. Gently, Linnea covered Nissa's old hand. When she spoke, she spoke softly. "I'd like to know about Melinda."

Nissa looked up. The oval lenses magnified her faded brown eyes and accentuated the wrinkles in the lids. She studied Linnea silently, considering. From outside came the call of a crow and the disappearing sound of horses' hooves. She glanced toward the farmyard where father and son could no longer be seen, then withdrew her hand from Linnea's to push the catalogue back with two thumbs. "All right. You want to know, I'll tell you. Much as I know about it. You mind if I get a cup of coffee first?"

Was it Linnea's imagination, or did Nissa appear weary for the first time ever? She braced her knees and pushed herself to her feet, found a cup, and filled it. But when she returned to the table, it wasn't weariness alone that weighted her shoulders. There was in her eyes the unmistakable look of sadness.

"It was the summer of 1900. My man, my Hjalmar, he thought Theodore Roosevelt was just about the greatest person that ever walked this earth. All the people around here loved Old Four Eyes, you know, liked to think of him as their native son, ever since he ranched down at Medora those couple o' years. Add to that the fact that he'd just been down to Cuba with his Rough Riders and rode up San Juan Hill, and he was nothing short of a national hero. But there was nobody admired him like my Hjalmar.

"Then that summer Roosevelt decides to run for vice-president with McKinley, and Hjalmar heard they was coming through Williston on a campaign train. Never forget that day he comes poundin' in the house bellerin' 'missus'—that's what he used to call me when he was excited—'missus,' he bellered, 'get your gear packed, we're goin' to Williston to see Roosevelt!'

"Why, land, I couldn't believe it. I said 'Hjalmar, what're you talking about? You been samplin' Helgeson's new batch of barley beer again?' Used to be this fellow named Helgeson, lived over in the next section and brewed homemade beer the two of them was always claimin' needed testin'. . . . " A light of remembrance softened Nissa's eyes, and the ghost of a smile tipped up her lips. Abruptly she cleared her throat, took a gulp of coffee, and drew herself back to the main point of the story.

"So Hjalmar, he says no boy that was named after Teddy Roosevelt should miss the chance to see his namesake in the flesh when he was gonna be no more'n sixty miles away, and so we was all three going to Williston to meet that train."

Nissa made a gavel of her fist and brought it down lightly atop the open catalogue. "Well, say, that's just what we did. Rode on down to Williston, the three of us, and took a room in the Manitou Hotel and got all gussied up in our Sunday clothes and went to the depot to watch that train come in." She waggled her head slowly. "It was somethin' to see, I'll tell you." She pressed her fist to her heart. "There was this big brass band playin' all them marching songs and school children waving American flags, and then the train come in, all decked out with bunting . . . and there he was, Mr. Roosevelt himself, standin' on the last car with his hands in the air and his cheeks as red as the stripes on them flags and that band boomin' out patriotic songs. I remember lookin' up at my Hjalmar and seein' the smile on his face—he had a mustache just like Roosevelt's—and he had his arm around our Teddy's shoulder and was pointing at the great man and shoutin' somethin' in Teddy's ear."

Watching the expression on Nissa's face, Linnea could see and hear it all. Then Nissa looked up, caught herself woolgathering, and dropped her hand from her heart to the handle of her cup. She sniffed, as if to clear more than just her nose.

"Well, she was there on the train somewhere, Melinda was. Her pa was on the McKinley/Roosevelt campaign committee and her ma was dead, so she went everywhere with him. As it turns out, they stayed in Williston for more than a whistle-stop. Seems there was some rich fellow there by the name of Hagens who had donated plenty to the campaign, and there was a regular rally where the farmers could have a chance to talk to the candidates and pin 'em down to some promises. Afterwards there was a dinner at the Manitou and they spread all of McKinley's key people around at the tables to answer questions, and Melinda and her pa ended up at our table.

"I don't remember much about it and maybe it was Hjalmar's and my fault for not payin' much mind to them young people, but he was busy talkin' politics and I was gettin' my eye full of that fancy hotel. I do remember there was a band playin' again and once I nudged Hjalmar's shoulder and said 'Would you look at there,' because lo and behold, there was our Teddy dancing with that young girl. Course Hjalmar, he was caught up in arguing the goods and bads of Mr. Roosevelt's new civil service system, and I don't just remember what time it was but our Teddy he comes and tells us he and the young lady are going out for a walk. Sure, I was surprised, but Teddy, he was seventeen, after all."

Linnea tried to imagine Theodore at seventeen, but could not. She tried to imagine Theodore dancing, but could not. She tried to imagine him taking a young woman out for a walk with her hand on his arm, but could not. Having seen only his irascible side, these pictures seemed out of character.

"But seventeen or not, that boy had us in a tizzy fit before mornin'. We waited and we waited, and we checked with Melinda's pa, but she wasn't back either, and it wasn't till nearly five in the mornin' them two got back and when they come down the hall they was holdin' hands." Nissa peered over the tops of her glasses and crossed her arms over her chest. "Now, you ever seen what it's like when a weasel sashays into a henhouse? That's about what it was like when we caught sight of them two in that hall. There was feathers flyin' in all directions, and some of 'em was from me. Granted, I was doin' my share of dressin' down, but, lord, I never heard such bawlin' and screamin' and shoutin' as when Melinda's pa hauled her off into their room down the hall, flingin' accusations at her. She was yowlin' fit to kill and claimin' they'd done nothin' to be ashamed of and that if she lived in a house and stayed put like other girls she wouldn't have to stay out all night to make new friends." Nissa rubbed her mouth, staring at the cold coffee in her cup. "I never asked where they was all that time, nor what they done. Truth to tell, I don't think I wanted to know. We hauled Teddy into our room and slammed the door while that girl was actin' like a wildcat in the hall yet, and heads was poppin' out of doors. Land, it was awful."

Nissa sighed. "Well, we thought that was the end of it and we hauled Teddy out of there in the mornin' without settin' eyes on Melinda again. But don't you know it wasn't a week later she showed up at my kitchen door, bold as brass—we was livin' in John's place then. That was the home place up there—said she wanted to see Teddy and would I please tell her where she could find him." Nissa shook her head disbelievingly. "I can see her yet, with that face lookin' like she wouldn't have the spunk to ask for second helpings, standin' there on my doorstep demanding to see my boy—it never fit, how she acted then and how she turned out to be. Guess it was just one of them crazy times of life some of us goes through when we're chafin' at the bit and think it's time to cut the apron strings."

Nissa faded off into memory again, pondering silently.

"What happened?" Linnea encouraged.

Nissa looked up, drew a deep sigh, and went on. "What happened is she marched right out there into the field where Teddy was cuttin' wheat with Hjalmar and the boys, and she says she had decided to come here and marry him after all, just like they talked about. Now, I never asked, but it appeared to me her showin' up sayin' that was as much of a surprise to Teddy as it was to the rest of us. But he never let on, and with a face like Melinda's, it was easy to see he was knocked off his pins.

"They married all right, and fast. Hjalmar, he give them this land here, and all the boys put up this house for them. We all wondered how it'd work out, but we hoped for the best. It come out later how she'd been fightin' with her pa about travelin' on the train with him, and I reckon what was actually behind it was she was nothin' more than a young girl being told to do one thing and decidin', by lizzie, she wasn't gonna be told what to do.

"So she married my boy. But she never suited." Nissa shook her head slowly. "Never. She was a city girl, and what she wanted with a farm boy I never could understand. First thing you know she got in a family way, and I can see her yet, standin' at the window staring at the wheat, sayin' it was drivin' her crazy. Lord, how she used to cuss that wheat. Trees, she said, there wasn't no trees out here. And no sound, she said. The sun gave her rashes and the flies drove her crazy and the smell of the barnyard give her headaches. How Teddy ever thought a woman like that could be a farm wife, I'll never know. Why, she had no sense about raisin' gardens—didn't like gettin' her fingernails dirty, didn't know how to put up vegetables." Nissa made a sound of humorless disdain: "P'chee." Again she shook her head, crossed her arms. "A woman like that," she ended, as if still mystified by her son's choice.

"I seen it happenin', but there wasn't nothin' I could do. Teddy, he was so happy when she first come here. And when he found out there was a baby comin', why, that boy was in his glory. But little by little her complainin' turned to silence, and she started actin' like she *was* gettin' a little tetched. At first, after Kristian was born, I could see she tried to be a good mother, but it was no good. Teddy never said so, but Clara used to come down here and play with the baby, and she'd come home and tell us how Melinda cried all the time. Never quit cryin', but what could he do about it? He couldn't change all that wheatland into woods. He couldn't put no city in the middle of this here farmyard for her.

"And then one day she just up and left. Left a note sayin' to tell Kristian she loved him and she was sorry, but I never saw it, nor did I ask to. It was Clara told me about it." Again her thoughts trailed off.

"And you took care of Kristian after that?"

A new sadness came into Nissa's eyes. "Me and Clara did. You see, my man, my Hjalmar, he'd died that year. We'd been up to church one spring evenin' to help with the grave-yard cleanin' like we always did every spring. We come home and was standin' just outside the kitchen door and I remember Hjalmar had his hands in his pockets and he looked up at the first star comin' out and he says to me, he says, 'Nissa, we got lots to be thankful for. It's gonna be a clear day tomorrow,' and just like that he pitches over and falls dead on our doorstep. He always used to say to me, 'Nissa, I want to die workin',' and you know, he got his wish. He worked right up to the very hour he died at my feet. No pain. No sufferin'. Just a man counting his blessings. Now, I ask you, what more could a woman ask for than to see her man die a beautiful death like that?"

The room grew quiet except for a soft sigh of ash collapsing in the stove. Nissa's stiff old hands rested, crossed, beneath her drooping breasts. In her eyes was the bright sheen of remembrance as she stared, unseeing, at the red flowered oilcloth beneath the catalogue. A lump formed in Linnea's throat. Death was an entity she hadn't pondered, and certainly never as a thing that could be beautiful. Studying Nissa's downcast eyes, Linnea suddenly understood the beauty of lifelong commitment and realized that for those like Nissa it took more than death to negate it.

Nissa lifted the cup to her lips, unaware that the coffee was cold. "The home place was never the same without Hjalmar, so I left it to John and came up here to take care of Teddy and the baby, and I been here ever since."

"And Melinda? Where is she now?" Linnea inquired softly, holding her breath for some inexplicable reason. She sat absolutely still while waiting for the answer.

"Melinda got run over and killed by a streetcar in Philadelphia when Kristian was six."

Oh, I see. The words were unspoken, but buzzed in Linnea's mind as she released the lungful of air in small, careful spurts that slowly relaxed her shoulders. The room grew still except for the soft, absent tapping of Nissa's fingertips upon the forgotten catalogue. Her apron swagged between her spread knees, and the afternoon sun lit the soft fuzz on her cheeks. Suddenly it seemed the kitchen was being visited by two people long dead, and Linnea strove to see their faces, but all she made out was a white drooping moustache on one and the drooping shoulders of the other as she stared out the window at the fields where even now Theodore was cutting grain.

She glanced at the window. *So that's why you're bitter. You were so young and the wound was so deep.* She felt a twinge of guilt for her impatience and anger with him. She wished she could somehow undo it, but even if she could, what good would it do? It wouldn't change what he'd suffered in the past.

And Kristian, poor Kristian. Growing up without a mother's love.

"Does Kristian know?" Linnea asked sympathetically.

"That she run away? He knows. But he's a good boy. He's had me, and Clara, and plenty of other aunts. I know it ain't the same as his real ma, but he's got along fine. Well . . . " The mood was broken as Nissa threw a glance at the catalogue. "We ain't gettin' them shoes picked out now, are we?"

They chose the storm boots of pebbled black box calf that tied up the front to mid-calf, and while Linnea was filling out the mail-order blank, Nissa added one last postscript to the personal story. "I'd appreciate it if you didn't tell Teddy I told you. He don't talk about her much, and, well, you know how men can get. I figured you ought to know, being Kristian's teacher and all."

But Linnea didn't know how men could get. She was only now coming to learn. Still, the story had had great impact on her, and she found herself promising to treat Theodore more patiently in the future.

The men returned late again, and when they shuffled in, Linnea realized she was studying Theodore as if expecting to find some physical change in his appearance. But he looked the same as ever—powerful, somber, and unhappy. All through supper she was conscious of the fact that he had studiously refrained from glancing her way; neither had he spoken to her since she'd upbraided him earlier that afternoon. As they all took their places at the table, John offered his polite, self-conscious nod, accompanied by a shy, "Hello, miss." And Kristian angled furtive glances her way after a stumbling greeting. But Theodore concentrated on his plate and nothing else.

When the meal was half over, she could tolerate his disregard no longer and found herself overwhelmed by the need to end the enmity between them. Perhaps what she really wanted was to make up in some small way for Melinda.

He was taking a bite of mashed potatoes and gravy when she fixed her eyes on him and spoke into the silence. "Theodore, I want to apologize for the way I spoke to you this afternoon."

His jaws stopped moving and his gaze rested on her for the first time that evening while he tried to mask a look of total surprise.

Completely dauntless and wearing an open look of ingenuousness, she went on, "I'm certainly glad none of my students was here to see me, because I didn't make a very good example. I was sarcastic and snappy, which is really no way to treat people when it's just as easy to ask nicely. So I'm asking nicely this time. In the future, Theodore, would you please speak to me directly when I'm in the room, instead of talking over my head as if I'm not there?"

Theodore stared at her for a moment before his glance flickered to Nissa, then Kristian.

Kristian had stopped eating to stare in surprise at Miss Brandonberg taking his father down a notch, and all with the coolest of courtesy and a direct look that Theodore was having trouble meeting. Furthermore, she'd done it again—started talking in the middle of supper. Nobody around here cared much for talking on an empty stomach, and he could see Theodore's eagerness to get on with his meal in peace. But she was staring him down, second for second, sitting as pert and straight as a chipmunk while beneath her steady gaze his face turned pink.

"Somehow," she went on benevolently, "you and I managed to get off on the wrong foot, didn't we? But I think we can be more adult than that, don't you?"

Theodore didn't know what to say. The little missy had apologized—to the best of his memory the first time in his life any female had ever apologized to him—yet she seemed to be calling him childish at the same time. *Him!* When he was nearly old enough to be her father! He swallowed, feeling confused and wondering what sarcastic meant. Nissa, John, and Kristian were all watching and listening, nobody moving a hand, and finally Theodore had to say *some*thing!

He swallowed again and it felt like the potatoes were stuck in his throat. He stared at the little missy's fresh, wide-eyed expression and realized what a pretty young thing she was.

"Yeah, maybe we could at that. Now eat." And he gratefully dropped his attention to his plate.

She had won a round at last. Realizing it, Linnea felt John's gaze still lingering on her in amazement. She gave him a wide smile, making him dig into his meal again with self-conscious haste.

The little miss was something new to John. Someone who could make Teddy blush and back down when nobody'd ever been able to do that except their ma. But the way Ma did it was a lot different than the way Little Missy did it. In his dull-witted way, John wondered just how she'd managed it. He remembered one other woman who used to be able to soften up Teddy. Melinda. She'd been somethin', that Melinda, pretty and tiny and big-eyed as a newborn colt. All she used to have to do was turn those big eyes on Teddy and he'd get pink around the collar. A lot like he just did when Little Missy talked soft and serious and looked him square. And Melinda used to talk at the table, too. Always sayin' how she couldn't understand their Norwegian ways, how they all bottled things up inside and never talked about what really mattered.

Not being one who talked much, John never had understood that.

He glanced up and met Ma's eyes.

You remember, John, don't you? Nissa was thinking. That's the way he used to act around Melinda. She turned her gaze to her right, to the girl politely eating and totally unaware of the undertones she'd just caused, then to Teddy engrossed in his supper but frowning at his plate.

I think, my crotchety son, that you've met your match at last.

*   *   *

It was Saturday night. Nissa got down her galvanized wash-tub, set it near the kitchen stove, and began filling it with steaming water.

"We take turns," she announced. "You wanna be first?"

Linnea gawked at the tub, at the wide-open kitchen, glanced at the living-room doorway, from beyond which the voices of John and Theodore could be clearly heard, then back at the tub beside the stove.

"I think I'll just take some water upstairs in my basin."

She filled the small speckled basin and took it to her room, only to find the amount of water inadequate. Still, the all-over bath felt glorious. While she was washing, she heard John leave for home. The house grew quieter and quieter. She dried, dressed in her nightgown, and sat in her rocking chair to study the notes she'd made beside her students' names. Nissa took her bath first, then her voice carried clearly as she called upstairs to tell Kristian it was his turn. She heard him go downstairs with his clean clothes, and some time later, come back up wearing them, she presumed. She heard the third bath in progress, and tried to picture those long legs folded into the tiny tub, and smiled. A few minutes later she heard Theodore call Kristian downstairs to help carry the washtub outside.

Then nothing but silence.

John, Nissa, Kristian . . . Theodore, she thought. My surro-gate family now. Each so individual, each raising a distinctly different reaction within her. She'd liked them all immediate-ly. Except Theodore. So why was it she thought about him longest? Why did his unsmiling face and contrary disposition remain in her thoughts even after the lantern was out and she found it impossible to feel sleepy? Why was it *his* bare limbs she thought about in the washtub?

The house was quiet, the lingering smells of supper mixed with the scent of homemade lye soap in the dimly lit kitchen as Theodore and his son carried the washtub out to the yard.

When the water had been slewed, Theodore stood a moment, studying the sky, contemplating. After some time, he said thoughtfully, "Kristian?"

"What?"

He reviewed the word carefully before pronouncing it exactly as she had. "You know what sarcastic means?"

"No, Pa, I don't. But I'll ask Miss Brandonberg."

"No!" Theodore exclaimed, then consciously dropped the anxiety from his voice. "No, it don't matter. Don't go askin' her nothin' on my account."

They stood in the darkness, the sound of early-autumn crickets harmonizing through the night, the tub weightless now between their two hands. The moon was at three-quarter phase, white as fresh milk in a star-studded sky, throwing their shadows long and deep.

"She sure is pretty, ain't she?" Kristian murmured softly.

"You think so?"

"Well, she sure ain't mousy and puny, like you said. Why'd you say that, anyway?"

"Did I say that?"

"You sure did. But she's no more mousy and puny than Isabelle, and you seem to think Isabelle's all right."

Theodore harrumphed. "I think you better take another look at Isabelle when she drives that cook wagon in here."

"Well, all right, there's a lot more to Isabelle compared to Miss Brandonberg, but still Miss Brandonberg isn't mousy and puny. She looks just right to me."

Theodore eyed his son askance, making out his clear, youthful profile beneath the bright moonlight. "You better not let her hear you say that, seeing as how she's your teacher."

"Yeah, I guess you're right," Kristian said dejectedly, dropping his glance to the dark earth, standing thoughtfully for a moment before suddenly lifting his face and asking more brightly, "You wanna know somethin' funny?"

"What?"

"She thinks Russian thistles are *pretty*! She said she's gonna have us go out in the field and paint pictures of them!"

Theodore grunted, then laughed once, joined by Kristian. "Yeah, well, she's a town girl. You know they ain't so smart about some things."

But later, when Theodore lay down in his double bed, where he'd slept alone for well over fourteen years, he tried to picture a Russian thistle blossom and realized he really wasn't sure

what one looked like. For though he'd seen thousands upon
thousands of them in his thirty-four years, he'd never looked
at one with anything but contempt. He decided next time he
saw one he'd take a second look.

5

LINNEA WASN'T PREPARED for the change she saw in Kristian and Theodore on Sunday morning. They'd looked the same as always when they returned from doing the morning chores to have their breakfast. But afterward, when Nissa called up the steps, "Come on! Buggy's waiting!" Linnea dashed outside to find father and son dressed in formal black suits and ties and crisp white shirts, sitting side by side in the front seat of a black four-passenger surrey.

She came up short, assessing Theodore's formal black hat and Kristian's freshly combed hair, still wet at the sides and gleaming in the sun. They both wore tight, tight collars that appeared to be cutting into their jaws.

"My, don't you two look handsome," she said, pausing beside the rig. Kristian lit up while Theodore's eyes lazily lingered on her ridiculous high hat, then dropped to her feet to assess the high-heeled congress shoes. He'd give them about six weeks out here on these rocky roads.

Neither of them, however, remembered to help the ladies board. When Nissa made a move to do so unaided, Linnea halted her as inconspicuously as possible.

"I wonder, Kristian, if you'd mind giving your grandmother a hand up. Her knees are bothering her this morning."

"My knees're as good—"

"Now, Nissa," Linnea hushed her with a light touch on the arm. "You remember how you just said your knees seem to be out of joint this morning. Besides, a young man like Kristian is only too happy to display his manners and help us ladies board."

He was down in a flash to hand up first Nissa then Linnea into the backseat, grinning widely. Theodore craned to observe, but said not a word. He just sat and watched the girl work her wiles on his son, who was falling all over himself to do her bidding. When everyone was seated, he caught the little missy's eye, lifted one brow sardonically, then turned to cluck at the horses, flick the reins, and order quietly, "Hup there, Cub, Toots." The whiffletree leveled and they were off at a trot.

The ride was very pleasant, though Linnea couldn't help wondering at the reticence these people practiced during times when her own family would have been chatting pleasantly. Why, the weather alone made her spirits bubble. A slight breeze rustled the grasses at the edge of the road; the mid-morning sun was a golden caress. And the smell—pure, clean, the way she imagined it must smell a mile up into the clouds.

She glanced up. A few meringue puffs floated high to the north, but straight ahead the westerly sky was hard blue, a blue so rich it smote the senses.

Against it, she saw the white steeple long before they reached it. It seemed to be resting on Theodore's broad right shoulder. The bell pealed, drifting to them quietly on the soft autumn wind. Again it pealed, louder, then again, diminished, its reverberations waxing and waning at the whim of the wind. Twelve times it chimed, until its canticle at last ushered their carriage into the churchyard.

Here, as at school, the wheat pressed close, surrounding the scores of horses and rigs tied at the hitching posts. The churchyard was filled with the congregation, all outside taking in a few extra minutes of the wondrous morning. The men stood in groups with their thumbs caught in their waistcoat pockets discussing the weather and the crops. The women gathered together, their bonnets nodding, discussing their canning. The children, their freshly polished boots already coated with dust, chased each other around the women's skirts while being warned to stop before their shoes got dusty.

When the surrey halted, Linnea didn't have to remind Kristian of his manners. He was johnny-on-the-spot, helping both women with a newfound sense of pride. But as they walked toward the church steps, Nissa commandeered her grandson's arm and Linnea found herself beside Theodore. She neither took his elbow, nor did he offer it, but moved through the crowd with him, offering quick smiles when her glance met those of strangers.

Immediately she sensed people falling back to give her a respectful distance, watching as she made her way toward the door. There, Theodore introduced her to the minister, Reverend Martin Severt, a spare, handsome man in his mid-thirties, and his wife, an angular, well-dressed woman with prominent teeth and a ready smile. The Severts seemed a charming couple, their handshakes warm, their welcomes genuine, and Linnea couldn't help but wonder if their son was really the mischief-maker Nissa said he was.

Inside, John was already waiting in their pew. As they filed in to join him, Linnea ended up between Kristian and his father. When the service began, Kristian followed along in his prayer book, but Theodore sat for the most part with arms crossed tightly over his chest. Until the hymns began. She was amazed, then, to hear him sing out heartily in a clear, resonant baritone, as true as the tone of a tuning fork. Joining him in her equally true soprano, she allowed herself a cautious upward glance.

It was impossible, she decided, for a person to appear hard-bitten while singing a hymn.

For the first time, she saw all that his face could be. His lips, now open wide in song, appeared less harsh than ever before. His jaw, dropped low to hold a note, had lost its stubborn set. And his eyes, lit by morning light streaming through an arched window, sparkled with a mellow expression. Shoulders squared, he stood with eight fingertips lightly tapping the pew in front of them, adding his robust voice to those around him.

He glanced down and caught her—singing, too—peering up at him. For only a moment his eyes seemed to radiate the smile his open mouth could not. Obviously, he knew the words by heart, but the moment was too perfect to pass up the opportunity of proffering an olive branch. It took only the slightest leftward shift for Linnea to lift her hymnal and offer to share it. Her elbow bumped his arm. A ripple skipped up her skin. She felt his uncertain pause, then he angled his body toward her. His fingers took the far edge of the book and they finished the hymn together.

In those minutes, while their voices blended toward heaven, she felt a reluctant accord, but by the time the song ended, a barrier had tumbled.

When the amen faded, Theodore waited until she began folding toward the seat before following suit. The sermon began and she struggled to concentrate on it and not the smell of lye soap and hair dressing coming from her left.

The service ended with Reverend Severt announcing, "We're pleased to have with us today our new schoolteacher, Miss Linnea Brandonberg. Please take a minute to greet her and introduce yourselves and make her feel welcome." Dozens of heads turned her way, but she was uncomfortably aware of only one, the one directly to her left. Realizing Theodore was scrutinizing her at closer range than ever before, she wondered suddenly if her hat was straight, her collar flat, her hair tight. But a moment later the church began emptying and she was swept into the bright autumn day. She forgot about appearances and concentrated on the new faces and names.

They were all such ordinary people, but in that very ordinariness Linnea saw nobility. The men were built broad and strong, their hands hard and wide, all of them dressed in stern black and white. The women dressed simply with much more attention to comfort than to style. Their hats, unlike hers, were plain and flat, their shoes sensible. But to a number, they afforded Linnea an unmistakable diffident respect. The women smiled shyly, the men doffed their hats, and the children blushed when being introduced to "the new teacher."

She met all of her students, but the two who stuck in her memory after they turned away were the Severt boy—a looker like his father, but with an unsettling nervousness about him—and Frances Westgaard, because Nissa had said she was slow. Perhaps it was the innate teacher in Linnea that made her radiate toward any child who needed her most, but her first glimpse of the thin girl with freckles and a corona of braids sent her heart out to the child.

Alas, there were so many Westgaard children she soon gave up trying to remember who belonged to whom. The adults were a little easier. Ulmer and Lars were simple to spot because they looked so much like Theodore, though Ulmer, the eldest, was losing his hair, and Lars had a far more ready smile.

And then came Clara—bulging with pregnancy, laughing at something private her husband had just whispered in her ear, and with eyes that smiled even before her lips did. Her hair was coffee-brown and she had beautiful skin, though her features were far less classically attractive than her brothers'. Her nose was a little too long and her mouth a little too wide, but when she smiled one scarcely noticed these imperfections, for Clara had something much more lasting. Clara had the beauty of happiness.

Linnea knew the minute their eyes met, she was going to like this woman.

Clara clasped Linnea's hand, held it firmly and let a conspiratorial grin play at the corners of her lips. "So you're the one who put my brother in his place. Good for you. He probably needed it."

Linnea was so startled she couldn't think of a proper response.

"I'm Clara."

"Y . . . yes," Linnea's eyes swept down to her gently rounded belly. "I thought so."

Clara laughed, caressed her high stomach, and pulled her husband's elbow closer against her side. "And this is my Trigg."

Perhaps it was the way she said "my Trigg" that made Linnea like her even more. There was such obvious pride in her voice, and for good reason. Trigg Linder was probably the handsomest man Linnea had ever seen. His hair glinted in the sun like freshly polished copper, his sky-blue eyes had the kind of lashes women envy, and his Nordic features had flawless symmetry and beauty. But what Linnea noted about Trigg Linder that remained in her memory was that all the while his wife talked, he kept one hand lightly around the back of her neck and seemed unable to keep himself from enjoying her face.

"So Teddy gave you a hard time," Clara commented.

"Well, he . . . he didn't exact—"

Clara laughed. "You don't have to whitewash it with me. I know our Teddy, and he can be a royal Norwegian pain. Mule-headed, stubborn . . . " She squeezed Linnea's wrist. "But he has his moments. Give him time to adjust to you. Mean-time, if he gets to you, come on over and let off some steam at my house. Coffee's always on and I sure could use the company."

"Why, thank you, I just might do that."

"And how about Ma? She treating you okay?"

"Oh, yes. Nissa's been wonderful."

"I love every wiry hair on her head, but sometimes she drives me plumb crazy, so if she gives you one too many orders and you have the urge to tie and gag her, come and see me. We'll talk about all the times I almost did." She was already leaving when she turned back and added, "Oh, by the way, I love your hat."

Unexpectedly Linnea burst out laughing.

"Did I say something funny?"

"I'll tell you when I come for coffee."

Even pregnant, Clara moved briskly, but when she was gone Linnea was the one who felt breathless. So this was Clara, the one who'd been closest to Theodore. The one who'd known Melinda. And she'd invited Linnea's friendship. There was no doubt in Linnea's mind she'd take her up on the offer.

Just then Kristian appeared and announced, "Pa says to come and ask you if you're just about ready."

She looked across the churchyard and found Nissa already in the wagon and Theodore standing beside his rig looking displeased, his foot tapping nervously.

"Oh, am I holding you up?"

"Well, it . . . it's the wheat. Out here, when the weather's good and the wheat's ripe, we work every day of the week."

"Oh!" So she'd given her landlord fuel for the fire. "Let me just say good-bye to Reverend Severt." She kept her farewell short, but even so, as she crossed to Theodore's wagon she saw the irritation on his face.

"I'm sorry I held you up, Theodore. I didn't know you'd be going out in the fields today."

"You never heard of making hay while the sun shines, missy? Just get up there and let's move." He grasped her elbow and helped her up with a shove that was more rude than no help at all. Singed by his abrupt change after the closeness to him she'd felt in church, Linnea rode home in confusion.

As soon as they arrived there was a quick scramble to change clothes. Linnea was in her room removing her hatpin when she remembered the coal. The last thing on earth she wanted to do was bring up the subject and rile him further, but she had little choice.

She intercepted him as he came out of his bedroom into the parlor, dressed in freshly washed and ironed bib overalls and a clean faded-blue chambray shirt. He was setting his shaggy straw hat on his head when he came up short at the sight of her. His arm came down very slowly, and they stared at each other for a long, silent moment.

She recalled sharing the hymnal with him in church and how for those few minutes he had seemed . . . different. Approachable. Likable. Suddenly it became difficult to talk to him. But at last she found her voice.

"I realize how busy you are at this time of the year, but I promised Mr. Dahl I'd remind you about the school coal."

"Dahl always thinks a blizzard's gonna blow up in the middle of September and he'll lose his job if that coal shed's not filled. But Dahl ain't got wheat to get in."

"*Hasn't* got wheat to get in," she corrected.

"What?" His brows drew together.

"Hasn't got . . . " Her fingers went up to cover her lips. *Oh, Linnea, must your tongue always work faster than your brain?* "Nothing. N . . . nothing . . . I . . . I told him I'd remind you, now I have. Sorry I held you up." What was it about the man that could make her so twitchy at times?

"If Dahl comes around pesterin' you about it again, tell him I'll get to it when I can. While the sun shines, I cut wheat." And with that he shouldered around her and left the house.

The afternoon stretched before her endlessly, so she decided to go down to the schoolhouse. Knowing more about her students now, able to put a few faces to names, she sat down and mapped out the first week's lesson plans, perusing her limited textbooks. There was *Worcester's Speller, McGuffey's Reader, Ray's Mental Arithmetic, Monteith and McNally's Geography,* and *Clark's Grammar.* The other books on the shelf were on varied subjects and appeared to have been donated from homes over the years. Most, such as the one she'd randomly selected the day she read to Kristian—entitled *New Era Economics*— were far too advanced to be of much use for her students, especially the younger ones.

But there was one thing children were never too young to learn, and that was table manners. She needed no books to help her teach this! And it was high on her list of priorities.

When her lessons plans were done, she unfurled the American flag and hung it from its bracket up front, printed the words to the "Pledge of Allegiance" on the blackboard, then her name in large block letters: MISS BRANDONBERG. She stood back, surveying it with smiling satisfaction, brushing the chalk dust from her fingers, almost giddy at the thought of ringing the bell at nine o'clock tomorrow morning and calling her first class to order.

It was only mid-afternoon, and she hated to leave the pleasant schoolhouse just yet.

On a sudden inspiration she sat down and began drawing a series of large alphabet cards to augment the textbooks, each with a picture to represent the letter. On A she drew an apple. On B a barn. On C a cat. She enjoyed drawing, and took time over the task, stopping often to ponder long and hard over what symbol should represent each letter. Striving to make them pictures of things to which the children could relate, she made H a horse, rather misproportioned, but she did her best—M a mouse, and S a sunflower. And with a smile, she began next on a thistle.

But upon beginning, she realized she'd need to see the plant to capture the Russian thistle accurately.

She walked down the road with the sun beating hot on her hair, dreaming idle dreams while the cottonwoods tittered in the gentle afternoon breeze. Spying a gleaming amber rock in the middle of the road, she squatted, plucked it into her palm, and remained hunkered for long minutes, chin on knees, savoring the warmth of the stone—smooth and weighty in her palm. In places it glittered, and in the center bore a translucent stripe reminiscent of the color of Theodore's eyes. She closed her own and remembered the touch of his arm next to hers in church, the odd sense of unity she'd felt while singing with him. She had never before been to a church service with a man.

She rubbed the stone with her thumb, popped it into her mouth, tasting its warmth and good earthiness, then spit it into her hand and studied the brown stripe, wet now, gleaming, its color intensified to the deep amber of Theodore's eyes.

She smiled dreamily, hunkering yet in the center of the road.

"Lawrence," she murmured aloud, "isn't it funny, I've known you all this time yet I've never noticed the color of your eyes."

She stood up, squeezing the stone in her palm. She looked into Lawrence's eyes. "Oh," she noted disappointedly, "they're green." Then she forced herself to brighten. "Oh, well. Come on"—she grabbed Lawrence's hand—"I'll show you a Russian thistle."

She found one in the ditch not far up the road. It grew in a ball. In winter it rolled before the prairie wind and caught on barbed-wire fences, causing thick drifts to build up around it. Come spring, it had to be manually dislodged. But now, in September, it was a perfect orb of tiny green flowers. A pair of blue-green bottleflies buzzed around it, and a fat bumblebee came to dip into its flowers.

Linnea leaned her drawing pad against her waist and began sketching. *"Now tell me, Lawrence, don't you find that a pretty plant? Look how the bee drinks from it."*

* * *

Coming over the crest of a small rise of land in the wheat
field to the northeast of the schoolhouse, Theodore raised his
eyes to the small building in the distance. From here it appeared
no larger than a dollhouse, but as the horses plodded along
the gentle slope he made out the coal shed, the swings, the
bell gleaming in the sunlight. A motion caught his eye and
he noticed a figure some distance from the school, standing
in the ditch near the far corner of the field. Unconsciously his
spine straightened and his elbows came off his knees. Beneath
the brim of his hat his brown eyes softened and a small smile
lifted his lips.

What was she doing out there, the little missy? Standing in
weeds up to her knees with something in her hands, something
he couldn't make out from here. Such a child, dawdling in the
ditch as if she had nothing better to do with her time. He gave
a silent, indulgent chuckle.

He knew the moment she spied him. She straightened, alert,
then lifted whatever she was holding to shade her eyes. An
odd exhilaration fluttered within him as she suddenly flung
both arms in the air and waved in wide arcs, jumping up and
down several times.

He shook his head a little, smiling as he eased forward again,
elbows to knees, and continued studying her.

Such a child, he thought. Such a child.

Linnea watched the three sickles cross the field, coming her
way, but too far to tell who was in the lead. It was a stunning
sight, and she wished she possessed the skill to capture it in
a painting, in bright yellows and blues to duplicate those of
the wheat and the sky. There was a magnificence about the
men and horses, so small against the majesty of all that land,
spread before her in vast oceans of undulating yellow. That
they controlled it and made it bountiful increased her admiration. Something clutched her heart with a wondrous ferocity
and the words of a song came with awesome clarity . . .

> *Oh, beautiful for spacious skies*
> *For amber waves of grain . . .*

Could there really be a war happening when before her lay nothing but beauty and bounty? And they said it was happening to preserve exactly what she was looking at. She thought of the flag she'd just hung, the words she'd just printed on the blackboard. She watched three men drive their teams through the thick stand of wheat. She breathed deeply. And leaped three times in sheer appreciation. And waved.

And one of them waved back.

6

LINNEA HAD SLEPT in a state of excitement. Awakening the first morning of school, she heard a rooster crowing out a reveille. Dawn promised a clear day through her little square of window. Downstairs, Nissa was making noises in the kitchen. Linnea bounded from bed with vitality and an avidity to begin the real thing at last.

She took great care with her hair, parting it down the middle, forming the tight twist that began just behind her ears and contoured her nape in a crescent shape. She donned her new green skirt and the matching Black Watch plaid shirtwaist, buttoning it high up the neck, then stretching the thin waist ties from front to back where she formed a bow before twisting on tiptoe to check the results in the mirror.

Though the skirt fit snugly across the front, its rear plaits were deep and full, billowing slightly across her spine, giving a faintly bustled shape that lifted the gathered tail of the shirtwaist. Seeing her reflection, she felt adult and confident. Still on tiptoe, she struck a pose, arms elevated, wrists gracefully cocked.

"Why, thank you, Lawrence. How I wish I could, but you see, today is the first day of school, and I'll have a building full of children by . . . " She suddenly looked down at her chest and gave a chagrined laugh. "Oh, dear, I've forgotten my watch.

You'll have to excuse me while I fetch it."

Dropping the whimsy, she moved to the dresser and took up a dainty gold pendant watch that hung suspended from a delicate bow-shaped pin. Over its face was a paper-thin gold cover etched with an all-over design of roses. It had been a graduation gift from her mother and father and was the first timepiece she'd ever owned. She pinned it just above the fullest part of her left breast, then stood back once again to admire herself with pride.

Yes, now I look the part. Miss Brandonberg, teacher.

With a smile, she went down to breakfast.

The others were there already, the men seated at the table while Nissa scuttled back and forth between it and the stove.

"Well, good morning, everyone! Mmm . . . that smells delicious, Nissa." Linnea sounded as cheerful as the wake-up rooster, and her step was sprightly as she crossed to her usual chair.

John pivoted in his, gave her a longer inspection than ever before, turned the color of a freshly cured ham, and seemed unable to find his tongue.

"John," she greeted, dipping her knees in a brief curtsy. "Kristian." She swung his way with a gay smile and found him wide-eyed and gawking.

"Good—" But his voice cracked and he had to start again. "Good morning, Miss Brandonberg."

"Theodore." She gave him her brightest smile, but he scarcely glanced up as he filled his plate.

"Mornin'," he mumbled.

Well, what have I done now, she wondered. Probably nothing. Theodore was just being his usual bright, sunny self.

"It looks like we're going to have a beautiful day for our first day of school," she chirped.

Nobody said a word except Nissa, who came to join them and offered, "Sure does. Everybody's here so let's pray."

Theodore again did the honors in Norwegian, and though Linnea tried several times to break the barrier of silence through the meal, she met with little success. She complimented Nissa on the breakfast, then brought up the subject of yesterday's lunch.

"If I keep eating this well, I'll be fat in no time. My sandwich Saturday was delicious, too." She looked up inquisitively. "What was in it?"

"Tongue."

Linnea felt her stomach lurch. "T . . . tongue?"

"Beef tongue," Nissa clarified.

"Beef t—" But she couldn't bring herself to say the word again. She gulped and felt slightly nauseated while four pairs of eyes slowly lifted to her.

"Never had tongue before?" Nissa inquired.

"N . . . no, thankfully."

"Thought you said you liked it."

"I thought I did. But . . . *tongue?*"

"Hadn't you heard? There's a war going on. We don't waste no part of the cow around here, do we, boys?"

She could feel their amused gazes on her and suddenly felt foolish. Still, she had to ask. "Did you put it in my sandwich again today?"

"Matter of fact, I did. It was the only cold meat I had. Course, I could fry you an egg and put it in there instead if you . . . "

"Oh, no . . . no," Linnea was forced to insist. "I don't want to make any extra work for you. The t . . . tongue will be fine."

For the first time that morning, Theodore's eyes rested on her for more than a flash. But they wore a glint of amused mockery as he said, "Wait till you taste Ma's heart stew."

A chuckle rippled around the table before the Westgaards returned to their eating, but Linnea found it impossible to take another mouthful.

Rising, she offered lamely, "If you'll excuse me, I have some things to get ready for school." She gestured limply toward the stairway, then made her getaway.

But not even the prospect of tongue sandwiches could daunt her later when she checked her watch and found it was at last time to set off down the road.

Nissa was waiting to bid her good-bye. Kristian must have been in his room changing clothes, and the other two had already gone off to the fields. At the door, Nissa said, "Kristian says to give you this. I put a chunk of cheese in your lunch pail to bait it with."

Linnea looked down at the mousetrap, accepted it gingerly

between two fingers, and placed it on top of her grade book.

"Oh, he remembered. I'll thank him when I see him." She looked up and smiled, drew a deep breath, held it several seconds, then said, "Well, here goes. Wish me luck."

"You won't need it, I don't think. Just make 'em know you're boss and you'll do good."

Linnea set out on her twenty-minute walk eager and happy, her step animated as she strode along the crunching gravel. Beside the road the tall grasses were sleek with dew, glistening in the low sun, bending toward her in lissome arcs that scarcely quivered in the windless dawn. Beyond the ditches the fresh-cut grains dried in the long-stretching fields like a woman's freshly washed hair. And everywhere was the scent of harvest: a nutlike quality tinctured with the dusty smell of chaff that hung before the sun in gilded motes.

A red-tailed hawk drifted high on an updraft, its wings as still as the grasses below, only its tail occasionally twisting as it circled and searched for its breakfast. The world was resplendent, silent, its night sounds ceased in the flush of early morning. The sun was an orange ball of flame, hot and blinding, warming Linnea's front but leaving her back cool. Even squinting she could not make out the bell tower of the schoolhouse only half a mile away.

She passed John's place and studied the small weathered house behind its windbreak of columnar cedars. A number of black-and-white cows stood beside the barn. A flock of song sparrows fluttered about the latticed derrick of his windmill, whose lower third was covered with thick morning glories lifting their blue trumpets toward an equally blue sky. Halfway between the house and the windmill sat an old washtub overflowing with bright pink and white petunias. Had he planted them? And the morning glories too? She felt a stab of loneliness for the shy, quiet man, then saw a patchwork cat sitting on the back step washing its white face with a gray paw. Somehow she felt better.

John, she thought. What a simple, dear man.

Theodore. She frowned. Anything but simple, and certainly not dear. How could two brothers possibly be so different? If only their personalities could in some way be homogenized— John could use some of Theodore's gall and Theodore some of

John's shyness. Odd, how in spite of Theodore's boorishness—
or was it because of it?—she couldn't stop trying to win him
over. There were times when she detected humor emerging,
but always he submerged it. How many days could a man go
without smiling? Without laughing? Did he never indulge in
gaiety? Surely he had when he was young, when he'd had
Melinda.

*You just wait, Theodore, you old sourpuss. I'll make you
smile yet.*

With that promise, she reached the schoolhouse. She paused
in the driveway to relish the scene—white building, azure sky,
emerald cottonwoods, gold wheat, birds singing somewhere
in the grain, the awakening breeze brushing her ear, not a
soul about . . . as if she were the only person arisen. *Mine,*
she thought, filing away the memory, promising herself she
would never forget these precious moments.

She walked to the concrete steps, touched the cool steel
handrail, and opened the wooden door. *Mine . . . at last.*

She moved through the cloakroom and stopped just inside
the double doors—everything was exactly as she'd left it.
She clasped her hands beneath her chin, savoring the anticipation of her first school day. Golden light poured through
the long, clean windows of the schoolroom. The shadows of
the desks angled crisp and black against the unfinished oak
floor from which Saturday's scrubbing had raised the smell
of fresh wood. The shade pulls swayed lazily, their rings
creating shifting oval shadows that undulated across a row
of desks. Between the windows, the lamp chimneys gleamed.
The flag hung motionless. The freshly blacked stove awaited
its first fire, the inkwells their first filling, the words on the
blackboard their first reading.

And the mouse was sitting in the middle of the floor.

She laughed. The sound sent the creature scampering toward
the front of the room. "Well, good morning to you, too." She
watched as it scurried across the creaky floor and disappeared
behind the bookcase. "So this is where you hide," she said as
she went down on one knee to peer behind the shelves. She
stood up, brushed off her hands, and said aloud, "I'll get you
soon enough, but till I do, don't stick your nose out, do you
hear?"

She sat at her desk, pried open the lid of her tin pail, and found the wedge of cheese Nissa had sent. But after she'd set the mousetrap, she glanced at the bookcase, back at the deadly steel spring, and at the bookcase once more. Finally she mumbled, "Oh, all right, just one more day." She tripped the trap and set it on the floor, harmless, cheese and all.

Next she went outside and filled the water pail, lugged it inside, and transferred the water to the water crock. Last, she filled the inkwells then checked her watch impatiently. Fifteen minutes to wait. She glanced at the closed doors, tipped her head thoughtfully, then rushed across to open both the inner and outer ones, leaving them wide and welcoming.

From the door she studied her table. Then from her table she studied the door. She sat, clasped her hands on the scarred oak table, and studied the view: the west schoolyard and cotton-wood windbreak framed by white walls and cleanly dissected by the black stovepipe.

She was sitting precisely that way when the first three heads appeared and peeked around the stovepipe.

"Good morning." Immediately Linnea was on her feet, moving toward them. Lars and Evie's children. Each of them held a theme book and a tin molasses pail, and they all stared at her. The boy was freckled, his hair parted on the side and severely slicked down. His dark-blue britches were held up by gray suspenders, and the toes of his boots hadn't a scuff mark on them. The taller girl held the hand of a younger one who tried to hide behind her sister's shoulder. The two girls were dressed similarly, in flowered cotton dresses reaching their high-top brown boots, which were obviously as new as their brother's. The younger girl wore a starched white pinafore over her dress. Both of them had their hair parted down the middle, slicked back into tight, neat pigtails bound by tiny yellow ribbons.

"Good morning, Miss Brandonberg," the older two sing-songed in unison.

Linnea's heart hammered as she tried desperately to recall their names, but dredged up only one. "You're Norna, aren't you? Norna Westgaard."

"Uh-huh. And this is Skipp and Roseanne."

"Hello, Skipp."

He nodded and colored while Roseanne stuck her finger in the side of her mouth and looked as if she were about to cry.

"Hello, Roseanne."

Norna nudged her with a knee and the little tyke recited the obviously rehearsed greeting. "Good morning, Mith Brandonberg." Norna leaned over and pulled her sister's finger from her mouth, ordering, "Say it nice now."

"Good morning, Mith Brandonberg." This time it came out a little more clearly, but with the same captivating lisp as the first time.

Linnea's heart melted immediately. She came forward, but not too near, afraid of rushing Roseanne. "Well, Roseanne, this is your very first day of school, I've heard."

Roseanne pulled out her cheek and nodded, her eyes never leaving Linnea's.

"Did you know it's mine, too? You're my very first students. And I'll tell you a secret if you promise not to tell anyone else." Linnea folded her hands, pressed them between her knees as she bent down, and confided, "I've been just a little bit nervous about meeting you."

Roseanne's finger came out of her mouth and she gazed up at Norna, who smiled down reassuringly.

Another figure came to the door just then. It was Frances Westgaard with a little brother in tow. Recognizing them as Ulmer and Helen's children, Linnea expected to see two older brothers join them momentarily. But as the children filed in to meet her, there were no older brothers.

After an exchange of greetings, they all went outside, the children to the playground and Linnea to the school steps to meet each student who came. She kept one eye on the road for the approach of the missing boys. But minutes passed and the oldest one to arrive was Allen Severt, who sauntered off to the playground where he immediately began pestering the older girls pushing the younger children on the swings.

At nine o'clock Linnea was still short of her four oldest male students and went back inside to check her class list to make sure she hadn't been mistaken about whom to expect.

But she couldn't be mistaken about Kristian! Where was he? Scouring her memory, she came up with a face to go with the name "Raymond Westgaard"—a tall, angular boy who, as soon as he'd been introduced to her on Sunday, had gone off with Kristian. And the Lommen girl had already arrived—she was the pretty one with trailing auburn hair and stunning, long eyelashes—but where was her twin brother? And who else was missing? Oh, yes—Linnea checked her list—Anton. Tony, Nissa had called him, and Linnea had marked his nickname in the margin. Tony Westgaard, age fourteen, was missing, too.

Linnea drew a deep breath and felt her stomach tense. Were they putting her to some test already, the older boys? Deliberately arriving late the first day just to see what her reaction would be?

Thinking of Kristian, she found it impossible to believe he'd be part of such maneuvering. But it was ten after nine already and she still hadn't rung the bell. Finally she looked over all the students and chose the one who looked the most sensible and trustworthy.

"Norna, may I speak to you a moment?" she called from the edge of the playground. Immediately Norna left the rest and came to stand before her.

"Yes, Miss Brandonberg?"

"It's ten after nine, and I'm missing four students. All the older boys. Would you happen to know where they are?"

Norna looked dumbfounded. "Oh, didn't you know?"

"Know? . . . Know what?"

"They won't be coming at all."

"Won't be coming?" Linnea repeated disbelievingly.

"Well, no. Not till the wheat's in and threshing's done."

Confused, Linnea repeated, "The wheat? You mean today? Somebody's threshing today?"

"No, ma'am. Not only today, but at the end of the season. The boys got to help with the harvest."

As a glimmer of comprehension surfaced, Linnea feared she was beginning to understand only too well. "The harvest. You mean the whole thing?" She waved a hand at the vast fields around the schoolyard. *"All that?"*

Norna glanced nervously at her hands, then up again. "Well, they need the boys, else how would they get it all in and threshed before the snow flies?"

"Before the snow flies? You mean they intend to keep the boys out of school all that time?"

"Well . . . yes, ma'am," the girl answered with a worried expression.

Realizing she was making Norna uncomfortable, Linnea disguised her dismay and returned mildly, "Thank you, Norna."

But she was already seething as she gazed off toward the northwest, in the direction the boys had been cutting yesterday. Not a soul in sight. And when she stepped into the cloakroom and yanked the heavy knotted rope from its bent nail, she rang the bell with such vehemence that it pulled her feet completely off the floor on the upswing!

What a disastrous beginning to the day that she'd built up in her mind with such idealism. They really got by with it, year after year? Robbing the older boys of valuable school time to help them get their precious wheat in? Well, they'd better think again, because this year Miss Brandonberg was here and things were going to be a little different!

The incident ruined Linnea's entire day. Though she went through the motions of setting up a routine and getting acquainted with her charges, whenever they were busy and she was not, her thoughts turned sour and she couldn't wait to get home and tie into Theodore.

She assigned seats and drew herself a name chart, then had all the children who knew it say the "Pledge of Allegiance" to begin the day. After that they all took turns standing beside their desks, stating their names, ages, and the approximate place each had been working in various subjects when school ended last year. Most of the books the children used had no demarcation indicating grade level.

In an attempt to familiarize herself with each student, both personally and academically, she assigned the older ones the task of writing a short essay about any one member of their family. Those who were in the middle grades were assigned to write a list of ten words they thought described their family, and the younger ones were asked to draw pictures of their family. Meanwhile, she gathered her "first grade" around her—cousins Roseanne and Sonny Westgaard—and began teaching them the alphabet with her prepared flash cards.

It was tricky, Linnea found, keeping seven grade levels going at once, and there were times when it seemed she'd given one or a pair of her students enough to occupy their time for a full hour when—presto!—there they'd be, all finished and ready for the next lesson, long before she'd completed a task with another group.

She was grateful for the midmorning recess break and the lunch break at noon, though she couldn't force herself to choke down the tongue sandwich. She ended up discreetly throwing most of it away and spending the afternoon with a growling stomach.

Because the children worked alone so much of the time it was easy to tell who applied himself and who didn't, who was fast and who wasn't, who could work without constantly being watched and who couldn't be trusted.

Allen Severt was the worst of the lot.

His written work was slipshod, his attitude bordering on insolent, and his treatment of the other children boorish and inconsiderate. During the lunch break he went off to drown gophers—there was a bounty of gophers, Linnea learned, so gopher-catching was the boys' favorite noon activity—and brought back not only two tails but one tiny, furry foot, which he quietly laid on Frances Westgaard's shoulder after class resumed. When she discovered it, her shriek unsettled the whole schoolroom as she leaped to her feet and brushed the thing off onto the floor.

"Allen!" Linnea ordered, "you will apologize to Frances immediately, then take that vile thing outside and dispose of it!"

He slouched in his seat indifferently and demanded, "Why? I didn't put it there."

"Weren't you the one who caught the gophers at noon?"

Instead of answering, he let the cynical curl remain on his lips as he slowly dragged himself to his feet. He bent from the waist with a cheeky attitude and swished the gopher foot from the floor.

"Whatever you say, teacher," he drawled.

The way Allen said the word *teacher* was like a slap in the face. It took every bit of fortitude Linnea possessed to keep from giving him the smack he deserved. Their eyes clashed— his lazily victorious, hers snapping—then he hooked a thumb in his back pocket and began to turn away.

"The apology first," she demanded.

He stopped, one shoulder drooping lower than the other with an air of persecution, and barely took his eyes off Linnea. "Sorry, twerp," he grunted.

"Outside!" Linnea snapped, realizing the psychological importance of getting in the last word. The boy shuffled to the door with a loose-jointed impudence, deliberately dragging his feet so they clunked on the hollow floor.

Thankfully, the incident happened near the end of the day, for it left Linnea in a state of trembling anger. She tried not to let it show as Allen shuffled back in and resumed his seat with the same bored attitude as before.

With a half hour to go before the dismissal bell, she sat at her table up front, going over the day's papers. Allen, who was part of the oldest group assigned to write the essays, had instead printed the list of words. Further angered by his willfulness, she read the list anyway, without taking him to task for deliberately disobeying instructions. The list itself revealed the boy's defiance:

> boring
> stoopid
> prayers
> pest (sister)
> black
> disterb

To Linnea's surprise he'd added two words totally incongruous with the rest:

> choclat cookys

She looked up from the paper to find Allen slouched over his desk with his chin resting on one curled fist, staring at her. He was supposed to be reading, but his hands covered the open book.

Choclat cookys. His mother's chocolate cookies? Was there a glimmer of appreciation inside the boy after all? But what about the word *disterb?* Too disturbed herself to try to figure it out, she turned the paper facedown and went on to the next. She felt Allen's eyes drilling the top of her head until she could stand it no more and checked her watch again.

The watch was retractable, its spring-wound cable concealed behind the gold bow. As she pulled it out and snapped the cover open she again felt a discomfiting scrutinization. She looked up to find Allen's eyes fixed on her breast where the fabric of her shirtwaist formed a point at the tug of the chain. A shiver rippled up her spine and she felt herself senselessly coloring, but then he turned his disinterested gaze out the window.

Don't be silly. He's only a fifteen-year-old boy, for heaven's sake.

She studied him covertly for a minute longer. He was gangly and thin, but tall and disproportionately wide at the shoulder, like a high building whose rafters are up and sturdy, but waiting for the walls to be fleshed out. He had none of Kristian's developing brawn, but then he didn't do strenuous work like the sons of farmers did. Still, approaching manhood could be seen in the bones of Allen's angular face and in his sardonic upper lip, which was already trimmed by a wispy shadow of soft whiskers matching those just below the hollows of his cheeks. His eyebrows appeared to be thickening, too, as if one day they would almost span the bridge of his nose. But when she considered what Allen would be like as a man, she shivered again, and quickly dropped her gaze as his head began turning her way again.

"Children, it's time to put your desks in order for the night. Please return your books to the front and wash your ink pens out in the pail in the cloakroom. We'll go by grades—Jeannette, Bent, and Skipp, you may go first."

When the room was in order, she wished them all good afternoon and walked toward the cloakroom to ring the bell. But when her arms were lifted high above her head and the children were dashing past, Allen Severt alone took his slow, sweet time. He ambled toward her, heels dragging, and this time there was no question about it—he was openly eyeing her breasts. Immediately she released the bell rope, facing him with as much confidence as she could muster.

"Good-bye, Allen. Let's you and I try for a better day tomorrow."

He gave a single, mirthless huff and sauntered past without saying a word.

All of which did little to ameliorate her temper for her meeting with Theodore.

Theodore was troubled by the amount of time he spent thinking of Miss Brandonberg. It was a hazard of his occupation, thinking too much. How many hours of his life had been spent behind the plodding horses, thinking? And what else was there to do while riding along, watching their shiny rumps sweating in the sun and their large heads nodding? As a boy, working for his father, he'd done his share of dozing to the horses' steady strut. As an adolescent, maturing, he'd done his dreaming to the scrape of earth against an iron plowshare. As a disillusioned husband, he'd done his worrying to the constant *ch-r-r-r* of seeds falling from the grain drill. And as a greenhorn father, abandoned with a year-old son, he'd done his angering in this same place.

Over the years the vista hadn't changed at all: horses, harvest, and horizon.

He had communicated chiefly with the land and animals for so long that he'd grown introspective and dour and had quite forgotten how to communicate with human beings. Oh, there were Nissa and John, and even Kristian. But they, like him, were private, at home with their own company for the most part.

But this little missy, she was something else again. Forever babbling, bubbling. She sure didn't know how to put a button on her lip. The fellow who married her had better be ready to put up with plenty of sass. How was it she could rile him so? Loosen his tongue? Make him think of such foolishness as Russian thistle blossoms and the meaning of fancy words?

He smiled, imagining how surprised she must have been when Kristian didn't show up at school today. Yeah, she was going to be slinging words, first chance she got. Well, let her sling. Kristian was already acting fidgety, gazing off toward the schoolhouse every time he came to the crest of a hill. Theodore wasn't blind: a fool could see the boy was smitten with the schoolmarm and would have dropped the reins and run off to practice his three Rs at a moment's notice. Puppy love. The corner of Theodore's mouth lifted in a grin, but a moment later it faded as he recalled that he himself hadn't been much older than Kristian when he'd made that fateful trip to the city and met Melinda.

Melinda.

Dressed in butter yellow, with her black hair bound in a love knot, her green eyes flashing approval. From the moment he'd seen her on that railroad car, he'd been unable to look away.

He shifted restlessly, transferring the reins to his other hand. What in tarnation had come over him that he was thinking of Melinda lately? Melinda was a thing of the past, and the less he thought of her, the better. He'd learned that years ago.

Theodore squared himself in the iron seat and squinted at the sun, riding down the western sky. Milking time. He flexed and twisted, massaged the back of his neck, and thought of how good it would feel to climb down from this rig and stretch his legs. From the bib of his overalls he pulled a huge old silver stem-winder, checked the time, and slipped it away. Ahh, Ma would have sandwiches and a hot cup of coffee waiting. He signaled the others, pulled up at the edge of the field, and released the horses from the sickle. And as he guided the team toward the familiar windmill for a well-deserved drink, he wondered if the little missy would be home from school by this time.

She was waiting to pounce, standing by the derrick with her fists on her hips when Theodore and Kristian entered the yard on foot behind the horses.

Theodore eyed her from beneath the brim of his straw hat, but made no indication he noticed her. Instead, he called, "Slow down, you two," as the horses spied the water tank and lengthened their strides. Deliberately, he guided Cub and

Toots within sniffing distance of her head, all the while ignoring the fact that she stood almost directly in his path.

"Mister Westgaard!" she accosted, turning to glare at his broad shoulders as he passed her without a word.

He'd come close enough to see sparks snapping in her blue eyes.

"Miss Brandonberg?" he replied, with deliberate coolness while she followed him, leaning forward, fists clenched and pumping with each step.

"I want to talk to you!"

"So talk."

"Your son was *not* in school today!"

Theodore nonchalantly dropped the reins and bent to loosen the cruppers.

"*Course not. He was out in the fields with me.*"

"Well, what—pray tell!—was he doing there!"

"Doin' what every able-bodied boy around these parts was doing. Helpin' with the harvest."

"On your orders?"

Theodore straightened just as Kristian pulled up with his team, but the boy sensibly kept his mouth shut.

"It don't take no orders. Boy knows he's needed and that's all there is to that."

"*Doesn't* take *any* orders!" she exploded. "Just listen to yourself!" She gestured at Theodore's chest. "Your grammar is appalling, yet you want him to grow up talking that way? Well, that's exactly what he'll do if you don't let him come to school!" She shook a finger under his nose for good measure.

Theodore colored and his mouth became a thin slash. Just who did she think she was talking to? "What does it matter how he talks, long as he knows how to run a farm? That's what he's gonna do all his life."

"Oh, is it? And what does he have to say about that?" Her angry eyes snapped to Kristian, then back to his father. "Or does he have *anything* to say about it?" Suddenly she turned and confronted Kristian directly. "What do you say, Kristian? Is this what you plan to do all your life?"

The boy was so startled, he made no reply.

"See there!" she continued. "You've got him so brainwashed

he can't even think for himself!"

"Missy, you'd better—"

"My name, when you are addressing me as your son's teacher, is Miss Brandonberg!"

Theodore glared at her, squared his shoulders, and began again. "*Miss* Brandonberg . . ." He let the pause ring mockingly before continuing, "There's a couple things you'd better get straight. Around here we live by the seasons, not by no calendar set by no lord-high-mukky-muk school superintendent. We got wheat to get in, and when it's threshed and in the granaries is time enough for boys to go to school." He raised a finger and pointed to the horizon. "We ain't tinkerin' in no old maid's garden here, you know. What you're lookin' at is fields measured in sections, not acres. Just when in the hell do you think he's gonna use all that fancy language when this land is his? His horses ain't gonna care one way or another if he talks proper or not." He thumbed over his shoulder at the horses whose noses were touching the water. "All they care about is gettin' fed and watered and harnessed proper when we expect 'em to work for us. Cows, horses, pigs, and wheat! *That's* what matters around here, and you'd best remember it before you start preachin' education."

She straightened and flung her palms up haughtily. "So what was I hired for? If that's all that matters, you can teach him! I thought my job was to make literates out of children, to prepare them for the world beyond *Alamo, North Dakota,*" she ended on a disparaging note.

If literate meant what he thought it did, the little snip had put him down again and he'd had about all of it a man could be expected to take from a wet-nosed brat sixteen years younger than himself!

"Alamo, North Dakota, *is* his world, and it always will be, so just be happy you get him for six months of the year instead of none."

He turned away, but she hounded him. "So you intend to jerk him out of school again in the spring, too, huh?"

Instead of answering, Theodore headed toward the barn. Incensed, she ran after him and caught him by an arm. "Don't you dare turn your back on me, you . . . you ornery . . . " She searched for an adequately scathing term, and finally spit, "*Cynic!*"

Theodore had no idea what the word meant, and the fact riled him all the more. "Watch who you're calling names, little missy." He yanked his elbow from her grasp.

"Answer me!" she shouted. "Do you intend to take him out of school to help you plant, too?"

Theodore's jaw grew stubborn. "Six months for me, six for you. That's fair, ain't it?"

"For your limited information, there's no such word as *ain't*, and we're not talking about what's fair for me and you. We're talking about what's fair for your son. Do you want him to grow up without knowing how to read and write properly?"

"He knows enough to get by."

"Get by!" Frustrated beyond tolerance, she clutched her temples and spun away. "Lord, how did you get so dense!"

Theodore's anger rose swiftly, and he blushed a bright scarlet. "If I ain't smart enough to suit you, you can go find somebody else to give you a roof over your head. It's for sure the school district don't pay me enough to make up for the food you eat, much less heatin' the upstairs."

Again he turned away. This time she let him go. When he'd disappeared inside the barn, she became aware of Kristian, standing beside the horses with the reins forgotten in his hands, looking very uncomfortable.

Suddenly it struck her what she'd done.

"Kristian, I'm sorry. I didn't mean for you to witness that. I . . . I was totally out of line to call your father names. Please forgive me."

Kristian didn't know where to look. He glanced at the reins, back at Linnea, then at the tugs running along Nelly's rump. "Don't matter," he mumbled, absently laying a hand on the horse's shoulder.

"*Doesn't* matter," Miss Brandonberg corrected unconsciously, then added, "Yes, it does. I had no right to lose my temper that way, or to call him dense." She glared at the barn, made two fists, and hit her thighs. "But I just don't know how to make him realize the importance of education when all he sees is that he's done very well without it."

"He's right, you know." Kristian looked up and met her

eyes. "I ain't going no place. This's where I'll probably live all my life. And anyway, I love this farm."

This time she didn't even bother to correct his grammar. Steeped in futility, she watched him walk toward the barn while from its far side came the sound of Theodore calling "Come, boss . . ." as he gathered the cows in for milking.

7

THEODORE TRIED TO remember when he'd felt this angry. A long time ago, maybe as long ago as when Melinda abandoned him and the baby. Then, as now, he'd felt inadequate, which only increased his anger. There were a thousand more churning thoughts seething for release, but Theodore had had long practice at keeping his rage concealed. Throughout supper he ignored Miss Brandonberg, unable to look at her without feeling a suffocating sense of inferiority. The table was silent again and, by God, that's how it ought to be! He'd had all he could take of her high-handed back talk, and he wasn't about to speak another civil word to a sharp-tongued little snot like her who had no idea how to respect her elders.

The minute the tense meal was over, Theodore sought solace in the place he loved best. He pushed away from the table and without a word to anyone took his hat from the hook behind the door, lit a lantern, and walked through the darkness toward the barn. The night was throbbing with the trill of crickets, but he scarcely heard. The moon was nearly full, but he scarcely saw. Head bowed, footsteps automatic, he made his way through the living night.

The barn door squeaked when he opened it, the first thing to register on his troubled mind. He moved through the barn to the door of the tack room and lifted the lantern high. He glanced across the whitewashed walls where harnesses draped thick in garlands of heavy leather, the order as meticulously maintained as in any woman's pantry. Here was his domain. Here he had total control. Here nobody laughed at him or found him lacking.

The lantern turned his face to gold as he reached to hang it on an overhead hook, then the shadow of his hat darkened his scowling eyes. He let his inward rage run its course, externally calm while unconsciously moving to touch familiar things, finding an oil can and returning to oil the hinges of the barn door, scarcely aware of what he was doing.

Words at whose meanings he could only guess roiled through his thoughts.

Cynic. Literate. Sarcastic. Pondering them, he felt ignorant and impotent. How many times had he wished he could read English? He had grown up to the sound of Norwegian being spoken around him. His ma had taught him to read it when he was a boy, but in those days no other language was necessary here. Things had changed though. Laws had changed. Children were now versed in the language of the new country rather than the old, and only the old-timers clung to the language of their native land.

How did you get so dense? The blood rushed to his face afresh as he recalled the schoolteacher's words. Vehemently, he whacked the barn door shut, returned to the tack room, slammed the can down, then snatched a horse collar from the wall. He hooked it over the arm of the chair and found a thick needle. But as he threaded it with black whipcord, his hands shook. The frustrating sense of impotence came back stronger than ever, and he flung down the needle and thread, closed his eyes, hung his head, and pressed his palms hard against the top of the tool bench. *Dense. Dense. Dense.* It was true. She was nothing more than a child and already she knew more than he'd ever know in a lifetime. But how dare she throw it in his face!

His hands still trembled but somehow managed to thread the needle. Then he fell into the worn chair, took up the collar, and propped it on the floor between his feet. The seam of the leather had torn, exposing a line of pale wood within. He stared at it absently for a long time before patiently beginning to stitch.

There's no such word as ain't.

There ain't? he thought. She might be right, but everybody he knew said *ain't,* even Kristian, and he'd been to school to the seventh grade already!

"She *ain't* goin' to make me feel like an ass again," he vowed aloud, deliberately using the word, "'cause I *ain't* going to talk to her and give her the chance."

His fingers fell still. He stared at the collar without seeing it. The light from the lantern fell upon his straw hat and slumped shoulders and threw a shadow over his hands and boots. Outside the crickets still sang. Inside, all was still. Then, hesitantly, he began speaking aloud once more.

"She . . . ain't . . . " He paused, thought, remembered the schoolteachers of the past and how they'd talked. "She's . . . not . . . goin' to make me feel like an ass again, cause I ain't . . . cause I'm not going to give her the chance."

He pondered again for some time, picked up the collar, and hung it over his crossed knees, continuing to mend it. "She ain't even dry behind the ears," he said to the collar, then amended, "She's . . . not . . . even . . . dry . . . behind . . . the . . . ears."

Her face appeared clearly, eyebrows angling, blue eyes intent and glistening as she stalked him with angry zeal and made *Alamo, North Dakota,* sound like the armpit of the earth. She was too good for Alamo, huh? Just like Melinda, though to Melinda's credit, she had never been nasty about it. But what did it matter now? She was gone.

What angered him now was the fact that the schoolmarm's coming had aroused his seething memories of Melinda, ones he'd successfully submerged for years.

He should have followed his initial instincts and tossed Linnea Brandonberg out on her smart little rump while he had the chance. He cut the whipcord, hung the collar up, and put the needle in its appointed place. *Well, when it comes right down to it, it don't matter. The schoolmarm will only be here one year, just like all the rest. She won't come back.*

He could ignore her for a year . . . couldn't he?

But when he'd hung around the tack room until weariness got the best of him, he found it impossible to ignore even so much as the fact that she was in his house. Making his way into the yard he eyed her tiny window. Though it was dark, lights burned yet in the kitchen. He halted, unnerved at the thought of running into her downstairs. *You ain't . . . you're not gonna let that little smarty-pants make you think twice about walkin' in your own house, are you, Teddy?* Resolutely he continued past the windmill toward the golden rectangle that threw an oblique slash of color into the yard. But he breathed a sigh of relief to find everyone had gone to bed. It must've been Ma who left the kerosene lantern on the kitchen table for him.

He took it along to his bedroom where he momentarily paused in the doorway. The room was simple, homespun, the furniture sturdy, old, but well-preserved. There was a mirrored dresser with bow-front drawers. It matched the heavy headboard of the bed, both stained as dark as a hickory nut. The bed was covered with one of Nissa's hand-stitched patchwork quilts in blue and red. The hand-loomed rag rugs brightened the wide pine floorboards, which were the color of coffee without cream. Upon the single window hung shirred lace curtains the color of coffee with cream.

Theodore crossed to the dresser whose top was protected by a white embroidered dresser scarf with blue crocheted edging. He stared at it a long time before setting the lantern down and touching an embroidered blue butterfly, remembering a woman's slim hands holding a needle and hoop, stitching, stitching, trying to stitch away her loneliness. He ran his fingers along the variegated edging until a callus caught the thread and pulled the scarf awry. Sadly, he straightened it, then with slow deliberation opened the top dresser drawer and searched beneath the clothing for the photograph he hadn't looked at in years. It was surrounded by a wooden oval frame with a domed-glass front and looked ridiculously feminine when contrasted against his wide, horny palm. The delicate likeness of a beautiful woman smiled up at him in sepia tones as colorless as she had become during the two precious years he'd had her.

A band of hurt cinched his chest. *Melinda. Aw, Melinda, I thought I'd gotten over you.*

He set the picture down atop the butterflies and flowers she had stitched, watching her as he drew his suspenders over his shoulders and methodically undressed. He turned down the lightweight patchwork quilt, folded back the coarse white sheet, extinguished the light, piled the goose-down pillows one

on top of the other, and stretched out with both hands beneath
his head. Even in the dark he could see her face smiling with the
winsome appeal no woman had had for him before or since. He
closed his eyes and swallowed hard, forcing himself to remain
as he was, forcing his hands to cup the back of his head instead
of running them over the empty half of the bed. Loneliness was
a thing he usually accepted with the stoicism peculiar to his
people and their way of life. But tonight it crept in stealthily, causing his heart to thump with a heavy ache he couldn't
control. He was only thirty-four years old. Had he lived three-
fourths of his life? Half? Had he thirty-four more years to sleep
in this large bed alone? To come in from the fields at the end
of the day to share a table with nobody but his ma and son
and brother? And when Ma and Kristian were no longer there
to share it, what then? Nobody but John, whom he loved—
yes—but who could scarcely compensate for the void left by
Melinda. Times were rare when he wished for a woman to
replace her. Common sense told him that even if he wanted
one there was none to be found around here, where half the
women in the county were related to him and the other half
either already married or old enough to be his mother.

He didn't understand what had brought on these thoughts of
women. He didn't understand why this sadness had struck now
at the height of the harvest season, which usually filled him
with a sense of fullness and contentment. He didn't understand
so many things, and if there was anything that made Teddy
Westgaard feel stupid and inadequate, it was not understanding. He wished there was someone he could talk to about it,
about Melinda, about the hurt she'd caused all those years
ago, about how the hurt could be so intense yet when he'd
thought it mastered. But who was there to talk to? And what
man would ever resort to spilling out his feelings that way?

Nobody he knew.

Not a soul he knew.

In her bedroom upstairs, Linnea listened to the sounds of
Theodore entering below, settling down for the night. She
recalled his icy treatment of her at supper and the isolation
she'd felt at being closed off that way. It made her feel like
crying, though she didn't exactly understand why. Theodore

was wrong and she was right. And just because she'd had a tiff with a bullheaded moose like him was no reason to bawl herself to sleep.

Resolutely she flopped over, burying her face in the pillow to stop the stinging in her eyes. Everything seemed so hopeless.

She recalled the conversation she'd had with Nissa right after her run-in with Theodore. She'd thought surely Nissa would see her side, but the older woman had offered little encouragement.

"We didn't tell you the boys wouldn't be in school cause we knew you'd be vexed," Nissa said. "And anyway, you ain't gonna change Teddy's mind. He's had the same fight with every schoolteacher that ever came here. Matter of fact, that's why most of 'em never come back a second year. Might as well get used to it. The boys won't be in school till the threshing crew's come and gone."

"And just when will that be?"

"Oh, about mid-October or so. Things move faster once the hired help comes in."

"Hired help?" Where were they going to get hired help when they were already using every available man and boy? And if Theodore could afford to hire help, why didn't he do it now when it would do Kristian the most good?

"Soon as the harvest is done in Minnesota, these boys come out here and hire on. We get some of the same ones, year after year."

So Linnea was alone in her fight to get the older boys the full nine months of education they deserved. Kristian was sixteen years old already and only in the eighth grade. Didn't they understand the reason was that he couldn't complete a full grade's work in six short months?

The tears were coming fast now. She blamed them on frustration and her shattered expectations and the trying day she'd had, what with her shortened roll and her confrontations with Allen Severt and Theodore. But when the tears turned to sobs it was not academics, or roll call, or Allen Severt of which she thought, but of Theodore Westgaard entering the kitchen, sitting at the table, eating an entire meal, and leaving the house without once glancing at her or acknowledging that she existed.

*   *   *

She was treated to more of the same whenever their paths crossed during the next several days. The only time he spoke to her was when she forced him to by greeting him first. But he never raised his eyes. And if she was in the room, he got out of it as fast as he could. On Sunday they ended up side by side in church, and she was conscious of the care he took to make sure his sleeve didn't brush hers. His enmity had by now become a winch about her heart. Each time he gave her the cold shoulder she wanted to clasp his arm and beg him to understand that in her position as a teacher she could not take any stand but the one she had. She wanted to bare her soul and admit that she was utterly miserable, living with his frigid detachment. She wanted him friendly again so the strain in the house would vanish.

Nothing like this had ever happened before in her life. She had never made an enemy of a friend—not that Theodore had ever really been her friend. But his point-blank snubbing was a far cry from the neutrality they'd managed to reach before she blew up at him and called him dense. To sit beside him, feeling his contempt, withered Linnea's heart.

Reverend Severt announced hymn number 203. The organ bellows swelled, the music spilled forth and the congregation got to its feet. It seemed providential that there was only one hymnal for each two people in a pew. Linnea picked one up and nudged Theodore's arm.

He stiffened. She peeked up from beneath her bird-wing hat and offered a hesitant smile. He realized she was offering much more than to share a songbook. He also realized he was in the House of the Lord—no place to practice hypocrisy. As he reached out to hold one edge of the book, he didn't consciously set out to dupe her into believing he could read the words.

Though his antipathy seemed to mellow in church, he said nothing to her during Sunday dinner. He ate stolidly, then left the kitchen to change into work clothes. When he came back through the room on his way outside, he came up short at the sight of her staring at him from across the room. She twisted her fingers together and opened her lips as if struggling to speak.

He waited, feeling a curious weightlessness in his stomach, an expectancy that thrust up against the underside of his heart. Her blue eyes were wide and timorous. Two bright splashes of color highlighted her cheeks. The moment seemed to expand into an eternity, but then her lashes swept down. She swallowed and her lips fell closed. Disappointed, he passed through the room without uttering a word.

She spent the afternoon in her room, correcting papers and planning the week's classes. Downstairs, Nissa retired to her bedroom for a nap. The house grew quiet, the rafter room stuffy. Outside, the sun disappeared and the sky took on a green-gray tinge while off to the north, thunder groaned softly.

Immersed in misery and feeling less self-righteous by the hour, Linnea found her concentration straying from her schoolwork. She glanced at the window, noting the changing weather. Her thoughts wandered for the hundredth time to the fight she'd had with Theodore and the resulting antagonism neither of them seemed able to end. Having no one to discuss it with, she decided to tell Lawrence.

"Remember Theodore? Well, I'm afraid he and I are still at odds. We've had a terrible fight, and now he won't talk to me or look at me!" Dressed only in her chemise and petticoats, Linnea confronted her reflection in the mirror, pressing a hand to her breast, fingertips touching the pulse in her throat while an expression of utmost dismay covered her face. "What am I going to do, Lawrence?" She paused, fluttered her fingers and replied, "Well, I suppose we're both at fault. He's being bullheaded and I . . . well, I was terribly nasty to him." Suddenly her back arched and her chin came up defensively. "Well, he deserved it, Lawrence. He's such a stubborn moose!" She flung herself away, taking care not to bump the commode this time. "He thinks the rest of the world is at fault for wanting a higher education than he, and all the while he's tak—" She stopped abruptly and turned back toward the mirror. "Well, yes, I . . . I . . . " She flung her hands up, disgusted with Lawrence's unwillingness to place the blame where it belonged. "So I called him dense! So what?" She moved to the stack of papers she'd been correcting and fiddled with the corner of one, then swung around, wide-eyed.

"Apologize? Surely you don't mean it! Why, he's the one who should be apologizing to me!"

At the first grumble of thunder Theodore turned toward the edge of the field. His backside was planted on solid metal, and in the middle of a wheat field he was a sitting duck in an electrical storm. A pale streak of yellow lit the gray horizon again, and he counted the seconds till the thunder reached his ears, then flagged the others in behind him.

He checked his watch. Four o'clock, and this would be the first day in well over three weeks they'd knocked off early. The break would do them all good, though if the rain came, it would cause delays in drying the wheat they'd already cut.

Back at the house Theodore left Kristian behind to water the horses. He stepped into the empty kitchen and crossed immediately to the stove to check for warm water. With the teakettle in hand he paused, cocking an ear. Now who in blazes could be here visiting with her in her room? He listened for another voice, but none came. There were pauses, then the soft muffled tones of the girl's voice. From a downstairs bedroom came the soft snuffle of Nissa's snoring, and with a puzzled glance at the ceiling, Theodore tiptoed to the stairway, the teakettle forgotten in his hand.

"I just don't know what I'd do without you, Lawrence. You're . . . well, you're absolutely the best friend I've ever had. Now be a dear and fetch my shirtwaist. It's suddenly grown quite chilly."

Theodore waited, but after that all was still. He heard the sound of her footsteps and his eyes followed them along the ceiling. *Lawrence? Who in thunder is Lawrence? And what was he doing in her room?* Again he cocked his head, waiting for a male voice to answer. But minutes passed and none came. What were they doing that could be done so quietly? Theodore poured water in the basin and scrubbed up as quietly as he'd ever done in his life, still curious, listening. But soon Kristian came in from the barn, slamming the screen door and awakening Nissa, who tottered out, hooking her glasses behind her ears and commenting on the brooding weather.

Theodore turned, drying his face and whispered. "Who's up there with her?"

Nissa stopped in her tracks. "Up there? Why, nobody."

"Then who's she talking to?"

Nissa listened intently for a moment. "She ain't talkin' to nobody."

"Oh, I thought I heard voices."

It didn't strike Theodore till he was on his way to the tack room that Ma had said *ain't*. Slipping both hands inside the bib of his overalls, he took on the appearance of a wise old monk as he walked along and corrected, "She's *not* talking to nobody."

The clap of the screen door and the conversation from below brought Linnea back to reality. Suddenly she became aware of how dark it had grown outside. Bracing her palms on the window frame she peered out and saw a flicker of lightning off to the north. So the men had come in early and wouldn't be going back out after the milking.

She plunked down on the edge of the bed and linked her fingers as they dangled between her knees. Flicking her thumbnails together, she studied them morosely.

"You'd better be right, Lawrence," she said, then rose to tidy herself up.

She need not ask where Theodore might be; somehow she knew. The lightning had drawn nearer and the first knives of rain were riveting as she scurried to the barn. The outer door swung open soundlessly. As it closed behind her, she paused, letting her eyes adjust to the gloom. The long row of windows to her left gave off only the vaguest light, but enough to reveal that the barn was kept as fastidiously as Theodore's private little domain at the near end. Its door was open, spilling a flood of orange lantern light across the hem of her skirts.

She saw only half of Theodore's back. After church he had changed into overalls, but had left his white shirt on. It stretched taut over his shoulders, crossed by striped suspenders as he bent forward in the old chair with his elbows resting on widespread knees. He held something in his hands and appeared to be polishing it, his shoulders rocking rhythmically. He bent, dropping a hand to a can between his feet, and she tiptoed one step farther, bringing him fully into view. She watched the play of muscles in his arm below the rolled-up

sleeve as he resumed his task. A strip of black leather dangled
from his fingers and, as he worked it, its hardware set up a
repetitive *ching*. The room was close, warm, and smelled of
saddle soap and oil and horses.

He looked so at home in it, everything as tidily in place as
when she'd inspected it before. But he looked lonely, too. His
hands stopped moving, but he sat on as before, as if absently
studying the rag in his hands. She held her breath and remained
stark still. She could hear him breathing and wondered what he
thought as he sat in solitude with his head bowed low.

"Theodore?"

He flew from the chair and spun to face her, sending the can
skittering and the chair balancing on two legs. Even before it
settled to the floor again he was blushing.

"Am I disturbing you?"

He'd been sitting there thinking of her, and having her
appear silently behind him was disturbing, yes. Her hands
were clasped behind her back, bringing her breasts into promi-
nence, and even though he kept his eyes skewered on hers, he
caught the wink of her gold watch hanging almost to the fullest
part of the left one.

"No."

"I didn't mean to startle you."

"I didn't know you was standing there."

"Were." It was out before she could stop it, and she bit her
inner lip.

"What?"

"Nothing." It was her turn to blush.

Silence fell again, strained, as when they'd met and passed
in the kitchen earlier.

"May I come in?"

"Oh, well." He waved the rag nervously, once. "Yeah, sure.
But there ain't much . . . " He shifted feet. "Isn't much room
in here."

His correction made her feel as uncomfortable as he.
"Enough for one more?" she asked. When he made no
reply, she eased into the room, affecting a casual air, with
her arms overlapped behind her waist, glancing up at the
wall wreathed with leather. "So this is where you spend your
spare time."

"There ain't . . . " He tried to think up the right term, but somehow his mind seemed jumbled with her in the room. "No such thing on a farm."

"Mmm . . . " She perused the neatly hung harnesses, ignoring his grammar this time. "So what were you doing?"

"Polishing tack."

"Oh. Why?"

He stared at the side of her head as she tilted it to study things high above her. What a question. And *she* thought *he* was dense?

"Cause if you don't, the sweat from the horses'll rot it, and if that don't get it, the fumes from the . . . the fumes from out there will." He nodded toward the main part of the barn.

"Really?" She turned to face him, wide-eyed. "I never knew *that before. That's interesting.*" Theodore had never before considered it interesting, only true. "But then, I guess you know absolutely everything there is to know about running a farm." She strolled farther into the room, and he watched, fascinated, unable to fathom why she'd come here. She ambled to the sawhorse, reached out to brush the sheepskin liner, and suddenly changed her mind.

"Oh! I almost forgot." She turned, producing a mousetrap from behind her back. "I have an unwanted guest at school. Kristian found the trap for me, but I'm afraid I didn't have much luck setting it. Could you show me how?"

He glanced at the mousetrap, then back at her, and she thought for an infinitesimal moment that he was going to grin. But he didn't, only thought for the second time in three minutes that for an educated woman she had her dense spots, too.

"You don't know how to set a mousetrap?"

She shrugged. "My father always did it in the store, so I never had to try before. Nissa sent some cheese in my lunch pail one day, but I kept springing the fool thing and I was scared I'd break a finger."

"What store?"

"My father owns a mercantile store in Fargo. The mice love to chew holes in the flour sacks."

His eyes narrowed slightly. "I thought your father was a lawyer."

She stared at him speechlessly, caught in her own lie. She dropped her eyes to the mousetrap, and when at last she spoke, there was contrition in her tone. "It was a fib. You ... you rattled me so badly that day that I had to think up something quick, because I was ... " She looked up appealingly, then dropped her eyes again. "Because I was afraid you weren't going to take me with you and I didn't know what else to say to change your mind."

So little miss righteous wasn't so righteous after all. But her cheeks were stained as bright as peonies and she concentrated on the mousetrap as if afraid to raise her gaze again. Her fingernails were neatly buffed and trimmed and she scratched at the stamped ink design around the edge of the wood.

He extended one wide palm. "So give it to me. It will be something new, me teaching you something."

Her head came up; and their eyes met. To her relief, she found in Theodore's a hint of amusement. She placed the mousetrap on his palm, and he stretched to pluck the lantern from its ceiling hook and took it to the workbench, presenting his back. But now that she'd come this far, she was reluctant to stand too close to him.

He looked back over his shoulder. "Well, are you coming?"

"Oh ... yes."

They stood side by side, and she thought she had never seen hands so big as she watched them set the trap. He produced a tiny square of leather to use in place of cheese. "First you bait it. Here."

"Well, of course, there. I'm not *that* stupid."

He looked down. She looked up. They both came very close to smiling. She noted that he'd removed the celluloid collar from his dress shirt, which was open at the throat, and that for a man he had extraordinarily long eyelashes. He noted that the depths of her blue eyes held tiny flecks of rust, almost as bright as the burnished glow of the lanternlight reflecting off the gold watch on her breast. They forced themselves to concentrate on the lesson at hand.

"Hold it down flat and force the bow back to the other side."

"Force the bow back," she repeated and looked up again. "It's called a bow?"

"Yeah."

"Why?" He made the mistake of glancing into her eyes again, and the trap snapped and bounced off the top of the bench onto the floor.

She started giggling and he felt his face heating up.

"*I* can do it *that* well," Linnea teased. She bent over and retrieved the trap, then handed it to him with an expression of mocking tolerance.

Flustered, he took it and began again—found the square of leather, put it in place, and forced the bow back. "Put the locking bar into place beneath the little lip . . . ." Carefully he withdrew his hands. "There." He was relieved to see he'd done it right this time. He reached to pluck a screwdriver from an orderly can of tools and tripped the trap with it. "Now you try." He slipped the screwdriver back into the can and pushed the trap her way.

"All right." He watched her hands perform the lesson, thinking of how the trap, if accidentally sprung, could bruise and probably break a finger that small. But she managed beautifully, and soon the baited trap lay on the workbench between their four hands.

Outside the storm had strengthened. In the little square of window their faces were reflected against a blue-black sky, while the tack room grew distractingly silent all of a sudden. The scent of leather, horses, and old wood sealed them in securely.

"Theodore?" She said it so quietly it might have been an echo. Rain was pelting against the window, but inside it was bright and dry. But not as dry as Theodore's throat, which suddenly refused to work as they both continued staring at each other's hands. "I didn't really come here to learn how to bait the mousetrap. I figured it out by myself on the second try. It was just an excuse."

He turned to look at her, but found himself staring at the part in her hair. Her head remained bowed as she went on. "I came to apologize to you."

Still he could think of nothing to say.

"I think I hurt you rather badly the other day when I ridiculed you for your improper grammar and called you dense. I'm very sorry I did that, Theodore."

He saw her chin lift and quickly glanced away before their eyes could meet. "Aw, it don't matter."

"Doesn't it? Then why have you refused to talk to me or even look at me ever since?"

He had no idea how to respond, so he stared at the piece of leather on the trap while an enormous clap of thunder made the sturdy barn shudder. But neither Theodore nor Linnea flinched.

"It's been very hard on me to share the same table with you and to pass you in the kitchen all the while you were trying to freeze me out. My family is very different from yours. We talk and laugh together and share things. I miss that very much since I came here. All week long, whenever you'd get all cold and stiff and turn away from me, I felt like crying, because I've never had an enemy before. Then today in church, I thought . . . well, I hoped maybe you'd warmed up a little, but when I thought about it a little more I realized you were probably very deeply hurt and if I wanted to be your friend again, I must apologize to you. Would you . . . would you look at me, please?" Their eyes met, his self-conscious, hers contrite. "I'm sorry. You're not dense, and I never should have said that. And I should have been more patient with you about your grammar. But, Theodore, I'm a teacher." Without warning she placed a hand on his arm and her expression became tender. Something awkward happened to his heart, and it felt like her light touch was singeing his skin. He tried to drag his gaze away but failed.

"Do you know what that means?" Her eyes glittered and he wondered frantically what he would do if she started crying. "It doesn't mean that I'm a teacher only when I'm in the schoolroom. I can't separate me into two different people— one who teaches when she's a mile down the road and one who forgets about it when she comes back here."

She gestured widely and, thankfully, he was free of her touch

and of the threat of tears. "Oh, I know I'm impetuous sometimes. But it happens automatically. I hear people speaking
improperly and I correct them. I did it again without even
thinking, when I came in here. And I saw how uncomfortable it made you feel." He began to turn away, to pick up
the rag and look busy, but she grabbed his shirtsleeve and
forced him to stay where he was. "And I'll do it again . . .
and again . . . and again before I'm through with you. Do you
understand that?"

He stared at her mutely.

"So what harm can it do if you know that I don't mean to
belittle you? There's no rule that says I must be a teacher only
to children, is there?" When he made no comment, she twisted
his sleeve impatiently and insisted, "Is there?"

She was an enigma. He wasn't used to dealing with direct-
ness such as this, and he waited too long, trying to decide what
to say to her. She flung away his arm irritably. "You're being
bullheaded again, Theodore. And while we're on the subject
of bullheadedness, you certainly don't set a very good example for your son when you sulk around and pull your silent
act. What do you think Kristian thinks about his father treating the schoolteacher that way? You're supposed to respect
me!"

"I do," he managed at last.

"Oh, of course you do." She squared her fists on her hips
and tossed a shoulder. "So far you've tried to pawn me off
on the Dahls and freeze me out. But I can't live this way,
Theodore. I'm just not used to that sort of enmity."

Out of the clear blue sky, Theodore made an admission such
as he'd never expected to hear himself make. "I don't know
what enmity means."

"Oh!" His admission went straight to her heart. Her eyes
softened and she dropped her belligerent pose. "It means hos-
tility . . . you know, like we're enemies. We're not going to be
enemies for the next nine months, are we?"

He seemed unable to summon up his voice again. All he
could think about was how fetching she looked in the lanternlight, and how her blue eyes came alight with those gold

sparkles, and how he liked the pert tilt of her nose. She grinned and added, "Because I'll be plumb crazy before then."

What could a man say to a feisty little firecracker like her? "You talk a lot, you know."

She laughed and suddenly swung across the room and mounted one of the saddles on the sawhorse. Astride, she crossed her hands on the pommel and hunched her shoulders. "And you talk too little."

"Quite a pair we make."

"Oh, I don't know. We were doing all right when I first came in here. Why, you were practically . . . " She grinned teasingly. "Rhapsodizing."

He leaned back against the workbench and crossed his arms over his bib. "So what does that mean?"

She pointed her nose at him and ordered, "Look it up."

Someplace in the house there was an English/Norwegian dictionary. Maybe he could puzzle it out or stumble across the word somehow.

"Yeah, maybe I'll do that." And maybe he'd see if he could find out anything about a few of the other words she'd harangued him with.

She took a big breath, puffed out her cheeks, and blew at her forehead. "Wow, I feel so much better."

She smiled infectiously, and Theodore found himself threatened with smiling back.

In her mercurial way, she slapped the saddle. "Hey, this is fun. Giddyup." With her heels she spurred twice. "I haven't been on a horse many times in my life. Living in town, we don't have any of our own, and whenever we travel, Father rents a rig."

A quarter grin softened his mouth as he leaned back, watching, listening. Forevermore, but she could babble! And she was, after all, really a child. No woman would sling her leg over a saddle that way while visiting a man in a tack room and run on about anything that popped into her mind.

"You know, little missy, it ain't . . . it's not good for a saddle to be set on that way when it's not on a horse."

"Sat on," she corrected.

"Sat on," he repeated dutifully.

She pulled a face and looked down at her skirts, then up at him while her expression changed to an impish grin. "Aww, it ain't?" Without warning, her foot flew over and she landed on her feet with a bounce. "Then next time maybe it better have one under it, wouldn't you say?" And with that she flitted to the door, pivoted, and waggled two fingers at him. "Bye, Theodore. It's been fun talking."

She left him studying an empty doorway as she ran out, heedless of the rain, and in her absence he found himself wondering again who Lawrence was.

8

THE FOLLOWING MORNING the rain had turned into a low-lying mist that clung to the skin and clothing and made hay cutting impossible. Kristian shivered, then sneezed twice as his feet went over the side of the bed. Even the linoleum felt damp. Over long underwear he drew on warm woolen britches, a long-sleeved undershirt, and an outer shirt of thick flannel. As he opened his bedroom door to go downstairs, Linnea Brandonberg opened hers to do the same.

Kristian's blood suddenly lost its chill.

Her hair wasn't combed yet but hung free to the middle of her back. She looked sleepy-eyed as she held the neck of her wrapper with one hand, the blue basin with the other.

"Good morning," she greeted.

"Good morning." His voice went from tenor to soprano in one crack. Flustered, he realized his shirt was only half-buttoned and hurriedly finished the job.

"Chilly, isn't it?"

"Damp, too." He'd never seen any woman besides Grandma in her wrapper and bare feet. The sight of his teacher in nightclothes made his throat feel queer and he wasn't sure where to let his eyes light.

"I guess you won't be able to go out to the fields today."

"Ahh, no, I ahh, guess not."

"You could come to school then."

He shrugged, not sure what his father's reaction would be to that. "One day wouldn't do much good, and the sun'll probably be out tomorrow."

"One day is one day. Think about it." She turned and hurried down the stairs, giving him a better view of her cascading hair, which bounced with each step. What was happening to him lately? He never used to notice things like girls' eyes or what they were wearing or whether their hair was up or down. Girls were just troublesome brats who always wanted to tag along hunting gophers or swimming in Little Muddy Creek. When you let them they always spoiled your good time.

He clumped down the stairs behind her and pretended not to be watching as she greeted Nissa, filled her basin, and scurried back upstairs for her morning bath. He pictured it . . . and his chest felt like it was caving in.

She's the schoolteacher, you jackass! You can't go around thinkin' about the schoolteacher that way!

But he was still dwelling on how pretty she'd looked on the landing as he made his way to the barn to help with the morning milking.

Dawn hadn't yet arrived but would soon sneak in undetected. The farmyard, shrouded in mist, was redolent with the smells of animal and plant life. Cattle, pigs, chickens, mud, and hay— they were all out there in the damp shadows. The dense air muffled all but the faraway sound of roosting chickens throatily clucking their prelude to rising. Upon the spillpipe of the windmill droplets condensed, quivered, then fell to a puddle below with an uneven *plip*. Beyond the looming derrick a row of golden windows glowed a welcome.

Opening the barn door, Kristian sneezed.

Entering, he gave an all-over shudder, happy to be out of the damp. There was a pleasantness to the barn at this time of day that could always manage to take the edge off a man's early-morning grumpiness, especially when the weather was bad. Even when snow, sleet, or biting cold pressed against the windows, inside, beneath the thick, cobwebbed rafters with the doors sealed tightly, it was never chilly. The cattle brought with them a warmth that dispelled the most insidious dampness, the most oppressive gloom.

Theodore had already let them in. They stood docilely, await-
ing their turns, rhythmically chewing their cuds, the grinding
sound joining the hiss of the lanterns that hung from the
rough-hewn rafters. The barn cats—wild, untamable things—
had decided against mousing in the rain and watched from a
safe distance, waiting for warm milk.

Kristian picked up his milk stool and wedged himself
between two huge warm black-and-white bellies. When he
sat and leaned his forehead against old Katy, he was warmed
even further. He filled the sardine cans, set them at his side,
and played the perennial game of waiting to see if the wary
cats could be enticed that close. They couldn't. They held their
ground with typical feline patience.

"You still asleep or what?" Theodore's voice came from
someplace down the line, accompanied by the liquid pulsa-
tions of milk falling into a nearly filled pail.

Kristian flinched, realizing he'd been woolgathering about
Miss Brandonberg, whose hair was quite the same caramel
color as one of the cats.

"Oh . . . yeah, I guess I was."

"All you took from Katy so far was two sardine cans full."

"Oh, yeah . . . well . . . " Guiltily, he set to work, making
his own milk pail ring. Then, for long minutes, there was only
rhythm . . . the unbroken cadence of milk meeting metal, of
milk meeting milk, of powerful bovine teeth grinding against
cuds, of the beasts' breaths throwing warmth into the barn with
each bellowlike heave of their huge bellies.

Kristian and Theodore worked in companionable silence for
some time before Theodore's voice broke in.

"Thought we'd drive over to Zahl today and get coal."

"Today? In this drizzle?"

"Been waitin' for a rainy day. Didn't want to waste a sunny one."

"Reckon you'll be wantin' me to hitch up the double box
then."

"Soon as breakfast is over."

Kristian went on milking for some minutes, feeling the
strong muscles in his forearms grow warm and taut. After
pondering at length, he spoke again.

"Pa?"

"Yuh?"

Kristian lifted his forehead off Katy's warm side. His hands paused.

"Long as I'm gonna have the wagon all hitched up, would it be all right if I took Miss Brandonberg to school?"

In their turn, Theodore's hands stopped pumping. He recalled warning Miss Brandonberg that he didn't have time to be hauling her to school. He thought of her on that saddle last night and his neck seemed to grow a little warm. He'd readily admit she hadn't looked much like a hothouse pansy then. She'd looked . . . ahh, she'd looked . . .

Something happened within Theodore's heart as the picture of Linnea appeared. Something a man of his age had no business feeling for a young thing like her.

Resolutely, Theodore continued milking. "I told her when she come here I didn't have time to be cartin' her off to school when the weather got bad. I got things for you to do."

"But she'll be soaked through by the time she gets there!"

"Tell your grandma to find her a spare poncho."

Kristian's lips hardened and he vehemently lit into his milking. Damn the old man. He don't need me and he knows it. Not for the ten minutes it'd take me to drive her to school. But Kristian knew better than to press the point.

Linnea was all dressed for breakfast when she heard the thud of Kristian taking the steps two at a time. Two sharp raps sounded on her door, and she opened it to find him standing breathless on the landing.

For the second time that morning there was a look on his face that warned her to keep things very impersonal between them.

"Oh, hello. Am I late for breakfast?"

"No. Grandma's just putting it on. I . . . ahh . . . " He cleared his throat. "I just wanted you to know I'd give you a ride to school if I could, but Pa said he needs me right after breakfast. But Grandma's got a spare poncho for you to wear. And an umbrella, too."

"Why, thank you, Kristian, I appreciate it." She flashed him a second smile, attempting to make it appreciative but not encouraging.

"Well, I . . . um . . . I gotta wash up. See you downstairs."

When Linnea closed the door, she leaned back against it, releasing a huge breath. Goodness, this was one problem she hadn't foreseen. He was her student, for heaven's sake. How would she handle his obvious attraction for her if it kept growing? He was a sweet, appealing boy, but he was—after all—just a boy, and while she liked him as she liked all her students, that was as far as it went.

Still, she couldn't help being touched by his blossoming gallantry, his visible nervousness, and the fact that he'd asked permission to give her a ride to school. Neither could she help being piqued by the fact that the permission had been denied.

At breakfast, several minutes later, Linnea covertly studied Theodore. She'd hoped that last night had seen the last of his orneriness, but apparently not. Well, if one could be ornery, so could two.

"It's too wet to work in the fields today. No reason why Kristian can't come to school."

Theodore stopped chewing and leveled her with a chastising stare while she innocently went on spreading raspberry jam on a piece of toast.

"Kristian ain . . . isn't going to school today. We got other things to do besides cut wheat."

She glared at Theodore. Her mouth tightened like a drawstring purse. Their eyes met and clashed for several interminable seconds, then without another word, she pitched her toast onto her fried eggs, her napkin on the toast, and ejected herself from the chair. She made as much racket as possible as she clattered angrily up the stairs.

In her wake, John, Kristian, and Nissa, astonished, stared at the empty doorway, but Theodore went on calmly eating his bacon and eggs.

Less than fifteen minutes later Kristian watched her trudge off down the road through the drizzle and wished again he were going with her. Still stewing, he harnessed Cub and Toots, then clambered onto the wagon seat to wait in irate silence for his father. He sneezed twice, hunkered forward, and stared straight ahead when the old man came out of the house, dressed in a black rubber poncho and his tattered straw hat. The wagon seat pitched as Theodore climbed aboard, and Kristian sneezed again.

"You gettin' a cold, boy?"

Kristian refused to answer. What the hell did the old man care if he was getting a cold or not! He didn't care about anybody but himself.

Even before Theodore was seated, Kristian gave a shrill whistle and slapped the reins harder than necessary. The team shot forward, setting Theodore sharply on his rump. The older man threw a look at his son, but Kristian, churning, only pulled his hat down further over his eyes, bowed his shoulders, and stared straight down the lines.

The day suited his mood—wet and cheerless. The horses plodded along through a sodden, colorless countryside devoid of moving life. Those fields already shorn looked dismal, their stubble appearing like tufts of hair on a mangy yellow dog. Those yet uncut bent low beneath their burden of rain like the backs of tired old people facing another hard winter. When Kristian had ridden in stony silence for as long as he could, he finally spouted, without preamble, "You shoulda let me give her a ride to school!"

Theodore cautiously studied his son, the profile set in lines of rebellion, the lips pursed in displeasure. Just when had the boy had time to become so dead set on squiring the school-marm around?

"I told her the first day I wasn't cultivating no hothouse pansies here."

Kristian glared at his father. "Just what is it you got against her?"

"I got nothin' against her."

"Well, you sure's hell don't like her."

"Better watch your mouth, hadn't you, boy?"

Kristian's face took on a look of intolerant disgust. "Aw, come on, Pa, I'm seventeen years old and if—"

"Not yet, you ain't!" In his ire Theodore realized he'd used *ain't,* and it angered him further.

"Two months and I will be."

"And then you figure it's all right to cuss a blue streak, huh?"

"Saying hell ain't exactly cussin' a blue streak. And anyway, a man's got a right to cuss when he's mad."

"Oh, a man is it, huh?"

"You don't ask that when you send me out to do a man's work."

The truth of the statement irritated Theodore further. "So what is it got you so nettled? And give me them reins. You ain . . . you're not doin' them horses' mouths any good." Theodore plucked the reins from Kristian's hands, leaving him to stare morosely between the horses' ears. Moisture gathered on his curled hat brim and dripped past his nose.

"You never ask me, Pa. You never even give me the choice about going to school or not. Maybe I want to be there right now."

Theodore had figured this was coming. He decided to confront it head on.

"To study?"

"Well, of course to study. What else?"

"You tell me." Kristian shot his father a quick look, set his gaze on the hazy horizon, and swallowed pronouncedly. Theodore studied Kristian and remembered clearly the pangs of growing up. He forced his voice to calm, and asked without rancor, "Got feelings for the teacher, do you, boy?"

Surprised, Kristian again flicked a glance at his father, shrugged, then stared straight ahead. "I don't know. Maybe. What would you say if I did?"

"Say? Not much I can say. Feelings is feelings."

Having expected an explosion, Kristian was surprised at his father's calm. Having expected reticence, he was even more unprepared for Theodore's apparent willingness to talk. But they never talked—not about things like this. It was hard to get the words out, but there were so many things mixing up Kristian lately. His own anger calmed and much of his youthful confusion became audible in his tone. "How's a person supposed to tell?"

"Don't know if I can answer that. I guess it's different for everybody."

"I can't quit thinkin' about her, you know? I mean, I lay in my bed at night and think about stuff she said, and how she looked at supper, and I come up with things I wanna do for her."

The boy was smitten, but good, Theodore realized. Best tread soft.

"She's two years older than you."

"I know."

"And your teacher, to boot."

"I know, I know!" Kristian stared at his boots. Water funneled from the front of his hat brim and rain wet the back of his neck.

"Come on kind of fast, didn't it? She's only been here a couple weeks."

"How long did it take for you and my mother?"

What should he answer? The boy was growing up for sure, to be asking questions like that. Truth was truth, and Kristian deserved to know. "Not long—I'll grant you that. I saw her standin' up there on that train beside her pa, wearin' a hat as yellow as butter, and I hardly looked at Teddy Roosevelt again."

"Well then why couldn't it happen to me that fast?"

"But you're only sixteen, son."

"And how old were you?"

They both knew the answer. Seventeen. In just two months Kristian would be seventeen. It was coming on faster than either of them was prepared for.

"What did it feel like, Pa, when you first knew how you felt about my mother?"

Like last night when I looked at the little missy sitting on that saddle. To Theodore's bewilderment the answer came at will. He was no more ready for it than for his son's imminent manhood.

"Feel like?" The feeling was with him again, new and fresh. "Like a strong fist in the gut."

"And do you think she felt the same?"

"I don't know. She said she did."

"She said she loved you?"

Slightly self-conscious, Theodore nodded.

"Then why didn't she stay?"

"She tried, son, she really tried. But right from the start she hated it here. Seemed like she was sad all the time, and after

you were born it seemed to get worse. Oh, not that she didn't
love you. She did. I'd find her layin' with you beside her on
the bed in the middle of the afternoon. She'd be playing with
your toes and talkin' and croonin' to you. But underneath,
she was pure sad, like women get after birthings. She never
seemed to get over it. By the time you were a year old she
was still starin' out across the wheat fields, claimin' the sight
of it wavin' and wavin' was drivin' her mad. There was no
sound here, she said." Theodore shook his head disconsolately. "Why, she never cared to listen. To her, sounds meant
streetcars and motorcars clanging by on a cobblestone street
and hawkers peddlin' and blacksmiths hammerin' and trains
whistlin' through the city. She never heard the wind in the
cottonwoods, or the bees in the caragana bushes." Theodore
squinted at the vast prairie and went on as if talking to himself. "She never heard them atall.

"She hated the stir of the wheat, she said after a while she
hated it worse than she'd hated travelin' on that train with
her pa. I watched the sparkle go out of her, and her laugh
disappeared, and I knew . . . " He looked at the runnels of
rain slipping down his wet poncho. "Well, I knew I wasn't
the kind of man who could ever bring it back. She thought I
was somethin' I wasn't, that night when we danced and talked
in Dickinson. That was some kind of fairy tale to her, but this
was the real thing, and she could never get used to it."

Kristian sneezed. Wordlessly, Theodore lifted a hip, produced a handkerchief, and handed it to his son. When Kristian
had blown his nose, Theodore went on.

"She just stared out over the wheat fields and got sadder
and quieter, and pretty soon her eyes looked all dull and . . .
well, nothin' like they were the day I first saw her on that
train. Then one day she was gone. Just gone."

Theodore's elbows rested on his knees. Sadly, he shook
his head.

"Ah, that day. I'll never forget that day. Worst day of my
life, I suppose." He shook off the memory and went on matter-
of-factly, "She left . . . but I never thought it was us she was
leaving as much as it was the place. It hurt her to leave you.
She said so in her note. Tell Kristian I love him, she said. Tell
him when he's old enough."

Kristian had heard it before, but his heart swelled at the words. He'd always understood that his motherless family was different from those of his cousins and schoolmates, and though he'd never known a mother's love, there had always been Nissa. But suddenly he missed the mother he'd never known. Now, on the verge of manhood, he wished he had a mother to talk to.

"You . . . you loved her, didn't you, Pa?"

Theodore sighed, and kept staring at the horses' rumps. "Oh, I loved her, all right," he answered. "A man sometimes can't help lovin' a woman, even if she's the wrong one."

They rode on in silence through the weeping day, with Theodore's last words reverberating in their minds. And if those words brought to mind Linnea rather than Melinda, it was nothing either man could control.

They came at last to the coal fields of Zahl. Theodore pulled the wagon onto the scale and stopped the horses with the old Norwegian term that was somehow comforting today.

"Pr-r-r," he ordered, the word blending with the mood set by both the story and the falling rain. Nobody was about. They were surrounded by the smell of wet coal and the sound of dripping water. Theodore turned to his son, rested one hand on his shoulder, and said, "Well, she's a pretty little thing, all right. I'll grant you that." Abruptly, he changed moods. "So, here we are. You up to loadin' eight tons of coal, boy?"

Kristian wasn't. He was feeling worse all the time. The sneezes were coming one right after the other, and it was a toss-up as to which was dripping faster, his nose or his hat brim.

"I ain't got much choice, have I?"

Theodore gently scolded, "There's no such word as ain't, boy." Then he vaulted over the side of the wagon and went to find old man Tveit to get the empty wagon weighed, so they could start loading.

The vast farmland that had driven Melinda Westgaard into a state of depression and caused her to desert her husband and son was, that day, as bleak as she'd found it on the bleakest of days. The rain fell dismally over the flat coal fields of Zahl with not a single tree to break the monotony of the featureless horizon. Aesthetically, nature had been unkind to North Dakota. But though she'd robbed the state of trees to provide precious fuel, she had offered something in their stead: coal. Twenty-eight thousand square miles of it. Soft, brown lignite, so accessible that man could simply scrape away the thin covering of surface soil and harvest the fuel with pick axes and shovels.

And so Theodore and Kristian harvested it that wet September day.

The weather was so grim that old man Tveit hadn't even hitched his team to the fresno. Instead, the earth-scraper sat idle, collecting rain in its scoop.

As Kristian worked beside his father, he paused often to blow his nose and sneeze. The damp chill crept up his legs and down inside his poncho. The inside of his collar grew wet, sending a shiver straight to his marrow.

By the time the wagon was loaded, he was utterly miserable. But he still faced the hour-and-a-half drive back home. Long before they got there Kristian felt weak from sneezing. His nose was rubbed raw from Theodore's damp handkerchief and the chills were shaking his body. Halfway home a timid sun began separating the clouds, peering through like a jaundiced eye, but it did little by way of warming Kristian.

"I s'pect you're feeling as soggy as you look," Theodore noted.

Kristian's mouth was open, eyes closed, nostrils flaring as he felt another sneeze coming. He peered at the sun to bring it on. When it erupted, it doubled him over and left his eyes watering.

"I'll drop you at home before I go on over to school to unload."

"I can help," Kristian felt compelled to insist, but there was little zest in the words.

"The best place for you is in bed. I can handle one wagon of coal by myself."

Kristian had no thought of objecting, and Theodore left him tucked securely in bed with Nissa fussing over him like a mother cat.

*   *   *

By the time he started for school it was late afternoon. The sun had chased away the remaining clouds and lay upon the ripe wheat like a benediction. Troubled, Theodore went over his talk with Kristian.

You'd best tread light around the little missy, too. Kristian's got no idea she sets off a spark in you too, and he'd better not ever find out.

The schoolyard was empty as he pulled the horses up before the steps.

"Pr-r-r," he ordered softly, studying the door as he secured the reins and leaped down. Crossing before the team, he distractedly fondled Cub's nose and headed for the schoolhouse steps.

The door opened soundlessly. The cloakroom was deserted, its inner doors ajar. The lunch pails were gone from beneath the long benches. A drip of water fell from the water spigot into a bucket with a lazy, echoing *blip*. The heavy knot of the bell rope swayed before Theodore's eyes and he backhanded it aside, moving toward the double doors. Suddenly, from inside, came the sound of Miss Brandonberg's angry, feminine voice. With his hand on the door, he paused.

" . . . next time I catch you up to your tricks, I fully intend to tell your parents about it. I will, in any case, be making visits to each home. You'd like me to have something good to report to your mother and father, wouldn't you, Allen?"

So the Severt kid was in there with her.

"You know, you've given me another one of those absolutely awful days. You and Theodore."

Theodore's eyebrows shot up and his chin drew in. Then he scowled. What business was it of the Severt kid's what went on between himself and the teacher?

"I do not understand that man. It wouldn't have hurt him one bit to let Kristian come to school today!" Her voice calmed and she added, *"But I guess that's none of your affair. You're excused, but tomorrow when you come to school it had better be with a changed attitude."*

Theodore backed away from the door, prepared to look as if he'd just entered the cloakroom when Allen walked past. But no footsteps sounded. No Allen appeared. Instead, all Theodore heard was the scrape and click of the chalk on the blackboard.

"All right, Theodore, he's gone and we can fight in peace!"

Theodore stiffened, chagrined at being caught eavesdropping. He was preparing to enter the schoolroom when her voice hurried on. *"Oh, all right, you know what I mean!"* Suddenly he realized she had no idea he was there, and smiled. So, what was she doing, *practicing* fighting with him? Apparently so, for she was putting plenty of gusto into her words as she scolded, *"It wouldn't have killed you to let Kristian come to school today, but no, you're too bullheaded stubborn to let me get one up on you, aren't you! So how did you keep him busy?"* Her voice turned sarcastic. *"Polishing harnesses in the tack room?"*

The chalk scraped on the board, and she started pronouncing disjointed words.

"Clock. Kite. Stuff. Fling. Wheel. Gullet."

Theodore smiled and inched toward the double doors. Silently, he pushed one wider and peered inside. She was writing a list of words on the blackboard, putting dots above some of them with an angry smack of the chalk. She's going to chip that blackboard, he thought, amused. He watched her slim back as her hand moved along and the movement of her skirts as she slashed a crossbar across the top of a letter. Then she began long strings of words.

The *clock* hung on the wall, she wrote, murmuring along with each word, while Theodore's eyes followed. And next, The *kite* had a blue tail. She snapped straight and appeared to be studying the blackboard thoughtfully. Then, with brisk, sure motions, she wrote and pronounced very clearly, "I would like to stuff Theodore."

He smiled so big it was all he could do to keep from laughing aloud. She backed off and studied the sentence, forcefully underlined *stuff*, then propped her hands on her hips and snickered. "Oh, would I ever," she repeated, her voice rich with anticipation.

But when she wrote the next sentence, she chose not to repeat the words aloud, and Theodore's smile faded as he puzzled over the writing he couldn't read. Again she backed off and giggled, obviously enjoying herself at his expense before bending toward the board again.

When she'd finished the next sentence, she covered her mouth with both hands and laughed so hard it rocked her forward.

"Hello, teacher," he drawled.

Linnea whirled around, mortified. There stood Theodore, lounging against the back wall with one thumb hooked behind a suspender clip. Her face took on the appearance of a slice of watermelon, and she twirled back toward the blackboard, frantically erasing the words.

"Theodore, what do you mean by sneaking up on me that way?" She wielded the eraser so hard Theodore thought she might push the front wall off the schoolhouse.

"What do you mean, sneaking? I drove up with a team of horses making enough noise to raise the dead, but there was just so much racket in here you wouldn't't've heard a mule train comin' through."

She swung around to face him with her palms pressed against the chalk tray behind her. "What do you want, Theodore? I'm busy," she finished superciliously.

His eyes lingered on the milky blackboard then came back to her as he tapped a pair of dirty leather gloves against his thigh. "Yeah, so I see. Getting ready for tomorrow's lesson?"

"Yes, I was, until you so rudely interrupted."

"Rude?" He touched the dirty gloves to his heart, as if unjustly maligned. "*I* am the rude one when I came to offer you a ride home from school?" That put her in a fine tizzy. She scowled like a great horned owl.

"Now's a fine time to offer me a ride home! Now that the sun's out and the rain has stopped! And where was your generous offer this morning, when you refused to let Kristian give me a ride to school?"

"He told you that?"

"He didn't have to tell me that. All he had to tell me was that he wanted to. And you don't fool me for one second. You didn't come to give this . . . this hothouse pansy any ride home, so what are you doing here?"

He pulled away from the back wall and clumped slowly up the left aisle, drawing on his gloves, all the time watching her. "Why, waitin' to get stuffed. Wasn't that what you said you wanted to do?" Reaching the edge of the teacher's platform, he spread his hands wide. "Here I am."

Linnea's embarrassment doubled, but her sense of theatrics came to save her. She pointed imperiously at the door. "And you can just turn around and head straight back out! I have no wish to either see or talk to you until you change your attitude about Kristian coming to school."

"My boy comes to school when I say he does, and not a minute sooner!"

She forgot theatrics and let her temper flare. "Oh, you . . . are . . . insufferable!" She stamped a foot and sent chalk dust swirling around her hem.

He lifted one boot to the edge of the platform and crossed both hands on his knee. "Yeah. And don't forget bullheaded."

"Well, you are, Theodore Westgaard."

"Yeah, I've been told that before, but who was the one that threw her napkin down and stomped out of the kitchen like a spoiled brat this morning? Not a very good example you set for your student."

Properly chastised, she faced the board and started erasing it more cleanly before listing the spelling words again.

"If all you came for is to criticize me, you may leave. And the sooner the better."

"That's not all I came for. I came with the load of coal."

"I could have used it this morning," she nagged. "My feet were squishing by the time I got here and the room was as chill as an icehouse."

The scrape of the chalk was the only sound in the room before his voice came again, kinder. "I'm sorry."

Her hand stopped moving over the blackboard. She peeked over her shoulder to see if he was serious. He was . . . and studying her feet. She turned to face him again, brushing the chalk dust from her hands. When their eyes met, she found only apology in his. Her gaze dropped to the soiled gloves, but even the sight of the aged, bruised leather became fascinating, simply because they encased his hands. How could he be so aggravating one moment and so appealing the next?

"You should be sorry. You made me so angry, Theodore, I did want to stuff you."

It was when she wasn't even trying that she achieved her goal: he reared back from the waist and broke into rich, resonant laughter. Never having seen him even smile before, she was unprepared for the impact. The sight was incredible; it completely changed him. She gazed at his beaming face with a feeling of profound discovery. She had not known his teeth were so beautiful, his mouth so handsome, his jaw so perfect, his throat so tan, or his eyes so sparkling. While his laughter filled the sunny schoolroom, the sight of him filled her heart. And suddenly she found herself incredibly happy. A first chortle of enjoyment left her throat, then a second, and soon her laughter joined his.

When the room stilled, they continued smiling at each other in mutual amazement. Her watch was lifting and falling very quickly upon her breast. He imagined that if he stepped close and placed his hand over it, he would find the gold warmed by her flesh.

He tried to swallow and couldn't.

She tried to think of something to say, but couldn't.

He tried to think of her as a child, but couldn't.

She tried to think of him as an older man, but couldn't.

He told himself she was the girl his son was falling in love with, but it didn't matter.

She told herself he was her student's father, she lived in his house, it wouldn't be fitting. But none of it mattered. None of it.

Common sense intruded, and Theodore withdrew his foot from the step. Briskly he tugged his gloves on tighter. "I'd better get that coal unloaded."

She stood with unformed words clogging her throat, watching him walk down the length of the room, noticing for the first time in her life how much narrower a man's hips are than a woman's, how beguiling bronze arms can be when protruding from rolled-up sleeves, how powerful a man's hands appear when sheathed in soft old gloves that have been with him through hours and hours of toil.

When he was gone, she tried returning to the sentences she'd been forming, only to be distracted time and again by the sight of him, just outside the window, shoveling coal. She moved closer. From her high vantage point she looked down upon his shoulders and the top of his head, captivated by the sight he made as he leaned to the task. How wide his shoulders, how spare his movements, how capable his muscles.

He paused, rested crossed wrists on the handle of the shovel, and she retreated one step into the shadows. The bright sun rained down on his rich walnut-brown hair, and she realized she rarely saw him without the straw hat he wore in the fields. She supposed it had gotten wet this morning and was at home, drying on the peg in the kitchen. He glanced in a circle, squinting, his face wearing a film of coal dust now. He was sweating, and she watched a droplet trickle along the edge of his hair, collecting black as it went. He pulled off one glove, searched his rear pocket, found no handkerchief, so donned the glove again and swabbed his forehead with a sleeve. Again he set to work, sending up a rhythmic clatter of coal falling upon coal.

He was so much a man, so much more mature than any of the boys to whom she'd ever been attracted. And he was attracted to her, too; she hadn't imagined it. For that brief, revealing second she had seen it in his eyes as clearly as she could now see the coal dust coating his handsome brown face. Something had sizzled between them while they'd stared at each other. Desire? Was that what it felt like? Her heart had caromed from the impact. She felt it yet. The awareness. The pull. The insistence.

But when he'd drawn the curtain over his eyes, she'd realized he still saw her as a child.

Most of the time.

9

WHEN THE COAL shed was full, he sailed the shovel onto the empty wagon bed and flexed his tired back. He wiped his forehead with an arm, checked the gray streak left there, tossed his gloves aside, and ambled across the schoolyard to the pump. Unhooking his suspenders, he sent them swinging, stripped off his shirt, and tossed it aside, then started pumping. With widespread feet he leaned over the stream of pure, icy water that splattered onto the dirt below. Alternately pumping and washing, he doused his face, splashed his chest, arms, and neck, then drank from his cupped palms.

When he straightened and turned, he found Linnea on the steps, watching him. She stood still as a stork with the fingertips of one hand lightly touching the iron handrail, the other palm clasping her elbow. Their gazes met and locked while he slowly wiped his mouth with the back of his hand, then became conscious of his bare, wet chest and the suspenders hanging down his thighs. He leaned from the hip and grabbed his flannel shirt from the ground, did a cursory toweling, then slipped it on and began buttoning it, all the while wishing she would move or at least stop staring.

But Linnea was intrigued by the sight of him. There were times she had seen her father's chest bare, but it hadn't nearly as much hair as Theodore's. And though her father, too, wore suspenders, they'd never dangled at his knees like dropped reins. And watching a father wash up was nothing whatever like watching Theodore pelt water over himself with such heedlessness that it went flying through the air, ran down his chest, and dripped from his temples and elbows.

But Theodore's heedlessness stopped abruptly when he spotted her.

She grew bemused by the sudden haste he showed in getting the shirt on and buttoned. He hung his head and half-turned away while stuffing the shirttails into his britches, snapping the suspenders back into place, and combing his hair with his fingers. At last he turned.

"Are you ready to go?" he called.

She flashed him a saucy smile. "Are you?"

She could have sworn Theodore began to blush, though he managed to hide it behind a wrist as he again swept a hand through his hair and broke into a purposeful stride.

"I'll bring the wagon around."

When they were sitting side by side, heading home, all was silent. Theodore rode with his back sloped, elbows to knees, thinking of how strangely self-conscious he'd felt when he'd turned around and caught her watching him wash up. Linnea balanced her grade book on her knees and glanced at the passing countryside, thinking of how dark and curly the hair at the back of his neck became when it was wet. Neither of them looked at the other, and neither said a word until they were past John's place. Then, out of the clear blue sky, Theodore stated, "Kristian caught a cold today. That's why he didn't come along to help unload the coal."

Her head swiveled around, but he stared straight ahead, offering nothing further. How odd that he felt compelled to explain why he'd come alone. She searched for something clever to fill the gap, but her thought processes seemed to be confounded by the memory of that well water running into the hair on his chest. "Oh, poor Kristian. It's much too beautiful a time of year to have a cold, isn't it?"

With the barest turn of the head he watched her study the landscape while she breathed deeply of the rarefied, fresh-washed air as if each breath were a blessing.

And he thought of how differently she studied the wheat than Melinda had.

Back at home he pulled up near the windmill. A soft breeze turned the vanes and a loose board rattled rhythmically above their heads. She craned to look up.

"There's something restful about a windmill, isn't there?"

"Restful?" His eyes made the same journey hers did.

"Mmm-hmm. Don't you think so?"

He always had but would never have dreamed of saying so for fear of sounding silly.

"I reckon," he admitted, ill at ease with her so close.

"I see John planted morning glories around his," she recalled, while they both squinted up at the revolving blades behind which the sky was tinted the same vivid blue as John's flowers.

"I remember John and me helping Pa build this one."

Linnea's gaze moved down the derrick to discover him still looking up. She found herself wondering what he'd looked like then, perhaps in the days just before full maturity set in, before he had whiskers and muscles and the brittle aloofness he preferred to display most times. Now, with his chin tilted, his jaw had the crisp angle of a boomerang. His lips were slightly parted as he squinted skyward, sending the fine white lines around his eyes into hiding. His eyelashes seemed long as the prairie grass, sooty, throwing spiky shadows across his cheek.

"Mmm . . . beautiful . . . "

"Melinda always said—" Suddenly his lips clamped, his head came down with a snap, and he shot her a cautious sideward glance. Enjoyment fled his face. "Got to fix that loose vane," he mumbled, then tied the reins and vaulted over the side of the wagon.

She clambered down right behind him and stood with her grade book against her breasts. "Who is Melinda?"

Refusing to look at her, he busied himself loosening the harness so the horses could drink. "Nobody."

She scratched on the red book cover with a thumbnail and rocked her shoulders slightly. "Oh . . . Melinda always said. Only Melinda is nobody?"

He knelt, doing something under the belly of one of the horses. The top of his hair was flattened, messed, and dulled by coal dust, but still damp at temple and nape. She wanted to touch it, to encourage him to confide. He seemed to take a long time deciding. Finally he stretched to his feet. "Melinda was my wife," he admitted, still refusing to meet Linnea's eyes while fussing with a strap just behind the horse's jaw.

Her shoulders stopped rocking. "And Melinda always said . . . "

His hand fell still, spread wide upon Cub's warm neck. Linnea's eyes were drawn to that hand, almost as brown as the sorrel's hide, wider than any she remembered, and certainly far stronger.

"Melinda always said windmills were melancholy," he told her quietly.

Countless questions popped into Linnea's mind while the sound of the loose board rattled above their heads. She stood nearly shoulder to shoulder with Theodore, watching his blunt fingers absently comb Cub's mane. She wondered what he would do if she covered the back of his hand with hers, ran a finger along the inner curve of his thumb where the skin was coarse from years of diligent work. But, of course, she couldn't. What would he think? And whatever was making her conjure up these fanciful thoughts about a man his age?

"Thank you for telling me, Theodore," she offered softly, then, discomposed, swung away toward the house.

Watching her, he wondered if he knew another woman who could turn her back on such a topic without prodding further. And he knew she'd been as aware of him as a man as he'd been of her as a woman. Woman? Eighteen years old was hardly a woman.

But then that was the trouble.

At supper that night, Kristian was absent, but Linnea announced to the others, "I've decided to visit all the homes of my students. Superintendent Dahl told me I should try to get to know them all personally."

Theodore looked at her squarely for the first time since they'd been in the schoolroom together.

"When?"

"As soon as I get invited. I'll send letters home with the children, telling them I wish to meet their families, then wait to see what happens."

"It's harvest time. You won't be meeting the men unless you go after dark."

She shrugged, glanced at Nissa and John, then back to Theodore. "So I'll meet the women." She spooned in a mouthful of broth, swallowed, then added, "Or I'll go after dark."

Theodore dropped his attention to his soup bowl while Linnea did the same. All was silent for several minutes, then to Linnea's surprise he spoke up again.

"You expect to be staying at their houses for supper?"

"Why, I don't know. I guess if I were invited I would."

Still giving all his attention to his soup bowl, he declared, "Dark sets in earlier these days. You'll need a horse."

Linnea stared at him in surprise. "A . . . a horse?"

"For riding." His eyes flicked to hers, then immediately away.

"If the children can walk, so can I."

"Clippa should do," he went on as if she hadn't spoken.

"Clippa?"

John and Nissa were observing the exchange with ill-concealed interest.

"She's the best horse we got for riding. Calm."

"Oh." Linnea suddenly realized her folded hands were clasped between her knees and she didn't recall setting her spoon down. Jerkily she picked it up and lit into her vegetable soup again, the words *hothouse pansy* cavorting through her mind.

"You ever saddled a riding horse before?" Theodore asked presently.

They braved a quick exchange of glances.

"No."

Theodore reached across the table, stabbed a thick slab of bread with his fork, started buttering it, and didn't look at Linnea again. "Come down to the tack room after supper and I'll teach you how."

There was still some fading light left in the sky as she walked down to the barn. Across the prairie she made out the silhouette of John's windmill, and from somewhere far off came the lowing of a cow. The chickens had gone to roost, and the chill of evening had begun settling in.

The outer barn door was open and she stepped inside to the mingled scents, both pleasant and fecund, that were now a welcomed familiarity.

"Hello, I'm here," she called, peering around the doorway of the tack room before entering.

Theodore stood at the wall, reaching up for a piece of equipage. He was dressed as he'd been earlier, in black britches, a red flannel shirt, suspenders, and no hat. He glanced over his shoulder, plucked down a halter, and handed it to her, backwards.

"Here. You bring this."

He swung the smaller of the two saddles off the sawhorse, nodded toward the door, and said, "Let's go."

"Where?" She preceded him into the main part of the barn, casting questioning glances over her shoulder.

He grinned—just barely. "Got to catch the horse first."

He placed the saddle down beside a box stall, looped a lead rope in his hand, and ordered, "Grab that pail."

Carrying a galvanized pail of oats, she followed him outside into the dusky twilight, across the muddy barnyard with its strong scent of manure and damp earth. He opened a long wooden gate, waited while she stepped through, then closed it behind them. They stood now on firmer ground bearded with short yellow grass. Near a barbed-wire fence some distance away, a dozen horses clustered, feeding. Theodore whistled shrilly between his teeth. Their heads lifted in unison. Not one took a step.

"Clippa, come!" he called, standing just behind Linnea's shoulder with the bridle behind his back. The horses disinterestedly stretched their necks and returned to cropping grass.

"Guess you've lost your touch," she teased.

"You try it then."

"All right. Clippa!" She leaned forward, clicking her fingers. "Come here, boy!"

"Clippa's a girl," Theodore informed her wryly.

She straightened and clutched the pail handle with both hands. "Well, how was I supposed to know?"

He grinned teasingly. "All you have to do is look."

"I was born and raised in town."

Behind her she heard the ghost of a chuckle, then over her

shoulder came his long arm. "Cub," he observed, pointing to the big sorrel workhorse that Linnea had never looked at closely. "Now he's a boy."

This time she looked closely, and even before Theodore's arm withdrew she felt her cheeks grow as pink as the streaks coloring the western sky behind them.

"Clippa, come here, girl," she tried again. "Sorry if I hurt your feelings. If you come over here I'm sure Theodore won't hurt you with that rope he's hiding behind his back. All he wants to do is take you to the barn."

Still the horse declined the invitation.

Greenhorn, Theodore thought, amused, watching as she leaned forward and talked to the horse as if it were one of her students, and all the while probably afraid the mare might decide to saunter over after all.

His eyes wandered down her slim back and hips. There's probably plenty I could teach her, he mused, and not only about catching horses.

Linnea straightened and declared petulantly, "She won't come."

"Bang the handle of the pail," Theodore whispered, almost in her ear.

"Really?" Her head swung around, catching him off guard, so close her temple almost bumped his chin. Her heart lurched at his nearness. "Will that work?"

"Try it."

"Here Clippa, come girl." At the first clatter of metal on metal, the horse came trotting, nose to the air, head bobbing. When Clippa's mouth hit the oat bucket, she caught the greenhorn unprepared and sent her thumping backward against Theodore. Instinctively his hands came up to steady her, and they laughed together, watching the horse bury her velvet nose in the grain. But when their laughter stilled and Linnea glanced over her shoulder, Theodore became aware of the warmth seeping through her sleeves. He dropped his hands with punctilious swiftness, then hastily moved around her to catch Clippa's bridle and snap the lead line to it.

Walking on either side of the mare, they led her back to the barn.

Inside, the shadows had grown deeper. Theodore lit a lantern and hung it safely above their heads, concentrating on the lesson at hand instead of the girl who seemed able to distract him far too easily. She stood close, watching intently, frowning and nodding as he demonstrated.

"Always tie the horse before you start cause you never know about horses. Sometimes they take to disliking the girth or the bit and get fractious. But if they're tied, they ain . . . they won't go no place."

"Anyplace. Go on."

He glanced at her sharply. She seemed unaware of having corrected him. Her concentration was centered on the lesson at hand.

"Anyplace," he repeated obediently before proceeding. "Make sure you pull the blanket well up past the withers so it pads the whole saddle and doesn't slip." When it was smoothed into place, he knelt on one knee, folded a strap back over the seat of the saddle, then looked up. "When you throw the saddle on, make sure the cinch isn't twisted underneath, or you'll have to take it off and throw it again. I reckon since this'll be the hardest part for you, you won't be wantin' to do it twice." He nodded at Clippa. "She's not as tall as some of the horses, so you oughta be able to handle it." He straightened with the saddle in his hands and tossed it on the mare as if it weighed no more than the horse blanket.

"Grab the cinch strap—" He ducked, and with a cheek pressed against the horse's side, reached beneath her belly. "—and bring it through this ring, then back up to the saddle ring as many times as you have to, till all you have left is enough to tie off. You tie it at the top . . . now watch." She moved slightly closer. "First take it to the back, then around, then up through. And make sure the knot is always flat— see?—then you give it a tug." With a few deft movements the knot was fashioned. One powerful tug made it secure, then his fingertips tucked the loose ends underneath.

"There. You think you can do that?"

He glanced down to find her studying the knot with a dismayed expression. "I'll try."

He reversed the process, then stepped back to watch. It was the first time he'd ever seen her so nervous. Having been around horses his whole life, he'd forgotten how intimidating they could be. He smiled secretly, watching her sidle up to Clippa cautiously.

"She knows you're here. No sense sneaking."

"She's really big, isn't she?"

"As horses go, no. Don't be scared. She's a gentle one."

But when Linnea reached under Clippa's belly, the mare sensed someone strange and pranced sideways, rolling her eye to check who it was.

Linnea leaped back.

Immediately Theodore stepped forward, taking the bridle, rubbing the mare's forehead. *"Pr-r-r."* At the soft, rolling sound, the horse quieted. Linnea watched Clippa's brown hide twitch and tried to submerge her fear, realizing how little it had taken for Theodore to calm the animal. Still holding the bridle in one hand, his expression softened. "You're strange to her. She had to look you over a little bit first. Go ahead. She'll be still now."

She was, though it was with great diffidence that Linnea reached a second time under the thick belly. But things proceeded without a hitch until it was time to tie the knot. She tried it once, twice, then raised her eyes guiltily.

"I forgot."

He showed her again. Standing at his shoulder she watched his strong, brown fingers fold the leather into the shape he wanted, his broad thumbs flattening the knot before drawing the end of the strap behind and giving it its final tug.

Their arms brushed as she reached toward the saddle. Neither of them spoke as she took the cinch and began undoing Theodore's handiwork, studying it carefully in reverse. He noted how she held the tip of her tongue between her teeth while concentrating. She made a false start and mumbled under her breath.

"Have you ever tied a man's necktie?" he asked.

Her fingers stilled and she looked up at him. "No."

Her face was lit from above by the golden lanternlight. He noticed for the first time the dusting of freckles across the crests of her cheeks. Coupled with her dark, studious eyes, they gave her a guileless look of innocent youth. Had she been laughing or angry his heart might not have fluttered. But her expression was sober, as if she approached the lesson with utter seriousness. It reminded him again of how truly young and inexperienced she was—so young she had never saddled a horse before, and certainly too inexperienced to have tied a man's necktie. He forced his attention back to the triangular knot.

"You have watched your father, haven't you?"

"Yes."

"So handle it like a necktie, keepin' it flat with your thumbs. Now start again."

She bit the tip of her tongue and started again. Halfway through, his thumb reached up and pressed hers. "No . . . flat," he ordered. His other hand clasped the back of hers and changed its angle. "The other direction."

Fire shot up her arm and she bit her tongue harder than she'd intended. But his hands fell away immediately and she was sure he had no idea how he'd affected her. "Now give it a good yank with both hands." She grabbed, gave a jerk, and secured a perfect knot.

"I did it!" she exclaimed jubilantly, smiling up at him.

His smile, when he turned it on full force, was numbing. It turned her bones to butter and made her heart dance. Had this been one of her daydreams, she would have awarded the heroine at least a hug of approval. But it wasn't, and Theodore only tapped the end of her nose with a fingertip and teased, "Yeah, you did, little missy. But don't get too smart yet. Not till you do it without help."

Little missy! Her cheeks grew pink with indignation at being treated like some adolescent in pigtails! She twirled toward the horse with a haughty lift of her chin and determination in each movement.

"I can and I *will* do it without your help!"

He stepped back and watched, grinning, while she not only untied the cinch, but reached up and whipped the saddle and pad off the horse's back. When her arms took the weight, it almost tipped her on her nose. Amused, he crossed his arms and waited for the show to go on. She narrated it in a piqued voice and never shot him so much as a glance.

"Blanket all the way up on the withers. Saddle ov-ver . . ." She grunted and puffed, lifting it off the floor. " . . . and make s-sure . . . " She boosted it with one knee, but not high enough. He suppressed a smile and let her struggle. "Make sure the cinch is . . . is . . . " She kneed the weighty load again and missed again, nearly pulling her arms from their sockets.

Theodore forced a sober expression and stepped forward, reaching to help.

"I'll do it!" At her angry glare he stopped cold, studied her puckered mouth, and backed off with a silent nod. Her shoulders weren't even as high as Clippa's back, but if the ornery little cuss wanted to prove she could do it, he wasn't about to stop her. There was a nice solid stool in the tack room for her to stand on, but he decided he'd let her suffer away until she grew tired and asked for his help. Meantime, he enjoyed the sight of her adorable mouth, pinched in irritation, and her dark eyes snapping like lightning bugs on a clear, blue night.

To Theodore's amazement, the saddle plopped over Clippa's back on the next throw, and his eyes took on a gleam of respect. She hung onto the stirrup for a moment, resting and panting, then stooped to capture the cinch. She executed a perfect flat knot, gave it a two-armed jerk, and spun to face him with her hands defiantly on her hips.

"There. What's next?"

The lanternlight caught in her dark pupils. She was breathing heavily from exertion. Theodore wondered what the law said about mature fathers making advances on their children's underage teachers. With forced slowness he closed the space between himself and Clippa, nudging Linnea aside with an elbow. He slipped two fingers between the cinch and the horse's hide.

"This could've been tighter. She starts runnin', and you'll find yourself upside down, little missy."

"Theodore, I told you once, don't call me that!"

He casually rolled a glance her way with his fingers still beneath the girth.

"Yeah. Miss Brandonberg, then."

Her eyes blazed brighter and her fists clenched harder. "And don't call me that either. For heaven's sake, I'm not *your* teacher. Can't you call me Linnea?"

Calmly he untied her knot and tightened it.

"Probably not. Wouldn't be seemly—not when you're the

schoolmarm. Around here teachers ain . . . are never called by
their first name."

"Oh, that's absolutely ridiculous."

He turned to face her, reached around her shoulder, and sent
her heart racing. But he only came away with the bridle from
the edge of the stall behind her.

"What're you so riled up about?" he asked coolly.

"I'm not riled up!"

"Oh?" With exasperating calmness he moved to Clippa's
head. "Guess I was mistaken. Here. You want to learn the
rest?"

She glared at the metal bit resting across his palm, then
whisked it up irately.

"Just show me what to do."

One last time he smiled at her charming display of temper,
then showed her how to place the bit in Clippa's mouth, adjust
the headstall, thread the mare's ears through the browband, and
buckle the throatlatch.

"All right, she's ready to ride."

To his surprise, Linnea hung her head and said nothing. He
studied her round shoulders and peeked around them. "What's
wrong?"

Slowly she lifted her eyes. "Why do we fight all the time,
Theodore?"

His throat seemed to close and blood surged through parts
of his body that had no business coming to life around a girl
of her age.

"I don't know."

Like hell you don't, Westgaard, he thought.

"I try very hard not to get angry with you, but it never
seems to work. I always end up spitting like a cat whenever
I'm around you."

He slipped his hands into his rear pockets and did his
damndest to look platonic. "I don't mind." He certainly
didn't. Being close to a riled Linnea was a good bit safer
than being around one like this. Disconsolately she studied
the rein draped over her palm, her lashes dropped like fans
to her smooth cheeks.

"I wish I didn't."

Everything hung too heavy and silent between them. He

gripped his own buttocks inside his pockets and tensed his leg muscles. When he knew he was in danger of touching her, he had to say something—anything to keep him from his own folly.

"You want to ride her?" He nodded toward Clippa.

Dejectedly, Linnea answered, "I guess not. Not tonight."

"Well, you better get up once, so I can adjust the stirrups for you."

For several seconds she stood still, silent. Finally she turned and reached up for the saddle horn. It was a long stretch, and to add to the difficulty her skirts got in the way. She hitched them up and hopped on one foot, making several false starts while Theodore fought the urge to put his hands on her backside and give her a boost. Persevering, she finally swung astride. But her skirts were caught, binding her legs. When she tried to stand and free them, her feet fell two inches short of the stirrups. She sat, waiting, looking down on Theodore's head as he adjusted first one stirrup, then walked around and adjusted the other.

She wished she were more experienced so she'd know how to handle the feelings that seemed to be springing up restlessly within her. She wanted to touch his gleaming hair, lift his chin and study his eyes at close range, hear his laugh and his voice speaking gently of what mattered most to him. She wanted to hear her name on his lips. But above all, she wanted to be touched by him. Just once, to find out if it would be as heady as she imagined.

He shortened the stirrups as slowly as possible, wanting to prolong their time together, wishing there were other favors he could do for her. It had been years since he'd felt this compulsion to be chivalrous. He'd thought it was something a man feels only when he's young and raring. What a shock to experience it again at his age. He felt her gaze following him as he moved about the horse, but controlled the urge to look up. To do so would be disastrous. But when he could think of nothing more to do for her, he stood staring at her delicate foot. How long had it been since he'd wanted to touch a woman this badly? But she wasn't a woman. Was she? Suppose he touched her—a simple touch, just once—what harm could come of that?

He reached for her ankle. It was warm and firm through the black leather of her new, sensible boots. His thumb bracketed her heel tendons, rubbing gently. There was no mistaking the touch for anything but what it was—a lingering caress. Nor was there any mistaking the fact that she sat with bated breath, waiting for him to look up, to go one step farther, to lift his hands and help her down. He thought of her name—Linnea—the name he refused to allow himself to call her lest it break down barriers better left unbroken. If he said it, if he lifted his eyes, he was certain of what would follow. Mistakes.

"Theodore," she whispered.

Abruptly, he dropped her foot and stepped back, realizing his folly. He stuffed his hands into his back pockets. When he looked up, his face was just as impersonal as usual.

"You're all set now. Make sure you put the saddle back in the tack room after you ride. I'll keep Clippa in the near pasture so you won't have to run clear to Dickinson to find her."

His attempt to lighten the atmosphere failed. There was too much burning between them.

"Thank you." Her voice held a faint reediness.

He nodded and turned toward the tack room with the pretext of searching for something, afraid if he stayed he'd reach up for her narrow waist to help her dismount and end up giving in to other urges.

By the time he returned she was removing the saddle.

"Here, I'll take that. You go on up to the house now. You probably got schoolwork to do yet."

When she was gone he turned Clippa out, then returned the saddle to its proper place. After throwing it over the sawhorse he stood a long time staring at it. He touched the curved leather. It was warm where she'd been sitting.

She's only eighteen and she's your boy's teacher. Closer to his age than to yours, Teddy, you fool. What would a girl like her want with a man damn near old enough to be her father?

A short time later, in her room beneath the rafters, Linnea prepared for bed with an odd feeling, like she'd swallowed a goose egg. Had she only imagined it all day long with him? No, she hadn't. He'd been aware of it, too. In the schoolroom.

Then again when she'd watched him wash at the well. And tonight in the barn when he'd held her ankle.

It was awful.

It was awesome.

It was—she grew more certain by the hour—desire.

She blew out the lantern and went to bed to consider it. Flat on her back, she tucked the blankets painfully tight over her breasts, as if to keep the feeling from escaping. She could feel her heartbeat, heavy and fast against the strictures. She conjured up Theodore's naked back as he'd leaned to throw water on his shoulders . . . his chest when he'd turned around with water dripping into the mat of dark hair . . . his thick hair as he'd moved about the horse refusing to look up and meet her eyes.

The desire centered in her nether regions.

He'd felt it, too. That was why he was afraid to look up, to say her name, to answer when she'd spoken.

She closed her eyes and subtracted eighteen from thirty-four. Sixteen. He had lived and experienced almost twice as much as she. There were so many things she wanted to know and be for him that by virtue of her immaturity she could not know or be.

Suddenly she was smitten by a strong wave of jealousy for his advanced age. Stubborn man that he was, he would probably never follow his instincts. Distraught, she rolled up on one elbow and gazed down at the white blot of her pillow in the dark.

"Teddy?" she queried in a soft yearning voice. Then she embraced the pillow tenderly and lowered her lips to his.

10

LINNEA'S LETTERS TURNED up immediate invitations to her students' homes, and within the week she began her visits. She chose Ulmer and Helen Westgaard's first because they had more children in school than any other family; also, because Ulmer was Theodore's brother. She'd developed a growing curiosity about anything relating to Theodore.

From the moment she stepped into their kitchen she sensed love present. The house was much the same as Theodore's, but far gayer and a lot noisier, with six children. The three oldest boys were out in the fields helping their father when Linnea arrived, the younger children helping their mother in the kitchen. But to Linnea's surprise, the field crew all came in for supper with their guest.

Eating, she observed, was as serious a business here as it was at Theodore's. They talked and laughed before the meal, and after. But while they ate—they *ate!*

However, several times during the course of the meal she looked up to find the oldest boy, Bill, studying her closely. Boy? He was no boy. He was a full-grown, strapping man of perhaps twenty-one or so, and he gave her a most disconcerting amount of overt scrutinization. His eighteen-year-old sister, Doris, also lived at home, though she was engaged and planning a January wedding. It seemed weddings, like education, had to be put off until after harvest season. Raymond and

Tony, Linnea's missing students, treated her with diffidence, as though forewarned that she was displeased about their not coming to school. The two youngest, Frances and Sonny, smiled and giggled whenever she caught their eye, and she suspected they felt highly honored to have the teacher choose their home first.

She delayed bringing up the subject of the school calendar until after dessert. When she did, she introduced it calmly, stated her case, and left the subject open for discussion.

There was no discussion. She was told politely, but in no uncertain terms, that the boys would come to school when the wheat was in.

The family all came out into the yard to bid her good-bye, but Bill left the others and appeared at Clippa's head to detain Linnea.

"Miss Brandonberg?"

"Oh . . . did I forget something?"

"No. I just didn't want you to think it's anything personal against you, them keeping the boys out to help with harvesting. It's always been that way, you know?"

"Yes, I know. But that doesn't make it right. The boys need the full school year, just like the girls do."

Linnea was so tired of going over the same argument. But just when she expected it to continue, Bill seemed to forget all about it. He stood looking up at her with one hand on Clippa's bridle, his attractive green eyes issuing a message of undisguised interest.

"Do you dance?" he asked.

For a moment she was too startled to answer. "D . . . do I dance?"

"Yeah—you know, one foot, two foot."

She smiled. "I . . . well, yes, a little."

"Good, then I'll see you at one barn or another when the threshers come. There's always lots of dances then."

In her experience there had never before been anyone who so blatantly showed his interest. She grew flustered by his open regard and the fact that his family looked on, waiting for her to ride away. Frances and Sonny were giggling again, heads close together. Linnea stammered, "Y . . . yes, I . . . guess you will. Well, good night then."

Riding home, with the night air cooling her cheeks, she considered Bill Westgaard. Sun-streaked blond hair, eyes as green as spring clover, a rather upturned nose, and a smile revealing slightly crooked teeth. He was a curious combination of boyish features and manly brawn.

So what did you think of him? Handsome?

A little.

Appealing?

Somewhat.

Bold?

Bolder than any other fellow I've met before.

So will you dance with him?

Perhaps.

But when she imagined it, it was Theodore with whom she danced.

Her intentions had been to leave the Severt home until last, hoping to give Allen time to become more cooperative at school so that her own feelings wouldn't be negative when she paid the visit. But Allen continued instigating more classroom disruptions than anyone else. During school prayers he invariably created a disturbance by tapping his pencil or his boot against the desk. He pestered the younger children by boldly snatching their cookies and taking bites, then calling them crybabies before giving them back—if he gave them back at all. As if sensing that Frances and Roseanne were two of Linnea's favorites, Allen singled them out to persecute more than any of the others. He taunted Frances, calling her a dummy, and sometimes pulled her skirt up to peek at her underpants. He turned the wood block on the girl's privy door while Frances was inside, and stuck a garter snake through the moon-shaped cutout. The resulting fit of hysteria had Allen beaming with joy for the remainder of the afternoon. He looked satisfied each time he managed to rile one of his classmates, or the teacher. And he was very good at making people angry.

Linnea was dreading the visit to Allen's house, but decided to get it over with immediately. She left school early on the day of home visits, so it was well before suppertime when she arrived at the Severt home. To her surprise, Allen came out and asked to see to Clippa. Reverend Severt was busy in his study, but Linnea enjoyed a pleasant visit with his wife while she made the final preparations for the meal.

Lillian Severt was a meticulously groomed woman with a neat finger-waved upsweep of pure black hair, held in place by unadorned tortoise-shell combs. She had flawless ivory skin and a face that was marred only by her upturned nose with its rather overlarge nostrils. But one tended to forget her nose in view of her clear, hazel eyes and square-set mouth and chin. Instead of the customary starched cotton housedress, she wore a stylish garment of ribbed amber faille with a white collar of pierced, embroidered organdy. And earrings—nobody else around Alamo wore earrings. Hers were small gold apple blossoms, with tiny citrine gems centered in each. Unlike most farm wives who often smelled of homemade lye soap and whatever they were having for supper, Lillian Severt smelled of her bureau, of spearmint and tansy and saxifrage and whatever other fragrant herbs she had mixed into her potpourri.

Her house was different, too. The front parlor had a bound carpet covering most of the floor. The kitchen had a cabinet with a self-contained flour sifter. And there was a formal dining room with built-in glass-fronted china closets and a colonnaded archway dividing it from the front parlor.

The cherry-wood table was covered with ecru lace, the food served in covered tureens, the napkins bound with Belgian lace, and when Lillian Severt took her chair, she left her cobbler apron in the kitchen.

Though Allen was a hellion at school, at home it was another story. Around his parents he was so polite as to appear almost ingratiating, even pulling out his mother's chair as the meal began. He bowed his head reverently when grace was being said, displayed impeccable table manners, and his voice lost all its schooltime flippancy.

To Linnea's surprise, when supper was finished Martin Severt ordered, "Allen, now you help Libby clear the table, then the two of you are excused."

In a pleasantly modulated voice, Mrs. Severt countered, "Now, dear, you know doing dishes isn't a man's work. Libby will do them."

Reverend Severt's fingers tightened on his cup handle, his eyes confronted his wife's, and for a moment tension was palpable in the room.

Then Allen squeezed his mother's shoulder, kissed her cheek, and offered, "Supper was de-lish. Nobody makes pumpkin pie like you do, Mother."

She laughed, patted his hand, and ordered, "Off with you, you flatterer."

Before he could escape, his father interjected, "Did you fill the woodbox when you came home from school?"

Allen was already heading out of the room. "Didn't have to. It was already full." His footsteps sounded on the stairs leading up from the front parlor, presumably to his room. When he was gone Libby cleared the table, then disappeared, too.

"Would you like more coffee?" Mrs. Severt inquired, refilling all three cups. A quiet fell upon the room. Linnea tried to screw up her courage to broach the subject foremost in her mind. She took a swallow of coffee and it seemed to drop twenty feet before it reached her nervous stomach.

"Mr. and Mrs. Severt . . ." The minute the words were out Linnea wondered if she should have addressed him as Reverend. She pushed the doubt aside and did her job, unpleasant though it was at the moment. "I wonder if we might talk for a while about Allen."

Mrs. Severt beamed.

Reverend Severt frowned.

"What about Allen?" he inquired.

Linnea planned her words carefully. "Allen seems very different here at home than he does at school. He . . . well, he doesn't seem to get along with the other children very well, and I was wondering if you might offer some insight as to why not, and what we might do to help him."

"We?" Mrs. Severt repeated, raising one eyebrow. "Allen has no trouble getting along anywhere else. If he's having difficulties, perhaps it's the school's fault."

The implication was clear: *school* meant *Miss Brandonberg*. While the teacher was still adjusting to the rebuff, Allen's mother went on. "I'm interested in what you see as . . . getting along." Her very inflection made the phrase sound suspect.

"Socially, it means he doesn't attempt to fraternize with the others, to join in the games, make friends. Academically, he doesn't always conform to the rules. He tends to . . . to ignore instructions and do things his own way."

"Fraternize with whom, Miss Brandonberg? Until the older boys come to school there's nobody for him to fraternize *with*. Surely you don't expect a fifteen-year-old boy to be overjoyed about playing hopscotch with the second and third graders?" Mrs. Severt's voice was a velvet ice pick chipping away at Linnea's self-esteem. Nerves prickled in places she hadn't realized she had them. She wished she were home at Nissa's where nobody talked at the table. Quivering inside, she nonetheless kept her voice placid.

"Perhaps fraternize isn't exactly the right term." Linnea searched for another, but none came, so she blurted out, "Allen teases the other children a lot."

"All children tease. I did when I was a child. I'm sure Martin did, too, didn't you, dear?"

But not all children take such perverse pleasure in it, Linnea thought, though she could hardly say so to the minister and his wife.

Reverend Severt ignored Lillian's question and posed one of his own. "Specifically, what has he done?"

Linnea hadn't intended to name specifics, but it appeared Mrs. Severt had a blind eye where her son was concerned. If Allen was to be helped, Linnea must be frank. She related the incident about Frances and the garter snake.

Lillian Severt demanded, "Did anyone *see* Allen put the snake through the moon?"

"No, but—"

"Well then." She settled back with a satisfied air.

Growing angrier by the minute, Linnea rushed on. "I was about to say that he was the only one not taking part in the kickball game that was going on in the playground at the time. And it happened right after he had stolen one of the cookies from Frances's lunch bucket and she'd complained to me about it."

Mr. Severt began, "Our Allen stole—"

"Frances?" his wife interrupted yet again. "You mean Frances Westgaard, that rather dim-witted child of Ulmer and Helen's?"

Under the table, Linnea's fists clenched in her lap. "Frances is not dim-witted. She's a little slow, that's all."

Lillian Severt took a ladylike sip of coffee. "Ah, slow . . . yes," she said knowingly, replacing her cup in its delicate saucer. "And you'd take the word of a child like that over the word of the minister's son?" One eyebrow raised in reproof, she let the question settle for several seconds, then brightened visibly. "And anyway," she flashed a smile at her husband, then at Linnea, "there would be absolutely no reason for Allen to steal someone else's cookies. I pack him an ample lunch myself every day, and as you just heard, he's more than appreciative of the sweets I make around here. Granted, he does love cookies, but I always see to it that he's well supplied."

Martin Severt leaned forward. "Miss Brandonberg, is there any chance you could be wrong about Allen stealing?"

Linnea turned to him with new hope. "This particular time, I'm afraid not. He snatched it from her while all the children were together, and gobbled it down before she could get it back. But there have been other times when he's managed to take bites and leave the cookies in their pails."

Again Mrs. Severt came to her boy's defense. "You may call that stealing, Miss Brandonberg, but I'd call it a childish prank."

"Given my vocation," the minister added, "you can well imagine that teaching the Ten Commandments has been of utmost importance to both Mrs. Severt and myself in raising our children. I know Allen isn't perfect, but stealing is a serious allegation against a boy who's been raised to read the Bible every night."

Allen's list of words came back to Linnea—*boring, stoopid, prayers, choclat cookys*. It had revealed more about Allen Severt than she'd realized at the time. She was beginning to see more and more reason to be concerned about Allen's behavior.

Sitting before his parents, feeling chastised and ineffectual, Linnea couldn't help but wonder what they'd say if she came right out and informed the Severts that their son spent an inordinate amount of time staring at her breasts. Undoubtedly, Lillian would intimate that Miss Brandonberg had done something to entice the boy. Having had a dose of the woman, Linnea wasn't too sure Mrs. Severt wasn't capable of costing a teacher her job on grounds much less serious than that.

Tact seemed prudent until she had gathered more substantial proof of Allen's misdeeds.

"Mr. and Mrs. Severt, I didn't come here to criticize how you raise your children. I wouldn't presume to do that, but I wanted you to be aware that things are not running smoothly for Allen at school. His attitude must change before he gets into even bigger trouble, and when I give him an order, I expect it to be carried out."

"Specifically what orders has he not carried out?" Mrs. Severt asked.

Linnea related the incident regarding the paragraph and the substituted list.

"And did the list tell you anything—now that you've seen his home?"

"Yes, but that's not—"

"The point is, Miss Brandonberg, Allen is an extremely bright boy. We've been told so ever since he began school. Bright children need constant challenge to perform at their best. Perhaps he isn't receiving that challenge under your tutelage." Linnea felt her face grow red and her anger multiply while Mrs. Severt went on almost indulgently. "You're new here, Miss Brandonberg. You've been with us less than a month and already you're labeling Allen a troublemaker. He's had five other teachers in the past, all of them older and more experienced than you . . . and men, I might add. Don't you find it strange that if our son *is* such a troublemaker we haven't heard about it before this?"

"Lillian, I don't think Miss Brandonberg—"

"And *I* don't think"—Lillian leveled her husband with a look that made Linnea expect a lightning bolt to come through the ceiling—"Miss Brandonberg has bothered to look for the positive traits of our son, Martin." If her words hadn't effectively silenced the minister, her condemnatory expression would have. "Perhaps she needs a little more time to do so. Let's hope that next time she comes to dinner her report will be less prejudicial."

To his credit, Martin Severt squirmed and blushed. Linnea wondered what to look at, and how long it would take to clear out of here so she could blow off the steam that was close to erupting.

"Yes, let's hope so," Linnea agreed quietly, then folding her napkin and pushing herself away from the table, added, "It was a delicious meal, Mrs. Severt. Thank you for having me."

"Not at all. You're welcome any time. The door of a minister's house is always open." She extended her hand, and though Linnea would rather have touched a snake, she took it and made her departure as gracefully as possible.

Upstairs, in the bedroom directly above the dining room, Allen Severt lay on his belly on the linoleum floor, his face directly above the heat register. Through its adjustable metal slats he clearly saw and heard what was going on in the room below.

"Allen, I'm gonna tell!" Libby whispered from the doorway. "You know you're not supposed to listen through the register. You promised Daddy you wouldn't."

Allen eased away from the grate slowly, so the floor wouldn't creak.

"Yeah, well, she's sittin' down there tellin' all kinds of damn lies about me, tryin' to make them think I cause trouble around school."

"You're not supposed to cuss either, Allen Severt. I'm tellin'!"

With a single insidious step he was at his sister's side, one hand painfully squeezing her arm. "Yeah, you just try it, pignose, and see what happens."

"You can't do anything to me. I'll tell Daddy and he'll make you recite verses."

Allen squeezed harder. "Oh, yeah, smarty? Well, how'd you like that cat of yours to get her tail dipped in kerosene? Cats dance real good when they get kerosene up their ass. And when you touch a match to 'em—poom!"

Libby's chin quivered. Tears formed in her wide blue eyes as she tried to pull free. "Ouch, Allen! Let go. You're hurting me."

"Yeah, and just remember it when you wanna go tattle to the old man. When the teacher starts spreading lies about me it's not my fault what happens around school after that." He glared at the register, then gritted evilly. "Just who does she think she is anyway?" Then, as if he'd no further use for his sister, he thrust her aside.

"Lawrence, I swear I've never—never!—been so mad in my life! Why, that... that supercilious, misguided old bag! I swear to God, Lawrence, if she'd've made one more nasty crack, I would've pushed that flat snout of hers clear to the back of her skull!"

Linnea bounced along on Clippa's back, so infuriated her eyes teared. A lump of rage clotted her throat.

"Clippa, slow down, you mangy old nag! And, Lawrence, come back here!"

But Lawrence slunk away and Linnea needed someone with whom to vent her emotions. Perhaps it was fortuitous that only a quarter mile down the road she passed Clara and Trigg's mailbox.

"Whoa."

She stared down their lane at the lights beaming from the windows, recalled Clara's invitation, and decided she had never before needed a friend as badly as she needed one now.

It was Trigg who answered the door.

"Why, Miss Brandonberg, what a surprise." He glanced beyond her and frowned. "Is anything wrong at Teddy's?"

"No, everything's fine. It's just—"

"Come in, come in!"

At that moment Clara appeared behind her husband. "Linnea! Oh, this is wonderful." She grabbed Linnea's hand and drew her inside. "But the little ones are going to be so disappointed. They're already in bed."

"Oh, this isn't an official visit. I was just passing by, and I remembered you said the coffee was always hot and..." Suddenly Linnea gulped to a stop, blinking rapidly.

"Something's wrong. What is it?"

"I think I n... need a friend."

The kitchen was warm, yellow, and cheerful, the welcome enthusiastic. Linnea's pent-up frustrations came to a head, and before she could stop them, tears glistened in her eyes. Clara immediately put an arm around the younger woman and drew her toward a round oak table where a kerosene lantern lit tomorrow's breakfast plates and cups already in place, upside down. While Clara urged Linnea into a chair, Trigg headed for the coffeepot.

"Your hands are cold. Where have you been, out there in the dark?" Clara seated herself facing Linnea and rubbed her hands between her own.

"I'm sorry to come here this way and . . . and wail on your shoulder, but I'm so upset and I . . . I . . . "

"Is it Teddy?"

"No, it's Allen Severt."

Clara sat back, her expression wry. "Oh, *that* little turd."

Unexpectedly, Linnea laughed. She looked at the down-to-earth Clara and a weight seemed to lift from her chest. The tears that had been threatening suddenly evaporated and things didn't seem nearly as exasperating. She was going to love this woman.

"He really is. I wonder how many times I've wanted to call him that myself."

"Bent tells me plenty about what goes on around school. So what has Allen done now?"

"This time it isn't him so much as his parents." Linnea shook her head in exasperation. "His mother! Lord!"

Smiling wryly, Clara overturned and filled three coffee cups. "So you've met Lillian the Hun." Again Linnea laughed at the woman's outrageous candor. Clara tipped her head aside and grinned. "Well, I'm glad you can still laugh. Feeling better now?"

"Immeasurably."

"Then tell us what happened."

Linnea related the highlights of the confrontation and could see the anger growing in Clara.

"She called our Frances *what?*"

"Dim-witted. Can you imagine a minister's wife saying a thing like that?"

"Lillian thinks that being a minister's wife covers a multitude of sins. Like criticizing others to make herself look good. You ought to hear her at Ladies' Circle." Clara waved the memory away. "Well, I don't want to get into that, but you won't find anybody around here who has one good thing to say about her. She hasn't been liked since the first Sunday she stood beside the reverend on the church step and basked in reflected glory.

"But to think she'd have the gall to tell *you* that you're not doing your job at school when that devil of hers has been driving teachers crazy for years. I know more than one of them who didn't stay because of Allen.

"But that's neither here nor there. Listen, Linnea, the stories coming home from school with the children are all good. And don't you forget it! Lillian's been whitewashing that brat's foul streak her whole life. And she's gonna keep on till one of these days he'll pull one that she won't be able to wish away." Clara stopped, considered a moment, then asked, "Have you told Teddy about this?"

Startled by the question, Linnea grew wide-eyed. "No."

"Well, if Allen keeps it up, I think you should."

Linnea shook her head. "No, I don't think so. Theodore doesn't like to be bothered with school business."

"Oh. He's been grumpy lately, huh? Well, don't let that fool you. Underneath he cares about more than you'd guess. Take my word for it, if Allen keeps it up, the one to talk to is Teddy."

"All right. I'll think about it." The coffeepot was empty and Trigg was stifling a yawn. "It's late," Linnea said. "I've enjoyed this so much, but I really must go."

At the door she and Clara exchanged the customary parting niceties, but at the last minute they couldn't resist sharing an impetuous hug.

"You be careful riding home now."

"I will."

"Come anytime."

"I will. And you do the same."

At home, when Linnea reached the barn it was dark and silent. She lit a lantern, going over all of Theodore's instructions for putting away the tack and turning Clippa out into the near paddock. But she had scarcely begun working on the girth knot when Theodore appeared silently behind her.

"You're late!"

She jumped and spun, pressing a hand to her heart.

"Oh, Theodore, I didn't know you were there."

He'd been so worried. Pacing, listening for hoofbeats, wondering what could have happened to her. Her safe arrival brought relief, but along with it an irrational anger. "Haven't you got more sense than to stay out this long? Why, anything could've happened to you!"

"I stopped to visit Clara and Trigg."

He stood close enough to touch, but his face wore a mask of displeasure.

"This isn't the city, you know."

"I . . . I'm sorry. I didn't know you'd be up waiting."

"I wasn't up waiting!"

But he had been and they both knew it. While he scowled down at her she felt it again, that wild, wondrous new thing that filled her breast to bursting.

Blast it, girl, don't look at me that way, he thought, looking down into her somber face that hid little of what she was feeling. His heart pounded. His hands itched to touch her. He wanted to say he was sorry he'd shouted—it had little to do with her being out late. Instead, he reached for the girth knot.

"You go on up to the house," he ordered, more gently. "I'll see to Clippa."

"Thank you, Theodore," she replied softly.

He nodded silently, concentrating solely on his task.

She studied him as he turned away, but again he closed himself away from her. *Why are you so afraid of what we're beginning to feel,* she wondered. *It's nothing to be afraid of. And you* were *waiting to see that I arrived home safely. You* were, *Theodore, whether you'll admit it or not.*

But she kept her thoughts to herself and slipped quietly from the barn, leaving him to wrestle with his emotions.

During the days that followed, Linnea visited the homes of the rest of her students, sharing meals and getting to know the people whose lives were all so closely intertwined. She found them to be basic, hardworking, rather too introspective—the effervescent Clara was the exception—but flatteringly polite to the new teacher . . . if one disregarded table manners.

The Lommen twins had a charm all their own, stemming from their constant good-natured competition with each other. It was a positive force in their lives, one that spurred them to try to please, not only at school but also at home.

At Oscar Knutson's Linnea was startled to find the house so cluttered with litter, they seemed to live in the paths between piles. Linnea made a mental note to create a desk-check day at school in an attempt to teach Jeannette the value of orderliness. Aside from the messy house, however, the visit was a success. Not only did Linnea enjoy a delicious meal, she had the chance to discuss such things as Christmas plays, county spelling bees, and a cakewalk she had in mind to raise funds for a real teacher's desk.

Her second visit to Clara and Trigg's house cemented the friendship between the two women, and Linnea went away considering Clara a confidante.

In making the rounds of the Westgaards, Linnea's respect for their mother grew. Nissa had raised sensible, loving children, with the possible exception of Theodore, who seemed the least pleasant, the least loving of the lot. Especially since that night in the barn. They'd said very little to each other since then, had managed to stay out of each other's way, but the fact that the older boys were still being withheld from school was like a rowel under Linnea's hide. Every time she sat down across the table from Theodore, she wanted to lash out at him and demand that he release his son into her daytime custody.

But October came and settled in with cooler weather, and still the older boys were missing.

At school, Allen Severt continued to persecute Rosie and Frances more than any of the others, but always sneakily enough to keep from getting caught. He hid Rosie's lunch pail, sometimes ate the choicest contents from it, then blamed it on someone else. When she ran to the teacher in tears, Allen taunted, mimicking her lisp in a singsong voice.

Systematically he worked on shortening Frances's left pigtail. Only her left. He did it in a way that could never be proven, somehow managing to trim off no more than a quarter inch at a time, leaving no fallen hair as evidence, no abrupt change in length to bring attention to what he was doing. It was only when Frances's pigtails began to look lopsided that it came to light.

Linnea found the ten-year-old crying in the cloakroom one day during noon recess. She was sitting in a dejected heap on one of the long benches, looking heartbreakingly forlorn with her pigtails drooping and her skinny shoulder blades protruding as she sobbed into her hands.

"Why, Frances, what is it, dear?"

Frances swiveled toward the wall and hid her face on a jacket hanging from a peg. But her shoulders shook. Linnea couldn't resist sitting down and turning Frances into her arms. Unadvisable as it was to have favorites, Linnea couldn't resist Frances. She was a sweet child, quiet, untroublesome, one who strove to please in every way, no matter how difficult it was for her academically. As if realizing her shortcomings in that department, she tried to make up for it with little kindnesses: a favorite cookie left on Linnea's grade book; a crisp, red apple placed on the corner of the teacher's table; an offer to collect the composition books or pass out crayons or tie the boot strings of the younger ones who didn't know how yet.

"Tell me what's made you so unhappy."

"I c . . . can't," the child sobbed.

"Why can't you?"

"B . . . because . . . you'll th . . . think I'm d . . . dumb."

Linnea gently pressed Frances back and looked into her puffy, downcast face. "Nobody here thinks you're dumb."

"Allen d . . . does."

"No, he doesn't."

"He d . . . does, too. He c . . . calls me d . . . dimwit all the t . . . time."

Linnea's anger flared, and with it protectiveness. "You are *not* dumb, Frances, so just put that out of your head. Is that what made you cry? What Allen said?"

Woefully, Frances shook her head.

"What then?"

It all tumbled out at last, the secret that "teacher" wasn't supposed to know, but part of which she already did. Frances's greatest wish was to be an angel in the Christmas play, because the angels always wore long white gowns and let their hair flow loose with a sparkly tinsel halo adorning it. But instead of growing, her hair was getting shorter, and not only did she fear missing the chance to be an angel, she was afraid she was going bald.

It took great self-control for Linnea not to laugh at this astounding revelation. She hugged Frances hard, then drew back to wipe the girl's cheek. Forcing a sober expression, Linnea cajoled, "Here now, have you ever heard of little girls going bald? Only grandfathers go bald."

"Th . . . then why is my h . . . hair getting sh . . . shorter?"

Linnea perkily turned the child around to investigate. "Doesn't look any shorter to me."

"Well, it is. But only one of my pigtails."

"Only one?"

"This one." She pulled the left braid over her shoulder.

Upon closer scrutiny, it was obvious the hair had been trimmed—and none too neatly. Linnea took the end of it and teasingly brushed Frances's nose. "Maybe you ate it off yourself. Isn't that the one you suck on when you're trying to figure out your arithmetic problems?"

Frances dipped her chin to her chest with a coy smile she couldn't quite hold back, though her cheeks were still tearstained.

"I have an idea," Linnea said, adopting a thoughtful air. "Until you find out if you're really going bald or not, and until you find out why it's happening to only one side of your head, why not have your mother tuck your pigtails up in a coil—like mine, see?"

Linnea twisted around, showing the child the back of her head, then faced her again, lifting the brown pigtails experimentally. "All it takes is a couple of hairpins, and they're tucked safely away so nobody can see how long or short they are."

Frances showed up the following day proudly displaying her new corona of braids, which Allen Severt could no longer crop. The change settled the symptom but not the problem, for only two days after that *somebody* drilled a peek hole through the back wall of the girls' privy.

Linnea felt certain the villain was Allen, but had no proof. And not only were his pranks growing more serious, she had the uneasy feeling he enjoyed seeing others suffer.

She decided to talk to Theodore about it.

11

SHE SOUGHT HIM out that night and found him in the tool shed fashioning a new vane for the windmill. One of his knees held a wooden slat across a barrel top, and he faced the rear of the building as she approached.

She stopped outside the high-silled door and watched his shoulders flexing, then glanced around the interior of the shed.

Here, as in the tack room, neatness reigned. She studied the almost fanatic tidiness, smiling to herself. Hilda Knutson could take a lesson from Theodore. The shed was cozy. The lantern created enough heat to warm the tiny, windowless building, which smelled of fresh-cut pine and linseed oil. A stack of paint cans took up one corner. On the wall hung snowshoes, traps, and a variety of pelt stretchers. There were two small nail kegs and a neat coil of barbed wire. In a near corner leaned a worn broom. Linnea's eyes fell to the sawdust drifting onto Theodore's boot, and she imagined him sweeping it up the moment the chore was finished. His penchant for neatness no longer irritated her as it had when she'd first arrived. Now she found it admirable.

"Theodore, could I talk to you a minute?"

He swung around so suddenly the board clattered to the floor. His cheeks turned crimson.

170

"Seems you and I are always startling each other," she ventured.

"What're you doing out here?" He hadn't meant to sound so displeased. It was just that he'd been doing his best to avoid her lately. The sight of her made his palm feel slippery on the saw handle.

"May I come in?"

"Not much room in here," he replied, retrieving the fallen board and setting back to work.

"Oh, that's all right. I'll stay out of your way." She entered and perched herself on an upturned keg.

"Theodore, I have a problem at school and I wondered if I could talk to you about it. I need some advice."

The saw stilled and he looked up. Nobody ever asked Theodore for advice, least of all women. His ma was a dictator and Melinda hadn't bothered letting him know that she was going to show up at his doorstep expecting to get married. Neither had she informed him she was running away two years later. But there sat Linnea, rattling Theodore with her mere presence, posed like a nymph on the nail keg, with her hands clasping her knees. Her big blue eyes were wide and serious, and *she* wanted *his* advice.

Theodore set aside his work and gave her his full attention.

"About what?"

"Allen Severt."

"Allen Severt." He frowned. "He giving you trouble?"

"Yes."

"Why come to me?"

"Because you're my friend."

"I am?" he asked, surprised.

She couldn't hold back a chuckle. "Well, I *thought* you were. And Clara said if Allen kept it up, I should talk to you."

Theodore had never had a friend before. His only friends were his brothers and sister and those they'd married. It sounded good, having a friend, though he wasn't sure how well being Miss Brandonberg's would work. But if Clara thought he should know, he'd listen. He set aside his saw, straddled the barrel, and crossed his arms.

"So what has Allen been up to?"

"Not much I can prove, but plenty I can't. He's been a troublemaker right from the first day of school—teasing the younger children, openly defying me, creating disturbances. Just little irritating things. Hiding lunch pails, taking bites of cookies. But now he's started in on Frances and I—"

"Frances? You mean *our* little Frances?" His shoulders squared and his arms came partially uncrossed. As he bristled defensively everything about him became more masculinely imposing.

So Frances was one of the things he cared about. Linnea found it touching that he'd referred to the child as *ours*.

"He calls her dimwit all the time. He's very good at picking out the children's weaknesses and teasing them. But that isn't the worst of it. I suspect he's the one who's been cutting off Frances's braid, and one day he locked her in the outhouse and stuck a snake through the hole in the door. Now the girls have found a peek hole drilled in the back of the outhouse wall. I can't prove any of it, but there's something about Allen that . . . " She shrugged, then rubbed her arms and shivered.

Theodore's air of displeasure doubled. Forcing himself to remain seated, he pressed the heels of both hands to the barrel edge between his thighs.

"Has he done anything to you?"

She glanced up quickly, not having intended to say that much. Her personal misgivings about Allen were too nebulous to put to voice. And besides, she'd feel utterly foolish telling Theodore that Allen stared at her breasts. All boys reached an age where they became interested in the development of girls. With Allen it wasn't the fact that he stared, but *how* he did so; trying to put this into words would be difficult.

"Oh, no, he hasn't *done* anything. And it's not even so much what he does to the others. So far it's been little things. But they're getting more serious all the time. And what I'm most concerned about is that I think he enjoys being . . . well, malicious . . . making people squirm."

Theodore rose in one swift movement. He gave the impression that he wanted to pace but was unable to in the confined space. His brow beetled, he swung on

Linnea. "You talk to his folks about this when you were at their place for dinner?"

"I tried. But I saw immediately that Allen's mother wasn't going to believe a word I said about her golden boy. She has him so spoiled and herself so deluded that there's no reaching her. I thought for awhile I might get some cooperation from Reverend Severt, but . . . " She shrugged. "He seems to think that if Allen reads the Bible all his life it'll keep him a saint." Linnea chuckled ruefully, looking at the floor.

"Martin's not a bad sort. It's just that that wife of his has led him around by the nose for so long he don't know how to stand up to her."

"Doesn't," she corrected absently.

"Doesn't," he repeated without a second thought.

Linnea looked up appealingly. "I'm not sure I can handle Allen without their help."

A warning stirred in Theodore. He pressed his hands more tightly against his armpits.

"You afraid of Allen?"

"Afraid?" Her gaze held his for a moment, then flickered aside. "No."

He didn't believe her. Not entirely. There was something she wasn't telling him, something she didn't want him to know. And even if she was telling him everything, there was still little Frances to consider. She had always been one of Theodore's favorites, the one who never forgot her Uncle Teddy at Christmas. One year she had given him a pomander ball for his bureau—a pomander ball, of all things. He'd taken one sniff of the feminine thing and wondered what his brothers would think when he showed up smelling like orange and cloves in his clean overalls. But he'd slipped it into his bottom drawer until Frances smelled the fruit and spice on him one time and grinned wide in toothless approval. Then and only then had he removed it from his drawer.

With the recollection fresh in his mind, he made a sudden decision.

"I want you to tell everything you just told me to Kristian, then pick out a desk for him cause he'll be in school Monday morning. After that Allen better watch out if he decides to pick on Frances. But Monday's the soonest I can spare him."

Linnea's lips dropped open in surprise.

"K . . . Kristian?" she repeated.

Theodore—stubborn—was a sight to behold! His eyes darkened to the color of wet Zahl coal, his jaw jutted, and his chest looked invincible as he stood like a Roman gladiator with his shoulders thrust back, lips narrowed with resolve. "What that little pip-squeak Severt needs is somebody bigger than he is to take him down a notch every now and then."

She stared at him while a smile spread slowly upon her face. "Why, Theodore!"

"Why Theodore what?" he grumbled.

"You'll give up your field hand to protect someone you care about?"

He dropped the warrier's pose and gave her a quelling frown. "Don't look so self-satisfied, teacher. Frances gave me a pomander ball for Christmas one year and—"

"A pomander ball!" Linnea squelched a giggle.

"Wipe that smile off your face. We both know Frances isn't nearly as bright as the rest of the kids, but she's got a heart of gold. I'd like to shake that Severt brat myself a time or two for pestering her. But don't worry. From now on Kristian'll be there to keep an eye on things."

On Monday not only did Kristian showed up at school, but all the other older boys as well. It appeared they'd been simultaneously released from field work as if by some mystical force.

Their coming brought a distinct change to the schoolroom. It seemed pleasantly full, taking on a busy air, a new excitement. It was especially apparent in the younger students, who idolized the older ones. There was a wonderful and unexpected camaraderie between the oldest boys and the very youngest children. Instead of shunning the small ones, the big boys indulgently included them, helped them, soothed them if they fell and hurt themselves, and, in general, tolerated their immature concerns with good-natured forebearance.

On the playground things were livelier. Gopher-hunting was finished for the season, and it wasn't uncommon during noon recess for the entire school, including the teacher, to take part in a ball game.

Linnea loved it. There was a wholly different feeling to a country school than to a town school. She'd never experienced anything like it before. It was wholesome and rich with sharing, much the same as in an extended family. Watching a sixteen-year-old boy pick up and dust off a howling seven-year-old girl who'd hit the dust during a game of red rover was a rewarding experience. And watching an older girl teach a younger one the intricacies of making French braids brought a smile to Linnea's lips. One day, looking on, she realized something astounding.

Why, they're learning to be parents!

And as long as they were, they'd better learn right.

Now that all the boys were present, she took up the subject she'd been dying to introduce.

"Shakespeare may have said 'Unquiet meals make ill digestions,' but Shakespeare, I daresay, never sat down to the table with a bunch of hungry Norwegians. We shall today take up the topic of table etiquette, including the social amenity of making graceful mealtime conversation."

The boys looked at each other and snickered. Steadfastly, she went on, pacing back and forth in front of the room, hands clasped dramatically at her waist. "But before we get to that, we will start with the subject of burping."

When the laughter died down, the students suddenly realized Miss Brandonberg was not laughing with them. She was standing with sternly controlled patience, waiting. When she spoke again, not a student in the room doubted her earnestness. "I will have it clearly understood that this schoolroom has heard the last unrestrained belch it will ever hear as long as I'm the teacher here."

No more than five seconds of silence had ticked by when, from the direction of Allen Severt, came a loud, quick rifle shot of a burp that echoed to the rafters.

Laughter followed, louder than before.

Linnea strode down the aisle, stopped calmly beside Allen's desk, and with a movement as quick as the strike of a rattler smacked his face so hard it nearly knocked him out of his seat.

The laughter stopped as if a guillotine blade had fallen.

In the quietest of voices, the teacher spoke. "The proper words, Mr. Severt, are, 'I beg your pardon.' Would you say them to your classmates, please."

"I beg your pardon," he parroted, still too stunned to do otherwise.

It was, indeed, the last burp Linnea ever heard at P.S. 28, but Allen Severt didn't forget the slap.

October settled in, bringing the first frosts and the first hired hands. Linnea ambled out of the house one afternoon to find a stranger in conversation with Nissa by the windmill.

"Linnea, come on over! Meet Cope!"

Cope, it turned out, had been coming to work for the Westgaards for twelve years. A stubby, ruddy Polish farmer from central Minnesota, he took his nickname from the round can of Copenhagen snuff ever present in his breast pocket. Doffing a flat wool cap, he shook Linnea's hand, called her something sounding like "a pretty little sitka," spit out a streak of brown tobacco juice, and asked where them other bums was.

Cope was followed by Jim, then Stan, and a string of six others. Five of the men were repeaters, three of them new to the Westgaards.

One of the first-timers was a young buck who had drifted through from Montana wearing scarred cowboy boots, a battered Stetson, and a platter-sized silver belt buckle bearing a Texas longhorn. His hair was as dark and shiny as polished onyx, his smile as teasing as a Chinook wind.

As Cope had been, he too was talking with Nissa the first time Linnea saw him. She returned from school one afternoon with her grade book and papers to find the two of them outside, near the kitchen door.

"Well, who's this now?" he drawled as she approached.

"This here's Miss Brandonberg, the local schoolteacher. She boards with us." Nissa nodded sideways at the man. "This here is Rusty Bonner, just hired on."

From the moment her eyes met his, Linnea became

flustered. In her entire life she'd never met a man so blatantly sexual.

"Miss Brandonberg," he drawled, slow as cool honey. "Happy t' meetcha, ma'am." When he spoke, one could almost smell sagebrush and whang leather. With one thumb he pushed his Stetson back, revealing arresting black eyes that hooked downward at the corners as he grinned, and untamable black locks that teased his forehead. In slow motion he extended one hand, and even before she touched it, she knew what it would feel like. Wiry and hard and tough.

"Mister Bonner," she greeted, attempting to keep the handshake brief. But he clasped her hand a moment longer than was strictly polite, squeezing his rawhide-textured hand against her much softer one.

"Name's Rusty," he insisted in that same drawn-out way.

The only rusty thing about him was his skin. Burned by the sun to a rich, deep mahogany, it framed his dark, lazy smile in a way that must have left a string of broken hearts from the Texas panhandle to the Canadian border. He was a head taller than Linnea, lean as a drought year, and put together mostly with sinew.

"Rusty," she repeated, flashing a nervous smile first at him, then at Nissa.

"Well now, you're a right pretty lady, Miss Brandonberg. Makes me wonder what I missed when I dropped out o' school to go rodeoin'."

Flushing, she dropped her gaze to his scarred boots and the bedroll lying on the ground beside them. He stood in the hipshot pose of a self-assured ladies' man, one knee bent, grinning at her lazily with those devilishly handsome eyes that looked as if they were figuring her body dimensions and her age.

Nissa sensed that Linnea was out of her league and ordered, "You can put your roll in the barn. You'll bunk with the other boys in the hayloft. Wash water'll be hot one hour before sunrise and breakfast'll be served in the kitchen till the cook wagon gets here."

Inveterate charmer that he was, Rusty Bonner wasn't choosy about whom he showered that charm on, long as

she was female. He swung his laconic gaze to Nissa with no
perceptible change in appreciation, doffed his hat, and drawled,
"Why, thank y', ma'am. That's most obligin' of y'."

Then he swung down lazily to snag his bedroll and
sling it over his shoulder by one finger. Tipping his hat
brim low over his eyes, he sauntered off toward the barn,
hips swinging like pines in a slow breeze.

"Whew!" Nissa puffed, shaking her head.

"Whew is right!" Linnea seconded, watching Rusty's back
pockets undulate on his tight blue Levi Strauss britches.

Eyeing Linnea, Nissa declared, "I think I mighta just
made a big mistake by hirin' that one on." She swung
and aimed a finger at Linnea's nose. "You keep away
from him, you hear?"

"Me?" Linnea's eyes widened innocently. "*I* didn't do
anything!"

Disgruntled, Nissa turned back toward the house. "With
his kind a woman don't have ta."

It was Sunday, the last lull before the roar of the steam
threshers broke over the prairie. Down along the creek bottom the poplars were already dropping gold coins into the
Little Muddy. The cottontails were fat as Buddhas, and as the
muskrats went about filling underwater larders, their pelts were
so thick they stood out like ruffs about their necks.

In the wind it was chilly, but in the shelter of the uncut
millet, with the sun pouring into their own private bowl,
Kristian and Ray lazed like a pair of contented coon hounds,
their bellies to the sun. The boys were shaped alike, all length
and angles, with too much bone for the amount of muscle they'd
grown. Cradling their heads, elbows up, they studied the puffy
white clouds scudding along the cobalt-blue sky.

"I'm gonna go after mink this year," Kristian announced.

"Mink?" Ray chuckled knowingly. "Good luck. You're
better off goin' for muskrats."

"There's plenty of mink left. I'll get 'em."

"You'll get one for every ten of my muskrats."

"That's okay. It's gotta be mink."

Something in Kristian's voice made Ray roll his head

to squint at his cousin. "What's gotta be mink?"

Kristian shut his eyes and mumbled, "Nothin'."

Ray eyed him a little longer, then settled back again, staring at the sky. From far away came a faint sound like old nails being pulled from new wood. It amplified into the unmistakable rusty squawk of Canadian honkers, heading toward the Mississippi flyway. The boys watched them grow from distant dots to a distinct flock.

"Hey, Ray, you ever think about the war?"

"Yeah . . . some."

"They got airplanes over there. Lots of 'em. Wouldn't it be somethin' to fly in one of those airplanes?"

The wedge of geese came on, necks pointing the way toward Florida, wings moving with a grace that forced a silent reverence upon the boys. They watched and listened, thrilling to a sound that stirred their blood. The cacophony became a clatter that filled the air over the millet field, then drifted off, dimmer, dimmer, until the graceful creatures disappeared and the only sound remaining was the rustle of the wind in the grass and their heartbeats against the backs of their heads.

"Someday I'm going to see the world from up there," Kristian mused.

"You mean you'd go to France and fight, just to fly in an airplane?"

"I don't know. Maybe."

"That's stupid. And besides that, you're not old enough."

"Well, I will be soon."

"Aww, it's still stupid."

Kristian thought about it a while and decided Ray might be right. It probably was stupid. But he was anxious to grow up and be a man.

"Hey, Ray?"

"Hmm?"

"You ever think about women?"

Ray let out a honk of laughter as raucous as the call of the geese. "Does a wild bear shit in the forest?"

They laughed together, feeling manly and wonderful sharing the forbidden language with which they'd only recently begun experimenting.

"You ever think about giving a woman something to make her look different at you?" Kristian asked, as if half asleep.

"Like what?"

It was quiet for a long time. Kristian cast a single wary glance at his cousin, returned to cloud-watching, and suggested, "A mink coat?"

Ray's head came up off the millet. "A mink coat!" Suddenly he clutched his stomach and bawled with laughter. "You think you're gonna trap enough mink to have a mink coat!"

He howled louder and rolled around like an overturned turtle until Kristian finally boosted up and punched him in the gut. "Aw, shut up. I knew I shouldn'ta told you. If you say anythin' to anybody I'll stomp you flatter'n North Dakota!"

Ray was still winding down, breathless. "A . . . m . . . mink coat!" Overdramatizing, he flopped spread-eagled, wrists to the sun. "You might just get enough mink by the time you're as old as your pa."

Kristian laced his fingers over his belly and crossed his ankles, scowling straight up. "Well, that was just a daydream, you jackass. I *know* I ain't . . . I mean, I'm not gonna get enough for a mink coat, but I could get enough to give her mink mittens, maybe."

Suddenly it dawned on Ray that his cousin was serious. He came up on one elbow, giving Kristian his wholehearted attention.

"Who?"

Kristian grabbed a blade of dry millet and split it with a thumbnail. "Miss Brandonberg."

"Miss Brandonberg?" Ray sat up, shifting his weight to one hip and raising one knee. "Are you crazy? She's our teacher!"

"I know, but she's only two years older than we are."

Too startled to be amused, Ray gawked at his cousin. "You *are* crazy!"

Kristian flung the millet away and crossed his hands behind his head. "Well, there's nothin' wrong with thinkin' about her, is there?"

Ray stared at Kristian as if he'd just sprouted horns. After a long stretch of silence, he flung himself onto his back and exclaimed, "Sheece!" in a breathy rush of excitement.

They lay flat, unmoving, thoughtful, staring at the sky to give themselves an air of controlled casualness while underneath their blood was running faster than Little Muddy Creek.

Ray broke the silence at last. "Is that what you meant when you asked if I think about women? You think about the teacher . . . like *that?*"

"Sometimes."

"You could get in trouble, Kristian," Ray declared dourly.

"I said, all I do is think."

Minutes passed. The sun dipped behind a cloud, then came back out to bake their hides and turn their thoughts hot.

"Hey, Kristian?" came a furtive inquiry.

"Hmm?"

"Anything ever . . . well, *happen* when you think about . . . well, about women?"

Kristian squirmed a little, as if trying to settle his shoulder blades more comfortably. When he answered, he tried his best to sound offhand. "Well . . . yeah. Sometimes."

"What?"

Kristian considered for a long time, formulating answers, disqualifying them before they were spoken. Looking askance, he saw Ray's head roll his way and felt his eyes boring for the truth. He met Ray's eyes squarely.

"What happens to you?"

The millet whispered around their heads. The silent clouds rolled on. A slow grin appeared at one corner of Ray's mouth, and an answering grin came to Kristian's. The grins became smiles.

"It's great, isn't it?" Kristian put in.

Ray made a fist, socked the air, flailed one foot, and gave a banshee yell. "Eeeeeee-yowww-eeee!"

Together they fell back and laughed and laughed, reveling in being almost seventeen and full of sap.

After a while Kristian asked, "You ever kissed a girl?"

"Once."

"Who?"

"Patricia Lommen."

"Patricia Lommen! That brain?"

"Aw, she ain't so bad."

"Yeah? So how was it?"

"Nothin' great, but that was a while ago. I wouldn't mind tryin' it again, except Patricia's the only one around here who's not my cousin, and I think she'd rather kiss you than me."

"Me?" Kristian popped up in surprise.

"Open your eyes, Westgaard. Every time you walk into the schoolroom she gawks at you like you were the eighth wonder of the world."

"She does?"

"Well, doesn't she?" Ray sounded a little envious.

Kristian shrugged, puffed out his chest like a strutting cock, and flapped his wings. Ray landed him a mock punch that doubled Kristian over. They shared a round of affectionate fisticuffs before the talk got serious again.

Kristian inquired curiously, "You ever think about your ma and pa together—you know?"

"Doin' it, you mean?"

"Yeah."

"Naw, I think they're too old."

"Mmm . . . I don't know. They might not be, cause I think my pa . . . "

When Kristian drew up short, Ray became all ears. "What? Come on, tell me."

"Well, I don't know for sure, but I've been thinking about every fall, when Isabelle comes."

"Isabelle!" Ray was flabbergasted. "You mean that fat woman who drives the kitchen wagon?"

"She's not exactly fat."

"You mean, you think your pa does it with her? Why, they're not even married!"

"Oh, don't be such an infant, Westgaard. Not everybody's married when they do it. Remember that girl who used to live over on the other side of Sigurd's place, the one that got pregnant and nobody knew who got her that way?"

"Well, yeah, but ... but ... that was a girl and ... well ..." His reasoning became muddy as he tried to puzzle it out. "You really think your pa does it with Isabelle?"

"I don't know, but every year during threshin', while she's got her cook wagon around here, my pa isn't in the house much at night. I can remember him not comin' in till it was nearly milkin' time, and when he did, if he wasn't sneakin', you could've fooled me. Now where would he be spendin' the night besides in Isabelle's wagon?"

They pondered the possibility for a long time, till the sun went under and their lair grew chilly. They thought of women ... those mysterious creatures who suddenly didn't seem like nuisances anymore. They thought of flying in airplanes as high up as the wild geese had flown.

And they wondered how soon they'd be men enough to do it all.

12

ISABELLE LAWLER'S COOK wagon, driven by the lady herself, rolled in the following morning. An ungainly looking thing, longer than a prairie schooner and fully as clumsy, it appeared on the road like a ramshackle railroad car that had somehow lost its tracks. From its roof projected a black stovepipe, and along its sides dangled pails and basins that sang out like glockenspiels whenever the cook wagon hit a pothole. The sight of its unvarnished boards rocking down the gravel road turned heads in every field it passed. The field hands waved a greeting and received a return flourish from Isabelle, who rode high atop the wagon, hunkered forward with her knees widespread, a battered felt "John B" perched on frizzy hair that blazed in the sun with the same hue and uncontrollability as a prairie fire.

There were those still alive who remembered the notorious Calamity Jane from down Deadwood way, who'd made her circuit through these parts many times with the Wild West shows in the 90s. Some said Isabelle and Jane would have been kindred spirits, had they met.

The only thing feminine about Isabelle was her name. She stood five foot eight in her bare feet. With four inches of wiry frizz on top of her head she appeared to tower over most men. She had the strength of a draft horse, the

184

invincibility of a mule, and less grace than either, which led men to treat her like "one of the boys."

She rode alone, claiming her only home was the prairie, and when harvest season was over, nobody knew where she holed up for the winter. Asked about her origins, Isabelle was fond of bawling uproariously, "I was sired by the devil when he tangled with a she-buffalo." She never failed to raise gusty laughs when she pulled her hat off to display her blinding hair and crowed, "Devil give me m' fire and the buffalo give me m' shape!" Then she'd slap some fellow's shoulder with her misshapen felt hat, clap it back on her gaudy hair, and stand foursquare with both hands planted on her beefy hips while laughter roared around her.

It took a woman like Isabelle to do what she did. The team she drove was a pair of cantankerous bay mules, the rig they pulled not only a mobile kitchen and dining room, but her rolling home as well. Maneuvering the clumsy cook wagon with such a pair of blockheaded creatures would have daunted many men. Isabelle, however, took it all in stride, just as she did the enormous task of feeding four robust meals a day to threshing crews numbering up to twenty. On most farms this was done by an army of cooks, but Isabelle did it single-handedly, bringing the food to the workers instead of the workers to the food. Breakfast and supper were served somewhere near the barn or bunkhouse, while midday dinner and afternoon sandwiches were served out in the vast wheat fields, near the steam engine, saving precious hours in transportation time. Those who hired her services provided the meat and vegetables, which Isabelle cooked and served right in her wagon at the long bench table that dominated its interior.

She'd been coming to Theodore's for nine years. The sight of her carrot-colored hair and splayed knees with the skirts drooping between them like a hammock brought smiles not only to the Westgaards but to most of the hired hands, who'd shared many a meal and laugh with her.

As her wagon appeared, bumping along the rough track at the edge of the field where the steam engine was already chugging, Theodore pushed his hat back. He rested his hands on the handle of his pitchfork and watched her progress. The expression on his mouth softened.

"Belle's back," John noted, turning to watch the wagon whose singing hardware was drowned out by the huff and puff of the steam engine behind them.

"Yeah, Belle's back," Theodore seconded.

"That Belle's a good cook," John praised simply.

"That's for sure."

Belle hauled the mules to a halt, got to her feet, and stood with the reins in one hand, waving her hat exuberantly.

The field hands set up a cacophony of calls, hoots, and whistles. "Hey, Belle honey! You still got the best shanks this side o' the Rockies?"

Belle glanced at her thighs, cupped her mouth, and bawled back in a voice like a guitar pick on a metal washboard, "You wanna talk about my shanks, you come up here where I can slap your mouth, you mangy little varmint!"

"*Beef* shanks, Belle!" the man called back.

"Beef shanks, my eye! You're talkin' about buffalo, and I know it!" Belle stood square on the high wagon, silhouetted against the pale-blue sky. Her fists were planted on her hips. At that moment, every man there loved her.

"Hey, Belle, you find that man who could throw you over his shoulder like a sack o' corn yet?"

"Hell no! I'm still single. Threw a few over m' own shoulder since I last seen y' though!"

She howled at her own joke as the men broke into gales of laughter, then another one called, "I get the first dance, Belle. You promised me last year!"

"Promises, hell! You git in line with the others!"

"Belle, you learn how to make potato dumplin's yet?"

"Who's that? That you, Cope, you little piss ant?" She shaded her eyes and leaned forward.

"It's me, Belle!"

"You still got that foul smellin' wad o' cow shit tucked in your cheek? Think I c'n smell it from clear over here!"

Cope bent over and laconically spit a brown streak, then hollered, "That's right. And I can still nail a grasshopper from twelve feet!"

Belle leaned back and bellowed with laughter, lifted one

knee, and whacked it hard enough to put it out of joint, then yelled, "Hey, Theodore, you pay these lazy no-counts to stand around jawin' with the cook?"

Theodore, who'd been standing aside enjoying the ribald interchange, only shook his head at the ground, centered his hat, and smilingly turned back to work, followed by the others, all of them refreshed and ready to roll.

Every year when Belle arrived it was the same: both the work and the fun could begin in earnest. The work was taxing, but lightened by the camaraderie she fostered in them all. Winter was coming, and soon they'd be back in their own homes, sealed in by snow. But for now there was the rhythmic rasp of the steam engine and the promise of hearty food and laughter around Belle's table. There would be dances, too, and more teasing, and at the end of it all, full pockets. So they labored in the autumn sun sharing a oneness of purpose and the grand sense of conviviality that came so naturally on the wake of Belle's arrival.

The morning had been rimed with hoarfrost, but long before noon the men were sweating in the sun as they fed bundles of wheat into the machine that separated grain from chaff and spewed the two out in separate directions. Periodically a full wagon of wheat would leave the field, headed for the granaries in the yard. And with each laden wagon the residual haystacks grew.

At noon Belle stepped out of her wagon and clanged a dishpan with a wooden spoon. The men dropped their pitchforks, wiped their foreheads, and headed for the welcome basins of warm water she had waiting beside the wagon. They washed beneath the sun while enticing aromas drifted out through the horizontal hinged doors that were lifted back along both sides of the wagon, giving them a view of its interior. At the front Belle scurried about before the big black cookstove, bellowing in her outrageously grating voice, "You spit that cud out before you put foot in my kitchen, Cope! Cause if you don't, I'm gonna take my potato masher and make it disappear, and you ain't gonna be too happy about where!"

Cope obliged, while the men nudged him and grinned.

Again came Belle's outrageous orders. "And I don't wanna hear no more mention of potato dumplin', you hear me, Cope? When you're done eating what I put on this table, if you can eat a potato dumplin', I'll sling you over m' shoulder and personally carry you onto that dance floor Saturday night!"

When the men clumped inside they were still chuckling. They filled the benches along the length of the table and dug into the generous meal amid more good-natured teasing and laughter. There was roast pork and beef, snowy mashed potatoes and succulent gravy, green beans and yellow corn, crusty buns and tart coleslaw, apple cobbler and strong coffee. And throughout its disappearance, there was always Belle, moving behind the men's benches, urging them to eat up, tossing out bawdy retorts, refilling bowls, slapping a shoulder here, pulling a hank of hair there.

She treated Theodore no differently from the rest. He took his share of teasing and back slapping, even added bits of wry humor now and then.

But that night, when the others had bedded down in the hayloft, on new, sweet wild hay, Theodore took a pail of cold water and a bar of soap to the tack room, closed the door, bathed, and donned fresh clothes. Buttoning his blue chambray shirt, he wondered if the others suspected what there was between Belle and himself. Then he put it from his mind, drew his suspenders over his shoulders, and pulled on a plaid wool jacket against the cool night.

When he slipped from the barn, the light from Belle's wagon glowed softly out beside the caragana bushes. As he'd known she would, Belle had lowered the hinged doors, hooking them tightly at the bottom, leaving only a tiny square of brightness glowing from the window on the rear door.

He knocked softly, then slipped both hands into the deep pockets of his jacket, studying the knee-level step.

The door opened and he lifted his head. The rich light filtered through Belle's hair, turning it the color of sunset before it fell across Theodore's upraised face. She wore a fresh muslin nightdress surrounded by a pale-green shawl, which she held together at her breast. Her face was in shadow as she leaned out and held the door wide in welcome. All traces of the salty, loud-voiced harridan were gone. In her place was a mellowed woman, her coarse facade replaced by a quiet dignity, neither shy nor bold.

"Hello, Belle," Theodore said softly.

"Hello, Ted," she replied. "Been expecting you."

Briefly, over his shoulder, he glanced at the quiet farmyard. "It's a nice night. Thought we might talk a while."

"Come in." She moved back, and Theodore stepped up and inside, closing the door quietly behind him, glancing slowly around in a circle, both hands still in his pockets. The benches were pushed beneath the table, the table against one wall. Upon it was spread her bedding: two thick goose-down ticks and a single fluffy pillow. With the shutters secured, the interior of the wagon was cozy and private. A teakettle sizzled softly on the cookstove, and beside the entry door a kerosene lantern sat on the seat of the room's only chair.

"Looks the same," he said, his eyes returning to her and sliding on past.

"It is the same. Nothing changes. Have a chair."

He moved as if to sit, noted the lantern, and straightened again.

"Here, I'll set it out of the way," she said, brushing near him in the limited confines to take the lantern and set it on one of the benches, which she pushed from under the table to the opposite wall. Theodore bent his frame to the chair, and she boosted herself up onto the edge of the makeshift bed. For a full minute neither of them said a word.

"So, how have you been?" she asked at last.

He flicked her a nervous look, his elbows resting on his widespread knees. "Fine . . . fine. Had a good year." Again he studied the floor between his feet.

"Yeah. Me, too. I see you got most of the same boys back."

"Yeah, they're good workers, Cope and the rest. Got a couple new ones though." Still he studied the floor.

"So I see. So how they workin' out?"

"Good . . ." Then quieter, with a nod of the head, " . . . good."

"That boy of yours is sure growin' up."

Theodore braved a brief meeting of her eyes, smiling with

banked pride. "Yeah, only an inch more and he'll be as tall as me."

"Gettin' to look more like you all the time, too."

Theodore chuckled silently, a little shyly.

"I notice he didn't come to help with the threshing till afternoon."

Theodore cleared his throat and met her eyes at last. "No, he's started school already. The new schoolmarm, she pitched a fit cause I was keepin' him out, so I finally let him go."

"Ah, I see."

Theodore put in quickly, "Course, he comes home and helps right after school."

That subject died, and when neither of them could think up a new one, Theodore dropped his eyes to the floor again. After some moments he rubbed the back of his neck.

Isabelle noticed and explained, "Gets a little warm in here when I close up. You want to take your jacket off, Ted?"

He stood to do so and found Belle there to help him. When she turned away to lay the garment on the bench, he watched her shoulders and the side of her breast, crisscrossed by the lattice stitches of the green shawl. When she straightened and turned, her eyes met his directly.

"I've thought about you, Ted."

"I've thought about you, too."

"You're not married yet?"

"Naw." He shook his head, dropping his gaze.

"You would be if I ever gave up this crazy life and decided to plant myself."

"Aw, Belle . . . "

"Close the curtain, Ted."

He looked up, and his Adam's apple bobbed once. Without further ado he crossed to the rear door and drew the little blue and red patterned curtain together on its drooping string. When he faced her again he found Belle back on the edge of her bed, still with her shawl on.

"You know what I always liked best about you, Ted?" She neither expected nor got an answer, only his dark, uncertain eyes that caught the orange lanternlight as they lifted, then blinked. "You never take me for granted."

He moved to stand before her, raised one big hand to her temple, and touched the bright hair which she'd drawn back and tied at her nape with a wilted white ribbon. The hair was damp, as if she'd just washed it, and she smelled of the only perfume she ever used—ordinary vanilla extract. Wordlessly he took the shawl from her shoulders, folded it in half, and carefully laid it on top of his jacket. He took the ribbon between his fingers and slipped the bow free. When he laid the limp scrap of white atop the green shawl, he did it with as much care as if it were a jeweled tiara.

Returning to the edge of the makeshift bed, he took Belle's face in both hands, tipped it up, and lowered his mouth to hers with singular lack of haste.

When the kiss ended, he drew back and gazed into her plain, clean face. "A person gets hurt, takin' others for granted," was his reply. Then he kissed her again and felt her hands reaching for his suspenders to push them down and open his shirt before gathering him close and urging him with her onto the feather ticks where, together, they found ease.

Afterward, relaxed and lazing, he rested with Belle's head in the crook of his shoulder. Her hand lay across his chest, and he lightly brushed his fingertips up and down her arm.

"What's the matter with the women around these parts? Why doesn't one of them nab you?"

"I don't want to be nabbed."

"What a shame, when you're so good at what we just finished."

He smiled at the ceiling. "Am I?"

"Why, of course you are. You think any of those other galoots care about what I'm really feeling? How lonely it gets in this stuffy wagon night after night, year after year?"

"Then why don't you get married, Belle?"

"You askin' me, Ted?" His hand stopped moving on her arm, and she playfully swatted his chest. "Oh, no need to tense up so. I was only teasin'. You know a gypsy like me'll never take to settlin' down. But now and then I like to dream of it. Now and then a woman likes to feel like a woman."

His hand detoured for a light pass over her breast. "You feel like a woman, that's for sure."

She chuckled, then absently studied the glowing lantern and sighed against his chest. "You ever stop to think, Ted, about how different you and me are on the outside than we are on the inside?"

"A time or two, I have."

"I don't think another man on earth sees anything in me but the width of two axe handles, a lot of red hair, and too much sass. All these years I been meanin' to thank you for takin' time to look a little deeper."

He spanned her with both arms, kissed the crown of her head, and said, "You're a good woman, Belle. And I was thinkin' lately, you're probably the only friend I've ever had besides my brothers."

She raised her chin and peered up at him. "Really?"

He grinned down and squeezed her lightly. "Really."

"You reckon that's a sign we're growin' old, Ted? Cause I been spendin' some time lately dwellin' on the same thing. Never stayed in one spot long enough to make friends. Guess that's why I'm always so anxious to get back here every year."

"And I'm always here awaitin'."

She tucked her head against his shoulder again, pondered silently for some moments, and asked, "You think what we do is wrong, Ted?"

He studied the circular impression from the lip of the lamp chimney thrown onto the ceiling in a wavering ring. "The Good Book says it is. But who we hurtin', Belle?"

"Nobody I know of. Unless, of course, your boy found out. Might not be so good if he did. Do you think he suspects?"

"I thought about it some before I came out here tonight. He's growin' up in more ways than just one. Lately he's been moonin' over that new teacher, and when that starts, boys usually get pretty observant about the birds and the bees."

"I can see why he'd moon over her. She's a pretty little thing, isn't she?"

Oddly enough, Isabelle's observation seemed to cause more reaction in his heart than anything else she'd said or done tonight.

"She's all right, I guess. Never really looked at her close."

"All right! Why, Ted, where's your eyes? A woman like me'd give what good teeth she had left in her head just to look like her for one day." While Ted chuckled, Belle rolled across his chest, reached beneath the table, and came up with a tablet of cigarette papers and a drawstring bag of tobacco. Laying back down, she expertly filled, licked, and rolled herself a smoke, closed the drawstring bag with her teeth, then pressed herself across Theodore again to come up with a wooden match and a sauce dish. She struck the match against the edge of the table, beneath the overhanging feather ticks, then laid back with the sauce dish on her chest, thoughtfully watching the smoke drift toward the ceiling.

He patiently waited until she was settled before observing dryly, "There's nothin' wrong with your teeth, Belle, nor with your face either."

She smiled and blew a perfect, round smoke ring. "That's why I like you, Ted, cause you never seem to notice what's wrong with me."

He watched her smoke half the cigarette, trying his best to keep the images of Linnea from popping into his mind and making comparisons. When he failed, he reached over and took the cigarette from Belle's lips, transferred it to his own, and took a single deep drag. Finding it as distasteful as ever, he tamped it out, rocking the sauce dish on Belle's chest.

"Got some time to make up for and I'm gettin' a mite impatient, Isabelle."

He set the sauce dish on the floor. Rolling to his back, he found Belle grinning at him with a hooded look about her eyelids. As her strong arms and legs reached to reel him in, she declared in her gruff contralto, "Yessir, there's some mighty stupid women around here, but I sure hope they never wise up, Ted, cause once they do—"

"Shut yourself up, Belle," he said, then his mouth did it for her.

It was Saturday night. The first dance of the harvest season would start at eight o'clock in Oscar Knutson's barn, the one with the emptiest hay mow.

Linnea had devoted the entire afternoon to preparing for the event. She could have done it in far less time if Lawrence hadn't constantly interrupted, circling her around the bedroom floor while violins and cellos played Viennese waltzes—and she in her petticoat!

He sat in her rocking chair now, watching as she experimented with two combs, catching her hair back this way and that, frowning at herself in the mirror.

"I suppose you're going to be the belle of the ball. Probably dance with Bill and Theodore and Rusty and—"

"Rusty! Oh, don't be silly, Lawrence. Just because he smiled at me and called me 'right pretty' doesn't mean—" Linnea angled closer to the mirror and ran four fingertips from jaw to chin, studying her reflection critically. "Do you think I'm pretty, Lawrence? I always thought my eyes were too wide apart. It makes me look like a calf." She covered one incisor with an index finger. "And this tooth is crooked. I've always hated it." She closed her lips and smiled, then frowned again at what she saw in the mirror.

"You wouldn't be fishing for compliments now, would you?"

She spun around with her hands on her hips. "I am not fishing for compliments! And if you're going to tease me, you can just go away." She swung back to the mirror. "Which you'd better do anyway, or I'll never get this hair ready."

She had washed and given it a vinegar rinse, and now that it was dry, curled it with the curling iron. Heating the barrel over the kerosene lamp, she hummed and pondered hair arrangements. She tried piling it up on the crown of her head, leaving little sausage curls to drift from the cluster. But it was too long; the weight of the tresses pulled out the curls and left them looking like stringy cows' tails. Next, she put it up in a loose topknot, leaving trailing tendrils around her face and on her neck. But it was difficult to get the topknot loose enough without losing it entirely—she could just see herself spinning around the dance floor with the hairpins flying. By the time she had tried and ruled out the two styles, she had to curl it all again.

This time she decided on a simple, girlish fashion, letting the back hang free and catching the sides up high in a crisp navy-blue grosgrain ribbon. Assessing the final results, she smiled and moved to the next decision: what to wear.

Looking through her limited wardrobe, she ruled out the wools, which would be too warm, and decided on the white-yoked shirtwaist and the green twill skirt because, with its three back plaits, it was sure to billow as she swirled around the dance floor.

On her face she smoothed a single precious dollop of Almond Nut Cream, which she saved for very special occasions. On her lips and cheeks she spread three dots of liquid rouge. Standing back, she looked at herself and giggled. *You look like a tart, Miss Brandonberg. What are the parents of your students going to think?*

She tried to rub the rouge off, but it had already stained her skin. She succeeded only in roughing up her cheeks and making them brighter. She licked and sucked her lips, but they, too, were tinted fast.

A knock sounded and Linnea glanced at the mirror, perplexed. Her lips were not only red, but puffy now! *How do women ever mature and become self-assured?* Realizing it was too late to do anything about her face, she went to answer the door.

"Why, Kristian! Look at you! Are you going, too?"

There he stood, all decked out in his Sunday trousers and a white shirt and shiny shoes, his hair slicked back with brilliantine and shaped into a peak at the top like a rooster comb. And he smelled absolutely fatal! Like a funeral parlor full of carnations. Whatever he'd put on, he'd put too much. Linnea submerged the urge to pinch her nose shut.

"Course I am. I've been goin' since last November, when I turned sixteen."

"Goodness, does everybody around here start dancing so young?"

"Yup. Pa started when he was twelve. But when I turned twelve he said things had changed a lot since he was a boy, so me 'n' Ray had to wait till we was sixteen."

"Were sixteen."

He colored, shifted his feet, and repeated meekly, "Were sixteen."

Noting his discomfort, she flapped a hand. "Oh, blast me! Do I always have to be a schoolteacher? Just a minute while I get my coat."

He watched her move away.

Jumping Jehoshaphat, look at her! That hair—all loose and curling-like. If you put your finger in one of those locks, it'd twine right around and grab ahold, like a baby's fist. And her face—what had she done to her face? It was all pink and soft-looking, and her lips were puffed out like she was waiting for somebody to plant a kiss on them. He tried to think of what a grown-up man would say at a time like this to let a woman know he liked her more than spring rain. But his mind was a total blank and his heart hammered in his chest.

Returning, she took one look at the rapt expression on his face and thought, oh no, what should I do now? But she was still his teacher and there definitely were things he needed to learn, and if one of them was that helping a woman with her coat didn't constitute an act of intimacy, so be it.

"Would you mind, Kristian?"

He stared at the wool garment, hesitant to touch it.

"Kristian?" She cocked her head, waiting.

"Oh!" He jumped and jerked his hands from his pockets. "Oh, sure."

He'd never held a woman's coat before. He watched her shrug into it, then reach up to free her hair from inside the collar—women sure moved different than men.

She lowered the lantern wick and preceded him down the steps with brisk, businesslike footsteps.

Downstairs, they collected Nissa, another surprise.

"You're coming, too?" Linnea asked.

"Just try and get away without me. M' limbs ain't rusted up yet, and dancin's more fun than rockin'!" She was gussied up in a navy-blue dress with a white lace collar, joined in the front by a ghastly brooch. And she was rarin' to go.

Outside, Theodore sat on the seat of a buckboard loaded with laughing men and the garish redheaded cook, who was regaling them with a loud story about somebody named Ole who could break wind on command.

As the trio approached from the house, Rusty Bonner leaped down, smiling with half his mouth. He tipped back his hat brim and hooked both thumbs beside his gleaming belt buckle.

"Evenin', Mrs. Westgaard, Miss Brandonberg. Allow me?"

He presented a palm to Nissa first.

"To do what?" she crackled, and ignoring his hand informed him, "I'll ride up front with Theodore. These old bones can still dance, but hunkerin' on that hay'd jar m' sockets." While the men laughed she hotfooted it to the front of the wagon, leaving Linnea facing Rusty, whose hand was now waiting for hers.

"Ma'am?" he drawled. What else could she do but accept it?

Theodore cast a baleful eye over the proceedings as Bonner turned on the charm and, smooth as rendered lard, captured her waist and lifted her bodily onto the straw. He followed with a long-legged leap that showed off his wiry agility to great advantage. Theodore scowled as Bonner settled himself about as close as he could get to Linnea's side.

Theodore turned away. "Giddyup!" It was none of his business if Rusty Bonner flirted with every woman whose breasts didn't sag—he glanced askance at his mother—and some whose did!

But the little missy would be easy pickin's for a smooth mover like Bonner.

She's got no pa to look after her here, so she's your responsibility! Bonner'll have her in a haystack faster than a weasel on a hen's neck, and she won't even know what he's aiming for till it's too late!

Riding, Linnea felt Rusty Bonner's hip and thigh press hers. Across the wagon, the boisterous cook was telling a story about skinning a bullhead fish with her teeth. The men roared. But from her right, she felt Kristian's outrage burning at Bonner. They sat with their backs against the sideboards, knees updrawn. She tried to ease over and put an inch between herself and Bonner, but when she did she encountered Kristian, and that certainly wouldn't do! She centered herself as best she could, but Bonner let his leg loll wider and stalk hers. She was conscious that he was the only man here wearing tight denim britches, so tight they were nearly indecent. They added to his sinewy look and that air of banked sexuality that made her feel awkward and a little frightened. She sensed him watching her from beneath the shadow of his cowboy hat while his shoulders slumped indolently, his knees lolled wide, and his wrists dangled lazily against his crotch.

Nissa's words came back clearly: *With his kind a woman don't have to*.

By the time they arrived at Oscar's place, Linnea's stomach was jumping. Rusty was johnny-on-the-spot to help her alight. But once she was down, he stepped back politely, then touched his hat brim in parting. "Y'all be sure to save me a dance, ma'am." Turning away from his unnerving grin, Linnea felt enormously relieved.

Theodore saw to the horses and entered the barn just as Linnea was taking her turn up the ladder to the loft. He watched furtively as Rusty Bonner stood back, eyeing her skirts and ankles as she made her way up. Theodore pressed his palms beneath his armpits and waited until Bonner, too, had gone up, then followed them and immediately searched out John.

"I got to talk to you." He took John's arm and angled him away from the crowd. "Keep your eye on Bonner."

"Bonner?" repeated John.

"I think he's got eyes for the little missy."

"The little missy?"

"She's awfully young, John. She's no match for a man like that."

John's face was an open book. When he became displeased it showed plainly.

"She all right?"

"She's all right. But tell me if you see him hounding her, will you?"

John wasn't bright, but his loyalty, when he bestowed it, was unshakable. He liked Linnea, and he loved Theodore. Nothing Rusty Bonner tried would escape his watchful eye.

The band was already tuning up—fiddle, squeeze-box, and harmonica, and it wasn't long before the music was in full swing. To Theodore's relief, the first one to ask Linnea to dance was his nephew, Bill. He watched her face light up with surprise as they stood talking for a moment.

"Hello, again," Bill said.

"Hello."

"Want to dance?"

Her gaze followed a smoothly moving couple. "I'm not very good. You might have to teach me."

He smiled and took her hand. "Come on. This one's a two-step. It's easy."

When he swung her onto the floor, he added,. "I wondered if you'd be here."

"Where else would I be? Everybody's here." She looked around. "But how did they all know where the dance was going to be?"

"Word gets around. So, how have you been?"

"Busy—Oops!" She tripped on his toe and broke their rhythm. "I . . . I'm sorry," she stammered, feeling foolish, then blushing as she saw Theodore standing on the sideline, looking on. She dropped her eyes to her feet. "I wasn't raised doing fancy steps like that."

"Then I'll have to show you." He softened the turns, shortened his steps, and gave her time to adjust to his style.

"I'll have a lot of catching up to do if what Kristian says is true. He said some of you started going to dances when you were twelve."

"Fourteen for me. But don't worry—you're doing fine."

She watched their feet for some time, then he playfully shook her a little. "Relax and you'll enjoy it more."

He was right. By the end of the dance, her feet were negotiating the patterns much more smoothly, and when the music ended she smiled and clapped enthusiastically.

"Oh, this is fun!"

"Then how about the next one?" Bill invited, smiling down appreciatively.

Bill was a smooth and artful dancer. Linnea was soon laughing and enjoying herself with him. Halfway through the second dance, she swirled around in his arms to confront Theodore, not six feet away, dancing with the redheaded cook. Though she knew she was gaping, Linnea found it impossible not to. Why, whoever would have thought Theodore could dance that way? He sailed around on the balls of his feet like some well-balanced clipper ship, guiding—what was her name again?— Isabelle . . . Isabelle Lawler. Guiding Isabelle Lawler with an easy grace that transformed them both. He caught Linnea's eye and nodded with a smile, then swung around leaving her to stare at his crossed suspenders and his incredibly wide shoulders with Isabelle Lawler's freckled arm spanning them. In another moment they were lost in the crowd. Linnea's gaze followed until all she could see was a glimpse of his outstretched right arm with the white sleeve rolled up to the elbow. Then even that was gone.

The song ended. She danced next with some stranger named Kenneth, who was about forty years old and had a pot belly. Then with Trigg, who said his wife would dance only on alternate songs, because she tired easily. Linnea found Clara looking on and waggled two fingers. Clara waggled back and they exchanged fond smiles. She'd intended to talk to Clara when the song ended, but Kristian appeared before her, wiping his palms on his thighs while asking her to dance. Goodness, was it all right for a teacher to dance with her students? She glanced at Clara for help. Clara shrugged, palms up, and smiled.

Dancing with Kristian, Linnea began to realize that rhythm came built into these Norwegians. Even he, with only a year's experience, made her feel like a bumbling beginner.

"Why, Kristian, you're as smooth as your father!"

"Oh, have you danced with him already?"

"No! No . . . I only meant, I can see he's very good."

Theodore was dancing with a buck-toothed woman now, laughing at something she'd said, and Linnea felt a small spurt of jealousy. But just then another couple danced by, distracting Linnea. "Oh, look at Nissa!"

They followed her as she whirled around on John's arm.

"And, mercy! John, too!"

Kristian laughed at her wide-eyed amazement. "Ain't much . . ." This time he stopped himself. "Isn't much else to do around here all winter except dance and play cards. We're all pretty good at both of them."

As the evening wore on, Linnea was paired off with one after the other of the Westgaard men, their helping hands, the fiddler (who took a conspicuous break), several neighbors she'd never met before, and even school-board chairman Oscar Knutson. They were all good, but none were as good as Theodore, and she was dying to dance with him. But he asked every woman in the place except her.

Once during a break between songs they nearly ran into each other in the crowd.

"You having a good time?" he asked.

"Wonderful!" she said, forcing a smile. She *was* having a wonderful time. So why did she have to force a smile?

She danced with John—he was almost as smooth as Theodore, but not quite—then twice more with Bill and even with Raymond. She visited with Clara while the red-headed cook was back on the dance floor with Theodore again. Her eyes met his across the noisy hay mow, and she flashed him what she hoped was an innocent smile of invitation, but he only twirled his partner away.

Blast you, Theodore, get over here and ask me!

When the song ended, he did cross to them, making Linnea's heart leap, but when he got there it was Clara he led back onto the floor. Next he chose the buck-toothed one again. A woman who could eat corn through a picket fence! *So what does he intend to do, ignore me all night?*

While Linnea was still seething, Rusty Bonner appeared before her, tipping his hat and smiling his crooked smile, the corners of his eyes hooking downward.

"Dance, ma'am?"

She'd been standing on the sidelines for two songs while Theodore blatantly ignored her.

Watch this, Theodore!

"That sounds fun."

When he swung her into his arms, he immediately held her closer than the others, and instead of sticking to the basic box waltz, he languidly shifted from foot to foot with a "one-two" rocking motion that gently pumped her arm. He leaned forward from the waist and held his elbows high in a fashion that made her feel out of her depth. He was nothing whatever like the other men. Even his shoulders felt different inside a streamlined denim jacket that matched his jeans. Beneath it he wore a red and white checked shirt with a red bandanna tied about his throat. When he turned his eyes directly to hers, she found his face so close that she could count the hairs in his sable eyelashes. He had a way of allowing his eyelids to droop half-closed that made her stomach start jumping again. She returned a quavering smile and he shifted his arms, locking both hands at the small of her back. She felt his big silver belt buckle graze her waist and sucked in her belly.

"You enjoyin' yourself, Miss Brandonberg?" he drawled, and she had the feeling he was indulgently laughing at her.

"Y . . . yes."

"You dance very well."

"No, I don't. The other women are much better than I am."

"To tell the truth, I haven't been watching them much, so I really wouldn't know."

"Mister Bonner—"

"Rusty." He smiled that lazy, melting smile, and nudged her thighs with his. "And what's your first name?"

"Linnea."

"Lin-nay-uh." He rolled it from his tongue, syllable by syllable, as if tasting it. "Now isn't that pretty?" Everything about him made her feel like somebody had just rammed a finger into the hollow of her throat, and she thought, *Damn you, Theodore, for making me do this!*

She was surprised when her voice came out smoothly.

"Are you from around here, Rusty?"

"No, ma'am. Drifted in from Montana, and before that Idaho and Oklahoma."

"M . . . my, that's a lot of drifting."

He laughed, giving a glimpse of straight white teeth, tipping his head back, then letting his indolent gaze drift to her face again.

"I ride the rodeos, mostly. It's a driftin' kind of life, Linnea."

"So what are you doing here harvesting wheat?"

"The rodeo season is over. Got to have a dry bed and three square ones a day."

It struck her why he was so honed-looking: more than likely there'd been many a day he hadn't had three square ones, living the life he did. She suspected he'd danced this way with strange women in every western state of the union.

"So tell me. Do you win at this rodeoing?"

"Yes, ma'am." His drawl was thick and teasing as he settled a little closer so that her breasts brushed the front of his jacket. "When I let you go, you take a look at my belt buckle. Won it for riding the steers down in El Paso last season."

She tried to pull away but couldn't; he'd drawn her so close she had to lean back to see his face.

"You ever seen a man ride the steers?"

She swallowed and tried to breathe normally. "N . . . no."

"You ever seen a man ride anything?"

"O . . . only horses."

"Broncs?"

She shook her head in two nervous jerks while he poured that molten, sexy grin over her at far too close a range.

"N . . . no. Just saddle horses."

"You notice my belt buckle?"

Her throat closed tightly and her face turned the color of his shirt. His arms were strong and commanding, his shoulders hard as hickory. His fingers trailed on her spine and fired warning shivers down her thighs. He chuckled, throaty and low, and fit his chin against her temple . . . and her breasts against his chest . . . and his Texas longhorn against her stomach.

Theodore, come and get me, please!

Lazily, he tilted his shoulders back and smiled down into her eyes, leaving his hips cradled squarely against hers.

"Your cheeks're all pink. You warm, honey?"

"A little," she managed in a reedy voice.

"Cooler outside. Want to go see?"

"I don't think—"

"Don't think. Just follow me. We'll check out the stars."

She didn't want to, but Theodore was laughing with Isabelle Lawler again, and before she could dream up an excuse, Rusty had tugged her to the ladder. He went down first, then looked up. "Sssst! Come on."

She glanced down at his face and wondered if Theodore would miss her if she disappeared. Suppose he did, and asked her where she'd been. It would feel mighty sweet to be able to tell him she'd been outside looking at the stars with Rusty Bonner.

"Hey, you comin' or what?"

Three feet from the floor, Linnea felt Rusty catch her waist and lift her down. She gave a surprised squeal as she felt herself suspended in his strong hands. Then he settled her against his hip, looped an arm over her shoulder and ushered her toward the door.

Outside, the harvest moon smiled down so brightly it faded the stars by comparison. The air felt good against her heated cheeks.

"Oh, it *was* warm dancing," she breathed, covering her face with both palms, then dropping them to shake back her hair.

"Thought you said you were a beginner."

"Oh, I am. It's just that you're—well, it was easy following you."

"Good. Then follow me some more." He captured her hand and tugged her around the corner of the barn, where the moonbeams couldn't find them. In the shadow of the building he stopped, clasped her upper arms, and turned her to face him, rocking her lightly.

"So . . . you haven't danced much. And you never saw a man ride a bull or a bronc. Tell me, Miss Linnea Brandonberg, pretty little country school teacher . . . have you ever been kissed?"

"Wh . . . why, of course, I've been kissed. And more than once!" she lied, inexplicably excited at the prospect of finding out what it was like to really kiss a man—at last.

"I reckon you're pretty good at it, then."

"I reckon," she replied, trying her best to sound confident.

"Show me . . . "

Her heart caromed and a thrill of the forbidden shot through her as his head slowly tipped and his mouth touched hers. It was warm and firm and not wholly unpleasant. It rested lightly against her closed lips for some time before he backed away a mere inch. She opened her eyes to only the black shadow of his face and the underside of his hat brim. "More than once?" he murmured teasingly, bringing the blood surging to her cheeks. Again he covered her mouth with his, and this time the hot, wet tip of his tongue touched her. *What was he doing? Oh, mercy, he was licking her!* The shock sizzled down to her toes. Instinctively she drew back, but he captured her head in both hands, clasping her ears and threading his fingers into her hair as he drew her almost on to tiptoe. He ran his tongue around the entire rim of her lips until they were wet and sleek. She pushed against his chest, but he only released her mouth long enough to order, "Open your lips . . . come on, I'll show you more . . ."

"No . . ." she tried to argue, but his forceful tongue found the break in her lips and thrust inside. She struggled against him, but he shoved her flat against the cold stone barn wall and clasped one breast to hold her in place. She pulled at his wrist, but it was as taut as new wire fence, and while panic gripped her, so did Rusty Bonner. Again and again and again, squeezing her breast while she whimpered against his driving tongue and a stone painfully pressed her skull.

"Stop . . ." she tried to say, but again his mouth stifled the plea. She twisted violently and managed to free her mouth. "Stop! What are you doing?"

He caught her elbows and pinned them hard against the wall and ground his hips against hers until she felt dirty and more scared than she'd ever been before. Wildly she struggled to break free, but he'd ridden down broncs and Brahmas—one skinny little schoolteacher was nothing for Rusty Bonner.

"You said you'd been kissed before. More than once."

Mortified by what his hips were doing, she felt tears burn her eyes. "I lied . . . please, let me go."

His wrists were hard and corded and could not be budged.

"Easy, honey . . . easy. There now, you're gonna like this. . . ."

She choked back a sob as he filled his hands with her breasts, nearly lifting her off her feet.

Then Theodore's quiet voice intruded. "Miss Brandonberg, is that you?"

The pressure on her breasts disappeared and her heels touched the ground.

Relief made her want to cry and take refuge against Theodore's solid bulk. But shame made her wish she could disappear from the face of the earth.

"Y . . . yes, Theodore, it's m . . . me."

"What you doing out here?"

Rusty's voice was thoroughly unruffled as he turned indolently and answered, "We're just talkin' about Texas bull ridin'. Any objection, Mr. Westgaard?"

Suddenly Theodore thrust himself forward, grabbed Linnea's wrist, and yanked so hard she thought her shoulder would come unhinged. "You little fool! What's the idea of coming out here with him like this? Don't you care what people think?"

"Now whoa, just a minute, Westgaard," the Texan drawled.

Theodore spun on Bonner, still gripping Linnea's wrist. "She's eighteen years old, Bonner! Why don't you pick on somebody your own age?"

"She wasn't objecting," Bonner returned in that same easy tone.

"Oh, wasn't she? That's not how I heard it. And if she's not, I am. You're done here, Bonner. Pick up your pay in the morning and that's the last I want to see of you." Bonner shrugged and moved as if to pass Theodore and head back toward the dance. "And you're not goin' back in there. I don't want anybody at that dance suspecting she was out here with you." Theodore turned on his heel, yanked Linnea along after him, and ordered, "Come on."

"Theodore, let me go!" She tried to squirm free, but his angry strides reverberated through her arm and made her head snap.

"I'll let you go when you learn some common sense. For now, you're coming with me. We're going back up there and make them think you were outside talking to me. And if you do one thing to make them think otherwise, so help me, I'll haul you into Oscar's toolshed and blister your rear end, which your own father would do if he was here!"

"Theodore Westgaard, you let me go this very minute!" Outraged at being treated like a recalcitrant child, she tried to pry his thumb loose from her wrist, but it was useless. He stalked across the barn, then gave her a push that nearly put her nose against the third rung of the ladder.

"Now get up there, and act like you ain't about to bust into tears!"

Angrily, she climbed the ladder, tripping on her skirts and cursing under her breath. All she'd done was exchanged one bully for another. By what right did Theodore Westgaard order her around?

Upstairs, he grabbed her elbow in a bruising grip, thrust her toward the dance floor, yanked her to face him, and started them waltzing without so much as a "May I?" She moved like a walking stick while he impressed a waxen smile on his face. Through gritted teeth he observed, "You're moving like a scarecrow. Pretend you're enjoying it."

She loosened up, let her feet follow his, and faked a smile. "I can't do this, Theodore, please let me go."

"You'll dance, little missy. Now get on with it."

She had wanted to dance with him, but not this way. Her stomach was quaking. Her eyes glittered dangerously. She was choking with the need to cry. Theodore's hand on her back was stiff with anger, the other clasping her fingers with suppressed fury. But their feet moved to the music, and her skirts flared out as he swirled her in circles, pretending that they were having a wonderful time.

She held up for as long as she could, but when the lump in her throat grew too large to contain, when the tears grew too plump to hide, she begged in a quavering voice, "Please, Theodore, please let me go. If you don't, I'm going to cry and embarrass us both terribly. Please . . . "

Without another word he turned her by an elbow and walked her directly to Nissa. "Linnea isn't feeling well. I'm driving her home, but I'll be back."

In a moment she was at the foot of the ladder again, crossing the barn with Theodore at her heels. Breaking into a run, she headed for the door, and once outside, dropped her face into her hands as a wretched sob broke from her throat. Uncertainly Theodore stood behind her, still angry, but moved by her tears more than he wanted to be. He finally touched her shoulder, but she spun away, burying her face in an arm and leaning against the barn wall.

"Linnea, come, let's get away from here."

She was too miserable to realize he'd called her Linnea for the first time. He led her, still sobbing, toward a grove of cottonwoods where the wagons waited. She stood drooping, crying, while he fought the urge to hold and comfort her.

"He'll be gone in the morning. There's nothing to be scared of now."

"Oh, Th . . . Theodore, I'm, s . . . so ash . . . shamed."

He stuck his hands hard into his pockets. "You're young. I don't suppose you knew what he'd do."

She lifted her face. He saw the silver tracks of tears on her cheeks and heard the plea in her voice. "I d . . . didn't. Oh, Theodore, honest, I didn't."

A cinch seemed to tighten about his heart. He trembled everywhere and felt his anger dissipating.

"I believe you, little one. But you must be careful around strange men, didn't your parents teach you that?"

"Y . . . yes." She hung her head until her hair covered her face. "I'm s . . . sorry, Theodore. H . . . he said we'd j . . . just go outside and c . . . cool off, b . . . but th . . . then he k . . . kissed me and I . . . I only w . . . wanted to know wh . . . what it was l . . . like." A sob lifted her shoulders and she bobbed her head. "S . . . so I l . . . let him." At the memory of what followed, she covered her face with both hands and leaned her forehead against Theodore's chest.

His hands came out of his pockets and caught her shoulders. "Shh, little one. There's nothing to cry about. So you've learned a lesson."

Against his chest she spluttered, "B . . . but ev . . . everyone will know, and I'm th . . . the schoolt . . . teacher. I'm supposed t . . . to set a g . . . good example."

"Nobody will know. Now stop crying." His thumbs stroked her arms, but he stood erect, barrel-chested, trying to keep some distance between them. With each sob, her hands bumped his chest. A damp blotch formed on his shirt, then stuck to his skin, and his resolution weakened. He chuckled, but the sound was strained. "You know, I'm pretty out of practice at handling crying women."

From beneath her trailing hair came a single choked laugh as she self-consciously tried to dry her cheeks. "My face is a mess. Have you got a hanky?"

He drew one from his back pocket and stuffed it into her hand, stepping back. When her face was cleaned he began to feel safer.

At last she looked up. In the dappled moonlight her eyes and lips appeared puffy, her hair in disarray. He thought of that bastard, Bonner, with his mouth and hands on her and felt the pagan urge to kill.

Without warning, she flung her arms about his neck and pressed her damp cheek to his. "Thank you, Theodore," she whispered. "I was never so happy to see anybody in my life as when you showed up outside the barn."

His eyes slammed shut. He stifled a groan and clasped her tightly to his breast. She clung tenaciously, pressing close, igniting his body. His hands found her back. Her skin smelled of almonds, and her soft, messed hair pressed against his jaw, her breasts against his throbbing heart.

Then he stiffened and gently pushed her away.

"Come, I'll take you home."

Obediently she withdrew but stared at the ground between their feet for a long time. At last she raised her head to gaze at him. The shadows couldn't quite hide the grave question in her eyes even before she spoke it.

"Why didn't you ask me to dance?"

He searched for an answer, but the truth was the last one he could give.

"You danced with everyone but me, and that's why I went outside with Rusty. To make you jealous."

"M . . . me?"

"Why didn't you ask me?"

He swallowed. "We danced, didn't we?"

"That wasn't dancing, that was two people butting heads." She waited, but he backed a step away. "All right then, why did you rescue me?" She advanced a step and he put his hands out to stop her.

"Linnea." A warning.

"Why?"

"You know why, and it ain't good for either one of us."

"Why . . . tell me, Teddy, why?"

The name went through him like flash fire. "Linnea . . . " He only meant to put his hands on her arms to stop her.

"Why . . . " A whisper.

She was close enough that he could smell the almond on her skin. She was insistent enough that he could feel the quivering in her arms beneath his hands. She was innocent enough that he knew, even as his hands tightened and drew her up, this was going to be one of the greatest mistakes he'd ever make.

"Because . . . " He dropped his lips to her waiting mouth, and his heart was a wild thing in his breast. Her arms came up and their bodies meshed, close and warm and hard. She's still a child. She doesn't even know how to kiss. But her young breasts, crushed against him, her fingers on his neck, her sweet, closed, untutored lips were his for that moment. He let the feelings take him, and when common sense grew strong again, he finally found the strength to push her back.

Their breaths beat hard into the autumn night.

"It d . . . didn't feel like that when Rusty Bonner kissed me."

"Shhh. Don't."

"Kiss me again, please, Teddy."

"No!"

"But—"

"I said no! I shouldn't have done it in the first place."

"Why?"

"Have you got a couple of hours? I'll give you the whole list." He took her elbow and turned her toward the wagon. "Up with you, now," he ordered briskly. But his voice rattled with emotion.

"Theodore—"

"No. Please, just get in the wagon."

They hadn't realized they'd left their coats behind until they were headed home through the frosty night. Linnea shuddered and hugged herself. Theodore silently rolled his shirtsleeves down and buttoned his cuffs.

"You want to go back and get your coat?"

"No, just get me home."

And though it pained him to watch her huddle, shivering, when he could have put his arm around her and kept her warm and shielded from the world, he didn't.

By all that was holy, he didn't!

13

IN THE MORNING, Nissa stayed in bed later than usual, and Theodore was headed upstairs to awaken Kristian just as Linnea was headed down for water. They both halted at once. He looked up and felt his heart race. She looked down and felt the same. In that instant they relived the impact of the single kiss they'd shared the night before, and neither could think of a thing to say. For long moments they only stared.

Her toes were bare and she held her wrapper together at the throat. She's just climbed out from under the quilts, he realized, and his heart tripped faster at the thought.

He wore his heavy wool jacket, his nose was pink, and he hadn't shaved yet. He's already been out to do chores, she thought, and the sight of him, all rugged and masculine, made her toes curl over the edge of the step.

Suddenly they both realized they were standing in a narrow stairwell gawking at each other as if they'd been turned to pillars of salt. Linnea was the first to recover her voice.

"Good morning," she whispered.

"Good morning," he whispered back.

"You've been out already."

"I did the chores alone and let Kristian sleep."

"Oh."

This was silly. Couldn't they pass each other on the stairs without getting all fidgety?

"How are you this morning?" he asked.

"Tired. I didn't sleep much last night. How are you?"

"A little slow on the draw." He wondered what had kept her awake. Had she, like he, lain for hours thinking of that kiss? "We got home late. Looks like Ma and Kristian are in the same shape. But I better wake them or we'll be late for church."

Their hearts pounded harder as he moved up the stairs and she moved down. But when they finally passed each other, they made sure not so much as a thread of their clothing touched. As she reached the bottom step, he called down softly, "Linnea?"

She spun and looked up. She thought she would never grow tired of hearing him use her Christian name in that tone of voice. He stood with one hand on the knob of Kristian's door. She imagined what it would be like if he ever came to her door that way, and quietly spoke her name as he had a moment ago.

"Yes?"

"Bonner is gone."

But Bonner already seemed a hazy memory to Linnea, eclipsed by the imposing man above her. She could have stood all day, looking at him. But he turned away, opened Kristian's door, and disappeared.

Inside Kristian's room Theodore paused, staring at his boots. He remembered Linnea in her bare toes and wrapper, looking warm and tumbled and morning-mussed. It had taken fortitude to pass her on the stairs and not touch her. He sighed heavily. So damn young. Last night, when he'd hauled her out of Bonner's arms, he'd told himself he was acting in her father's stead, but it wasn't strictly true. All that anger hadn't been spawned by paternal protectiveness alone.

Aw, hell, Westgaard, you're just a middle-aged buck who feels like he's sipping from the fountain of youth whenever she's around. Are you forgetting you're a good five years older than Rusty Bonner, and you warned *Bonner* to pick on somebody his own age!

Theodore sighed and glanced at the bed. Kristian lay sleeping peacefully. His arms were thrown back and the quilt left part of his chest exposed. There was a fairly good crop of hair on it already. Now when had that happened? Next month he'd be seventeen. Seventeen already, and—Theodore had to admit—Kristian's seventeen to Linnea's eighteen was far less shocking than the sixteen years separating her from himself.

He recalled Kristian's uncharacteristic frankness in admitting he had feelings for the girl, and Theodore experienced a queer compulsion to sit on the edge of his son's bed and confess that he'd kissed her last night and ask the boy's forgiveness. Guilt. She'd only been here a month and she already had him feeling guilty. That was silly. Or was it? Kristian had marked her first, and had trusted Theodore enough to confide his feelings. Theodore considered the possible eventualities should his son ever find out what went on last night. Lord, suppose it got out and people started wondering what was going on over here with both father and son hankering after the same girl? Wouldn't they blow *that* all out of proportion?

You start anything with her, Westgaard, and you'll have one fine mix-up on your hands. She's too young for you and you know it, so leave her to your son and act your age.

The following night, who should show up at the door but Bill Westgaard, all spit-shined and brilliantined. The men were in from the fields and supper dishes were already put away when the knock sounded and Kristian went to answer it. When Bill stepped into the kitchen it was assumed this was nothing more than a family visit. They all sat around the table and Nissa brought out coffee cups and date cake and asked after Ulmer and Helen and the rest of the family. Bill politely gave an update and dutifully partook of the snack.

They talked about the war, President Wilson's military draft law, and how the American people were arguing about it everywhere. Few thought the nation's strength could be brought to bear on the battlefields of France in time to stave off an Allied disaster, and Theodore agreed. Bill, however, argued that with the German armies already having driven Russia to the brink of collapse and the invading German and Austrian forces now inflicting smashing defeats on the Italians at Caporetto, we had to get behind Wilson's effort one hundred percent.

Linnea's eyes opened wide at the men's understanding of

the happenings overseas. Even Kristian joined in the discussion, showing a vital interest in the subject of airplanes and the battles being fought in the air.

When the subject had run its course, they moved on to talk of winter trap lines, a fox that had been killing chickens in the area, and the possibilities of early snow.

They'd exhausted a variety of impersonal subjects when Bill announced, "I brought the rig. I thought you might like to go for a ride with me, Linnea."

An awkward silence fell. Linnea's eyes sought Theodore's. For an instant she saw startled disapproval, then he consciously wiped it away. What should she say?

"A ride. Oh . . . well . . . "

"We could go down along Holman's Bridge. It's pretty down along the creek, especially when there's a moon."

"It's rather chilly."

"I brought a lap robe," he added hopefully.

She glanced again at Theodore. His face was carefully blank, but across his belly his knuckles stood out like alabaster.

Nissa spoke up. "Sure, you young people go. Get out for a while."

"What do you say, Linnea?" Bill persisted.

And what could she say?

"That sounds wonderful. I'll get my coat."

They drove through the clear, cool night to Holman's Bridge, and counted the muskrat mounds on the river below. Bill was enjoyable to be with, polite and easy to talk to. He inquired about her Christmas holiday, her family, her plans for next summer. She asked about his plans for the future, and was shocked to hear that he was considering signing up for the army. The war, always so remote, was growing closer and closer, it seemed. Though she hadn't known Bill long, he was real flesh and blood, part of the Westgaard family. And he was thinking of going off to fight!

"Roosevelt said it was the thing to do, for us to join the Allies and declare war on Germany. Now that we have, I'd like to do my part."

Around here people paid more heed to Roosevelt than to Wilson.

"But you are doing your part. You're a farmer."

"There's plenty of men to raise wheat. What they need is a few more to fight."

Linnea pictured Bill in a trench with a bayonet in his hand . . . or in his heart . . . and shuddered. Guilelessly, she slipped her arm through his.

He chuckled, pleased. "Well, I'm not going yet, Linnea. I haven't even mentioned it to my folks."

"I don't want you to go, ever. I don't want anyone I know to go."

In less than an hour they were turning into the driveway again. When the horses stopped, Bill's gloved hand covered Linnea's.

"There'll be a dance again next Saturday night. Will you go with me?"

"I . . ." What should she say? She found herself comparing his upturned nose to Theodore's aquiline one, his clear green eyes to Theodore's brown ones, his blond hair to Theodore's plain brown. Bill's nose seemed too boyish, his eyes too pale, and his hair too wavy for her taste. Since the advent of Theodore in her life, no others seemed to measure up. He was the one with whom she wanted to go to the dance, but there was little hope for that.

"What do you say, Linnea?"

She felt trapped. What logical excuse could she concoct for refusing Bill? And maybe going with him would stir a reaction in Theodore. So she accepted.

Bill walked her to the house as if in no hurry to get there. Beside the back door he took her shoulders and gave her a single undemanding kiss. Yet it was lingering enough that if sparks were going to fly, they would have. None did. Absolutely none.

"Good night, Linnea."

"Good night, Bill."

"See you Saturday night."

"Yes. Thank you for the ride."

When he was gone she sighed, comparing his kiss to Theodore's. It wasn't fair that the kiss of a grouchy man should excite her more than that of a young interested buck like Bill.

Inside, a single lamp had been left burning low on the

kitchen table. She felt tired and suddenly despondent, filled
with endless questions about where her life was leading. And
what about those she cared about? Would Bill really go off to
war? Would other young men she knew? Absently she wandered around the table and rested her hands on the back of
Theodore's chair. Thank God, if it came to that, he was too
old to join.

"So, did you have a nice ride?"

Her blood fired at the sound of his voice in the shadows
across the room. She turned to find him leaning against the
living-room doorway, his arms crossed loosely. He wore black
trousers and black suspenders over the top half of his union
suit. He filled out the underwear like an apple fills its skin,
each bulge and dip emphasized by the form-fitting cloth. His
sleeves were pushed up to the elbow, revealing thick, muscular
forearms shadowed with dark hair. At the open buttons near his
throat more dark hair showed. He was so much more of a man
than Bill.

"Yes," she replied, standing straight and still.

He waited, silent, willing away the jealousy, telling his
heart to calm down. Her skin in the lamplight took on an
apricot hue. Her lips were slightly parted. Her eyes seemed
filled with challenge. And she made no effort to look as if
she weren't caressing his chair. Damn girl didn't know what
she was inviting.

"We rode down to the creek."

He knew perfectly well what she was up to, but leaned in the
doorway with feigned indolence, pretending his vitals weren't
wrenching him as he wondered what else they'd done.

"Pretty down there at night."

You stubborn Norwegian! Can't you tell what's in my heart?

"He asked me to the dance Saturday night."

"Oh? And what did you say?"

"I said yes."

For a long time Theodore stared at her, unmoving. Bill was
young; he had the right. But that didn't make it any easier to
accept. At length he forced himself to glance away. "That's
good," he said, pulling away from the door.

She felt like bursting into tears. "Y . . . yes." She drew a
deep breath and asked, "Will you be there?"

He seemed to consider for a long time before answering, "Guess I will."

"Will you dance with me this time?"

"You'd best dance with the young guys."

Her hand lifted in appeal. "Teddy, I don't wa—"

"Good night, Linnea." Swiftly he turned and left her standing in the kitchen.

In his bedroom he sat on the edge of the bed with his head in his hands. Her face glowed before him, that pretty young face with the expression that hid nothing. With those blue, long-lashed eyes that were incapable of concealing the truth. He flopped back, eyes closed, arms outflung. Lord, lord. He was the one with the age, the wisdom. It was up to him to hold her at arm's length. But how?

During the week that followed, the weather turned cold and the hay mows began filling. Oscar Knutson stopped by on Thursday to let Linnea know Saturday's dance would be held in the schoolhouse.

"The schoolhouse?"

"You got a stove here, and we just pile the desks against one wall. Most of the dances'll be here till the haylofts get empty again, on toward spring. Just wanted you to know so you have them kids empty their inkwells. Generally Theodore comes down here to light the stove and get the place ready."

Theodore again. He hadn't said two words to her since she'd told him she was going to the dance with Bill—the last thing she wanted to do was ask him to come down and light the stove before the dance.

"Do I have to ask him?"

"No, it's all taken care of."

They all went down early, Bill and Linnea in one rig, Theodore, Nissa, Kristian, and all the hired hands in another, to light the fire and fill the water crock and push the desks aside.

The schoolhouse seemed cozy at night, with blackness pressing at the windows, the lanterns lit indoors. Linnea pushed her table against the front blackboard so the band could set up on the teaching platform. Nissa set up a refreshment table in the cloakroom, sliced a high lemon cake that would be joined by more cakes and sandwiches when the other women arrived. Kristian sprinkled cornmeal on the floor. Theodore got the fire lit, then sauntered around the edge of the room, tipping his head to study a line of childish drawings strung along the wall on a length of red yarn.

From behind him came a quiet voice. "Russian thistle."

He glanced over his shoulder to find Linnea observing him with her arms crossed. She was wearing a navy-blue middy dress tonight and looked no older than the young ones who'd drawn these pictures.

"I thought so, but on some of these it's hard to tell."

He turned back to study the clumsy attempts at artwork, thumbs hooked around his suspender clips, a benevolent smile on his lips. She idled along the line with him.

"The Halloween ones are a little better." She pointed. "Pumpkins . . . corn shucks . . . ghosts." The farther along they moved, the more polished the work became, until it changed from outsized drawings to written compositions with smaller illustrations at the top.

"Kristian isn't much at artwork, but when it comes to rhetoric he shows great promise. Here, this is his." She removed a straight pin from the corner of one paper and proudly handed it to Theodore. "Read it and you'll see."

Read it? He gaped first at the paper, then at her, taken by surprise. Unable to think of what else to do, he reached out woodenly for his son's composition and stared at it while she waited at his elbow, beaming with pride. He stood beside her for several long minutes, feeling ignorant as a stump. He wondered what the paper said. The black writing on the white page reminded him of straight, parallel rows of corn stubble sticking out of a fresh snow, but beyond that it meant nothing. He was thirty-four years old and his son was smarter than he.

And now Linnea would know.

She tipped her head and pointed to a spot on the page. "See what he chose to discourse on? Wouldn't you say that shows an inquisitive mind?"

The blood climbed Theodore's chest. It climbed his neck. It reached his ears and they seemed to grow hot enough to singe the hair above them. He hung his head, swallowed, and stared at the paper, mortified.

Blithely, she crossed her forearms behind her back, waiting for him to finish reading and offer some comment. When he didn't, she glanced up with a perky smile. "Well, isn't it wonderful?"

One glimpse of his face and Linnea realized something was very wrong. He'd turned fiery red and refused to look up.

"I . . . I guess so," he stammered at last.

"Well, you don't seem . . . " She glanced from his face to the paper and back again, her words slowing like an engine losing steam," . . . very . . . impr . . . " Something tripped in her mind. One hand came from behind her back and covered her lips. "Oh . . . " she breathed, the truth at last registering. "Oh, Theodore . . . you can't read?" They stood close, so close she heard him swallow convulsively while his thumbnail dented the right margin of the paper.

He shook his bowed head.

Oh my dear stubborn Theodore, why didn't you tell me? She was abashed for him. Her heart melted. She, too, felt herself blushing. They stood in a cocoon of discomfort that bound them mercilessly, while behind them the band started tuning up. Slowly, he handed her the paper, meeting her eyes at last, still red to the hairline.

"B . . . but what about the hymnal at church?" she whispered.

"I know those songs by heart. I've been singing them for thirty-odd years now."

"And the sentences on the blackboard?" She recalled her own chagrin the day he'd caught her poking fun at him with all those outlandish insults. She empathized with him now when he was the one being found out.

His glance rested steady on her. "The only one I understood was that you'd like to stuff Theodore."

"Oh." She studied the tocs of her shoes. "When I heard you behind me that day, I thought you'd been standing there reading them all the while I was writing them, and I just wanted to die."

"Not half as bad as I want to right now."

She lifted her face and their eyes met, a little of the strain eased. The band struck up a first number. "Theodore, I had no idea. I really didn't."

"There was no school here when I was a boy. Ma taught me how to read a little Norwegian, but she never learned English herself, so she couldn't teach the rest of us."

"But why didn't you tell me? Surely you didn't think I'd think any less of you."

"After us arguin' about Kristian goin' to school? How could I?"

"Ah," she voiced knowingly, "pride." She reached to hang the piece of paper on the yarn again. "Men have such silly notions about it. So Kristian knows a little more than you do about the English language. But you know more than he does about a lot of other things." She faced him, gesturing toward herself. "Why, for that matter, you know more than *I* do about a lot of things. The other night when you were talking about the war—Well, I had no idea you knew so much about what's been going on over there. And you know how to fix windmills and set mousetraps and . . . you taught me how to catch a horse and saddle him—"

"Her," he corrected.

Their eyes met. Something good happened between them. Something warm and rich and radiant that held the promise of enjoyment. Matching grins grew on their lips. Linnea bowed formally from the waist. "I stand corrected again, sir. Her. Which proves my point exactly. Why, you don't have to feel—"

"There you are, Ted!" It was Isabelle Lawler, appearing to interrupt the harmonious moment. "My feet are itching and there's only one cure." Without troubling herself to apologize for the interruption, she appropriated Theodore and hauled him off to dance.

Linnea's happy mood turned sour. She glared after the outrageous redhead who seemed to follow no code of manners whatever. How dare that . . . that orange-haired hippopotamus commandeer a man that way, and trumpeting like a bull elephant yet! I'd like to get her into my etiquette class for just one day. Just one!

Suddenly something else struck Linnea.

Ted. She'd called him Ted!

"Come on. Let's dance." It was Bill, coming to claim his date. Linnea forced herself to smile and be gay, but she kept catching glimpses of *Ted* and the hippo and it practically ruined her evening. As before, Linnea had plenty of dance partners . . . with one obvious exception. Circling round and round the black stovepipe, she cast occasional furtive glances his way. Theodore was probably the best dancer in the place— damn his hide!—and he'd dance with that redheaded hussy till they'd have to put in a new schoolhouse floor! But he wouldn't dance with the *little missy* to save his soul. After what had passed between them last Saturday night, and earlier tonight, she'd hoped he'd finally begun looking at her as an adult. But apparently not, and she was sick and tired of being treated as if she were still wet behind the ears! But then, *she* wasn't built as wide as a gang plow. And *she* didn't have vocal chords like a mule skinner. And *she* didn't have hair the color of a Rhode Island rooster.

Petulantly, Linnea tried to turn a blind eye on them, but it didn't work. Finally, after Theodore had ignored her till nearly the end of the evening, she put on her best posture and most supercilious face, walked out on the floor, and tapped the red-head on the shoulder.

"I beg your pardon, Miss Lawler, may I cut in?"

To Linnea's acute embarrassment, the fool woman yelled in a voice loud enough to raise the dead, "Why, I should say not! When I get my hands on a man, I make damn good use of him before I cut him loose!" Then she collared Theodore in a death grip and whirled him away.

Linnea wanted to die on the spot. What could she do but withdraw to the edge of the room and burn? Just what did he see in that overblown floozy? She was rude and sweaty and she hauled Theodore around the dance floor puffing like an overweight draft horse.

Let him have her—it's no more than he deserves.

She was still standing petulantly at the edge of the dance floor when the song ended. She saw Theodore say something to Isabelle, then escort her to the cloakroom. Momentarily he reappeared alone, scanned the crowd, and crossed directly to Linnea. Her gaze shifted to the fiddler, and she tightened her mouth as if she'd just eaten a bad pickle.

"Come on, little missy, it's your turn."

Her turn! As if she'd been pining away the whole evening

until he could free a spot on his dance card.

"Don't bother yourself, Theodore." Haughtily, she turned up her nose.

"Well, you wanted to dance with me, didn't you?"

She glared at him, chagrined at how impotent she felt against his teasing. Give a man a few beers and a few dances with a redhead and he became noxiously jocular.

"Just wipe that smug expression off your face, Theodore Westgaard. No, I did *not* want to dance with you. I had something to tell you, that's all."

Theodore had all he could do to keep from laughing aloud at the little spitfire. She was something when she got riled and turned up her saucy nose that way—looked about fourteen years old, too. Though he'd told himself to lay low when it came to the little missy, there was no danger in taking her around the floor a couple of times while the whole family looked on. As a matter of fact, dancing with every woman in the place but her might look more suspicious than giving her a turn.

"So come along. You can tell me now."

He gave her no choice. He swung her onto the floor with loose-limbed ease and grinned down at her with the most annoying air of amusement.

"So, what was it you wanted to tell me?"

To dry up and blow away—along with that redheaded sweatbox! Linnea pursed her mouth and gazed over his shoulder pettishly. He tipped his head, bent his knees, and brought his eyes to the same level as hers.

"Cat got your tongue now that you finally got me?"

She glared at him, sizzling.

"Oh, quit treating me like a child. I don't like being condescended to!"

He straightened up and executed an adroit circle step, advising gaily, "You'll have to explain that one to me."

She punched him on the shoulder. "Oh, Theodore, you're exasperating! Sometimes I hate you."

"I know. But I sure can dance, can't I?"

Did the man have to be humorous just when she wanted to stay good and irritated with him? Her lips trembled, threatening a smile.

"You're a conceited pain! And if school were in session right now, I'd stand you in the corner of the cloakroom for treating me so rudely."

"You and what army?" he inquired with a devilish grin.

She laughed, unable to hold it back any longer. And when she laughed, he laughed. Then they forgot about bickering, and danced.

Mother MacCree, was he smooth. He even made *her* look good! He held her away from him, but guided her so masterfully that rhythm and pattern became effortless. How different he was on the dance floor than any other place. It was hard to believe this Theodore was the same one who'd greeted her that first day dressed in bib overalls and a battered straw hat, and had treated her so rudely he'd nearly sent her packing.

"So, are you going to tell me or not?"

They both leaned back from the waist while their feet glided effortlessly. "Tell you what?"

"Whatever it was you poked Isabelle's shoulder for."

"Oh, that!" She lifted her chin with an air of unassailability. "I'm going to teach you to read."

He grinned. "Oh, you are, huh?"

"Yes I am, huh," she mimicked.

"I'm gonna look pretty dumb tryin' to fit my knees under one of those toy desks."

"Not here, silly. At home."

"At home," he parroted sarcastically.

"Well, do you have something better to occupy your long winter evenings?"

He gave a snorting laugh and a slight lift of one eyebrow. "You sure you want to take me on? Men my age get pretty thick-headed and forgetful. I might not soak things up as fast as your first and second graders."

"Honestly, Theodore, you talk as if you're in your dotage."

"Prett' near."

She cast him a quelling look. "Men in their dotage have rheumatism. You don't dance like you've got a rheumatic bone in your body."

"No, by golly, my bones are pretty wonderful, at that, aren't they?" He preened and admired his elbow.

"Straighten up and be serious!" she chided, trying not to snicker. "When the schoolteacher is lecturing, you can't be making smart cracks."

His amused eyes met hers while they went on dancing smoothly, enjoying each other more all the time. "And what if I do, what's the little whippersnapper gonna do about it?"

"Whippersnapper!" she retorted indignantly, and stamped her foot. "I'm not a whippersnapper!"

But at that very moment the music had stopped. Quiet descended upon them while her words carried like a Swiss bell over a fjord. Several inquisitive heads turned their way. Linnea felt herself beginning to blush, but thankfully he guided her from the floor by an elbow. In parting, however, he added insult to injury by saying, "Thank you for the dance, little missy. Don't stay out too late now."

For two cents she would have kicked him in the seat of his britches!

She was still stiff and prickly as a new rope when Bill saw her home. As soon as the carriage stopped, he put an arm around her shoulders, pressed her back against the leather seat, and kissed her. She was just angry enough at Theodore to capitulate and hope to high heaven the kiss would raise some reaction in her heart. But it raised nothing.

"I've wanted to do that all night long."

"You have?"

"Mmm-hmm. Mind if I do it again?"

"I . . . I guess not." *Not if Theodore's going to keep thinking of me as a child. Maybe this will become more fun.*

But it became just the opposite when Bill's tongue entered her mouth and he rolled to one hip and tried to insert his knee between her legs. She jerked back and let out a squawk.

"I have to go in."

"So soon?"

"Yes, right now. Bill, don't!"

"Why not?"

"I said, don't!"

"Nobody ever done this to you before?"

Lord, how many hands did he have? "Stop it!" She shoved him so hard he clunked his head on a bonnet brace.

"Well, all right! You don't have to get pushy!"

"Good night, Mr. Westgaard!" With a jerk of her coat front, she leaped down.

"Linnea, wait!"

He caught up to her halfway to the house, but she shrugged his hand from her arm.

"I don't appreciate being mauled, Bill."

"I'm sorry . . . listen, I promise I—"

"No need for promises. I won't be going out with you again."

"But, Linnea—"

She left him spluttering in the path. Inside the kitchen she closed the door and leaned back against it, relieved. She felt her way up the stairs, undressed in the dark, and huddled under the covers, shuddering.

She wanted very badly to cry, but tears didn't come as easily as they used to. Wasn't this supposed to be a carefree, fun time of her life? But it wasn't carefree and certainly not much fun. What was she doing, anyway, kissing men like Rusty Bonner and Bill Westgaard when the only one she really wanted to kiss was Theodore?

But in the days that followed, he treated her like nothing more than a child. Always a child.

Linnea arose one morning shortly thereafter to a wind that whistled out of Saskatchewan bringing with it the chill promise of snow. Dutifully she drew on warm cotton snuggies and long wool leggings, but the walk to school seemed twice as long as it had when the reapers could be seen in the distance.

Arriving at school, she stood in the cloakroom doorway, studying the familiar room. Odd, how it took on different personalities under the different situations. On a sunny morning there was no place cheerier. On the night of a dance, no place more exciting. But today, totally devoid of children's voices, and with gray clouds churning beyond the long, bare windows, the little room brought an icy shiver.

She hurried outside for coal. The wind formed a funnel near the door of the coal shed and plucked at her scarf tails. She wondered how soon they'd see their first snow. Back inside she kept her mittens on while loading the stove, the sounds of the clanging lids and lifter resounding eerily through the schoolroom. When the fire was finally going, Linnea lingered near it a long time, warming her toes. Finally she forced herself back to the cloakroom, where she discovered the water crock topped with a disc of ice. She chipped it free and returned outside to the pump, feeling again the immense difference between doing this chore on a sunlit September morning and a dismal November one.

When Kristian arrived, she was terribly happy to have his company. Together they moved the water table to a rear corner of the main schoolroom. He and several of the other children brought potatoes to lay on the fender of the stove for their lunches, and by midmorning the room was fragrant with the aroma. At recess time only half the students chose to go outside. The other half turned their potatoes and passed the time visiting or drawing on the blackboard.

On the way home that afternoon, a few dry, hard snowflakes were falling. The brown grass in the ditch shivered and seemed to hunch low, preparing for its winter mantle. There was a menacing look to the clouds. They gamboled faster across the slate sky, their underbellies dark and heavy.

She entered the yard and discovered Isabelle Lawler's cook wagon gone. She glanced around, but there were no hired hands in sight. Somehow she knew they were gone and wouldn't be back till next year.

It was quiet in the house.

"Nissa?" she called. Nobody answered. "Kristian?" The kitchen was warm and smelled of roasting pork and new squash, but the only sound to be heard was the wind soughing bleakly outside. "Nissa?" she called again, searching the front room, but finding it empty, too. Cautiously, she peered into Nissa's bedroom. It was shadowed and unoccupied, the chenille spread tucked neatly beneath the pillows and everything in perfect order. Upon the dresser stood a gallery of photographs—her children as infants, toddlers, youngsters; on their confirmation days with Bibles in hand; on their wedding days with their spouses posing stiffly beside them. Without conscious volition, Linnea moved toward the dresser, bending to study them at closer range.

And there was Theodore with his bride. His hair was cropped painfully close above the ears and his face looked almost childish in its thinness. His neck appeared half its present girth, and his left ear seemed to lap over slightly at the tip. Funny, she'd never noticed it before.

Linnea's eyes moved to the image of the woman sitting erect on a straight-backed chair just in front of him. She had a face as serene and delicate as a violet blossom. Her eyes were very beautiful and her lips the kind—Linnea supposed—that men found dainty and vulnerable.

So you're Melinda. She studied the pretty face a moment longer. They don't say much about you around here, did you know that?

In keeping with the day, she shivered, then backed from the room. She paused, staring at the door to the adjacent bedroom. Unlike Nissa's, which had been left wide, it stood only slightly ajar. She had never seen what lay behind it.

"Theodore?" she called softly. His door was painted ecru, like all the woodwork in the house, and was of double-cross design with a white porcelain knob on a black metal escutcheon. "Hello?" She rested five fingertips on the wood and pushed. The door swung back soundlessly; as with everything, Theodore kept the hinges well oiled.

Guilty, but curious, she stared.

This room was lonelier than the last. The bed appeared to have been put into order this morning by Theodore himself. The spread was thrown over the pillows but not tucked beneath them as a woman would have done. There was no closet, only a hook board on one wall holding his black Sunday suit on a hanger, his overalls by their straps. On the floor his best boots nestled side by side like a pair of sleeping coots. Looking at them, she felt a ripple of guilt run through her—there was something so personal about abandoned shoes. She glanced away.

The wallpaper was floral and faded. Beside the nightstand perched a low, miniature footstool with a hand-creweled cover that must have belonged to Melinda. It seemed the kind of thing a shy-looking violet like her would have liked. It looked very sad and out of place in the dim room, as if waiting for the return of the woman who was gone forever.

On the bulge-fronted dresser lay a photograph in an oval frame, the kind that should have been hanging on a wall.

Unable to make it out from her oblique angle, Linnea moved closer.

There was Melinda again, only more beautiful—if that were possible—than in her wedding picture. Linnea's hands were drawn to the photograph. She lifted it, touched the domed glass. Such melancholy eyes, such haunting exquisiteness. How hard it must be for a man to forget a woman like that. Melinda had been so young when the photograph was taken—as least as young as Linnea was now. The thought saddened her and she rued the years that separated now from then, and her own youth, which she'd gladly forfeit if she could make Theodore look at her just once as he must have looked upon this woman.

Sighing, she replaced the likeness in the exact spot where it had been before. Once more she glanced at the double bed, then stealthily withdrew from the room, setting the door at the same angle she'd found it.

The house felt lonely, and Linnea suddenly didn't want to be in it without the others. She wanted to find them and shrug off the lingering effects of the brooding weather, the photos and the deserted feeling lying over the whole farm. She tightened the wool scarf beneath her chin and headed out the door.

The cook wagon was really gone. Funny she should miss it when she'd been so jealous of Isabelle Lawler. Just the caragana bushes remained, dressed only in their long banana-shaped pods that clicked together forlornly in the wind. It wasn't the cook wagon she missed, but the passing of the season it represented. What was between Theodore and Isabelle? If there really was something, how could a man be attracted to her when she was so diametrically opposite of Melinda?

The wind pressed Linnea's coat against the backs of her legs as she turned toward three diminutive figures in a distant paddock. Even from here she could tell it was Theodore, Kristian, and Nissa. What were they doing out there by the horses? Again she tugged her scarf tighter and sailed downwind, buffeted by the Saskatchewan nor'westerly. It appeared that all of Theodore's horses were gathered in one spot, their tails lifting like spindrift while they shifted restlessly. As Linnea approached, she saw Theodore caressing the broad dappled nose of a mare named Fly.

"Is anything wrong?" she called.

The three turned. Kristian answered. "No, just saying good-bye."

"Good-bye?" Puzzled, she looked from one face to the next.

"This is the day we turn the horses loose. Harvest is all done. The crew is gone," Nissa explained.

"Turn them loose?"

"Yup."

"Where?"

"Open range."

"Range? You mean, they just run free?"

"Yup."

"But how can you do that? They're worth a lot of money."

This time Theodore answered. "We've been doing it for years. They always come back in the spring, just like clock-work, when it's time to get the fields plowed."

Linnea's face reflected amazement. "But how can they know when that is?"

Theodore jerked his head out of harm's way as Fly threw her powerful head up and shook her mane.

"They're smart. They know where they belong and what their jobs are."

"But why turn them loose?"

"To save on feed. They'll be back all fat and sassy, come April."

"And you've never lost one?"

"Never."

She watched the three Westgaards take turns scratching Fly's nose, sensing their subdued sadness at the good-bye. Such trust, she thought, to free the creatures who meant so much to their livelihood.

"Do they all have to go?"

"All but old Cub and Toots," Theodore answered. "I keep them in every winter, just like my pa did. Got to have a way to get into town and to church. They always seem to know they're being kept behind and get a little let down."

There were twelve horses in the paddock. They shifted con-stantly, tossing their heads and whickering into the wind while Cub and Toots thrust their noses over the fence from the adjoining padlock where they were confined. A sturdy buckskin named Chief pranced around the pack, rearing once, then neighing as if to scold Theodore for delaying their release.

"Guess they're getting impatient. They know what's gonna happen." Theodore grabbed Fly's halter. "Don't you, girl?" He glanced at Kristian. "Well, I guess we better do it, huh, son?"

"I guess."

Linnea moved closer to Nissa, watching as the men circulated through the stirring herd, removing bridles. The animals shook their heads, their restlessness growing more palpable as the moment of release grew closer. "You want to let 'em out?" Theodore asked Kristian.

Without replying, Kristian transferred his bridles to Theodore's arm, then Theodore stepped to Linnea's free side.

They watched silently while Kristian opened the pole gate on the far side of the paddock, then circled the herd and flapped his arms, giving a sharp whistle through his teeth. The sound pierced the steely late afternoon and set twenty-four equine ears up straight. For one infinitesimal moment the animals stood still, caught in relief against the roiling leaden sky that seemed to personify their moods. Linnea shivered in appreciation. It was one of those moments of sterling clarity, a niche out of her life that would, in memory, forever remain as rich and real as the moment in which it was happening. Theodore on her left, Nissa on her right, Kristian with the herd, tiny bites of snow pelting her skin, the horses pawing, their nostrils dilated. There was a raw beauty to the scene that made Linnea swallow thickly.

Then the horses moved. Out through the gate and off to freedom, all tails and rumps and flexing flesh. The thunder of their hoofbeats came up through the soles of Linnea's shoes. Cub and Toots trotted to the far fence, their heads high, whinnying as if to call, "Wait for us!" They ran the fence line back and forth, back and forth, bugling in distress.

Standing between Nissa and Theodore, so close their shoulders nearly touched, Linnea hugged her arms. It wasn't the cold. It was the rapport she felt with all three of the Westgaards at that moment. She had never before stopped to think of the skein of feeling between a farmer and the beasts who fed him, clothed him, kept him safe from peril, but she felt it now intensely. It was beautiful . . . and sad . . . and poignant.

Good-bye, horses. Keep safe.

Linnea leaned forward just enough to press her arm to
Theodore's. He neither pulled away nor returned the pressure, but stood with his hands in his pockets, watching his
horses gallop off to their winter world of freedom.

"Where will they go?" she asked quietly.

"Down to the bottomland first, probably, along the creek.
We let the hay grow wild down there, and we put in a crop
of millet that we don't cut. They love the millet."

"And after that?"

Theodore shrugged.

"How far away do you suppose they get?"

"Eight, ten miles or so. There's a lot of government land
and school sections, plus what we all leave unfenced."

"Are you sure they'll have enough food?"

Theodore looked down at her head. The red plaid scarf was
tied in a double knot beneath her chin, making her look more
like a little girl than ever. But her concern came from the
heart and made her seem as much an adult as he. He thought
again of the wonderful gift Linnea had for finding beauty in
things others sometimes took for granted. So different from
Melinda.

She looked up and found him studying her, and they both
returned to watching the horses move off. "They'll have enough.
When the millet and hay run out, they'll start in on the stacks we
left out in the fields."

"They look so cold, don't they?"

"Don't worry about them. They're off to find the others, and
they'll bunch up thirty or more in a herd. When the blizzards
come, they'll huddle in a coulee someplace and press up close
to keep each other warm."

Suddenly Linnea realized her arm was pressed close and
warm against Theodore's. He felt it, too, and stayed where
he was.

"Will we see them at all till spring?" she asked.

"Might, now and then. They make a sight, with their coats
all shaggy, churning through the snow on a gray and windy
afternoon like this one. Only the ground will be all white until

you can't tell it from the whirlwind they leave behind. There's nothing prettier."

At his words, she looked up, he looked down. They felt the pull again, strong, undeniable, elemental. She thought of the woman whose picture remained on his dresser and wondered what it would take to get him to put it away and never bring it out again. He thought of how welcome her warmth felt, through his jacket sleeve, and realized they had shared an accord here today that went far beyond anything he and Melinda had ever shared.

Then they both became aware of Nissa's presence and cautiously drew apart. They returned their gazes to the horizon, but the horses had disappeared.

14

THE END OF harvest truly signaled the onset of winter. They awakened one morning in early November to a world of white. Linnea peeŕed out her tiny window and gasped in delight. Overnight North Dakota had been transformed into a pristine fairyland.

But before she was halfway to school, she stopped considering the snow as quite so romantic and began looking upon it as a nuisance. Trudging along, she moved with all the agility of a freshly wrapped mummy. Lord, couldn't somebody invent something better than these miserable leggings to keep the snow out?

The leggings weren't the only problem. Underneath them she'd donned thick long underwear that covered her from waist to ankle, and over these, full-length black wool knit stockings rolled at the top around a tight rubber ring that pinched and cut into her groin. Over all this bulk went the khaki-colored canvas leggings—stiff, unbending things with stays running from ankle to knee, the entire contraption lashed together at the sides with eyelets and strings that cut off her blood supply even further. Added to it all were rubber overshoes. She felt as if she were walking in kegs!

At school the snow brought excitement. And puddles. And the smell of wet wool. And runny noses. And a mess in the cloakroom, where leggings lay strewn beneath the benches and wool scarves fell onto the dirty floor and got wet and mittens got lost and overshoes mismatched. After recess came the worst smell of singed wool from the mittens drying on the fender of the stove.

Linnea assigned a cloakroom monitor, gave orders that no child was to come to school without a handkerchief, and made a mental note to ask Superintendent Dahl about a wooden folding clothes rack.

But the snow brought gaiety, too. At recess they played fox and goose, Linnea running the rim of the wheel with as much exuberance as the first graders. The younger children made "angels" in the snow and chattered about Thanksgiving, which was just around the corner. The older boys made plans to run trap lines down along the creek bottom in the hope of earning money over the winter.

With the arrival of snow, things were different at home, too. The routine around the farm changed. Everything relaxed. The family was all together at mealtime again, and Kristian was beginning to show a marked improvement in table manners. In the mornings, the kitchen smelled milky. The cream separating was done inside now instead of outside. Two of the barn cats took up residence underneath the kitchen stove. In the evenings, Nissa was often seen with knitting needles in her hands. Linnea, taking her cue from the cats, corrected papers in the kitchen instead of in her drafty upstairs room.

The weather turned frigid. Like her students, Linnea wrapped a warm woolen scarf around her face when she walked, and even in thick knit mittens her fingers were often numb before she reached P.S. 28.

She returned home from school one day to find Theodore and John working by a small shed near the well. She crossed the yard, pulled her scarf down, and greeted them. "Hello, what are you two doing?"

"Getting ready for butchering," John answered, his breath a white cloud.

"In *here?*" The shed was only six feet square, built of wood, with a crude floor in the middle of which was a square hatch.

Theodore and John exchanged smiles. Sometimes the little

missy asked the most ridiculous questions. "No," Theodore clarified, "this is where we store the meat. Gotta make the ice before we kill the cow."

"Oh."

They were busily pumping water into a deep, square hole beneath the floor. The following day she observed the ingenious efficiency of the meat house when she found them spreading a layer of clean straw over the huge solid block of ice, all now in readiness for the freshly cut beef.

The next afternoon, butchering day, she came home to a kitchen that quite turned her stomach. The two men were busy sawing up the carcass of a cow right on the kitchen table, and Nissa was busy with the sausage stuffer.

Walking in on the messy operation, Linnea turned a little green. Theodore grinned and teased, "So where did you think beef came from, missy?"

She hustled through the kitchen and burned a trail up the stairs in her haste to get away from the nauseating sight.

That evening, after supper, Theodore, Nissa, and Kristian sat at the table patiently cutting thin, long strips of beef and dropping them into a keg of brine.

"What's that now?"

"Gonna be jerky when we're through," Nissa replied without looking up. "Soak 'em a couple weeks, hang 'em in the granary to dry—ain't nothin' better."

The kitchen smelled delicious the following night, and at suppertime Linnea was passed a bowl containing a thick concoction of meat, potatoes, carrots, onions, and gravy. She buttered a slice of Nissa's fresh-baked bread, loaded her bowl with the scrumptious-smelling stew, and dug in. It was absolutely delicious. And how much more pleasant mealtime was around here now that they'd learned how to talk!

Kristian asked Nissa where Thanksgiving dinner was going to be held this year.

"Ulmer and Helen's turn," Nissa answered.

"Aw, Aunt Helen's dressing isn't as good as yours, Grandma. I like it best when we have Thanksgiving here."

"Christmas'll be here. You'll be eating my dressing then."

John put in, "Ma's dressing's good, but it can't hold a candle to this heart stew."

"Heart stew?" Linnea's jaw dropped and her eyes fell to her bowl.

"One of the biggest beef hearts I ever seen this year," added Nissa. "Eat up."

Linnea's innards seemed to roll and pitch violently. The spoon slipped from her fingers while she gaped at the half-finished serving before her. What was she going to do with the mouthful she was holding?

Just then Theodore spoke up. "I don't think Miss Brandonberg holds with John's opinion."

Every eye turned to her. She drew a deep breath, steeled herself, and bravely swallowed. Immediately the heart stew tried to come back up. She grabbed her coffee, sucked in a huge gulp, and burned her mouth. Her eyes started watering.

"Somethin' wrong with the heart stew?" Nissa inquired, peering at Linnea over her oval spectacles.

"I . . . I . . ."

"I don't think it's good table manners for her to answer, Ma," Theodore put in archly, hiding a grin.

"E . . . excuse me," Linnea managed in a weak, shaky voice. She pushed her chair back, dropped her napkin, and made a beeline for the stairs, running like a coon before a pack, a hand covering her mouth.

Upstairs, her door slammed.

The four at the table exchanged meaningful glances. "She's a fussy one at the table, ain't she?" Nissa observed wryly, and calmly went on eating.

"I reckon we should've told her. Especially after the tongue sandwiches," Theodore said, but inside he smiled.

"Thought she was Norwegian. Never heard of no Norwegian bein' so fussy."

"She's only half Norwegian," Kristian reminded them. "The other half's Swedish. Remember?"

"Oh. That must be the fussy half then," Nissa decided.

Upstairs Linnea curled on her bed, motionless. Each time she pictured the unsavory sights in the kitchen yesterday and thought of a big pumping beef heart, the queasiness peaked. She forced her thoughts to more pleasant things: the horses running free in a cool, fresh wind; the morning glories climbing John's windmill; the children playing fox and goose in the fresh, clean snow.

A gentle knock sounded on her door.

"Yes?" she answered weakly.

"Miss Brandonberg, are you all right?" It was Kristian—thoughtful, considerate Kristian.

"Not exactly."

"Can I do anything for you?"

"I'm afraid the heart stew already did it."

"Are you really sick?"

She drew a deep lungful of air. "Close."

Looking at her closed door, Kristian couldn't help smiling. "Grandma says to tell you if it's bad, you can take some peppermint extract."

"Th . . . thank you, Kristian."

"Well, g'night then."

"Good night."

That night, as he lay in bed, Theodore couldn't help smiling again at the memory of Linnea's face when she heard what she was eating. It was times when she appeared youngest that he was most attracted to her: when she balked at strange foods, when she stood looking down at an ice hole with her scarf tied tightly beneath her chin, when she stood in a middy dress with her arms crossed behind her back, when she caught her hair up in a crisp wide ribbon and let it fall free over her high collar. And, of course, when she looked at him across a dimly lit kitchen with innocent blue eyes that refused to admit the obvious reasons why the two of them must fight the attraction they felt for one another.

Since that night there'd been no further opportunities to be alone with her. Thank heaven.

But at bedtime, when he lay flat on his back staring at the ceiling, he pictured her in the room above. Sometimes he allowed himself to imagine what it would be like if she were thirty, or even twenty-five. The thoughts made him miserable. He ended up rolling to his stomach, groaning into his pillow, wishing for sleep to clear his mind of forbidden wishes.

Linnea's thoughts were far different. As the days went by, she found their age difference mattering less and less. Theodore's maturity only made him grow more desirable in her eyes. His body, fleshed out, honed by years of hard work, held far more attraction for her than the thin ones of younger men. The pair of creases that bridged his eyes only added character to his attractive face. And she knew how to make him laugh so they'd disappear. Though he didn't know how to read, he had knowledge of things that mattered more than written words: of horses and crops and weather and machinery and the thousand things about farm life she found fascinating. The few times she'd shared these with him only made her want to share more.

She thought of him sleeping below her, and remembered the night he'd kissed her. She closed her eyes and let the feelings sweep through her vibrant young body. Kissing her pillow no longer sufficed as a substitute for the real thing, and she was bound and determined to have more of the real thing.

On a night in mid-November the entire Westgaard family piled into Theodore's house for an impromptu card party. In no time at all the house was overrun with relatives. The adults set up several tables in the kitchen while the youngsters holed up in Kristian's and Nissa's rooms and the front parlor. While the children giggled, played paper dolls, or organized card games of their own, Linnea was invited to join in the adults' game of "smear."

In it, bids were announced as each hand began. Partners went for designated points: high, low, jick, jack, joker, and total game points. Linnea ended up as John's partner and sat across from him at a table of four, Lars on her right and Clara on her left.

As the cards were being dealt, she asked, "What's jick?"

"Left jack," John answered, scooping up his cards. "You never played before?"

"Oh, yes, but we never had anything called 'jick.'"

"Opposite jack of the same color as trump," he explained succinctly. She blinked at John, surprised. When play commenced she saw immediately that though he was slow at most things, cards wasn't one of them. Together they made an unbeatable team. In no time at all she and John were creating a sensation by winning nearly every hand. They took the first game easily, and as the evening wore on they remained consistent winners.

Between games, Ulmer passed out tiny glasses of a transparent liquid, placing one at Linnea's elbow, just as he did at everyone else's. She sipped and gasped, then fanned her open mouth.

"Aquavit," John informed her, grinning over his cards.

"Ah . . . ah . . . aquavit?" she managed, catching her breath. "What's in it?"

"Oh, a little potatoes, a little caraway seed. Pretty harmless, huh, Lars?" Linnea caught the devilish grin that passed between the two brothers. John tipped up his glass, downed the potent Norwegian liquor in one gulp, and closed his mouth tightly for a full ten seconds before breathing again.

Linnea expected to see the top of his head blow off. Instead, when he finally opened his eyes, he smiled appreciatively and nodded in satisfaction.

As the night rolled on, the glasses were refilled time and again, and though Linnea drank far less than the men, she mellowed at the same rate as everybody in the room. She couldn't say when the mood went from mellow to silly, then from silly to boisterous. But it all seemed to work in rhythm with the accelerating excitement over the card game. They whooped and hollered and leaped to their feet on big plays. Often a card would be played with a slam of the fist that sent the table jumping clear off the floor. Then everyone would roar with laughter or cuss good-naturedly.

Behind Linnea, Trigg bawled, "Damn you, Teddy, I figured you had that jack hiding someplace!" Linnea looked over her shoulder to see Theodore smiling like a new moon, his face flushed from the liquor, a hank of hair coiling down his forehead.

He caught her eye as he played another winning card and gave her a broad wink while scooping up the trick.

She spun to face her partner again, but she spun too fast and the room became a little bit tilted. The bottle labeled LINJE AKEVITT made the rounds again. By this time Linnea realized she was pleasantly drunk, and two-thirds of her students were in the house to witness it! She stopped imbibing, but the damage was already done. She giggled often and seemed to be observing everything through a golden haze.

Still, she and John continued winning. At the end of one close hand, Lars leaned his chair back on two legs and bellowed at Nissa, "Hey, Ma, we could use a little heart stew over here!"

Linnea's head snapped up—at least she thought it snapped, but everything seemed to be moving in slow motion now.

Without even looking up, Nissa called, "Why? You got somebody you wanna get rid of, Lars?"

Obviously, they had all heard of her green-faced flight from the supper table, and she wondered who'd spread the tale. She focused on Theodore, but he wore a tight-lipped grin. "All right, who's the loudmouth?" she demanded.

"John," Theodore accused, pointing a finger at his brother.

"Theodore," John accused, pointing back.

They all began chuckling, and suddenly the whole heart-stew episode became hilarious to Linnea. She giggled and giggled while the whole kitchen broke into an uproar of laughter.

It had been years since Linnea had laughed so much. When they let down their hair, these Westgaards really knew how to have a good time. She felt as much a part of the big, boisterous family as if she bore their name.

Midway through the evening everybody stretched, took a nature break, then returned to form up new tables.

"What do you say there, Heart Stew, you wanna take me on?"

Linnea turned around to find Theodore at her shoulder, grinning, the lock of hair still trailing down his forehead, his eyes dancing mischievously.

She lifted one brow cockily. "You think you're good enough . . . " She paused before adding, "Teddy?"

He pressed a hand to his chest and looked injured. "Me! Good enough? Why, I been playin' smear since before I had whiskers."

"Since before you had whiskers?" She gave a mock frown and pursed her lips. "Tsk! Tsk! Tsk! What a l-o-o-ong time! You're probably too good for me. And anyway, Trigg has already asked me to be his partner. But have a chair and we'll give you a chance to beat us." She pulled out the one at a right angle to hers. "Come on, Trigg. Let's show this big talker who knows how to smear whom!"

The playing began again. With Theodore so close, Linnea was conscious of his every movement. Occasionally he sipped aquavit, studying her from the corner of his eye. Sometimes he rested his elbows on the table, other times he tipped his chair back on two legs, knees splayed, considering his cards. Then he'd narrow his gaze, studying her over his hand as if to determine her next play before making his. Occasionally he'd flip a card out as if there were no question that it would take the trick. And sometimes she'd come back with a better one, loudly snapping the corner of her card on the table before pushing the trick toward Trigg to collect.

Linnea and Trigg took four games over Teddy and Clara's two. When the games ended, Theodore tipped back and called to John, "I get Heart Stew for my partner next week, John."

"I don't think so," John called back. "I found her first." Under cover of the noise and confusion of pushing chairs and clearing the tables, Theodore and Linnea exchanged a brief burning glance, then she murmured, low enough for only his ears, "Yes, he found me first," and turned away.

They cleaned away the cards and spread out dinner on the great oak table, and all the while she felt Theodore's eyes on her. "Dinner" was a regular feast: deep-fried cookies called *fattigman,* tasty cheese known as *gammelost,* and a suspicious-looking entry they referred to as *blodpose.*

Turning up her nose, Linnea inquired archly, "And what does *blodpose* mean?"

She directed the question to Theodore, expecting some teasing retort. Instead, he only sipped his coffee and glanced away. John answered instead. "She caught you this time, Ma."

Chuckles sounded, but Theodore remained sober. "What does it mean?" Linnea asked, clutching John's arm.

"Blood sausage."

"Blood sausage!" She groaned and did her best swooning heroine, grabbing her stomach and pitching forward across the table dramatically. Everyone laughed except Theodore.

When the food was cleared away, the adults collected their sleepy children, tucked them in the hay-filled wagons, and headed their horses home.

Kristian, who'd been tippling on the sly, immediately disappeared upstairs to escape the close scrutiny of his grandmother. Nissa made "the long walk" out back in the cold, and when she returned, Linnea did the same.

On her way back to the house, she tried to puzzle out the abrupt change in Theodore's mood. But her mind wasn't working well. She dropped her head back and sucked in deep breaths, trying to neutralize the effects of the potent aquavit. But in spite of the food, coffee, and fresh air, her head was still light and buzzing.

Back in the house the lamp had been left on the kitchen table for her. Not trusting herself to carry it up the steps in her tipsy condition, she lowered the wick until blackness settled over the room. As she tiptoed toward the stairway, Nissa's bedroom door opened, casting a pale gold splash of lanternlight across the living room and into the dim recesses of the kitchen.

"Nissa?" Linnea inquired softly.

"No."

Linnea drew a sharp breath and held it as Theodore appeared around the doorway and stopped in her path. His feet were bare and he'd removed his outer shirt. In the muted glow the top of his underwear became a pale blur. She made out the silhouette of his suspenders, trailing beside his knees as they had that day by the school well, and the neck placket of his underwear, with several buttons open. His face was in shadow, but she sensed belligerence in the wide-set feet, the stiff arms at his sides.

"Oh, it's you."

"You weren't really expecting Nissa anyway, were you?"

"I wasn't *expecting* anyone!" She edged around him and stalked toward the stairs, but hadn't touched the first step before he spun her around by an arm.

"Oh, weren't you?"

In the dark confines of the narrow landing, their chests almost touched. His grip was bruising.

"What's gotten into you all of a sudden, Theodore, you're hurting my arm. Let go!"

Instead, he gripped it tighter. "Little missy, if you can't keep levelheaded when you drink aquavit, maybe you should stick to milk. It's better suited to somebody your age anyway!"

"My age! I'm eighteen years old, Theodore Westgaard, how dare you treat me like a child!"

"Eighteen, and all grown up, is that it?" he mocked.

"Yes!" She spit in a whisper, enraged at being unable to shout at him, but afraid of waking the house. "Not that you've noticed!"

He laughed derisively, his voice low. "Just because you left home and wear a bird-wing hat and drink aquavit doesn't make you grown up, little missy."

"Stop calling me that! I told you before—"

"What was the idea of flirting with John tonight?" Two hands clamped her upper arms and drew her almost to tiptoe. "He's not very bright, don't you know that? But just because he's not doesn't mean he hasn't got feelings. So what do you think you're doing, teasing him that way? And if he falls for your shenanigans, then what? He's not like other men— he won't understand when you tell him that you were only fooling."

"You're crazy! I wasn't flirting with John!"

"Oh, what would you call it then? All that hanging on his arm and being his partner and claiming John found you first?"

She suddenly saw how it must have looked to Theodore. "B . . . but I didn't mean anything by it."

"That's not how it looked. That's not how it looked at all." He gave her a little shake that further threatened her equilibrium. "A lesson, huh? What happens when a little girl tries to act like the grown-ups and drinks too much aquavit."

She neither fought nor conceded, but let him grip her arms until she knew there'd be a string of black-and-blue marks on each. She sighed. "Oh, Theodore, you're so blind," she said softly, resting her fingertips against his chest. "When will you see that I'm not a little girl any more than you're an old man?"

His hands fell from her as if she'd turned into a living torch. She grabbed the front of his underwear to hold him. Beneath her knuckles his heart knocked crazily. "Admit it, Theodore."

He clutched her wrists and forced them down. "You've had too much to drink, Miss Brandonberg."

"Have I?" she asked calmly.

His head loomed over her. His grip was deathly on her wrists, his voice tight with anger. "First John and now me. Brother against brother, is that it?"

"Don't," she begged softly, understanding his need to erect barriers. "Please . . . don't."

They stood poised in the clutches of a tension more powerful than anything either of them had ever experienced before. His fingertips sank into the soft skin of her wrist where her pulse thrummed hot and fast. The shadows of the stairwell hid all but the vague outlines of their faces as they stared at each other in silence. The night seemed to throb about them with a seductive insistence all its own.

Suddenly, with a soft, mewling sound, Linnea pulled free, flung her arms around his neck, and pressed her lips to his. He made absolutely no response, holding himself rigid, with his lips sealed tightly for a full ten seconds. Then his hands came down on her shoulders, trying to force her away. But she clung to him, fervent and eager, knowing she would die of humiliation if he remained stubborn and refused to return the kiss. His thumbs dug into her shoulder blades, his fingers into her back. He pushed and she clung until they both trembled in silent combat, their breathing heavy.

Suddenly he gave in. His powerful hands drew her up until their chests touched. With a groan of reluctant capitulation he slanted his head and began returning the kiss, moving his lips over hers without restraint, opening his mouth to graze his tongue along her childishly locked lips. At the first touch she stiffened slightly, then shuddered with surprise. Against her lips he whispered, "You asked for it, little missy, so open your mouth and learn to kiss the way a woman does."

His tongue returned insistently, and at its touch Linnea realized a sharp difference between this kiss and those she'd experienced before. The others had slightly revolted her. This one asked to be answered in kind. She opened her lips experimentally and felt the wondrous shock of heat and wetness as Theodore's tongue boldly entered her mouth and slipped in a full, voluptuous circle around its confines. Shyly, she followed his lead, returning the intimacy, tasting him, sampling his texture—all sleek and heated and flavored of aquavit and coffee. Her body came alive with sensations more compelling than any she'd known before.

So this is what it's supposed to be like! Oh, Teddy, Teddy, teach me more.

She strained closer and he crushed her against the wool texture of his underwear for altogether too short a time. Even before she could tell if Theodore's heart hammered as wildly as her own, he drew back and lifted his head, holding her away. His breath pelted her face, beating back a loose strand of hair from her forehead while her vitals pulsed, unrequited. When he spoke, the words were wrenched out angrily from between clenched teeth.

"You're playing with fire, little girl."

Then he was gone, leaving her shaken. She touched her moist, trembling lips, her heart, her stomach. Confused, aroused, she stumbled up the stairs, into the safe familiarity of her icy attic room, to lay beneath the covers and shiver. Her breasts ached pleasantly and her head spun crazily. But it wasn't all from aquavit.

Linnea awakened the following morning with the kiss still fresh on her mind. She touched her lips, as if the imprint of it remained. She flung her arms above her head, closed her eyes, and saw his face as it had looked when he'd winked at her last night, flushed, merry, with the lock of hair trailing down his forehead. A handsome face whose smile she'd come to crave, in whose gaze she longed to lose herself. The thought of him filled her with a giddiness to see him again. But when she did, what would she say to him? What did one say to a man the morning after you'd forced him to kiss you thoroughly?

They met at breakfast and she stared at him with open fascination, as if she'd never seen him before, feeling her cheeks grow hot.

For a fraction of a moment his footsteps paused when he saw her across the kitchen. The aquavit had left his head thumping with a slow, incessant ache. The pain increased at the sight of her, looking rather breathless and uncertain, her hands clasped just below her breasts.

Move, fool, before Ma sees the two of you gawking this way.

"Morning," he said, forcing himself to turn away from her bright, expectant face.

"Morning."

For the first time ever, he felt self-conscious washing up in front of her. This is crazy, he thought. Yet he avoided her eyes all during breakfast. And he avoided her all during the day.

But Linnea had something she wanted to say to him. She finally tracked him down to the tack room in the late afternoon. He sat in his worn wooden chair, rubbing soap on a saddle, unaware that she stood behind him. She drew a deep, shaky breath, and tried for a steady voice.

"Hello, Theodore."

The sound of her voice created havoc in his heart, but he forced himself not to jump. It was risky business, stealing kisses in the dark with a girl like her. One of them had to come to his senses and there seemed only one way to do it. He gave her a desultory half-glance over his shoulder and kept on working.

"Oh, it's you."

"I'm sorry about last night."

He looked over his shoulder once more, unsmiling.

"For what?"

She was stunned. *For what?* He could sit there looking as unemotional as one of his field horses and ask, For what? She dropped her eyes to the floor and said softly, "You know."

"Oh, you mean you drank too much, too?" He turned back to his task, hunching over the saddle. "My head still feels like there's a steam engine running inside it."

She gulped and stared at his broad shoulders. "You mean you . . . you don't remember?"

He chuckled softly, remembering everything. Vividly. "Not much. You were my partner for the second set, weren't you?"

The blood surged to her face, but he didn't turn around to see it.

"Yes, I was. And you got upset with me because I agreed to be John's partner next week. Don't you remember that either?"

"Afraid not. That aquavit is powerful stuff. Today I pay the piper."

Linnea stood rooted for several more seconds, abashed that he should have forgotten something that had rocked her to her very core, no matter how much aquavit she'd drunk! Suddenly her eyes narrowed and a spurt of anger flicked through her. Why, he's lying! The stubborn Norwegian mule is lying! But why?

The answer was obvious: the kiss had affected him as deeply as it had affected her.

Stiffening, she spun on a heel and slammed out of the barn.

He swiveled on his chair, frowned at the empty doorway, then stretched to his feet. He stepped over the saddle and flung the oily rag down. Bracing his hands on the edge of the tool bench, he stared out the small window at the snowy paddock, remembering her pressing warmly against his arm the day they'd turned the horses loose, and last night, feeling her breasts flattened against his chest, and her arms clinging to his neck . . . her mouth offered freely . . . tempting . . . innocent . . .

He clamped his jaw. The muscles of his cheeks twitched.

Wet behind the ears! Didn't even know how to kiss yet!

Grim-faced, he rammed a fist down on the rough-hewn tool bench. But it didn't help a bit. It didn't make her any older or himself any younger.

The extended Westgaard family was much closer than Linnea had at first realized. It had only been harvesting that had kept them apart. Now that winter had set in she grew used to seeing them often. Quite naturally they gravitated toward Nissa, so Theodore's house became the gathering spot more often than the others'.

Linnea came to learn their individual places within the family clan. Of Ulmer, the oldest, the others most often asked advice. John, being slow, was the most protected and cosseted. Theodore received their gratitude for giving "Ma" a home. He also received their sympathy, for they knew he was the one, ironically, whom Nissa had always picked on the most and made work the hardest. Lars was the happiest, the one who brought out the humor in all the rest. Clara, being the baby, and the only girl, and pregnant to boot, was doted on shamelessly by all her brothers. But it hadn't spoiled her one bit. The longer Linnea knew Clara, the better she liked her and the greater grew her urge to confide more deeply in Theodore's sister.

There were countless reactions roiling within Linnea since the night she'd kissed Theodore. Chagrin, curiosity, irritation, and fascination. Theodore was fascinated, too—Linnea could tell. There were times when she'd glance up unexpectedly and find him watching her across the room. Times when they met in a doorway and he stepped back too quickly to keep a safe distance as she passed. And once, getting settled in their chairs at the table, when their backsides bumped and his face turned scarlet. But there were other times when he acted as if he were irritated simply by being in the same house with her. Others when he seemed unaware of her existence. She had no idea from day to day what thoughts churned behind his silent scowl or flat expressionlessness.

As her frustration mounted, she felt drawn toward Clara. But Clara was Theodore's sister. Perhaps it was unseemly of Linnea to want to air her feelings with someone so close to him. But there was no one else, and when Linnea found herself becoming short-tempered with the children at school, she realized they should not be the ones to pay for her frustration. She *must* have a confidante.

She walked over to the Linder farm one Saturday, and Clara herself answered the door. After a fond hug of greeting the two sat at the kitchen table, where Clara resumed cleaning eggs with a sanding block. She picked up a brown egg from the wire basket. As she stroked it with the sandpaper, it made a soft *shh-shh* in the cozy room.

Linnea fidgeted on the edge of her chair, staring at Clara's busy hands, wondering how to begin.

"How about some coffee?" Clara asked.

"No, thanks. I . . ." Linnea folded her hands between her knees. "Clara, could I talk to you?"

"So tense. It must be something serious."

"It is. To *me* anyway."

Clara waited. Linnea shifted nervously. *Shh-shh. Shh-shh.*

"You're going to wear the varnish off the edge of that chair. Now what is it?"

"Remember the night I got a little tipsy on aquavit?"

Clara chuckled. "Of course. Some of your students haven't quit talking about it yet."

"I suppose I made a fool of myself."

"No more than the rest of us."

"Maybe not while you were there, but later I did."

"Later?" Clara selected another egg from the basket. The sandpaper rasped rhythmically again.

Linnea felt as if the egg were in her throat. Before she could lose her courage, she gulped and stated baldly, "I kissed Theodore."

The sanding block stopped in midair. "You kissed Theodore?" Clara's eyes widened. "*Our* Theodore?"

"Yes."

Clara leaned back and gave a full-throated whoop of laughter. "Oh, that's wonderful." She rested the hand holding the egg on top of her head. "What did he do?"

"Kissed me back, then got mad at me."

"Why?"

Linnea shrugged, joined her hands on the table, and fit her thumbnails together. Scowling at them, she answered, "He says I'm too young for him."

Clara began sanding again. "And what do you think?"

"I guess I didn't think. I just felt like doing it so I did."

Clara noted the younger woman's frown. She couldn't resist grinning. "So, how was it?"

Linnea's head came up. Their eyes met. *Clara wasn't upset!* Her grin evaporated Linnea's fears and left her feeling free to confide what she would.

"Better than with Rusty Bonner, I can tell you that."

Again Clara acted surprised. "You kissed Rusty Bonner, too?!"

"The night of the barn dance. But Theodore discovered us and got upset. That's why Rusty disappeared so suddenly the next day. Theodore threw him off the place."

Clara fell back against her chair and gave up cleaning eggs. "Well, I'll be."

"You aren't mad? About me kissing Theodore, I mean?"

"Mad?" Clara chuckled. "Why should I be mad? Teddy gets too broody. He needs somebody to liven him up a little bit, and I think you're just the one who can do it."

Linnea hadn't realized how concerned she'd been about what the family would think of her interest in Theodore until Clara accepted it so blithely.

If only Theodore would accept it as blithely.

He didn't. He remained stubbornly aloof.

Linnea and Clara visited again on a Sunday when the Linders dropped in for an afternoon visit. When they arrived, Linnea was in her frigid room correcting papers because Theodore was sitting downstairs at the kitchen table. A light tap sounded, then Clara's head popped around the door.

"Hi, am I disturbing you?"

"No, I'm just correcting papers. Come in!"

"Heavens, it's cold up here." She rubbed her arms as she entered.

"Too cold for you?" Linnea glanced at Clara's popping stomach. "I mean, is it all right if you stay a while?"

Clara's eyes followed Linnea's. She fondled her belly and laughed. "Oh, heavens, yes, it's all right." Inquisitively, she prowled the edge of the room. "I haven't been up here in years. Are you sure I'm not disturbing you?"

Linnea set her work aside and tucked her stiff fingers between her knees. "Believe me, it's a pleasure to be disturbed when you're correcting papers."

Clara lifted the top paper, studied it absently, then set it back down. "You know, a lot of times I envy you, having the job you've got, being away from home and on your own."

"*You* envy *me?*"

"Well, why not? I've never been farther away from here than Dickinson. Your life is . . . independent. Exciting."

"And don't forget scary."

"I haven't seen you scared too many times."

"No? Well, I hide it well, I guess."

Clara laughed.

"Did I ever tell you how your brother scared me the day he picked me up at the station?"

"Teddy?" Clara chuckled, strolled to the dresser, and glanced at Linnea's personal items. Among them was an agate bearing a beautiful translucent stripe of amber color. She held it up to the light. "Oh, Teddy's just an old softie underneath—what'd he do, make you carry your own bags?" She replaced the agate and looked back over her shoulder.

"Worse than that. He told me I'd have to find someplace else to room and board because he didn't want any *woman* living in his house."

"Probably because of Melinda."

Linnea's eyes grew wide, interested. "He never mentions her. What was she like?"

Clara dropped to the edge of the bed, pulled one knee up, and became thoughtful for several seconds. "Melinda was like two people. One was gay and gutsy—that was the one we saw first, when she came here unannounced, saying she was going to marry Teddy. The other was the opposite. Quiet and broody. I was only eleven at the time, so I didn't realize it then, but I've thought about it since I've grown up and had children of my own. I think part of Melinda's problem was that she was hit harder than most by the baby blues and—"

"Baby blues?" Linnea interrupted, puzzled.

"You don't know what that means?"

Linnea shook her head.

Clara rested one hand on her mounded stomach and leaned back on the other. "Baby blues is after the baby is born when a woman gets real sad and cries all the time. It happens to all of us."

"It does?" Linnea's eyes dropped to Clara's burden. The sight of it filled her with awe.

"Strange, isn't it?"

"B . . . but, why? I mean . . . it seems to me that would be one of the happiest times of your life, right after a new baby is born."

Clara smoothed the skirts over her abdomen and smiled down wistfully. "Seems that way, doesn't it? But for a while after the birth you get so very sad, and you feel foolish because you know you have everything in the world and should feel lucky, but you just want to cry and cry. Husbands just hate it. Poor Trigg, he always hangs around feeling helpless and clumsy and asks over and over what he can do for me." She spread her palms and let them drop. "Only there's nothing. It's just got to run its course."

"And Melinda cried and cried?"

"Did she ever. Seemed like she'd never stop. I guess she hated it here. Claimed the wheat was driving her crazy. Then that fall, when the wheat was all in and the hired hands left, she disappeared, too."

"Oh!" Linnea drew a sharp breath and covered her lips. "You mean she . . . she ran away with one of them?"

"That part I don't know. If she did, they made sure I never heard the details. We lived in John's house then. That was the home place up there when Pa was alive. But Pa had been dead two years already. John was able to handle the home place alone and Teddy needed somebody to look after Kristian, so Ma and I moved in here. This used to be my room then. I can remember bringing Kristian up here and tucking him into bed with me when he was just a little mite." A soft smile crossed Clara's face. "Oh, he was the sweetest little thing you ever—" Suddenly she drew a sharp breath, closed her eyes, and tensed backward, one palm pressed to her stomach.

Linnea's eyes rounded in fright.

Momentarily, Clara relaxed again. "Oh, that was a hefty one."

Mystified, Linnea asked, "What happened?"

"The baby kicked."

"K . . . kicked?" She couldn't stop staring at Clara's protruding stomach, wondering about all the mysteries of childbearing.

"Don't you know anything about pregnant women?"

Linnea's gaze lifted, dropped again. "No . . . you're the first one I've ever talked to."

"The baby's alive already, you know. He's moving around in there."

"He is?" Linnea jerked as if from a reverie, and added, "I mean, of course he is. Otherwise how could he have kicked?" Fascinated, she had to learn more. "What does it feel like?"

Clara laughed, then invited, "Want to feel?"

"Oh, could I?"

"Come on. He'll move again. He always does, once he gets rolling."

Diffidently, Linnea perched beside Clara and reached out a timid hand.

"Oh, don't be shy. It's just a baby."

Shyly, Linnea touched. Clara was hard, and warm, and carrying a precious life. When it moved beneath her hand, Linnea's eyes widened in surprise, then a smile spread upon her face.

"Oh, Clara. Oh golly . . . feel."

Clara chuckled. "Believe me, I feel. More than I want to sometimes."

"But what does it feel like—I mean inside you when he rolls like that?"

"Oh, kind of like a gas pain rumbling around."

They laughed together. Linnea dropped her hand, envying Clara her headstart on her family.

"Thank you for letting me feel."

"Oh, don't be silly. A woman's got to know these things, otherwise she's in for some big surprises once she gets married."

Linnea pondered for a moment, thinking of Theodore touching Melinda's stomach as she'd just touched Clara's, feeling his child's movements, holding his child for the first time. Birth . . . the greatest miracle of all. She tried to comprehend the depth of sadness a man would feel at being deserted by a wife with whom he'd shared that miracle.

"I guess what happened pretty much soured Theodore on women," she ventured, running her thumbnail between the rows of chenille on the bedspread.

"A lot of questions about Teddy today."

Linnea's gaze lifted. "I was just curious, is all."

Clara studied the young woman's face closely, inquiring, "So how are things going between you two?"

"About the same. He's grumpy most of the time. Treats me as if I had the bubonic plague." Suddenly Linnea jumped up and stamped one foot. "He treats me like a child all the time and it makes me so mad!"

Clara studied Linnea's back, surprised by her vehemence. So she wants to be treated like a woman. Well, well.

"You *do* have some feelings for our Teddy, don't you?"

Linnea slouched, returned to the bed, and dropped down disconsolately. "Lordy, I don't know." She lifted pleading eyes to her friend. "I'm so mixed up."

Clara recalled feeling mixed up herself during the days when she and Trigg had courted. She reached out to touch Linnea's hand, convinced of the young woman's affection for her brother. "Could it be you're still doing a little growing up?"

"I guess I am." Linnea's expression turned doleful. "It's awfully confusing, isn't it?"

"We all go through it. Thank heavens only once, though. But I suspect that it's a little harder when you find yourself falling for someone like Teddy." Clara sat back and asked casually, "So what is it you want to know about him?"

"Has he ever had anyone else besides Melinda?"

"I've had my suspicions about that Lawler woman, but I'm not sure."

"So have I."

Clara cocked her head. "You jealous?"

"No, I'm not jealous!" Linnea at first appeared defensive, then dropped the facade. "Yes, I am," she admitted more quietly. "Isn't that absolutely silly? I mean, he's sixteen years older than I am!" Exasperatedly, she flung her hands up. "My mother would absolutely lay an egg if she knew."

"Knew what?"

"That I kissed him."

"Ah, that."

"Yes, that. I don't understand him, Clara. He kissed me as if he enjoyed it, too, but afterward he got so angry, as if I did something wrong. But I don't know what," she finished in a near wail.

Clara squeezed Linnea's hands, then dropped them. "More than likely it's himself he's upset with, not you. It's my guess that Teddy is feeling a little guilty because you're so young. And he's probably wondering what people would think—you living in this house like you do."

"But that's silly! We haven't—"

"Of course it's silly. No need to explain to me. But there's one other thing you should remember. He's been hurt awfully bad. I lived here after Melinda ran away. I saw how he suffered, and I'm sure it isn't easy for him to break down and get close to someone again. He's probably a little scared, don't you think?"

"Scared? Theodore?" She'd never thought about him being scared before. Not the way he blustered around all the time. The idea was sobering. "I'm probably making too much out of just a couple of kisses. Like I said, he still treats me as if I'm in pinafores. But, Clara, please don't tell anybody I told you."

"Of course not."

"And thank you for telling me about Melinda and about your condition."

"You're almost like one of the family now. And being

Kristian's teacher, you should know about his mother. As far as the other questions go—about personal matters—you can ask me anything, anytime. How are you supposed to know what to expect when you get married if you don't ask questions?"

In the weeks that followed their first confidential exchanges, Linnea voiced countless other questions. As the two women grew closer, Linnea learned more about a woman's body than she'd ever imagined there was to learn. There were times Clara shared some of the deeper intimacies of her marriage, revelations that sent Linnea's imagination spinning.

Each time after such a heart-to-heart talk, Linnea would lie in bed at night—still in her leggings and covered to the eyes—and try to imagine herself and Theodore doing what Clara and Trigg had done to get their babies. Oh, she'd heard rumors about copulation before, but never from any such reliable source as Clara, who should certainly know!

After all Clara had done it with Trigg *three times!*

Then in one of their confidential exchanges, Clara revealed that it was something men and women did together much more often than when they wanted to have babies. It was too much fun to reserve only for begetting!

They rolled their eyes at each other and giggled.

But Linnea went away feeling even more confused than before. She spent hours wondering about the logistics of such an act, and how on earth two people ever brought themselves to begin it. Did the man just say it was time and then you crawled in bed with him and did it? And *how,* for heaven's sake? Picturing it, she was sure it would be awkward and clumsy and grossly embarrassing, even if you loved the man. She recalled how repulsed she'd been by Rusty's groping, and how angry the night Bill had tried to wedge his knee between hers. Yet, the two times when she'd been pressed against Theodore—oh, mercy, it had been grand.

But to take off her clothes and let him do what Clara had talked about? Not on her life! In the first place, the size Theodore was, he'd squash her dead!

November waned and Kristian turned seventeen. At school, everybody geared up for the Thanksgiving and Christmas holidays. Linnea began planning the Christmas program, and she spent her evenings writing the script for the nativity play, conveniently forgetting about Theodore's reading lessons since they were still avoiding each other at every turn.

One day at noon recess the boys came back with a rabbit they'd snared. Excitedly, they asked Miss Brandonberg's permission to dress it then and there. Linnea reluctantly approved, though she steered clear of the coal shed where they skinned and gutted the poor creature.

When the job was done, Raymond, Kristian, Tony, and Paul came back, bright-eyed and eager. "Miss Brandonberg?" Tony acted as spokesman. "We were wondering . . . well, since we caught the rabbit ourselves, could we cook him?"

"Cook him? You mean here?"

"Yeah, see, we thought maybe if you'd let us we'd bring a frying pan and ask our mas how to do it, and we'd fry him up to go with our potatoes tomorrow."

Linnea's stomach turned at the thought of possibly being offered a hunk of rabbit meat, cleaned and cooked by four proud novices. Wasn't there such a thing as rabbit fever one could get from eating the creatures?

"I . . . well, goodness!" she exclaimed evasively.

"Please!" went up the chorus.

What could she do but consent, hoping that one small rabbit wouldn't go far, and she'd escape having to eat any?

"Well, all right." Hastily she added, "Provided you go home and find out exactly how to do it, and how long it has to be cooked to make sure it's safe. *And* clean up after yourselves."

They cut up the carcass, cleaned Paul's lunch pail, and packed it inside, then left it in a corner of the cool cloakroom overnight. The next day Raymond arrived with a cast-iron skillet. The boys had a consultation and approached their teacher, shifting their feet nervously.

"Well, what now? Did you forget the onion?" She had made sure to ask Nissa directions for cooking rabbit so things would be done properly.

This time Kristian had been elected to speak. "We thought, if it was all the same to you, we'd save the one rabbit we got and freeze him while we go out lookin' for more. Then, when we get enough, we'll fix them for the whole school. One won't hardly be enough," he reasoned.

Dear, no, Linnea thought, feeling her gorge rise in anticipation.

"But there are fourteen of you," she reminded them, carefully excluding herself.

Tony beamed. "Fifteen, countin' you, Miss Brandonberg."

Linnea despaired, unable to deny them permission when their intentions were so forthright and generous. She remained silent for so long that Raymond took up their plea.

"See, we were thinking how all the girls always get to learn to cook cause their mas teach them. But us boys, nobody ever teaches us."

"We boys," Linnea corrected automatically, her thoughts on the bloody patch of snow near the coal shed and the pinker patch beneath the pump.

"Yeah, we boys," Raymond repeated dutifully, rushing on eagerly. "We might end up living alone some day, like Uncle John, then where would we be if we didn't have our ma close by like Gram, to cook for us?"

How could she argue with that? What more important duty had any teacher than to prepare young people for life—whatever that life might bring?

"All right. You have my permission."

They howled in approval, socked the air, then babbled excitedly as they hit for the door.

"And boys?"

The four turned back.

"If you do a good and a neat job of it, there'll be extra credit for you at grade time. We shall call it 'domestics.'"

It took the boys a week to catch four rabbits. During that time there was much whispering and secretiveness. Linnea suspected some of the girls were in on the plans, too, because every day during afternoon recess, Patricia Lommen and Frances Westgaard had their heads together with the boys, talking animatedly, occasionally breaking out in excited giggles, then quieting suddenly when a loud "Shh!" would go up from the group.

Raymond finally announced that they had all the rabbits they needed—by now they were frozen in several tightly covered pails in the snow by the coal shed—but informed Miss Brandonberg that they were saving the meal for the day before

Thanksgiving, so could she set that day aside and give them a little longer dinner break than usual?

Libby Severt was somehow in on the act, too. She asked permission to take the smaller children aside for one hour of secret consultation early in Thanksgiving week. While Linnea sat at her desk, correcting arithmetic papers and trying her best not to appear inquisitive, a giggle went up from the youngsters in the back corner. She glanced up to see Roseanne and Sonny jumping up and down and clapping excitedly.

Then, with only one day to go before the event, another special request was made: they needed to use the cloakroom for a while and be left alone. Would Miss Brandonberg please stay out until they were done?

By this time Linnea was so curious it was all she could do to stay at her desk while the door opened and closed repeatedly and children came in and took things from their desks, then ran back and slammed the door. The cloak room was so cold they'd donned their jackets, yet nobody seemed to mind in the least.

At last the big day arrived and it was impossible to carry on normally with reading, writing, and arithmetic lessons. The children were simply jittering with excitement.

At midmorning the older boys started frying rabbits in two enormous iron frying pans. Potatoes ringed the entire fender of the stove, and soon the savory scent of cooking onions filled the schoolroom. Skipp and Bent proudly marched to the cloakroom and came back with a metal corn-popper on a long handle and set to work popping corn. Jeannette and Roseanne produced a reasonable facsimile of a basket—woven by their own immature hands?—of fresh, dry cornstalks, into which the popcorn was dumped. Several of the children took over pushing the rows of desks back against the walls. They swept the floor, then ringed the stove with fifteen plates and forks confiscated from their mothers' pantries. A fruit jar of bright, golden butter appeared, and salt and pepper shakers.

Roseanne marched up to Linnea's desk and announced, very soberly, "We know the Pilgrimth din't have plates, but we—"

"Shh! Roseanne!" Libby came by and almost yanked Roseanne off her feet. A moment later the cloakroom door slammed behind them.

Next, Norna came out and ran up to the big boys by the stove, whispering urgently into Kristian's ear. Kristian, Ray, and Tony followed her back into the cloakroom and returned moments later sporting wide white Pilgrim collars made of paper, and black paper hats that made them look more like warlocks than Pilgrims.

Finally, when Linnea's excitement was as great as that of her students, Bent and Jeannette came out of the cloakroom, marched with all due pomp and importance to "teacher's desk," and escorted her to the place of honor near the stove—one with a perfect view of the cloakroom door.

Libby Severt stepped out, closed the door, and announced clearly, "The first Thanksgiving." There followed a brief recitation on the history of the Pilgrims at Plymouth Colony in 1621, then Libby took her place on the floor next to Miss Brandonberg. Linnea squeezed her hand and solemnly returned her attention to the cloakroom door.

Out stepped Skipp and Jeannette nervously glancing at each other for a cue, taking deep breaths, then reciting in unison: "Thanksgiving was to give thanks for a good harvest or for rain after a drought." Each of them carried a sheaf of wheat in their arms. In procession they marched forward and laid the symbolic wheat on the floor within the circle of plates. When they were seated, Raymond hustled forward and whisked one bundle a safer distance from the stove, and at Jeannette's crestfallen expression assured her in a loud whisper, "You did just fine, Jeannette." Then he gave her a broad wink, which staved off her tears.

Linnea controlled the urge to chuckle, truly touched by the solemnity with which the children carried out their parts in the pageant.

Next came Frances, dressed in a brown blanket, with a chicken feather in her hair. "The Indians brought gifts of food," she announced importantly. Behind her entered four other Indians in feathers and blankets. First came Norna.

"Corn," she announced, bearing forth a lopsided basket of popcorn.

Then came tiny Roseanne.

"Nutth!" she blasted, so loud it raised an undertone of laughter. The sound faded as she solemnly came into the room with a dishtowel tied neatly in a bundle. Kneeling at the circle, she tried to untie it. When the knot refused to budge, she glanced with a trembling lip toward Patricia—obviously the play director—hovering near the cloakroom door. Patricia hustled over to lend a hand, and together she and Roseanne opened the towel, revealing a pile of crisp, brown walnut meats.

Roseanne settled down cross-legged, and the next Indian entered.

"Wild fruits." Sonny's offering was a wooden bowl full of quartered apples.

"And berries," Bent ended. Another series of snickers arose as he came forward with two quart jars of home-canned raspberry sauce, explaining, "We couldn't find no fresh berries." The younger children covered their mouths and giggled.

Libby rose to her feet and recited, "The Pilgrims taught the Indians about God, and they all asked for thanks together, for the year had been bountiful and they had food enough to see them through till spring."

To Linnea's surprise, Allen Severt stepped from the cloakroom, looking completely out of character in one of his father's white collars, which hung around his neck like a band around a chicken's leg. He held a Bible and grudgingly mumbled his way through the Thanksgiving Psalm, then sat down.

Again, Libby began, "And they all sang—"

Over by the stove, Kristian interrupted, "And they all decided that they would sing the Thanksgiving song later so the rabbit wouldn't be burned to a crisp."

They broke into gales of laughter. Then Tony and Paul passed around piping-hot potatoes, followed by the fruit jar of butter. Kristian and Raymond served the rabbit, and there was cold milk for everyone. They had all brought cups from home, and Miss Brandonberg got the one from the water jug.

When the food was all served and the big boys seated, Linnea sat back and smiled at them all, tears flooding her eyes. She reached for the hands of those closest to her. Never in her life had she experienced a feeling like this. These wonderful children had done this all for her. Pride shone in their eyes. A lump formed in her throat.

As they all joined hands in a circle, she found room in her heart to love every one of them.

"I give thanks for each and every one of you dear, dear children. You've given me a Thanksgiving I shall never forget." A tear trembled and rolled over her lashes, followed by another. She unashamedly let them fall. The children gazed at her in awe, and nobody seemed to know how to end the awkward moment.

Then, Roseanne, with her uncanny sense of timing, lightened the mood by informing "teacher" with all due seriousness, "Thkipp, he forgot the disheth for the rathberrieth, tho we can't really eat 'em."

When the laughter died down, Linnea suggested, "Maybe we don't need dishes if we finish our milk first and put our sauce in the cups."

The Thanksgiving feast began, and a queasy Miss Brandonberg had her first bite of rabbit. She chewed cautiously, raised her eyebrows, licked her lips, and declared in genuine amazement, "Why, it tastes just like chicken!"

And it really did!

15

THEY WERE ALL in the front parlor at Ulmer and Helen's house, gathered around a Thanksgiving table so long the far end seemed to vanish in the distance. It was much more formal than Linnea had expected. The table was set all in white: white china on white damask linens. The only color came from a luscious ribbon of translucent jellies, relishes, and preserves that lined the length of the table and caught the sun like a strand of jewels spread upon the snow. In the center was a glorious crown of tomato aspic.

When everyone was seated, Ulmer said grace. A moment later Helen swept in, triumphantly bearing a wide silver platter of steaming *lutefisk* glistening with drawn butter.

Oh no, Linnea thought. The Curse of Norway!

It passed from hand to hand accompanied by oohs and ahs while Linnea frantically wondered where the turkey was. But no turkey appeared. She watched the malodorous steaming cod come closer with all the eagerness of St. Joan watching the firebuilder search for a match.

When it reached her, she passed it on to Frances as unobtrusively as possible.

Frances bellowed, "You mean you don't want any *lutefisk?*"

"No thank you, Frances," Linnea whispered.

"But you have to eat *lutefisk!* It's Thanksgiving!"

Frances might as well have hired a barker. Everyone turned horrified glances on the recalcitrant Miss Brandonberg.

"I never learned to like it. Please, just . . . just pass it on to Norna."

At her left, Clara—bless her heart—was snickering. Across the table Linnea saw Theodore hide his smile behind a finger. The hostess bustled in with the next Norwegian delicacy, *lefse,* a flat potato bread that had, in Linnea's opinion, all the attraction of a platter of gray horsehide. Every eye in the house surreptitiously watched to see if the little missy would commit her second sin of the day. But this time she took a piece and plopped it on her plate to satisfy them. She slathered it with butter and lifted it to her lips. Looking up, she found Theodore lifting his own *lefse*—wrapped around a hunk of *lutefisk.* She bit into hers. He bit into his. She crossed her eyes and made a disgusted face. He chewed with exaggerated relish, then licked his lips ostentatiously while his eyes twinkled at her from across the table. It was their first friendly exchange since the night they'd kissed. Suddenly the *lefse* tasted nearly tolerable.

When the *lutefisk* and *lefse* courses were completed—ah, bliss—the turkey and dressing arrived. It was accompanied by snowy whipped potatoes, scalloped corn, peas in thick cream, and a rich apple and walnut salad in whipped cream.

Throughout the meal Linnea was conscious of Theodore's eyes roving her way again and again, but whenever she glanced up, he looked somewhere else.

When the meal ended she helped the women with the dishes while the men sprawled out and one by one drifted off to sleep.

When the dishes were finished Linnea peeked into the front parlor. The table had been taken down. The children had disappeared. John was snoozing in a rocker, Trigg was on his back on the floor. All was quiet except for the sound of soft snoring and the women settling at the kitchen table to chat. At one end of the horsehair sofa Lars was stretched out, eyes closed, hands laced across his stomach. At the opposite end, Theodore looked like his brother's bookend. Between them was the only available wedge of sitting space in the room, wide enough only for a small throw pillow that nobody had nabbed.

Her eyes traveled over Theodore. His suit jacket and tie were gone, his collar and vest buttons were open, white sleeves rolled to the elbow. His tan had begun fading; the pale strip of skin at the top of his forehead contrasted less sharply with the rest of his face than it had two months ago. His lips were parted, his chin was on his chest, his fingers relaxed, scarcely holding together as they lifted and fell with his slow breathing. He looked serene, imperturbable, even a little vulnerable.

She crossed the room, picked up the square pillow, and sat down. Theodore opened his eyes, smacked his lips, and sighed gently.

"Didn't mean to wake you," Linnea said quietly. "This is the only place left to sit."

"I wasn't really asleep." He closed his eyes again.

"Yes, you were. I was watching you."

He grinned with one corner of his mouth, chuckled, and closed his eyes. "Oh you were, huh?"

She hugged the pillow and slouched down, resting her head on the sofa back. "You haven't been saying much to me lately."

"You haven't been saying much to me either."

"I know."

She rested her chin on the pillow and studied his shiny Sunday boots, crossed at the ankle, then his bare arm, where brown skin met white cotton, the sun-bleached hair beginning to come in darker.

He opened his eyes slightly and watched her without moving another muscle. "You still mad?"

"What's there to be mad about?"

Desultorily, he rolled his head toward her. "Don't know. You tell me."

She felt her cheeks warming and lowered her voice to a murmur. "I'm not *mad* at you."

A full thirty seconds passed while their gazes held and the sound of the men's soft snuffling continued through the peaceful room. At last he said, in a voice so low it was barely audible, "Good." Then he settled his head squarely again and went on. "I hear you had quite a feast at school yesterday."

"And you're gloating, no doubt."

He feigned an injured expression and they grinned at each other. "Gloating. Me?"

"About the rabbit."

"Would I gloat?" But he arched one eyebrow, inquiring, "How was it?"

"I bow to your peculiar tastes. Delicious."

He chuckled. "But you couldn't quite bring yourself to bow to our peculiar tastes today, could you?"

"Nothing against Helen's cooking, but there wasn't any way I could bring myself to eat that . . . that Norwegian atrocity."

Theodore laughed so unexpectedly his heels came up off the floor. Beside them, Lars shifted. Across the room John's snoring halted, he snuffled, rubbed his nose, and slept on. Theodore grinned at Linnea with pure enjoyment.

"You know, I might learn to like you yet, even though you don't eat *lutefisk*."

"Only a Norwegian would come up with a ridiculous standard like that. I suppose if I suddenly discovered I loved that rotten-smelling stuff, I'd pass muster, huh?" He took his sweet time deliberating until finally she advised wryly, "Don't strain yourself, Theodore. I wouldn't want to be responsible for your committing any ethnic sins."

He inquired, good-naturedly, "What's that mean, then— ethnic?"

"Ethnic . . . " She gestured searchingly. "You know—peculiar to your nationality."

"I didn't know sins came in Norwegian. I thought they was all the same in any country."

"Were all the same."

"Well, I see you're back to correcting me. That must mean you got over whatever had you all dandered."

"I was not dandered. I told you—"

"Oh, that's right. I forgot." He wriggled into a more comfortable position with an air of disinterest that made her want to knock him off the edge of the sofa. How was a girl supposed to get his attention?

"Theodore, you know what I wish you'd do?" He didn't even bother to grunt. "Go soak your head in the *lutefisk* barrel!" She hugged the pillow, crossed her ankles, and slammed her eyes closed. If he was grinning at her, let him grin, the damn fool!

She'd lay there till she turned into a fossil before she'd let him see how his teasing riled her!

Several minutes passed. Her eyelids started twitching. Theodore sighed, wriggled down more comfortably, and let his arm touch Linnea's. Her eyes flew open. Sure enough, he was grinning at her.

"I was thinking about your offer to teach me to read. When can we start lessons?"

She jerked her arm away and huffed, "I'm not interested."

"I'll pay you."

"Pay me! Don't be ridiculous."

"I can afford it."

"That's not what I meant."

"Oh. What did you mean?"

"Friendship cannot be bought, Theodore."

He considered a moment, then told her, "You look about twelve years old when you stick out your bottom lip like that."

She sucked it in, sat up, produced her most syrupy smile, and pointed. "The *lutefisk* barrel is that way." She was half off the sofa when he grabbed her arm and hauled her back with a bounce. To her utter amazement, all his teasing disappeared.

"I want to learn to read. Will you teach me, Linnea?"

When he said her name that way she'd have done anything he asked. He had beautiful eyes, and when they rested on hers without teasing she wanted more than anything in the world for them to see her as a woman instead of a girl.

"Will you promise never to call me little missy again?"

Before speaking, he released her arm. "I promise."

"All right. It's a bargain."

She stuck out her hand and he shook it—one sure, powerful pump.

"Bargain."

She smiled.

"Miss Brandonberg," he added.

"Theodore!" she scolded petulantly.

"Well, you're my teacher now. Got to call you like your kids call you."

"I *meant* I wanted you to keep calling me Linnea."

"We'll see about that," was all he'd promise.

* * *

They began their lessons the following night. As soon as the supper dishes were done, Nissa settled down with her mending in a rocker by the stove. Kristian took a book to the kitchen table where he was joined by his father and Linnea.

Linnea was accustomed to facing a class full of fresh-scrubbed childish faces. It felt odd having to teach the ABCs to a full-grown man whose jaw showed the day's growth of whiskers, whose enormous hands dwarfed a pencil, and whose brawny chest and arms filled out a red plaid flannel shirt the way fifty pounds of grain fills a seed bag. On the other hand, she didn't have to put up with the attention lapses and fidgeting inherent with younger childrᐱn. She couldn't have asked for a more eager or attentive student.

"We'll start with the alphabet, but I'll try to make it interesting by giving you something to spur your memory on each letter." Having left all her books at school, Linnea took out a large tablet. After a minute's thought she filled the first sheet with a sketch of a half-filled bottle, giving it a tall, narrow neck. In the upper right corner she formed a capital and small A.

She turned the tablet to face Theodore. "A . . . is for aquavit." Her eyes met his over the thick pad. A slow smile spread over his face, a soundless chuckle formed in his chest.

"A is for aquavit," he repeated obediently.

"Very good. Now don't forget it." She tore off a sheet of paper and formed two perfect A's. "Here, you make each letter as you learn it. Make a row of them."

He bent over the paper and began following orders while she explained. "A has several different sounds. A is for aquavit, and apple, and ace. Each word starts with an A, but as you can hear, they all have different sounds. A is for arm, and for always, and for automobile. Now you name me one."

"Autumn."

"Exactly. Now one that starts with a sound like apple."

"Alfalfa."

"Right again."

"Now one with a sound like ace."

"Eight."

Linnea threw up her hands and let them flop to the table. "You should be right, and the dictionary should be wrong, but the first thing you have to learn about the English language is that its rules seem to have been made only to be broken. Eight starts with E, but we'll get to that later. For now, just remember what A looks like, both capital and small."

While Theodore worked on his small A's, Linnea sketched a string of link sausages, forming them into a capital B.

"B is for blood sausage," she announced, flashing the picture at him.

"Blood sausage?" he repeated, surprised again by her quick wit. She turned up her nose in distaste. "B is for bad, blukky, buckets of blood sausage!"

"B . . . blukky?" He laughed. Her sense of humor made the lesson anything but dull.

Across the table, Kristian listened and watched the proceedings with a grin, wishing it had been this much fun when he'd been in first grade.

Next Linnea ordered, "Name me a word that starts with B."

Theodore's answer was immediate. "Bird wings."

She feigned an injured expression, then scolded, "B is also for brat, so watch yourself, Theodore."

Nissa peered over the top of her glasses at the sound of her son's laughter, wondering when she'd last heard it. She glanced at Linnea, grinned appreciatively, and returned to her knitting. As the evening advanced, they laughed often. Nissa listened with one ear, yawning now and then.

C was supposed to be for Clippa, but Theodore declared that the horse Linnea drew looked more like a moose, so they changed C to coal. They progressed through the alphabet, searching for familiar items with which to associate the letters. D was for dipper. E was for eggs. F was for fence. G was for grain. H was for hymnal.

I was a little tougher. While they puzzled over it, Kristian began nodding heavily over his book. I became ice house as Nissa set aside her knitting, lumbered to her feet, and said, "Kristian, come along before you slip off your hand and break your chin." The two of them toddled off to bed as Linnea and Theodore agreed on jar for J.

Theodore watched while Linnea sketched a fruit jar and put the appropriate letters in the corner. The kitchen was quiet without the creak of Nissa's rocker and Kristian's page turning. The kerosene lamp hissed softly and the room was warm and cozy.

Then came K.

"K is for—"

Kiss. The word popped into Linnea's mind, and her blue eyes seemed to crash with the brown ones across the table. The memory came back, as vibrant and unnerving as if it had just happened, and she saw in his deep, dark eyes that he was remembering it, too.

"K is for—" he repeated quietly, his gaze unwavering.

"You think of one first this time," she returned, hoping her face didn't betray her thoughts. "It should sound just like the letter."

"You're the teacher."

Becoming flustered by his steady regard, Linnea frantically searched for inspiration. "K is for *krumkaka!*" she rejoiced.

"No fair. That's Norwegian."

"So is aquavit, but we used it. Besides, *krumkaka* is one Norwegian food I love, so allow me." She busied herself drawing the sweet Christmas delicacy she'd eaten so many times in her life, and came up with a perfect likeness of the delicate cone-shaped cookies.

Glancing at it, he praised, "Very good." But she had the impression his mind wasn't on *krumkaka* any more than hers was. In an effort to leaven their mood again, she went on to L.

"L is for all the worst ideas Norwegians ever produced. *Lefse*, liver loaf, and *lutefisk*. Pick one."

Theodore's eyes met hers, his face golden and attractive in the lamplight as he leaned back and laughed. "Let's make it *lutefisk*."

She drew her lower lip between her teeth, concentrating, trying to block out the electricity between Theodore and herself while she made the illustration. When the picture was done, she held it up. His head was bent low over his paper, the pencil moving.

"Theodore?"

He looked up. The tablet covered her face from the nose

down. She peered at him over her depiction of a serving platter
heaped high with chunks of nebulous matter emanating waving
stink lines.

"L is for *lutefisk*," she reiterated.

He broke out laughing—how mischievous she looked, eyeing
him from behind the silly sketch. She laughed, too, happier than
she'd been in a long time. Then suddenly their laughter dwin-
dled, fell away completely, and left a room so silent they could
hear the cat breathe, curled up in Nissa's abandoned chair. They
stared at each other, stirred by feelings neither could control.
She laid the picture down as if it were made of spun glass,
nervous under his watchful eyes, casting about for something
to say to end the gripping awareness they suddenly felt with
each other.

She looked up. He studied her as steadily as before, his jaw
resting on one hand, the index finger along his cheek. Was that
how he used to look at Melinda?

"It's late," she noted quietly.

"Oh . . . yes, I suppose it is."

He made fists, stretched them out at shoulder level, quivering
and bowing backward against the chair.

"I'd best get upstairs." But instead she remained, bewitched
by the sight of his flexed muscles, the fists bunched beside his
ears, his trunk twisting while the chair went back on two legs.
It was a heavenly spectacle.

The stretch ended.

She dropped an elbow to the table and propped her chin
on a palm. "We worked a long time. I didn't mean to wear
you out."

He grinned lazily. "I never knew going to school would be
such fun."

"It's not always. I can be an old witch when I want to."

"That's not what Kristian says."

Her eyelids drooped with veiled curiosity. "Oh? And do you
spend time talking to Kristian about me?"

"He's my son. It's my job to know what goes on down at
school." She picked up a pencil and began absently fanning it
across the tablet, sketching arc after arc.

"Oh."

Eyes locked with hers, Theodore set the chair rocking . . . backward . . . forward . . . backward . . .

The house, cozy, silent, wrapped them in privacy, making them seem the only two in the world. She hooked the nail of a little finger into the corner of her mouth, lifting and misshaping her lip in an unconsciously sensual fashion while studying him: white underwear beneath red plaid shirt, both opened at the throat, exposing a wisp of dark curling hair; six inches of underwear showing at the wrist beneath the rolled-up cuffs of red plaid; thumbs hooked behind brass suspender clips, black trousers hugging spread thighs that straddled the chair; the shadows of his eyelashes throwing darker shadows upon his upper lids as he watched her unflinchingly, continuing the mesmerizing rocking motion.

When he spoke, his voice was no louder than the creaking of his chair. "Kristian says you're the best teacher he's ever had. After tonight, I can believe him."

Something singular was happening here. She felt it in her vitals. The spark of a change in him, a change she liked immensely.

Quietly, she spoke. "Thank you, Teddy."

His chair stopped rocking. His lips opened slightly. Her pencil stopped fanning. "Is there something wrong with my calling you that?" she inquired innocently.

"I . . . I don't know."

"Everybody else does. Would you prefer I stick to Theodore?"

He carefully lowered the chair to all fours. "Suit yourself," he offered, not unkindly, but breaking the spell nevertheless. He reached for the papers and began shuffling them together.

Disappointment pressed heavily on Linnea's chest. "Here, I'll take care of those." She took the papers from his hands.

He got to his feet and pushed his chair in, then watched her tap the sheets into a neat stack. Tempted to touch. Tempted to end the evening the way they both wanted it to end. Instead, he turned and crossed the kitchen, lifted a stove lid, and slid in a scoop of coal. He heard her cross behind him and pause at the upstairs doorway. "Well, good night, Theodore." Her voice held the faintest tremble, and a touch of disappointment.

He clinked the lid back on the stove and swallowed thickly, wondering if he could handle turning around and looking at her and still stay levelheaded. In that moment it seemed he had to prove to both of them he could. He slipped both hands into his hip pockets and faced her, wiping all but a brotherly look from his countenance.

She held the papers in one hand, pressed against her ribs, the tiny watch peeking from above them on the fullness of her breast. He knew beyond a doubt that if he took a single step toward her those papers would go scattering to the floor and her watch would be ticking against his chest.

Their eyes clung while the decision hung in the balance.

"Good night," Theodore managed.

Her face became a curious mixture of disappointment and hope. "Should we do the second half of the alphabet tomorrow night?"

He nodded.

"And I'll think up some good funny ones that'll be easy for you to remember."

He nodded again, digging his fingers into his buttocks, thinking, Git upstairs, girl, go on!

"Well . . . " She waggled two fingers, but they fluttered to a stop. "Good night."

"Good night."

She turned and fled. Behind her, Theodore released a rush of breath, his shoulders sagged, and his eyes closed.

In the days that followed, Linnea found herself kissing things. The most curious things. Mirrors. The back of her own hand. Icy window panes.

One day little Roseanne caught her at it. Returning to school to get the lunch bucket she'd forgotten, Roseanne asked from the back of the room, "What you doin', Mith Brandonberg?"

Linnea spun around, leaving two damp lip marks on the blackboard. "Oh, Roseanne!" She pressed a hand to her heart. "Gracious, child, you scared me half to death."

"What were you doin'?" Roseanne persisted.

"Trying to get a thick chalk mark off, that's all. Really, though, it isn't a very sanitary way. You must never lick the blackboard. Promise? It's just so icy outside I didn't want to go out to the pump and wet a rag to wash it off."

"You mean you was gonna lick off the whole thing?" Roseanne screwed up her face in disgust.

Linnea tilted back, laughing. "No, not the whole thing. Now, you'd better get what you forgot and scoot. The others will be waiting for you."

After that Linnea worked harder at controlling her impulse to drift into fantasies of Theodore. At home the lessons continued, but the mood remained light and often comical: as long as they were laughing they were safe.

She taught him to recite the alphabet by teaching him a simple song she used with her first graders, sung to the tune of "Twinkle Twinkle, Little Star."

> *A, B, C, D, E, F, Geee . . .*
> *H, I, J, K, L-M-N-O-Peee . . .*
> *Q, R, S, and T, U, Vee . . .*
> *Double-ewe, and X, Y, Zee . . .*
> *Now I've learned my ABCs,*
> *Tell me what you think of me.*

"You expect me to *sing* that!" he balked.

"Well, of course. It's the easiest way to learn the letters."

By now she'd grown accustomed to his tilting the chair back on two legs and could read his every mood. This one was stubborn. His crossed arms were lashed around his chest. His brow puckered obstinately.

"Not on your life."

"You know what I do to my students when they cross me?"

"I'm thirty-four years old, for cryin' out loud!"

She smirked. "Never too old to learn."

The look he gave her could have singed hair at thirty feet.

She got him to sing it once, but never again, because Kristian made the mistake of snickering. But she suspected Theodore practiced it when he was alone in the tack room or working around the place, for once she came upon him in the kitchen, regluing the sole on one of Kristian's boots and whistling "Twinkle Twinkle" softly between his teeth.

She stood behind him, smiling, listening.

When he heard her humming along softly with him, the whistling stopped. He turned around to find her with her hands clasped behind her back, picking up where he'd left off. In a very soft, very teasing voice she sang, "Now I've learned my ABCs, tell me what you think of me."

He scowled and pointed the toe of Kristian's boot at her nose. "What I think is that you'd better watch yourself, missy, or—"

"Tut! Tut!" She pointed back at him warningly.

He backtracked. "I think you'd better watch yourself, *Linnea,* or you're going to lose your only thirty-four-year-old first grader!"

The lessons progressed rapidly. Theodore was a very fast learner. He grasped concepts quickly. Having marvelous recall, he scarcely had to be told things twice. Possessed of a desire to learn, he worked hard. Blessed with natural curiosity, he asked innumerable questions and recorded their answers carefully in his brain.

In no time at all he had memorized all the single consonants, so they moved on to combinations such as *ch* and *sh,* and began working with vowel sounds. Then came the first simple words, and once taught, they were rarely forgotten. Within two weeks he was writing and deciphering simple sentences. The first was, *The cat is mine.* Then, *The book is red.* And, *The man was tall.*

She taught him his name. Thus came the first personal sentence: *Theodore is tall.*

The night he wrote it, she said apologetically, "I'm afraid we'll have to forgo the lessons for a while." At his look of consternation, she hurried on. "It's the school Christmas program. I have so much to do to prepare for it."

"Oh . . . well . . . that's all right." But she sensed his disappointment.

"We'll pick up again right after New Year's."

His head snapped up, his face blank. "New Year's? But that's three weeks."

"I'm going home for the holidays."

His lips slowly formed a silent oh while he nodded. But the nod echoed his disappointment at the news. He ran a hand down the back of his head and studied his lap. "Well,

I've been thirty-four years learning to read, what's a few more weeks?"

But it wasn't the lessons he was thinking of, it was Christmas without her. Odd, how lonely it suddenly sounded.

"I can bring a reader and speller home for you to keep during Christmas vacation, and Kristian can teach you some new words. Then when I get back, you can surprise me."

"Sure," he said, but his voice was curiously lackluster.

She got up and began clearing the table. He did the same. When she'd pushed her chair under the table, she stood with her hands resting on its back. Her voice came quietly. "Teddy?"

"Hmm?" He looked up distractedly.

"I'll need a favor."

"I'm not paying you for the lessons. I owe you more than one favor."

"A ride into town to catch the train."

The picture of her leaving on the train seemed to drain all the joy out of Christmas.

"When you planning to leave?"

"The Saturday before Christmas."

"Saturday . . . well . . . " All was quiet for some time, then Theodore remarked, "You never said you were going home for Christmas."

"I assumed you knew."

"You don't talk about your family much. You miss them?"

"Yes."

He nodded. "Christmas'll be here at our house this year."

"Yes, I know." She gave a wisp of a smile. "I found out the night of the heart stew, remember?"

"Oh, that's right."

He looked at his feet. She looked at the way he hooked his thumbs into his side pockets, his fingers tapping restlessly against his hips. It was bedtime. The same thing seemed to happen every night at bedtime. After a pleasant two hours of lighthearted study, the minute they got to their feet their talk grew stilted, then fell away entirely. She searched for a way to tell him she'd miss him, too, over the holidays.

"I wish a person could be in two places at once."

He forced a laugh, but its melancholy note made her heart trip faster. So many times she thought he was about to voice his feelings for her, but he always backed off. Linnea's own feelings were running stronger by the day, yet she was helpless to force him to make the first move. And until he did, she could only wait and wish.

"You seem very sad all of a sudden. Is something wrong?" she asked, hoping he'd offer her the consolation of admitting he'd miss her.

But he only drew in a quick sigh and answered, "I'm tired tonight, that's all. We worked a little later than usual."

She studied his downcast face, wondering what it was that kept him from displaying his feelings. Was it shyness? Didn't he like her as much as she thought? Or was it that damnable difference in their ages? Whatever the reason, he was caught in its clutches. It seemed she might wait fruitlessly if something wasn't done to prod him.

She reached out and touched his forearm. His chin lifted and his eyes took on a dark, probing intensity. Beneath the sleeve of his underwear the muscles tensed. A pulse raced in her throat as she declared simply, "I'll miss you, Theodore."

His lips parted, but no words came out.

Her fingers tightened. "Say it," she requested softly. "Why are you afraid?"

"Aren't you?"

"Oh, no," she breathed, lifting her eyes to his hair, his brow, returning to his familiar, stubborn, confused brown eyes. "Never. Not of this."

"And if I say it, then what?"

"I don't know. I only know I'm not afraid like you are." She watched him hover, considering the options, the probable outcomes.

"You teach children arithmetic. Maybe you should try doing a little yourself. Like subtracting eighteen from thirty-four." His hand closed over her wrist and placed it at her side. "I want you to stop looking at me that way, you hear? Cause if you don't, these lessons are gonna stop permanently. Now go up to bed, Linnea." Her troubled eyes clung to his. Her heart clamored at the sound of her name falling softly from his lips.

"Theodore, I—"

"Just go," he interrupted with throaty urgency. "Please."

"But you—"

"Go!" he barked, thrusting her away, pointing to the stairway. Even before she obeyed, tears stung her eyes. She wanted to run not from him, but to him. But if she was miserable, she had one consolation.

So was he.

16

AS WINTER NEARED her solstice, the weather grew bitterly cold. Linnea's morning treks to school seemed to grow longer and longer and start earlier and earlier. Trudging down the road in the murky, predawn hours, with her breath hanging frozen in the cold-white light of the setting moon and the snow cracking beneath her feet like breaking bones, it seemed the fields had never worn their coats of gold, nor the cottonwoods their capes of green.

At school, the morning chores were the worst part of her day. The wind whipped around the coal shed, lifting the ground snow into a swirling funnel. Inside, the little lean-to was dark and icy, the sound of the coal chilling as it rattled into the tin hod from her shovel. The schoolroom itself was cheerless. The stove lids rang eerily as she removed them to lay the fire. Shivering and hunching before the crackling kindling, it seemed the room would never warm.

If there was fresh or drifted snow, she had to shovel the steps and the path to the outhouses. Then she shuddered over the worst chore of all: getting the day's water in. Even through thick wool mittens the pump handle numbed her fingers, and sometimes, while transferring the water to the crock, she got her fingers wet. One morning she froze her little finger, and it hurt for the rest of the week. After that, it seemed more vulnerable to the cold than the rest of her body.

It was on a particularly bitter morning while pumping water that she had the idea about the soup: if the boys could cook rabbits, why couldn't the girls cook soup?

When she presented them with the idea, it caught on immediately, not only with the girls, but with the boys, too. So Fridays became soup days. They agreed to work by fours, two older ones and two younger ones, taking turns getting recipes from their mothers, bringing ingredients from home—beef bones, potatoes, rutabagas, carrots. In the process of the soup-making the children learned planning, cooperation, and execution. Linnea often smiled as she watched the younger ones plying a paring knife for the first time under the tutelage of an older student. And for their efforts they were given a grade. But the biggest bonus was the soup itself.

During those cold December days nothing smelled better or tasted more delicious than Friday's soup.

The work began in earnest on the Christmas play, both at home and in school. Everyone at P.S. 28 looked forward to that most special Friday of all, the last one before Christmas vacation.

Linnea prevailed upon Kristian to help her make a rough wooden cradle for the manger scene and begged Nissa's help in creating costumes for those who lacked enough originality or materials to make their own. At school the children worked on a backdrop made of a cast-off sheet with the Christmas star, palm trees, and desert dunes drawn upon it in colored chalk. Those with more artistic ability cut out cardboard sheep and camels and drew in their features.

Frances wore a smile from day's beginning to day's end: she was going to be an angel. Linnea chose Kristian to be Joseph—after all, she told the others, he had turned seventeen in November and was now the oldest boy in the school. Patricia Lommen, with her long, dark hair would make the perfect Mary.

Linnea's plea for musical instruments turned up nothing more than one accordion. When she asked for a volunteer to play it, the only one who raised his hand was Skipp. The best he could do was pick out the tune to "Silent Night" with a single finger.

A note went home with each student asking for a Christmas tree. Shortly after four the next afternoon the children were all gone and Linnea was writing the program of Christmas songs on the blackboard, when a shy knock sounded on the door. John's head appeared, wearing a red and black plaid cap with ear flaps.

"John! Well, hello!"

He doffed the cap and hovered half in the cloakroom half in the schoolroom. "H'lo, Miss Linnea."

She stepped down from the platform and briskly crossed the room with a pleased smile. "Well, this is a surprise."

"Heard you needed a Christmas tree."

"Word travels fast."

"Kristian, he told me."

Suddenly she caught a whiff of evergreen. "Oh, John, you've brought one?" Her eyes shone with excitement as she reached the door and opened it wider. With a dip of the knees and a single clap she exclaimed, "Oh, you have! Well, bring it in here, it's cold out there!" She nudged him inside and the tree along with him. Quickly slamming the door, she whirled to examine the tree, clapped once more, then impetuously raised up on tiptoe to peck John on the cheek. "Oh, thank you, John. It's a beauty."

John turned plum red, shuffled his feet, and tapped his cap against his thigh. "Shucks, no, it ain't, but it's the best I could do. Kinda scraggly on that there side, but I figgered you could turn that to the wall."

She made a full circle around the tree. "It is *too* a beauty!" she scolded cheerfully. "Or it will be by the time the children get the decorations on it tomorrow. And the smell!" She leaned close and sniffed. "Isn't it glorious, John?"

He watched her dance around all giddylike, looking as pretty as a brand-new china doll and wondered why Teddy didn't snap her up and marry her. She'd make a man a mighty fetching little wife, and it was plain as the nose on his face she had eyes for Teddy. You'd think Teddy'd see that.

"Sure is, Miss Linnea. Ain't nothin' smells prettier than a pine fresh brung in."

Gaily, she whirled off toward the front of the room. "Where should we put it, John? In this corner, or that one? Look, didn't the children do a wonderful job painting the Bethlehem star?"

John perused the star, the palm trees, the sheep, and gave two bearlike nods. "It's pretty, all right. You want I should bring the tree up there?"

"Yes, right here, on the left, I think." Suddenly she twirled to face him, wearing a look of dismay. "But what'll we put it in?"

John leaned it in a front corner and lumbered back toward the door. "Never you worry, I got the stuff to make a stand. It's out in the wagon."

He returned with hammer, saw, and wood, and set to work. Looking on, she observed, "I swear, you Westgaards can fix anything, can't you?"

On one knee, sawing over the edge of the desk platform, he answered, "Pretty 'bout."

John was one person whose grammar she never corrected. She enjoyed it just as it was.

"Theodore fixes everything from shoes to harnesses."

"Teddy's a smart one, all right."

"But he has a terrible temper, doesn't he?"

John looked up blankly. "He does?"

Surprised, she shrugged. "Well, I always thought so."

John scratched his head, then righted his cap. "Teddy, he never gets mad at me. Not even when I'm slow." He paused, thinking for a full ten seconds before adding, "And I'm pretty slow." He studied the saw blade a long moment, then leaned back into the work at his usual plodding pace. Watching, she felt a warm, sympathetic spot in her heart, different from the warm spot reserved for Theodore, but every bit as full. She had never before realized that John knew he was slower than most, or that it must bother him. She could sense in him the quiet love he felt for his brother, and because Theodore was patient with John, she suddenly had even more reason to love him.

"You're not slow, John, you're only . . . unrushed. There's a big difference."

He looked up, the wool flaps of his cap sticking out like broken wings above his ears, their wrinkled black ties dangling below. He swallowed and his raw-boned cheeks took on color. The expression on his face said her words had made him happier than any gift she might have wrapped and left beneath a tree.

"Will you be coming to the Christmas program, John?"

"Me? Sure thing, Miss Linnea. Never missed it since Kristian's been in it."

"And . . . and Theodore, too?"

"Teddy? Why, he wouldn't dream of missin' it. We'll all be here, don't you worry."

The night of the big event they were all there, just as John had promised. Not only her own "family," but the families of all her students. The schoolroom was filled to capacity. Even the recitation benches from up front and the boot-changing benches from the cloakroom were pressed into service to seat the crowd.

Linnea's stomach had butterflies.

The "curtain"—two sheets confiscated from Nissa's bureau drawer—was strung across the front of the stage and behind it Frances Westgaard's face beamed as brightly as her tinsel halo as she stood in a long white angel costume with her bright hair flowing past her shoulder blades. Little Roseanne began crying because she'd misplaced her halo. Norna was dispatched to find it, but just when that problem was solved Sonny stepped on the backdrop and jerked it from its string line above. Linnea's face fell, but Kristian lifted Sonny bodily, set him to one side, and reached up easily to secure the clothespins once again. From out front came the smell of coffee brewing on the stove, and hot chocolate heating. Linnea peeked between the sheets and felt all the trepidation of a stage director on opening night. Nissa and Hilda Knutson were setting out cups and arranging cookies and nut breads on a table. The younger brothers and sisters of her students were climbing on their mothers' laps, agitating for the program to begin. And there was Superintendent Dahl! And the lady beside him had to be his wife. Linnea found Theodore and her heart skipped. There was no denying, she wanted everything to go smoothly not only for the children's sake but to prove herself in his eyes.

Bent Linder tugged her skirt. "I can't get my head thing on right, Miss Brandonberg."

She leaned to take the red farmer hanky from Bent and twist it into a rope, then secure it around the white dishtowel on his head. After checking to make sure he had his sprig of "myrrh," she stood him in place.

"Shh!"

It was time to begin.

The program went off without a hitch, but through it all, Linnea clutched her fingers and waited for someone to forget their lines and start crying. Or for the shaky cradle to collapse, or for somebody to step on the backdrop again and send it to the floor. But they were flawless, her children. And when the last stroke of applause died and she stepped before the curtain, Linnea's heart felt filled to bursting.

"I want to thank you all for coming tonight, and for helping at home with the costumes and the cookies. It's hard to say who's been more excited about tonight, the children or I." She realized she was still clutching her hands. Glancing down, she separated them and gave them a nervous flip. The audience laughed. She picked out Mr. and Mrs. Dahl. "We're honored to have Superintendent Dahl and his wife with us tonight— an unexpected surprise. Thank you so much for coming." Her eyes sought out John. "A special thanks to John Westgaard for providing us with our Christmas tree this year, and for delivering it and building the stand." She gave him a warm smile; he hung his head and blushed a holly-berry red. "John, thank you."

Her gaze moved past the spot where Theodore had been sitting, backtracked at finding him gone, then moved on to Nissa. "And to Nissa Westgaard for letting me raid her linen supplies. And for putting up with me when any less patient person would have told me to quit bothering her and find my own costumes.

"I want to take this opportunity to wish each and every one of you a blessed Christmas. I'll be leaving in the morning to spend Christmas with my family in Fargo, so I won't be seeing you in church. But Merry Christmas, one and all. Now, before we enjoy the treats you mothers have provided, let's give the children one more round of applause for a job beautifully done."

The sheets were drawn aside on cue and she stepped back, reached for the hands of those in the center of the line, and they all took a final bow.

When the performers and director lifted their heads again in unison, Linnea's mouth dropped open. Coming in the rear door was a robust red-cheeked Santa Claus with an enormous bag slung over his shoulder. Down each red pant leg ran a string of sleigh bells that sang out merrily as he moved.

"Wh . . . why . . . who in the world . . . " she breathed.

From behind the white beard and mustache came a deep, chortling voice. "Merrrrrry Christmas, everybody! Santa smelled coffee!"

The young children started whispering and giggling nervously. One of the pre-schoolers in the audience stuck his finger in his mouth and began to cry. Linnea had all she could do to keep from bursting out laughing. Why, Theodore Westgaard, you lovable sneak!

He closed the cloakroom door with more jingling of bells while from beside her came a murmur of awe. "It'th Thantaaaa!"

She leaned over to find Roseanne and Sonny with eyes like full moons. She nudged the two seven-year-olds gently. "Why don't you go invite him in?" she whispered. Then she turned to include all the small children in her suggestion. "Go on, make him feel welcome. Remember your manners."

It was quite a sight to watch the younger set shyly make their way to the rear of the schoolroom and reach for Santa's hand, then lead him to the front.

Tony rushed forward. "I'll get teacher's chair for you, Santa!"

As Santa stepped up onto the stage, a familiar brown eye gave Linnea a covert wink.

"Santa's been riding a long time. A little set-down'd feel mighty good." He lowered himself into the chair with a great show of breathlessness, bending over his enormous belly and bracing his knees as he plopped back, letting the top of his bag fall over one thigh. The eye of every believer in the room followed it excitedly.

He played the part to the hilt, inquiring archly how many of them had been good little boys and girls. In the audience little sisters and brothers furtively sneaked from their mothers' laps and inched forward, drawn irresistibly. As the man in red reached for the drawstring bag, one voice piped up boldly, "I been good, Thanta!"

Roseanne.

All the adults tried to muffle their laughter, but Roseanne approached him confidently and stood in her angel gown, with her belly thrust out. "You have?" Santa exclaimed, then with exaggerated motions, lifted one hip and searched his pocket. "Well, now, let's see who we have here." He produced a long white paper, ran a finger down it, stopped momentarily to peer more closely at Roseanne's face from beneath bushy white eyebrows. She waited before him, composed, her adorable face drawn into a sober expression of respect. "Ahh, there it is. This must be Roseanne."

She laughed like a lilting songbird and turned to Skipp. "Thee? He knowth me!"

When she was perched on his knee, she peered inside the bag until her head got in Theodore's way, and everyone laughed again. Roseanne offered, "I can reach."

Linnea could tell Theodore was having trouble keeping a straight face. "Oh, well, you go ahead then." He held the sack open and Roseanne almost fell into it, leaning over and groping. She came up with a brown paper bag. On it a name was printed in black.

"Who's it for?" Theodore asked.

Roseanne studied the name, then shrugged and looked up angelically into his eyes. "I can't read yet."

"Oh, well, let Santa try." Theodore checked the name. "Says here Frances Westgaard."

"Theeth my cuzzint!" Roseanne exclaimed.

"She is! Well, what do you know about that."

Frances came forward to accept her bag, and Roseanne dipped in for another. There was one for each child in the room, even those not yet attending school. Each of the young ones sat on Santa's knee and was given his personal approval. Linnea watched one after the other dig into their gift bags and pull out rosy red apples, green popcorn balls, peanuts, and peppermint sticks. Someone—she realized, gratified—had done a lot of planning. And someone else—Linnea studied the Santa whose cheeks glowed red with rouge and whose eyes twinkled gaily as he doled out the sacks to the tiny tykes

on his knee—had done some extra studying to be able to
read all those names. Her eyes glowed with pride, not only
for Theodore who made such a marvelous Santa, but for the
older children who gamely played along. Even Allen Severt
accepted a gift, though he dragged his feet as he went to get
it. Linnea was watching him when she heard her name being
called and looked up in surprise.

Her gaze met the familiar brown eyes beneath the bushy
white eyebrows. "Got one here says Miss Brandonberg on it,"
Theodore stated in a forced bass.

"For me?" She pressed her chest with her hands and chuckled nervously.

Santa glanced conspiratorially at the cherubic faces around
him. "I think Miss Brandonberg should come up here on
Santa's lap and tell him if she's been a good girl, don't you?"

"Yeah!" they all chorused, jumping and clapping. "Yeah!
Yeah!"

Before she could protest, Linnea found her hands captured. Resisting all the way, she was led toward the merrily
dancing eyes of Santa Westgaard. "Come on up here, Miss
Brandonberg." He patted his knee, snagged her hand, and
hauled her onto his lap while she blushed so brightly she
wished she could crawl into his sack and draw the string
over her head. "There now." Theodore bounced her a time
or two and the bells jingled. She lost her balance and grasped
his shoulder while his steadying hand stole to her waist. "Tell
me, young lady, have you been good?" The children howled
in laughter, joined by the adults.

She braved a look into his mischievous eyes. "Oh, the very
best."

He glanced at the children for confirmation. "Has she been
good?"

They nodded enthusiastically and Roseanne piped up, "Thee
let uth make thoop!"

"Thoop?" he repeated.

Everyone howled and Theodore's hand seemed to burn into
Linnea's waist.

"Then she should get her present. But first, Miss Brandonberg, give Santa a little kiss on the cheek."

She wanted to die of embarrassment, but she dutifully leaned over and pecked his warm cheek above the wiry whiskers that smelled strongly of mothballs. Under the guise of the kiss, she whispered, "I'll get you for this, Theodore."

When she pulled back he was handing her a rectangular brown package. His eyes glinted merrily and his lips looked rosy against the snowy beard and mustache. For a brief moment his hand squeezed her waist. Under cover of the noisy crowd he ordered, "Don't open it here."

He set her on her feet and the place broke into raucous applause as he grunted his way off the chair, took up the empty bag, then, escorted by the gleeful children, made his way to the door. There he paused, turned, gave them all a wave, and bellowed, "Merrrry Christmas!"

There was no doubt about it: his appearance had made the evening an unqualified success. Children and adults alike were in gay, laughing moods as refreshment time came. Moving through the guests, sharing hellos and holiday greetings, Linnea kept one eye on the door. She found Superintendent Dahl and put in a request for a soup kettle and a wooden clothes rack, but while she was explaining what she needed them for, Theodore reappeared and her words trailed away into silence. His eyes sought her out immediately and she felt as if they were the only two in the room. His cheeks were shiny and bright, chapped pink—Lord, had he washed at that icy well? His hair was inexpertly combed and there was a bit of straw on the shoulder of his jacket—and had he changed clothes out on a wagon? It struck her that there were qualities in Theodore she had scarcely tapped. Never before had she guessed how good he'd be with little children. He would be that way with their own, if only . . .

She blushed, turned away and took a bite of marzipan.

They met near the refreshment table some minutes later. She sensed him at her shoulder and gave a quick backward glance, then poured him a hot cup of coffee. In an undertone she teased, "Santa Claus had *lutefisk* on his breath." Turning, she offered him the cup. "A little something to cover it up, and to take the sting out of those icy cheeks."

He laughed softly, looking down at her. "Thank you, Miss Brandonberg." She wished no one else were in the room, that she could kiss more than his cheek, in more than gratitude. She wondered what was inside the brown package, and if he'd miss her after all while she was gone. But she couldn't stand here all night, riveting her attention solely on him. There were other guests.

"Don't mention it, Mr. Claus," she returned quietly, then reluctantly moved off to visit with someone else.

In the cloakroom Kristian and Ray were secreted in a corner, rehashing the Santa Claus scene and Miss Brandonberg's part in it when a feminine voice intruded, "Excuse me."

They both swung around to find Patricia Lommen behind them.

The two boys glanced at each other, then stared at her. She wore her auburn hair caught up at the top of her head in a wide red bow. Her dress was gray and red plaid with a high round collar, and for the play she had rouged her cheeks and darkened her eyebrows slightly.

"Could I talk to you alone for a minute, Kristian?"

Raymond said, "Well, I'll just go in and have some hot chocolate," and left the two of them alone.

Kristian stuffed his hands into his pockets and watched Patricia as she made sure the door was closed then crossed to his corner of the cloakroom. "I have a Christmas gift for you, Kristian." She brought it from behind her back—a balsam-green package with a dotted-swiss bow.

"F . . . for me?"

"Yes." She looked up brightly.

"B . . . but why?"

She shrugged. "Does there have to be a reason?"

"Well . . . gosh, I . . . gee . . . for me?" He accepted the gift, gawking at it self-consciously. As he took the delicate box he became aware of how ridiculously big his hands seemed to have grown this last year, with knuckles the size of baseballs.

He looked up to find her staring into his eyes, and his heart lurched into a queer, dancing beat. He'd been noticing things about her lately—how good she was with the younger children while directing the Thanksgiving play; what a perfect madonna she made, standing on the other side of the cradle in the manger scene; how her pretty brown eyes tilted up at the corners and had thick, black lashes; how her hair was always washed and curled and her nails neatly trimmed. And she'd developed breasts the size of wild plums.

"I don't . . . " He tried to speak, but his voice croaked like a bullfrog at mating time. He tried again and managed in a soft, throaty voice, "I don't have anything for you, though."

"That's all right. Mine isn't much. Just something I made."

"You *made* it?" He touched the bow, gulped, then looked up again and whispered reverently, "Gosh, thanks."

"You can't open it now. You have to wait till Christmas Eve."

Her mouth seemed to be smiling even though it wasn't really. A gush of rapture sluiced down his body. Oh, jiminy, were her lips ever pretty. The tip of her tongue came out to wet them and his heart slammed into double time. She stood before him straight and expectant, her chin tilted up slightly, her hands crossed behind her back. There was a look in her eyes he'd never seen in any girl's eyes before. It sent his heart knocking. His eyes dropped to her lips. He gulped, drew a deep breath for courage, and bent toward her an inch. Her eyelids fluttered and she held her breath. Kristian felt as if he were choking. They tipped closer . . . closer . . .

"Patricia, Ma wants you!"

The pair in the cloakroom leaped apart guiltily. Her brother stood in the open doorway, grinning. "Hey, what're you guys doin' out here?"

"None of your business, Paul Lommen, just go back and tell Ma I'll be there in a minute."

With a knowing leer, he disappeared inside.

Patricia stamped one foot. "Oh, that dumb Paul! Why can't he mind his own business!"

"Maybe you'd better go in. It's awful chilly out here and you might catch a cold." He wondered how it would feel to reach out and rub her arms lightly, but the mood was shattered and he'd lost his courage. She hugged herself and he observed the lift of her breasts above her crossed arms. He looked into her eyes, thinking about braving it again. But before he could she answered.

"I guess so. Well, I'll see you at church, okay?"

"Yeah, sure." She turned away with ill-disguised reluctance.

"Patricia?" he called just before she opened the door.

"What?" She faced him eagerly.

He gulped and said the manly thing that had been on his mind ever since Christmas play rehearsals had started. "You made the prettiest madonna we ever had."

Her face broke into a radiant smile, then she opened the door and slipped inside.

When the schoolhouse lanterns had been doused and the door closed behind them, they all rode home together. Theodore and John sat up front on the cold, wooden seat; Nissa, Linnea, and Kristian in the back with a motley assortment of sheets, dishtowels, Nissa's soup kettle, tins of leftover *sanbakkels* and *krumkaka,* coffee cups, a bag of Christmas gifts Linnea had received from her students, and one Santa suit buried under the hay. Theodore had brought the buckboard tonight, its summer wheels replaced by wooden skids that squeaked upon the snow. The sleigh bells he'd worn on his legs were now strung around Cub's and Toots's necks and jangled rhythmically through the clear, star-studded night. The air was stingingly cold, cold enough to freeze the nostrils shut, but the group in the sled was in a spirited mood. Linnea had to endure a description of her blushing face while she was sitting on Santa's knee, and plenty of teasing about the entire charade. Theodore took his share of good-natured jest, too, and they all laughed about the fact that his beard smelled like mothballs. They rehashed Roseanne's remark about "thoop." They were still laughing when they dropped John at his house.

"We'll be by in the morning to pick you up on our way to town," Theodore reminded John as his brother stepped down from the wagon.

"Sure enough," John agreed as they said their good nights.

Linnea's heart fell. She'd hoped to be alone with Theodore on their ride into town, but it appeared he wasn't risking it. He could set her on his knee, squeeze her waist, and even let her kiss his cheek in front of the entire school population, but he took great care to keep her at arm's length when nobody was around. She realized the importance of traveling by twos out here in the winter and knew she shouldn't resent John's coming along to keep Theodore company on his way back, but when would she get a minute alone with Theodore before she left? It was really the only thing she wanted for Christmas.

At home, Theodore pulled up close to the back door and they all helped unload the wagon. She rehearsed the things she wanted to say to him if only she'd get the chance. But it was late, and when morning came there'd be chores, then breakfast with the entire family, then John beside them every minute.

Theodore came into the kitchen with a last armload and turned back toward the door to see to the horses. If she didn't act now, her chance would be lost.

"You two go on to bed," she advised Nissa and Kristian. "I want to talk to Theodore for a minute." And she followed him back outside.

He was already climbing onto the sleigh when she called, "Theodore, wait!"

He dropped his foot, turned, and asked, "What're you doing out here?" The way he was feeling, the last thing he needed was to be alone with her—tonight of all nights, when a two-week separation loomed like two years.

"I just wanted to talk to you for a minute."

He glanced surreptitiously toward the kitchen windows. "It's a little cold out here for talkin', isn't it?"

"This is nothing compared to pumping water at school in the morning." In Nissa's bedroom a lantern came on. "Let me come down to the barn with you."

Forever seemed to pass before he made his decision. "All right. Get in." He handed her up, followed, and sent the team plodding slowly along. In the milky moonlight the windmill stood tall and dark, casting a long, trellised shadow across the face of the snow. The outbuildings were black shadows with glistening white caps. The skids squealed softly, the sleigh bells jingled, the horses' heads nodded to the rhythm.

"You made a wonderful Santa Claus."

"Thank you."

"I wanted to choke you."

He laughed. "I know."

"Why didn't you tell me?"

"And spoil the surprise?"

"Do you do it every year?"

"We pass it around. But it's got to be somebody without little ones, else they'd recognize their pa."

"And you did very well reading all those names off the sacks. How did you learn them all so fast?"

"Kristian helped me."

"*When?*" she asked, surprised.

"We did it in the tack room."

"Oh." She felt a little cheated, but insisted, "Promise me you'll keep on practicing hard while I'm gone?"

His only reply was a quick smile. He guided the sleigh beneath a lean-to roof behind a granary. It was suddenly very dark with the moonlight cut off, but the horses pulled through the blackness and stood again with the white rays falling on their backs. Theodore hopped over his side, and Linnea followed suit. He moved around the horses, disconnecting them from the whiffletree, and she helped him spread a crackling canvas tarp over the sleigh.

"I'm surprised Roseanne didn't say you sounded just like her Uncle Teddy."

He chuckled. "So am I. She's a smart little cookie, that one."

"I know. And one of my favorite pupils."

"Teachers aren't supposed to play favorites."

She let the silence hang poignantly for several seconds before replying softly, "I know. But we're only human, after all."

He straightened. All movement ceased. They stood on either side of the team, staring at each other in the thick shadows of the lean-to.

Think of something, Theodore warned himself, anything, or you'll end up kissing her again.

"So John brought you the Christmas tree."

"Yes. He's so thoughtful."

He moved to the horses and she followed at his shoulder as he drove them toward the barn. Even in the sharp, fresh air she smelled like almonds. He was getting to like the smell altogether too much.

"He's smitten with you, you know."

"John! Oh, for heaven's sake, where did you get that preposterous idea?"

"John never took a Christmas tree to any of our men teachers."

"Maybe they didn't send out a plea for one."

Theodore chuckled sardonically and ordered, "Open the doors."

She folded back the big double doors, then closed them when he'd driven the team inside. Just as the latch clicked, a lantern flared and Theodore hung it overhead, then concentrated on removing the harnesses from Cub and Toots and turning them into their stalls. She was right on his heels.

"Theodore, I don't know where you get these ideas, but they're just not true."

"Then there was Rusty Bonner and Bill. Yup, you sure do collect 'em, Miss Brandonberg, don't you?" Nonchalantly he reached overhead for the lantern and took it away.

"Rusty Bonner!" she yelped. "He was a . . . a . . . Theodore, come back here! Where are you going?"

The lanternlight disappeared into the tack room, leaving her in near darkness. She stalked after him, with her fists on her hips. Did the infernal man always have to pick a fight with her when she wanted just the opposite?

"I don't *collect* them, as you put it, and I resent your implying that I do!"

He hung up the collars, looped the lines in neat circles, then turned with a leather bell strap in his hands. "And what about in Fargo? You got some more you're collectin' over there?" He stood with feet spread wide, knees locked, the string of sleigh bells doubled over his palm.

"There is nobody in Fargo. Nobody!" she declared vehemently.

With a sideward toss he threw the bells onto the workbench. They made a muffled *ching* before the room fell silent. Theodore rammed his fists into his pockets.

"Then who is Lawrence?" he demanded.

Linnea's belligerence abruptly disappeared.

"L . . . Lawrence?"

"Yes, Lawrence."

Her cheeks grew blotchy pink, then deepened to an all-over heliotrope. Her eyes rounded and her lips parted uncertainly.

"How do you know about Lawrence?" she finally managed in a choked whisper.

"I heard you talking to him one day."

She absolutely wished she could die. How long had it been since she'd fantasized about Lawrence? Why, she'd practically forgotten he'd ever existed. Now when she kissed windows and blackboards and her pillow, it was Theodore she kissed, not Lawrence! But how could she explain such childishness to a man who already considered her far too much of a child?

"Lawrence is none of your business."

"Fine," he snapped and turned away, taking a rag to a bell strap and rubbing it punishingly.

"Unless, of course, you're jealous."

He reared back and barked at the ceiling, "Hah!"

She stomped to within a foot of his back, wishing she could whap him a good one and knock some sense into his head. Lord, but he was such a chicken!

"All right, if you're not jealous, then why did you bring him up . . . and Rusty . . . *and* Bill?"

He flung down the bells and swung on her. "What would a man of my age be doing getting jealous over a . . . a whelp like you?"

"Whelp?" she shrieked. "Whelp!"

"Exactly!" His hand lashed out and turned down one of her ears. "Why lookit there, just like I thought, still wet back there!"

She twisted free, hauled off, and kicked him a doozy in the shin.

"I hate you, Theodore Westgaard! You big lily-livered chicken! I never saw a man so scared of a girl in my life." She was so angry tears stung her eyes and her breath lost control. "And furthermore, I c . . . came out here to thank you f . . . for the Christmas present and you . . . you . . . sp . . . spoil it all by p . . . picking a fight!" To Linnea's horror, she burst into tears.

Theodore cursed and grabbed his bruised leg as she whirled and ran from the barn.

Utterly miserable, he breathed a sigh of relief. What else was he supposed to do except pick a fight when she came following him with those big blue eyes all wide and pretty and tempting him to do things no honorable man would think of doing with a girl barely out of normal school?

He sank to his chair, dropping his face into his hands. Lord God, he loved her. What a fine mess. Old enough to be her father, and here he sat, trembling in a tack room like some boy whose voice was just changing. He hadn't meant to make her cry—God no, not cry. The sight of those tears had made him want to grab her close and apologize and tell her he hadn't meant a word of it.

But what about Lawrence? Who was he? What was he to her? Most certainly someone she'd left behind, judging from her reaction when his name was mentioned. Someone who made her blush like summer sunset and argue hotly that he was nobody. But no girl got that upset about a man unless he was *somebody*.

Theodore puttered around the tack room until he was certain she was safely in bed. Wretched, he wiped off the harnesses and the strands of bells.

He thought of her returning to her gay life in the city with all its conveniences and old friendships, comparing some young buck eighteen or twenty years old to an old cuss like himself. At length he stretched and sighed, feeling each and every one of his thirty-four years in the heaviness of his heart and the stiffness of his bones.

Let her go and make comparisons, he decided sadly. It's best for all concerned.

In the morning neither of them spoke during breakfast. Nor on the ride to John's house. Nor on the long ride to town. The sun beat down blindingly upon the glittering snow. The sleigh bells had been left in the tack room, and the horses seemed less spirited without them. As if he sensed the strain, John, too, remained silent.

At the train depot, both men accompanied Linnea inside, and when she made a move toward the barred window, Theodore unexpectedly clasped her elbow.

"I'll get it. Wait here with John."

She went into the ladies' room and replaced her scarf with her bird-wing hat, and upon returning to the waiting room, studied Theodore's broad shoulders and the upturned collar of his heavy wool jacket. Within her was a hollow space where her holiday spirit had been the night before. A single word from him would revive that spirit and take away this terrible urge to cry again. But he turned and handed her the ticket without so much as meeting her glance. John picked up her suitcase and they moved toward the long wooden waiting bench with its thirteen matched armrests. She sat, flanked by the two men. Her elbow bumped Theodore's and he quickly pulled away.

Somewhere in the station a pendulum clock ticked, but other than that it was dreadfully silent.

"Something wrong, Miss Linnea?" John asked.

She felt as if she'd swallowed a popcorn ball. The tears were very close to showing.

"No, John, nothing. I'm just a little tired, that's all. It was a big week at school, and we got home late last night."

Again they sat in silence. Askance, she saw Theodore's jaw working, the muscles clenched so tightly they protruded. His fingers were clasped over his stomach, the thumbs circling each other nervously.

"She'll be in any minute," the station agent announced, and they went outside to wait on the platform.

Theodore scowled up the tracks. The train bleated in the distance—once, twice.

Linnea reached to take her suitcase from John's hand and saw that his eyes were very troubled in his long, sad face. The tears were glistening in her eyes now—she couldn't help it. Impulsively she flung an arm around John and pressed her cold cheek to his. "Everything's okay, John, honest. I'm just going to miss you all so much. Thank you for the present. I'll open yours first." His arm tightened around her for a moment, and she kissed his cheek. "Merry Christmas, John."

"Same to you, missy," he returned with gruff emotion.

She turned diffidently to face Theodore. "Merry Christmas, Theodore," she said shakily, extending one gloved hand. "Thank you for the g . . . gift, too, it's p . . . packed in . . ." But as his hand came out slowly to clasp hers, she could continue no longer. His deep brown eyes, filled with unspoken misery, locked with hers. He squeezed her hand so hard, so long, it took an effort not to flinch. The tears splashed over her lashes and ran in silver streaks down her cheeks. He wanted to brush them away, but resisted. Her heart felt swollen and bruised, and it beat so heavily it seemed she felt the reverberations at the bottom of her boots.

Down the track to the west the train wailed into view beneath its bonnet of white steam.

Theodore swallowed.

Linnea gulped.

Suddenly he grabbed her wrist and yanked her after him so abruptly that she dropped her suitcase and her hat tipped sideways.

"Theodore, whatever—"

Across the platform and down the steps he strode, in footsteps so long it took two of Linnea's to make up one of his. His face was set and thunderous as he towed her along the tracks and around the end of the building. She had no choice but to stumble after him, breathless, holding her hat on with one hand. He hauled her between a baggage dray and the dun-colored depot wall, then swung her around without warning and scooped her into his arms, kissing her with a might and majesty rivaling that of the locomotive that came steaming past them at just that moment, drowning them in noise. His tongue swept into her mouth and his arms crushed her so tightly her back snapped. Desperately, wildly, he slanted his mouth over hers, clutching the back of her head and pressing her against the wall. The tears gushed down her cheeks, wetting his, too.

He lifted his head at last, his breath falling fast and hard on her face, his expression agonized.

His mouth moved.

"I love you," it said, but the train whistle blasted, covering the precious words she'd waited so long to hear.

"What?" she shouted.

"I love you!" he bawled in a hoarse, miserable voice. "I wanted to tell you last night."

"Why didn't you?"

They had to shout to be heard above the couplings clanging against each other as the train came to a stop. "I was scared, so I trumped up that nonsense about John and Rusty and Lawrence. Are you going to see him in Fargo?"

"No . . . no!" She wanted to cry and laugh at the same time.

"I'm sorry I made you cry."

"Oh, I'm just foolish . . . I . . . oh, Theodore—"

"*Boooooard!*" the conductor called from around the corner.

Theodore's mouth swooped down again, open and hungry, and this time she clutched him as desperately as he clutched her. Her hat was smashed under his left boot. A piece of siding on the depot wall creased the back of her head and the clip of her watch was stamping its shape into her left breast. But Theodore had said it at last!

As abruptly as he'd lunged, he pulled back, holding her face, searching her eyes with a harrowed look.

"Tell me."

"I love you, too, Teddy."

"I know. I've known for quite a while, but I don't know what we're going to do about it. I only know I've been miserable."

"Oh, Teddy, don't waste precious time. Kiss me again, please!"

This time it was sweet and yearning and filled with good-byes that were really hellos. Their hearts thrust mightily. Their bodies knew want. They tore their mouths apart long enough for her to cry, "I don't want to go."

"I don't want you to either," he returned, then impaled her mouth with his warm, wet tongue a last time.

John came barreling around the corner, yelling, "Are you crazy, you two? The train's leaving!"

Theodore twisted from her, pulling her practically off her feet as he headed for the moving train.

"My hat!"

"Leave it!"

They raced for the doorway of the silver car that was sliding away in a billow of steam, and at the last possible moment, Linnea caught the handrail and was lifted from behind and swung safely aboard.

She leaned out and waved, then threw two kisses to the receding figures with hands raised over their heads.

"Merry Christmas! Merry Christmas!"

It would be the happiest of her life. As she found her seat and fell back with her eyes closed, she wondered how she'd live through it.

17

LINNEA'S FATHER WAS waiting to greet her at the train station, smiling and robust. His hair was parted in the center and paralleled the sweeping line of his thick blond moustache. Wrapped in his strong arms, with her face pressed against his storm coat, she smelled the familiar bay rum on his jaw and felt tears spring to her eyes.

"Oh, Daddy."

"Dumpling."

She had worked so long and hard at acting grown up that it was an unexpected relief to be his child again.

"What's this? A tear?"

"I'm just so glad to see you." She kissed his jaw and held his elbow tightly as they went outside.

He had bought a brand-new Model T Ford touring car that nobody had told her about.

"What's *this*?" She stared at it, awestruck.

"A little surprise. Business has been booming."

"Y . . . you mean it's yours?"

"You betcha. Get in."

They drove down the streets of Fargo, startling horses, laughing, peering through the horizontal split in the windshield. It was thrilling, but at the same time the new automobile made Linnea feel she had been away for years instead of months.

It created an odd, sad feeling she tried her best to hide. She wanted to come home and find everything as she'd left it.

"Do you want to stop by the store on our way?" he asked.

The store, where she'd been her father's clerk ever since she was old enough to make change. The store, with its intermingled smells of coffee and sweeping compound and oranges. The store would be the same.

"Let's," she answered excitedly.

But there were changes at the store, too. From the front window James Montgomery Flagg's frowning Uncle Sam pointed a bony finger at Fargo's men, admonishing, "I want you for the U.S. Army." A scratchy radio—a new addition—sat on a shelf, transmitting the new George M. Cohan song, "Over There." Beside the counter sat a collection barrel for empty tin cans. On the counter stood a "Blot it out with Liberty Bonds" poster. And behind the counter stood a total stranger.

"Here she is, Adrian, home from Alamo. Linnea, I'd like you to meet Adrian Mitchell, the fellow who took your place as my right hand. Adrian, my daughter Linnea."

Resentment prickled even as Linnea shook hands across the counter. Mother had written that they'd hired a new "boy," and here he was, measuring six feet tall and wearing a natty plaid bow tie.

"Pleasure, Miss Brandonberg."

"Mr. Mitchell," she said politely.

"Adrian is a sophomore at the university this year. Putting himself through," announced her father with a discernible note of pride.

Adrian smiled at Linnea. "And I understand this is your first year out of normal school. How do you like teaching so far?"

While they chatted she noticed he had an innate sense of cordiality, the most perfect teeth she'd ever seen, and a face almost unfairly handsome. It only made her resent him further for usurping her place.

The stop at the store was brief. Before long they were in the Ford again, heading home.

"I thought you said you hired a new *boy*," Linnea commented dryly.

Her father only chuckled.

"Well, where did you find him?"

"Walked in one day and said he needed a job to put himself through college, and he promised to increase my business by five percent within the first six months or he'd refund half his salary, and damned if he hasn't done it in three!"

To Linnea's resentment was added a tinge of jealousy. More than ever, she wanted to get home where things would be just as when she'd left.

Her mother was preparing her old favorite, fricasseed chicken, and Linnea's heart swelled with gratitude. Upstairs, Carrie and Pudge had their bedroom all spic-and-span, but when Linnea came back down to the kitchen and asked where they were, her mother answered, "Oh, I'm afraid they're gone, but they'll be here in time for dinner."

"Gone?" repeated Linnea, disappointed. She'd expected them to rush her with a thousand questions displaying the same girlish awe they'd shown upon learning that their big sister was going out into the world.

"Their Girl Scout troop is cutting and stitching comfort bags for departing soldiers."

Comfort bags? Her baby sisters?

"So did you stop at the store?" her mother inquired.

"Yes, for a minute."

"Then you met Adrian."

"Yes."

"What did you think of him?"

Linnea threw a suspicious glance at her mother, but Judith was busily shaping dumplings, dropping them into the kettle.

"I was only there five minutes." *Don't even think it, Mother. He's not my type.*

Carrie and Pudge arrived in time for dinner, overjoyed to see their big sister, but breathless and gushing about their own activities, scarcely asking about Linnea's. During the meal Linnea learned that their scout troop had spent weeks collecting peach stones to be burned into charcoal for gas-mask filters and was now engaged in a campaign to solicit soap, needles, thread, and other necessities for filling the comfort bags. Carrie was all excited about the fact that each individual who filled a bag was allowed to include a name card. She was hoping to hear from the soldiers who received hers. They bubbled on

about the white elephants they were collecting for a rummage
sale their school was planning to earn the $125 they'd pledged
to the War Fund Drive.

Linnea was quite disconcerted. When she'd left home, the
girls were climbing trees and skinning knees. Carrie had been
clumsy. Now she wore a new willowy silhouette. Her honey-
colored hair touched her shoulders and her blue eyes would soon
start capturing the boys' attention. Pudge, too, had changed. Her
nickname scarcely fit anymore. She was thinning out and her
pigtails were gone, replaced by a fall of caramel-colored curls
held by a ribbon. When she talked about their Girl Scout work
her hazel eyes lit with excitement that gave Linnea a glimpse
of the pretty young lady she would soon become. How could
they have changed so much in four months?

Her mother's interests had changed, too. She was no longer
sitting home darning socks in her spare time. She was in charge
of the women's committee for the Belgian and Armenian Relief
Fund at church, working with the Supplementary Military Aid
committee to meet trains and provide meals for enlisted men
passing through the city on their way to army camps. She was
taking a Red Cross class to learn how to make surgical dress-
ings and spent two evenings each week at the public library
picking oakum.

"What's oakum?" Linnea asked, and they all looked at her
as if she'd spoken a profanity.

But that wasn't all. Her father had spent a day recently with
a group of citizens who'd laughingly dubbed themselves "The
Amalgamated Order of Wood Sawyers." A river-bottom wood
lot had been donated to the Red Cross by the Fargo Tile Company, and the men had spent the day felling the trees and
sawing them into cordwood. It was auctioned off and $2,264
was raised for the war effort.

Her father, sawing wood?

Christmas would be less lavish this year, he said, because
they were giving instead to the soldiers who needed so much
so badly.

It wasn't that Linnea needed a lavish Christmas. She simply
wanted things as they were. She had rather expected her return
to be the axis upon which her family revolved while she was
at home. Instead, their axis seemed to be the war effort.

That night, when she went to bed, she lay in the dark pondering her disappointment. Four months—not *even* four months, and it seemed she'd left no more vacancy in their lives than a cup of water drawn from a full barrel. Her emotions were in turmoil. She wanted nothing so badly as constancy from her family. But they were all so busy. So involved! She wanted to cry, but tears didn't come as easily as they had last summer, before she'd started her plunge into maturity.

At least the house hadn't changed. The bedroom she and her sisters shared was as bright and cheerful as ever with its flowery wallpaper and long double windows. When she got up in the mornings the floor wasn't icy beneath her feet, and she didn't have to walk down a snowy path to an outhouse, or bathe in a washbasin, or trudge a mile to school, or shovel coal, or build a fire or pump water.

But she missed it all terribly.

On Christmas Eve day her father asked her to come and help him at the store, as she used to. "So many of my customers ask about you; I know they'd love to see you. And I'd really appreciate the help today. It's going to be a race right up till closing."

"But you have the new boy."

"Adrian will be there, but there'll be enough business to keep us all busy. What do you say, dumpling?"

She couldn't resist her father when he called her the old pet name, and no matter how things had changed, she loved it at the store.

When they arrived Adrian was already there, dressed in natty collegiate clothes, sweeping snow off the front sidewalk.

"Good morning, Mr. Brandonberg!" he greeted, doffing a tweed golf-style cap, smiling at Linnea at the same time. "And Miss Brandonberg."

"Good morning, Adrian. I talked her into coming down and giving us a hand today."

"And we can certainly use it. Are you enjoying your vacation?"

Standing with his hands crossed on the broom handle, Adrian Mitchell chatted as amiably as if they were old friends. He had a wonderful smile, which he wore nearly all the time, and the kind of natural courtesy Linnea tried so hard to instill in her

boys at school. He doffed his hat to passersby and bid each
a pleasant good morning. When Linnea and her father moved
toward the front door, he opened it for them before returning
to his sweeping.

When he followed them inside minutes later, she watched
him move around the store. He hung his stylish coat and suit
jacket on a coat tree in the back, then donned a starched white
apron, whistling softly between his teeth as he doubled the ties
around the front and secured them in back. He moved with a
briskness and confidence that made him appear as much the
proprietor of the store as the proprietor himself. He sprinkled
sweeping compound on the floor and swept the whole place
without so much as a word from her father. When the job was
done and the pleasant oily smell clung to the air, he marched
to the double front doors, pulled up the green shades to the
tall windows, and turned over the OPEN sign.

The first customer was a little boy Linnea didn't recognize
who had been sent by his mother to pick up a last-minute
pound of lard. Before the boy left, Adrian dropped something
into his bag and said, "Now you give that to your mother,
Lonnie, okay?"

"What's he giving him?" Linnea whispered to her father.

"An egg separator. It was Adrian's idea, to give out some
small kitchen item as a gesture of goodwill during the holiday season. Shows the customers we appreciate their business."

She studied her father's profile as he beamed at Adrian.
Obviously the new employee was his golden boy.

The twinge of jealousy returned, but as the day progressed
she came to see why her father valued Adrian so immensely.
The customers loved him. He knew them all by name and
inquired after their families and asked if they knew Miss
Brandonberg was here today, back from school and in just
to say hello to all of them. As each customer left, he called,
"Merry Christmas."

He had a way about him, all right. There were times when
Linnea studied him covertly and wondered if it was phony. But
long before the end of the day she'd decided he was strictly
genuine, a natural-born businessman who loved people and
wasn't afraid to let it show.

When the store closed at four that afternoon, Linnea's father gave Adrian a ham as a Christmas gift. Adrian had something hidden in the back room—a long, tall box—which he gave to his boss before the two exchanged a fond handshake. Then he turned to Linnea with his radiantly handsome smile.

"Miss Brandonberg, I hope we'll meet again while you're home. As a matter of fact, if it's all right with your father, I'd like to stop by the house some evening and pay a call."

He turned to seek Selmer Brandonberg's approval, and before Linnea could object, her father answered, "Anytime, Adrian. You just let Mrs. Brandonberg know and she'll set an extra place at dinner."

"Thank you, sir. I'll do that." Turning to Linnea, he added, "One evening next week then, after the Christmas rush slows down."

She was quite flabbergasted. He was so straightforward and confident that he hadn't really given her a chance to decline before he bid them a last holiday wish and left. Linnea stood gaping at the swinging shade pulls on the windows.

"So what do you think of him?" her father asked.

Hands on hips, she affected a scolding pout. "And you told me you'd hired a new *boy*. Why, he's no more boy than you are."

Selmer slipped on his coat, cocked one eyebrow, and grinned. "I know." Buttoning his coat, he repeated, "I asked what you thought of him."

Linnea threw him an arch, amused glance. "He isn't running for Congress yet, is he?"

Selmer laughed. "No, but give him time. I'm sure he'll get around to it."

"My point exactly."

They eyed each other a few seconds, then burst out laughing. But as they were leaving the store, Linnea pressed a gloved hand to her father's lapel.

"He's handsome and dynamic and a real up-and-comer, and though at first I was frightfully jealous of him, I can see what an asset he is to you. But I'm not looking for a boyfriend, Daddy."

He patted her hand and steered her out the door. "Nonsense, dumpling. You said it first—Adrian's no boy."

Immediately upon reaching home, Linnea was asked three times, "What did you think of Adrian?"

It was obvious the entire family fancied themselves match-makers. They oohed and aahed upon discovering Adrian had given Selmer a bottle of fine Boston brandy, Selmer's favorite brand, but one he rarely bought because of its prohibitive price.

"Oh, Selmer," his wife crooned, "isn't that boy thoughtful? And while he's struggling to put himself through college yet."

Linnea had all she could do to keep from rolling her eyes. She wanted to tell them they were wasting their time trying to foist Adrian on her, because there was another man in her life.

She thought of Theodore and wondered what they'd say if she told them about him. Would they understand if she said that beneath his gruff exterior lay a man with deep vulnerabilities? That his greatest wish was to know how to read? That he defended his family, down to the last niece, with a quick, noble ferocity? That he could tease one moment and share a hymnal the next? That he grew heavyhearted when it was time to turn his horses loose for the winter?

But the fact remained that she had fallen in love with a thirty-four-year-old illiterate wheat farmer who wore bib overalls, still lived with his mother, and had a son nearly Linnea's age. How could she possibly make a man like that compare favorably to an enterprising twenty-one-year-old college student with brains, ambition, good looks, and charisma enough to charm the molars out of a mother's head?

Linnea was very much afraid she couldn't, and so she said nothing of Theodore Westgaard.

They opened gifts, and true to her word, Linnea chose John's first. She was truly touched by the hand-carved likeness of a cat with its paws curled beneath it, like the one she often saw sitting on his step. From Frances she received a homemade pin cushion fashioned from a puff of steel wool inside a piece of strawberry-colored velvet. Nissa's gift was a beautiful handcrocheted shawl of white wool shot with tiny threads of silver; Kristian's—she gasped—the most beautiful pair of mittens she'd ever seen in her life. They were made of mink, and when she slipped one on she realized she'd never felt anything as warm. The girls leaned over to have their cheeks stroked, and her mother tried one on, rubbed it on her neck, and cooed with delight.

"What a beautiful gift," Judith said, passing the mitten back. "How old did you say Kristian is?"

Linnea felt slightly uncomfortable and wondered if her cheeks were pink. "Seventeen."

Selmer and Judith Brandonberg exchanged meaningful glances. "Very thoughtful for a boy of seventeen," Judith added.

Linnea met her mother's eyes squarely, hoping to dispel the erroneous impression. "Kristian traps down on the creek bottom. That's how he got the mink."

"How resourceful." Her mother smiled, then pointed. "You have another gift left, dear. Who is it from?"

"Theodore." She had intentionally saved it for last. It was weighty, wrapped in the same brown paper as that in which the children's treats had been bagged. Caressingly, she ran a hand over it.

"Ah, yes, Kristian's father." Her mother's words brought Linnea from her reverie. She realized she'd been daydreaming while her whole family looked on. "Well, go ahead, open it!" demanded Pudge impatiently.

Removing the wrapping, Linnea remembered the teasing brown eyes of a Santa Claus as she'd sat on his lap, and the feeling of her lips against a firm rosy cheek above a scratchy white beard. And the whispered words, "Don't open it here." She wished, suddenly, that she were in a weather-beaten house on the snow-swept prairie at this moment.

It was a book of Tennyson's poems, beautifully bound in brown and gilt, with engravings of angelic beings in wispy gowns whose bare feet trailed in drifting roses.

On the endleaf, in ink, he had meticulously printed, "Merry Christmas, 1917. To Linnea Brandonberg from Theodore Westgaard. Some day I will know how to read all these too."

Linnea carefully hid her secret pleasure as she showed her family the beautiful book. "I'm teaching Theodore to read and write, but I didn't think he knew how to spell my name yet. Kristian must have helped him with the inscription." Her mother reached for the book, brushed her fingertips over the expensive gilt lettering on its cover, read the inscription, looked up at her daughter's wistful expression, and murmured, "How nice, dear."

Several times during Christmas dinner Judith glanced over to find Linnea staring into her plate with a faraway look in her eyes. It wasn't the first time she'd noticed it. There was an unusual reticence about Linnea since she'd been home, an occasional withdrawal totally unlike her.

Later that night, she asked Selmer, "Have you noticed anything different about Linnea since she's been home?"

"Different?"

"She's so . . . I don't know. Subdued. She just doesn't seem to be her old bubbly self."

"She's growing up, Judith. That was bound to happen, wasn't it? A young woman with adult responsibilities, off in the world away from her mother and father." He lifted his wife's chin and kissed her nose. "She can't stay our little girl forever, you know."

"No, I suppose not." Judith turned away and began undressing for bed. "Did she . . . well, did she say anything at the store today?"

"Say anything about what?"

"Not about what. About whom."

"About whom? Whom did you expect her to say something about?"

"That's the puzzling part. I'm not sure whether it's Kristian or . . . or his father."

"His father!" Selmer's fingers stopped freeing his shirt buttons.

"Well, did you see her face when she opened that book from him?"

"Judith, surely you're wrong."

"Let's hope so. Why, the man must be nearly forty years old!"

Selmer became visibly upset.

"Has she said anything to you?"

"No, but do you think she would, considering the man has a son almost as old as she is and she . . . she lives in his house?"

Selmer forced himself to calm down and took his wife by the arms. "Maybe we're wrong. She has a good head on her shoulders, and besides, she's always confided in you before.

And I haven't told you the good news. Adrian Mitchell asked my permission to pay a call on her sometime this week."

"He did?" Judith brightened. "Did he really?"

"How do you feel about throwing an extra carrot in the soup for our daughter's dinner guest?"

"Oh, Selmer, really?" Her eyes lit up like Christmas candles as she clasped his hands tightly. "Can you imagine the two of them together? He'd be absolutely perfect for her."

"But we have to be careful not to push too hard," he scolded gently. "You know how single-minded that girl can be when she thinks she's being coerced. Still, it wouldn't hurt to have him over maybe a couple times before she has to go back, then this summer when she comes home to stay—who knows?"

Judith spun away and began pacing, one hand on her waist, the other squeezing her lower lip. "Let's see . . . I'll fix something splendid—stuffed pork chops maybe, and mother's hazelnut torte. We'll use all the best china and . . . "

Judith was still matchmaking when Selmer drifted off to sleep.

Adrian came on Wednesday, thoughtfully bringing his hostess a round tin of parfait mints to serve with after-dinner coffee. He sat and visited in the front parlor with the whole family until after ten P.M., then wished Linnea a polite good night when Judith insisted she see him to the door.

He came again on Thursday, around seven P.M., visited with the family for half an hour, then suggested that he and Linnea go for a walk.

"Oh, I don't—"

"That's a wonderful idea," Judith cut in. "Goodness, dear, all you've done since you've been home is sit here cooped up with us old folks."

"Linnea?" Adrian asked quietly, and she was too kind to embarrass him by saying no.

They walked around the bandstand in the city park and talked about their families, their jobs, his school, her school, and what they'd received for Christmas. She slipped once, and he took her elbow and walked her back home through the softly falling snow, then turned her to face him on the front porch and gave her a soft kiss on the mouth.

She pulled back. "Don't, Adrian . . . please."

"And how else should I state my case?" he asked pleasantly, still holding her arms.

"You're a charming man and I . . . I like you . . . but . . . " Discomfited, she fell silent.

"But?" He tipped his head.

"But there's someone else back in Alamo."

"Ah." They were quiet a while. She studied his chest while he studied her face, then asked, "Is it serious?"

"I think so."

"Are you promised to him?"

She shook her head.

"Well, in that case, would there be any harm in your coming to a party with me on New Year's Eve?"

She looked up. "But I told you—"

"Yes, there's someone back in Alamo. And I'll respect that, but I'd like your company just the same. And I'll bet you don't have any other plans, do you?" He tipped her chin up with one finger. "Do you?"

Good heavens, there was no justice in the world when one man could be so handsome.

"No."

"It's just some of my friends who are all about our age. We're going to go ice-skating, then go back to one of the girl's houses for something to eat. I'll have you home by one o'clock. What do you say?"

It sounded fun, and it had been so long since she'd been with people her age. And if she didn't go with him, she'd probably usher the New Year in by lying in her bed wishing she'd said yes.

"No kissing at midnight?" she insisted.

He raised a palm, Boy Scout fashion. "Promise."

"And no laughing if I take a few spills on the ice?"

He laughed, flashing his dazzling white teeth. "Promise."

"All right. It's a date."

He brought her violets. Violets for a skating party! Where he managed to find them in the middle of winter in Fargo, North Dakota, remained a mystery, but they were the first flowers Linnea had ever received from a man, and as she accepted them she thought of Theodore and had a flash of guilt.

Adrian had borrowed his father's automobile for the evening, and getting into it with him redoubled her guilt, but as the night progressed, she found herself forgetting about Theodore and having a wonderful time.

They skated on the river, warmed themselves with hot apple cider, returned to the home of a girl named Virginia Colson and played parlor games, danced, and toasted the New Year with a light champagne punch. But—true to his word—Adrian remained the consummate gentleman all night long.

When he took her home she tried to make a quick getaway, but he walked her to the porch, captured both of her hands, leaned one shoulder against the porch wall, and studied her with disconcerting thoroughness. "You're the prettiest thing I've ever met, you know that?"

She dropped her gaze to his chest. "Adrian, I really should go in."

"And you're all the things that your father said you'd be. I'd seen your picture, of course—he's so proud of you. But when you came into the store that day and I saw you in person for the first time, I thought right off the bat, that girl's for me." He paused, squeezed her hands, and said more softly, "Come here, Linnea."

Startled, she lifted her head. "Adrian, you promised."

"I promised no kisses at the stroke of midnight. It's now quarter to one."

He slowly eased his shoulder away from the porch wall while it struck her afresh how nature had played favorites with him. He was almost unfairly handsome. And she had never met a man who smelled better, nor one more polite, charming, or winning. Her parents were smitten with him. They were going to be outraged when she told them about Theodore. Suppose . . . just suppose she kissed Adrian back and discovered it was as shattering as it had been with Theodore? All her worries would be over. . . .

His lips were soft and silky as they opened over hers. When his tongue slipped inside her mouth, hers hesitantly answered. When he wrapped her tightly in his arms, she let herself wilt against him. When his hands caressed her back, hers caressed his shoulders. But instead of her mind filling with skyrockets, she found herself analyzing the smell of his hair pomade and the starch his mother put in his collars. She let him have as long as he liked . . . waiting . . . waiting . . .

But nothing happened.

Nothing.

When Adrian lifted his head, his hands slipped discreetly to the sides of her breasts and he breathed on her lips, plucking at them gently—once, twice. "Linnea, darling girl," he whispered, "summer can't come fast enough."

But she knew that even in summer there would be no acceleration of her feelings for Adrian. If it were going to happen, it already would have.

Later, in bed, the guilt struck. She'd never kissed any man up until a couple months ago, and now she'd kissed four. She suspected all four really knew what they were doing, and wondered if kissing four men qualified her as a loose woman. She supposed it did, and that Theodore was too honorable to deserve a loose woman.

Yet her reaction to each had been decidedly different.

She shuddered at the thought of Rusty Bonner, so practiced in his approach. Rusty'd probably left a trail of bastard babies from the Rio Grande to the Canadian border! How naive she'd been. It was rather embarrassing to recall it now.

And Bill—every time she met up with him she thought of how he'd forced his knee between her legs, and got angry all over again.

And of course there was Adrian, perfect, flawless Adrian. She almost wished she'd felt that keen fire in her blood when he'd kissed her; it would have simplified everything. After all, he was the most logical choice.

Love, however, paid little heed to logic. And she loved Theodore. Only his kiss had the power to shake her to the soles of her feet, to make her feel right, and eager, as though their love had been destined. It mattered little his age, his illiteracy, his simple upbringing, the clothing he wore, or the fact that he'd been married before and had a son who was nearly Linnea's age.

What mattered was that he was honorable, and good, and at the thought of going home to him tomorrow her heart soared and her blood pounded.

* * *

In the morning she was packing to go when her mother came to the bedroom doorway, crossed her arms, and leaned against the door frame. The girls had gone off skating and the house was quiet.

"Linnea, I've been waiting for you to tell me about it ever since you've been home, but I guess if I don't ask, you won't say anything."

Linnea turned with a stack of freshly laundered underwear in her hands. "Tell you about what?"

"What's bothering you."

For a moment she considered a denial, then sank to the edge of the bed, staring morosely at the clothing on her lap. "How do you know when you're in love, Mother?" she asked plaintively.

"In love?" Judith straightened, then crossed the room to perch beside Linnea. She took her daughter's hand.

"With Adrian?" she asked hopefully.

Linnea only shook her bowed head disconsolately.

"With . . . with Kristian then?"

Again Linnea shook her head, then lifted it slowly to meet her mother's questioning eyes.

"Oh, dear . . . " Judith breathed, dropping Linnea's fingers and resting four of her own against her lips. "Not . . . not the father."

"Yes . . . and his name is Theodore."

Alarmed, Judith leaned forward to grasp Linnea's hand again. "But he's got to be—what?—thirty-some years old."

"Thirty-four."

"And he's been married."

"A long time ago."

"Oh, my child, don't be foolish. This can't be. How far has it gone?"

"It hasn't *gone* anywhere." Linnea jerked her hand away in irritation and rose to put the underwear in her suitcase. "He's fought it every inch of the way because he thinks I'm just a child."

Judith pressed her heart and exclaimed quietly, "Oh, thank goodness!"

Linnea swung around and flopped down dejectedly. "Mother, I'm so mixed up. I don't know what to do."

"Do? Well, for heaven's sake, child, put him out of your head. He's almost as old as your father! What you can *do* is continue to see Adrian Mitchell when you get back here next summer. He certainly seems interested enough." She stopped, beetled her brow, and inquired, "He is, isn't he?"

"I guess so." Linnea shrugged. "If kissing me means he's interested."

"He kissed you." Judith sounded pleased.

"Yes. And I think this was about as experienced as a kiss could get. I tried to put my heart into it—honest, Mother, I did—but nothing happened!"

Judith began to show renewed concern. "Nothing is *supposed* to happen till after you're married."

"Oh, yes it is. I mean, don't you ever watch Daddy just . . . well, just walk into a room, and your stomach goes all woozy and you feel like you're choking on your own spit?"

"Linnea!" Judith's eyes widened in shock.

"Well, don't you?"

Judith would have jumped from the bed, but Linnea detained her with a hand on her shoulder. "Oh, Mother," she went on urgently, "don't tell me it's not supposed to happen, because it does. Every time Teddy comes around a doorway. Every time I see him pulling the horses into the yard. It even happens when we're fighting!"

Befuddled, Judith only stared at her daughter and asked, "You . . . you fight with him?"

"Oh, we fight all the time." Linnea got up and resumed packing. "I think that for a long time he picked fights with me to keep himself from admitting how he felt about me. And because he knew I felt the same and it scared him to death. I told you, he thinks he's too old for me, of all the preposterous things."

Judith fought down the panic, got to her feet, and went to take her daughter by her shoulders. "He is, Linnea."

"He's not," the girl declared stubbornly.

"He has a son nearly your age. I was upset at the thought that it was the boy you had feelings for, but to even consider yourself in love with his *father!* Linnea, it's absurd."

Their troubled gazes locked. Then Linnea said quietly, "I think you just want me to end up falling in love with Adrian and marrying him. I really wish I could—I mean it, Mother. But I'd better warn you right now, I don't think it's going to happen, not judging by what happened when he kissed me last night. Or rather, what didn't happen."

"Puh!" Judith huffed, releasing her daughter's shoulders with a slight shove. "You've always been single-minded, and I suppose nothing I say is going to change that now. But you listen to me. . . . " She shook a finger beneath Linnea's nose. "That . . . that *man,* that . . . that . . . Theodore? At least he's got some common sense. He knows better than you that there are too many years difference between you, and you'd best accept the fact before this thing goes any further!"

But Judith Brandonberg might as well have shouted down the rain barrel. Linnea only turned once more to do her packing with a stubborn set to her shoulders. "I didn't choose to fall in love with him, Mother. It just happened. But now that it has, I'm going to do everything in my power to make him see that what we've been given is a gift we must not squander." She straightened, and Judith saw the determined look in her eyes. Linnea's voice softened to a wistful, womanly tone. "He loves me, too, as much as I love him. He's told me so. And it's too precious to risk giving up, don't you see? What if I never find it again with a man my own age?"

Judith's troubled eyes lingered on Linnea with a sad, certain recognition. Yes, her little girl was growing up. And though her heart hammered in trepidation, Judith had no reasonable argument.

It was difficult to argue against love.

18

IT WAS OVERCAST the following day as Linnea rode the westward train. Beyond the window the sky was the color of ashes, but it couldn't dull the excitement she felt: she was going home.

Home. She thought of what she had left behind. A cheery house, a mother, a father, two sisters, the city where she'd been born. All the familiar places and people she'd known her whole life . . . yet it wasn't home anymore. Home was what tugged at the heartstrings, and the steel wheels were drawing her closer and closer to that.

When the train was still an hour out, she pictured Theodore and John already on the road to town, but when she stepped down from the car onto the familiar worn platform of the Alamo depot, only Theodore was waiting. Their eyes met immediately, but neither of them moved. She stood on the train step, clutching the cold handrail. He stood behind a cluster of people waiting to board: his hands were buried in the deep front pockets of a serviceable old jacket buttoned to the neck with the collar turned up. On his head was a fat blue stocking cap topped with a tassle; in his eyes, an undisguised look of eagerness.

They studied each other above the heads of those separating them. Steam billowed. The train breathed in gusts. The departing passengers hugged good-bye. Linnea and Theodore were aware of none of it, only of each other and their buoyant hearts.

They began moving simultaneously, suppressing the urge to rush. He stepped around the group of passengers, she off the last step. Eyes locked, they neared . . . slowly, slowly, as if each passing second did not seem like a lifetime . . . and stopped with scarcely a foot dividing them.

"Hello," he said first.

"Hello."

He smiled and her heart went weightless.

She smiled and his did the same.

"Happy New Year."

"The same to you."

I missed you, he didn't say.

It seemed like eternity, she swallowed back.

"Did you have a nice ride?"

"Long."

Words failed them both while they stood rapt, until somebody bumped Theodore from behind and said, "Oh, excuse me!"

It brought them from their singular absorption with each other back to the mundane world.

"Where's John?" Linnea glanced around.

"Home nursing a cold."

"And Kristian?"

"Checking his trap line. And Ma said she wanted me out from underfoot anyway while she fixed you a come-home dinner."

So, they were alone. They need not guard their gazes or measure their words or refrain from touching.

"Home," she repeated wistfully. "Take me there."

He took her suitcase in one hand, her elbow in the other, and they moved toward the bobsled. He had missed her with an intensity akin to sickness. The house had been terrible without her and Christmas only a day to be borne. He had been silent and withdrawn from the rest of the family, preferring to spend his time in the tack room alone, where his memories of her were most vibrant. He had even imagined that once she got a fresh dose of her old life in Fargo, she might not come back. He had worried about Lawrence and how he himself would compare to any man she'd known in the city, how Alamo and the farm would compare.

But she *was* back, and he was touching her again—though only through her thick coat sleeve and his leather glove.

She glanced up as they walked, her smile sending currents to his heart. "You have a new cap."

He reached up and touched it self-consciously. "From Ma for Christmas." He stowed her grip in the rear of the wagon and they stood beside the tailgate, trying to get their fill of each other, unable.

"I love my book, Theodore. Thank you so much."

He wished he could kiss her right here and now, but there were townspeople about. "I love my new pen and ink stand and the slate, too. Thank you."

"I didn't know you knew how to write my name."

"Kristian showed me."

"I thought as much. Have you been working with the speller since I've been gone?"

"Every night. You know, that Kristian, he isn't such a bad teacher."

"Kristian isn't a bad teacher," she corrected. "Not Kristian *he* isn't a bad teacher."

He flashed her a lopsided grin. "First thing back and she's pickin' on me already." He tightened his grip on her elbow and handed her up. A moment later they were heading home.

"Well, you might think you collected the wrong girl if I didn't pick on you a little bit."

His slow smile traveled over her, and he took his sweet time before replying, "Naw, not likely."

Her heart danced with joy.

"So how was your family?" he inquired.

They talked unceasingly, it mattered little of what, riding along with their elbows lightly bumping. Though the sun remained a stranger, the temperature was mild. The snow had softened, gripping the runners like a never-ending palm. It was pleasant, gliding along to the unending squeak and the clop of hooves. All around, the clouds hung like old white hens after a dust bath. They sulked churlishly overhead. Where they met the horizon, little distinction was visible between earth and air, just a grayish-white blending with neither rise nor swale delineating the edge of the world.

Theodore and Linnea were a half mile east of the schoolhouse when he squared his shoulders, stared off to the north, and drew back on the reins. Cub and Toots stopped in the middle of the road, pawed the snow, and whinnied.

Warily, Linnea glanced at the team, then at Theodore. "What's wrong?"

"Look." He pointed.

"What? I don't see anything."

"There, see those dark spots moving toward us?"

She squinted and peered. "Oh, now I see them. What is it?"

"The horses." Then, excitedly, "Come, get down." He twisted the reins around the brake handle and leaped from the wagon, distractedly reaching up to help her alight. Down the ditch they went, and up the other side, giant-stepping through knee-deep snow until they stood at a double strand of barbed-wire fence. Standing motionless they gazed at the herd that galloped toward them, unfettered, across the distant field. In minutes the horses drew near enough to be distinguished, one from another. But only their heads. Their bellies were obscured by loose snow moving like an earth-bound cloud around them. Their hooves churned it up until it blent with the white-clad world below and the milky clouds above. The sight was stunning: a swirling, whirling mass of motion.

As they neared, Linnea could feel a faint tremor beneath her soles, a singing in the thin wire between her mittens. There must have been forty of them, their leader a proud piebald prince with streaming gray mane and thick dappled shoulders of gray and white that seemed an extension of the dirty-linen clouds behind him.

Sensing their presence, he whinnied and lifted his head, nostrils dilated and eyes keen. With a snort and lunge, he veered, taking the herd off in a new direction. What a majestic show of power and beauty they made, their hooves charging through whorls of white, tails trailing free, coats long and shaggy now in high winter.

No sleek Virginia trotters, these, but thick-muscled giants of questionable breed whose chests were massive, shoulders strapping, legs thick, beasts who knew the plow and harrow and had earned their temporary freedom.

The pair who watched shivered in appreciation. Absorbed, Linnea clambered up to the lower fence skein to get a better look. Balancing there, watching the horses thunder off, she was scarcely aware of Theodore's steadying arm around her hips. The reverberations faded. The cloud of snow became dimmer.

Theodore looked up.

She might have been one of the unbridled creatures, reveling in her freedom. He had the feeling she'd forgotten he was beside her as she stood on the lower rung of barbed wire with her knees pressed flat against the upper rung, neck stretched, nosing the air, straining for a last glimpse of the disappearing herd. He wondered if she even realized she'd climbed up there. She looked more childish than ever, with a plaid wool kerchief over her hair, knotted beneath her chin.

But it didn't matter. All that mattered was that she saw the majesty in the horses just as he did.

It struck him afresh, how much he'd missed this poppet of a girl in the childish scarf, whose nose was as red as a cherry and whose mitten rested on his shoulder.

He chuckled, hoping it would relieve the sudden tension in his loins.

She glanced down.

"Come down here before you topple over to the other side and I lose you in a snowdrift." He took her by the waist and she leaped down. They stood for a moment with her mittens resting on his breast pockets.

"Wasn't that something, Teddy?" She glanced wistfully after the horses once more. All had grown silent, as if the herd had never appeared.

"I told you we'd see them sometime."

"Yes, but you didn't tell me it would be this beautiful . . . this . . . " She searched for an adequate word. "This awesome! How I wish the children could draw them, just as they looked, all mighty and snorting and throwing snow up everywhere!" Without warning she bent and scooped up two handfuls and tossed it over their heads. It drifted down on her upraised face while he laughed and backed off to avoid it. "Chicken, Theodore!" she taunted. "Honestly, I never saw such a chicken."

"I'm no chicken. I just got more sense than some teachers I know who're gonna end up in bed with the sniffles, like John."

"Oh, phooey! What's a little snow gonna hurt?" She stooped over, scooped again, and took a bite. He could gauge almost to the exact second when she changed from woman back to child. It was part of why he loved her so much, these quicksilver changes of hers. Nonchalantly she began shaping a snowball, patting it top and bottom, transferring it from mitt to mitt, arching one eyebrow with devious intent.

"You just try it and you'll find out what it's gonna hurt," he warned, backing off.

"It's just clean snow." She took a second taste and advanced lazily. "Here, try a bite."

He jerked his head back and grabbed her wrists. "Linnea, you're gonna be sorry."

"Oh yeah? Bite . . . here . . . bite it, bite it, have a b—" They began struggling and laughing while she tried to push the snowball in his face. "Come on, Teddy, good clean *Nort* Dakota snow." She mimicked the Norwegian accent that sometimes crept into his words.

"Cut it out, you little twerp!" She nearly got him this time, but he was too quick, and much stronger.

"Don't you call me a little twerp, Theodore Westgaard. I'm almost nineteen years old!"

He was laughing unrestrainedly as they continued struggling in hand-to-hand combat. "Oh, how about that—she goes off for two weeks and comes home a year older."

She gritted her teeth and grunted. "I'm gonna get you yet, Theodore!" He only laughed, so she hooked a heel behind his boot, gave one mighty shove, and set him on his backside in the snow. There he sat, with an amazed expression on his face, sunk in up to his ribs and elbows while she covered her mouth and rocked with laughter. He picked up one hand and peered into the sleeve. Snow was packed against the lining. He gave it a slow, ponderous shake, all the while skewering her with a feral gleam. He picked up the other hand, dug the snow from around his wrist, and eased to his feet with deliberate slowness. Linnea started backing away.

"Theodore, don't you dare . . . Theodore . . . "

He dusted his backside and advanced, leering wickedly. "Now she begs when she knows she's in for it. What'sa matter, Miss Brandonberg, you scared of a little good clean *Nort* Dakota snow?" he teased.

"Theodore, if you do, I'll . . . I'll . . . "

Unfazed, he advanced. "You'll what?"

"I'll tell your mother!"

"Tell my mother! Ha ha ha!" He came on steadily.

"Well, I will!"

"Yeah, you do that. I'd like to know what she'd say." Suddenly he lunged, caught her wrists, and tried to knock her backward. She squealed and fought. He pushed harder and she braced deeper, struggling, laughing. "I didn't mean it, honest!"

"Ha ha!" He took another step and she grabbed his jacket to keep herself from going over, but she was too late. Whoosh! Back she went, hauling him with her into the puffy pillow of snow, landing in a tangle of arms and legs and skirts, with Theodore sprawled over her like a human quilt. He fell to his side, one leg trailing across her knees while they laughed and laughed and laughed.

As suddenly as it started, it ended. The world grew silent. The weight of his leg across hers grew heavy. A pulse seemed to rise up out of the earth itself, through the snow, into their bodies.

He braced up on an elbow and looked down at her. Their gazes grew intense. "Linnea," he uttered in a queer, strained voice. Snow clung to the back of his collar, his shoulders. She saw him for a brief moment, his blue hat gone, his face framed by the pewter sky above him, his breath labored through open lips. Then his mouth took hers and his weight pressed her deeper into the snow. Their tongues met, mated, warm against their cold lips while he settled full length upon her and she drew him in with eager arms.

When he lifted his head, their hearts were crazy, erratic, and they knew an impatience to make up for lost time.

"I missed you . . . Oh, Teddy . . . " He kissed her again, holding her head in both gloved hands, and it felt as if the herd galloped by once more and made the earth tremble. The kiss ended with the same reluctance as the first.

"I missed you, too."

"I kept thinking of how I was home, but it didn't seem like home anymore because all I wanted was to get back here to you."

"I wasn't fit to live with so I spent most of my time in the tack room." A dollop of snow fell from his collar onto her cheek and as he licked it away her eyes closed and her lips opened. His mouth slid back to hers, reclaiming it with a fervor that vitalized both of their bodies.

Reluctantly he rolled from her and lay on his back.

"I even thought you might not come back," he confessed.

"Silly." She felt denied with his weight gone, and rolled across his chest.

"Am I silly? I don't think I've ever been silly before."

She kissed his eye, then lay with her lips there, breathing on him, smelling him—leather, wool, snow.

"Did you mean what you said at the station?"

"Oh, God, Linnea." He clutched her tightly, closing his eyes, wondering what to do.

She pushed back to see his face. "Y . . . you mean, you didn't?" Her fear sent another shaft of love to his heart.

"Yes, I meant it. But it's not right."

"Of course it's right. How could love be wrong?"

He took her arms and pushed her up, and they sat hip to hip. He wished he could be young again, plunging into life with the same recklessness she had. But he wasn't, and he had to use the common sense she hadn't grown into yet.

"Linnea, listen. I told you I didn't know what to do about it and—"

"Well, I do. I've thought about it a lot and there's only one thing *to* do. We have to get—"

"No!" He lunged to his feet, turning away. "Don't go getting ideas. It just wouldn't work."

She was up and at his shoulder in an instant, insisting, "Why not?"

He picked up his hat from the snow and whacked it against his thigh. "Linnea, for heaven's sake, use your head."

She swung him around by an arm. "My head?" She gazed

into his eyes, forcing him to look at her. "Why my head? Why not my heart?"

"Have you thought about what people would say?"

"Yes. Exactly what my mother said this morning. That you're too old for me."

"She's right." He settled his cap on his head and refused to meet her eyes.

"Theodore." She clutched his arm. "What do years have to do with this feeling we have? They're just . . . just numbers. Suppose we had no way of measuring years and you couldn't say you're sixteen years older than I am."

Lord in heaven, he loved her so. Why did she have to be so young?

He took her upper arms in his gloved hands and made her listen to reason.

"What about babies, Linnea?"

"Babies?"

"Yes, babies. Do you want them?"

"Yes. Yours."

"I've had mine already and he's seventeen years old. Almost as old as you."

"But, Teddy, you're only thirt—"

"What about Kristian? He's sweet on you, did you know that?"

"Yes."

He'd expected her to deny it. When she didn't he was non-plussed. "Well, don't you see what a mess that could make?"

"I don't see why it should. I've made it very clear in every way I know how that I'm his teacher and nothing more. I'm the first infatuation he's ever had, but he'll get over it."

"Linnea, he *told* me. I mean, he came right out and told me the day we went to get coal together how he felt about you. He trusted me for the first time ever with his feelings! Imagine what he'd feel like if I tell him now that I'm going to marry you."

But she sensed what was really bothering him. "You're scared, aren't you, Teddy?"

"Y' damn right I'm scared, and why shouldn't I be?"

She held his face in her soft mink mittens, capturing his eyes with her own. "Because I'm not Melinda. I won't run off and abandon you. I love it here. I love it so much I couldn't wait to get back."

But she was too young to consider that if they had children, by the time they left home he'd be a very old man—if he lived that long. He swung away and strode toward the wagon. "Come on. Let's go."

"Teddy, please—"

"No! There's no use even talking about it anymore. Let's go."

They rode in silence until they approached the driveway to P.S. 28.

"Could we stop at school for just a minute?"

"You need something?"

"No, I've just missed it."

He looked her full in the face. "Missed it?" She'd actually missed this little bump on the big prairie?

"I missed a lot of things."

He adjusted his cap and tended his driving again. "We can stop for a minute, but not long. It's cold out here."

When they pulled into the schoolyard, she exclaimed, "Why, somebody's shoveled the walks!"

He drew the horses up, went over the side, but avoided her eyes. "We had a little snow one day, and it drifted."

"You did it?" she asked in pleased surprise.

He came around to her side to help her down. They both recalled the first day she'd come here, how he'd claimed he had no time to be looking after hothouse pansies. "How sweet of you. Thank you, Teddy."

"If you wanna go inside, go," he ordered gruffly.

He watched her trot toward the door and shook his head at the ground. So young. What was he doing, fooling around in the snow with her when nothing could come of it and he knew it.

He followed her in and stood near the cloakroom door watching as she made a quick scan of the room. She observed it lovingly, and on her way to the front, touched the stove, the desks, the globe, as if they had feelings. The place was frigid, but she didn't seem to notice; her face wore a satisfied smile. What she'd said back there was true. She was nothing whatever like Melinda. But—hang it all!—she didn't stop to think that when she was thirty-four like he was now, he would be gray and long past his prime.

She mounted the teacher's platform, picked up a piece of chalk, and printed across the clean blackboard, "Welcome back! Happy New Year, 1918!"

She set the chalk down with a decisive click, brushed off her palms, and marched back to Theodore, then turned to inspect the message.

"Can you read it?" she asked.

He frowned, concentrating for several seconds. "I can read back and New." He struggled with the first word. "Wwww . . ." When it dawned, his face relaxed. "Welcome back."

"Good! And the rest?"

She watched him trying to figure it out.

"The next word is Happy," she hinted.

"Happy New Year, 1918," he read slowly, then reread the entire message. "Welcome-back-Happy-New-Year-1918."

She smiled with pride. He *had* been busy studying. "By the end of which you're going to be reading as well as my eighth graders." As he returned her smile the buildup of tension eased.

"Come on. Let's go home. Ma's waiting."

Stepping into Nissa's kitchen was like taking off new dancing shoes and putting on worn carpet slippers. Everything was just the same—the oilcloth on the table, the jackets on the hook behind the door, the pail and dipper, the delectable smell coming from the stove.

Nissa was making meatballs and potatoes and gravy for supper, and the windows were thick with steam. The old woman turned from her task and came with open arms. " 'Bout time you was gettin' back here."

Linnea returned the affectionate hug. "Mmm . . . it smells good in here. What're you cooking?"

"Heart stew."

They laughed and Linnea pushed her away playfully. "I'll tell Theodore to take me back to the depot."

"Don't think you'd have much luck. Think he was a little lost without you."

"Oh, he was, was he?" She arched one brow in Theodore's direction. "I wouldn't have guessed. He pushed me into a snowbank on the way home."

"A snowbank!"

Across the room Theodore scowled. Just then Kristian, fresh back from his trap line, came barreling down the stairs and careened to a halt before Linnea, wearing a smile so wide it seemed to lift his ears. His cheeks were still rosy, his hair stood in peaks, and the red toes of his wool socks belled out. Linnea could almost feel the strain as he held back from hugging her. She would marry his father. She *would!* And this entire family had better get used to the fact that she didn't intend to tiptoe around Kristian feeling guilty every time she had the urge to touch Theodore. She rested her mink mittens on his cheeks.

"Kristian, they're the warmest, most beautiful mittens I've ever seen. Did you make them?" He blushed and shifted his feet.

"They fit okay?"

"Perfectly. See?"

He thanked her for the rosewood brush and comb set, and she thanked Nissa for the slippers, and the awkward moment was behind them. Nissa quipped wryly, "Thank you, too, missy, but what's an old coot like me gonna do with that fancy lilac toilet water you give me? Ain't no man within forty miles'd wanna get close enough to sniff it." While they laughed and filled each other in on the last two weeks, Linnea set the table. Just before mealtime, John showed up, bundled in the new fine navy-blue wool scarf Linnea had given him for Christmas, though he wore it tied over his earlapper cap.

"John, I thought you were sick!"

"Was. Ain't no more."

Linnea gave him a quick hug then backed off to assess him critically. "You are too. Look at that red nose and those watery eyes. You shouldn't have walked clear over here in the cold."

Like Kristian, he self-consciously shuffled his feet and turned pink. "Didn't wanna miss out on anything."

Everyone laughed. Ah, how good it was to be back. This was what homecomings were supposed to feel like.

When they sat down to supper Linnea couldn't resist studying Theodore as he prayed—his bent head, his hair slightly flattened from the wool cap, his lowered eyelids, the corners of his lips behind his folded hands.

"Lord, thank you for this food, and for all You provided for us today, but especially for bringing our little missy back home safe. Amen."

He looked up and found her watching him, and they both knew perfectly well this was where she belonged, in this niche they had made for her in their lives.

Her gaze circled the table. Something sharp, very akin to pain, clutched her heart.

Why, she loved them. Not just Theodore, but all of them—Nissa with her gruff affection, Kristian with his quick blush of admiration, and John with his heart of gold and slow, plodding ways.

Theodore watched her eyes return to him. He quickly reached for the bowl of meatballs, though he'd been studying her ever since the prayer ended, thinking of how empty mealtimes had seemed without her. During her absence the family had reverted to their old accustomed silence, eating with the sole purpose of filling their bellies. But the minute she entered the house, gaiety came along with her, and they all seemed to find their tongues again.

He thought of spring, of her leaving, and the succulent meatballs seemed to turn to sawdust in his mouth.

When supper ended, Linnea said, "I'm anxious to see what you've learned. Care to show me?"

Though he answered off-handedly, "If you're not too tired," he came as close to fidgeting as he ever had when Ma said, "Teddy'll drive you home, John." John tugged on his overshoes, buttoned his jacket, and buckled his earlappers like a snail with low blood pressure. Laboriously, he tied his new scarf over his head and patted his pockets, searching for mittens. Theodore stood with one hand on the doorknob, but didn't say a word. There was an additional delay while Nissa tucked a fruit jar of vegetable soup under John's arm and gave him orders to stay home in bed the next day.

By the time he got John home, returned, put the horses away, and entered the kitchen, Theodore was fairly jittering with excitement. Both Nissa and Kristian were sitting at the table with Linnea. The books and new slate were spread out in readiness, and Kristian had the speller opened to the last page they'd been working on, eager to demonstrate all he'd taught his father.

Theodore had worked insatiably on his reading while Linnea was gone. He had hounded Kristian to help him, and now, as Kristian proudly dictated a spelling test, he became totally immersed in writing the words. He formed each one carefully: Theodore, know, knee, blood, sausage, fence, Kristian, heart, Cub, Toots, since, sense, John, mother, stove, Linnea, *lutefisk*.

"*Lutefisk!* You taught him to spell *lutefisk?*"

"He made me."

Linnea laughed, but when Theodore began reading aloud to her, she realized what remarkable progress he'd made, partly due to his own determination and partly due to their unorthodox method of choosing words hither-thither.

"Why, Theodore, you're already reading as well as my fifth graders!"

"He nearly drove me crazy, that's why!" Kristian put in. "He barely left me enough time to check my traps." Theodore's face turned pink, but she could see how proud he was. "One day I even found him writing words in the snow with a stick."

"In the snow?" She glanced at Theodore and his blush brightened. His eyes met hers and flickered away.

"Well, I didn't have my slate and I couldn't remember how to spell a word and it was easier if I saw it."

The only other time she'd seen him so vivid and flustered was the night she'd discovered he didn't know how to read. When he blushed and acted bashful he looked so young it made her heart thump.

The following night they were at the table again with Kristian and Nissa sitting by when Linnea decided to try to stump him. She wrote on the slate, "Did I tell you my father bought an automobile?" She turned it around to face him, watched as he read along smoothly, then frowned over the last word. His lips moved silently as he tried to puzzle it out. After several seconds she flipped the board around and put a slash through the word—auto/mobile—then turned it to him again.

He mouthed the word and his face split in a smile. But instead of answering aloud, he took the slate, erased it, and wrote, "No. Did you ride in it?"

She erased it and wrote, "Yes, it was delightful."

He puzzled for a full minute and finally gave up. "I don't know that one," he said.

"Delightful."

"Oh." He suddenly grew pensive and forgot about the slate as he studied her.

An automobile, Theodore thought. She would be the kind to like an automobile. When spring came and she returned to her life in the city, with the family automobile and all the other conveniences, surely she would compare it to the life out here and find this backward. Why ever would she want to return next fall? And there was one other thing that he hadn't been able to get off his mind but had felt foolish to ask.

He rubbed the chalky rag over his slate, then wrote, "Did you see Lorents?" He pondered the question for a long moment, trying to dredge up the nerve to show her. He cast an eye at Nissa and Kristian across the table. But his mother was mending a sock and his son was bent over a book. Theodore looked up to find Linnea with one fist bracing her jaw as she waited idly to see what he'd come up with. Slowly—very slowly—he angled the board so only she could read it.

She studied it, frowning, puzzling it out. Did you see . . .

Her eyes flashed up to his and her jaw came off her fist. Her heart did a quickstep and she threw a cautious glance at the two across the table, but they were paying no attention whatever.

She eased the board from his fingers, but left his question and wrote beneath it, "Lawrence?"

Theodore studied the name, properly spelled, feeling awkward and a little warm around the neck. He erased *Lorents,* rewrote it correctly, turned it to her, and nodded.

For interminable seconds their dark, intense gazes locked above the slate. Kristian turned a page. Nissa's scissors snipped a thread. In the final moment before Linnea's hand went back to her slate, Theodore thought he saw a flicker of amusement in her eyes.

No, she wrote.

When he read it, he quietly released a long breath and his shoulders relaxed against the back of the chair.

Though neither of them said a word about the message exchanged on the board, it was on both of their minds as they went to bed that night.

It won't work, having her so close all the time. You either got to marry her or get her out of here.

It won't work, living under the same roof with him. If he won't marry you, you'll have to find someplace else to teach next year.

The following day, when Linnea returned from school, an envelope was propped against the potted philodendron in the middle of the kitchen table. The return address said Adrian Mitchell.

She came up short at the sight of it and suddenly felt a pair of eyes censuring her. She looked across the room to find Theodore standing in the doorway to the front room, glaring at her as if she'd just announced she was a German spy. Between them Nissa worked at the stove, ignoring them. The silence was broken only by the sound of onion spattering into hot grease. Theodore spun and disappeared, and Linnea thought, Oh, you don't want me for yourself, but nobody else can have me either, is that it?

She snatched the letter off the table and went bounding up the stairs.

Adrian was as good at writing letters as he was at handling customers and parents. Some of his compliments made Linnea blush. And his plans for summer made her hide the envelope beneath her underclothes in a drawer where Nissa wouldn't spot it when she came up to change the sheets.

That night as they sat over their lessons, the tension between Linnea and Theodore was palpable. He wished for once they could be alone and have words, but Nissa sat on her usual chair, knitting, and Kristian was mending a snowshoe and chewing jerky. When Theodore could stand it no longer, he wrote on his slate, "Who is Adrian?"

When he turned it to face Linnea, his eyes were hard, his lips set in a thin line.

"He works in my father's store," she wrote back.

Though no further personal messages were exchanged that night, Theodore was stiff and sulky. He did his writing exercises without once looking at her, and at the end of the evening, when she offered a good night, he refused to answer.

The following morning Linnea awakened to a thermometer reading of thirty-eight degrees below zero and a wind keening

out of the northwest so forcefully it appeared the windmill was
going to go flying off to Iowa.

They took turns washing in the kitchen: there was no question of doing it upstairs where the temperatures were nearly
as cold as outdoors. The windows were so thick with ice
it was impossible to see out. John didn't even show up for
breakfast.

When the meal was done, Theodore pushed his chair back,
reached for his outerwear, and without bothering to glance
Linnea's way, ordered, "Get your things. I'll be taking you
to school."

"Taking me?" She glanced up, surprised.

"That's what I said. Now get your things."

"But you said—"

"Don't tell me what I said! You wouldn't make it to the end
of the driveway before your eyeballs froze." He jerked on his
wool jacket, buttoned it, turned up the collar, and jammed a
battered felt Stetson low on his head. Yanking the door open,
he repeated cantankerously, "Get your things."

Obediently she hustled upstairs. Five minutes later, when
she ran down the freshly shoveled path, she came up short at
the sight of the strangest looking contraption she'd ever seen,
hitched behind Cub and Toots. It appeared to be a small shed
on runners, with a chimney stack sticking out its roof spouting
smoke and reins stretching inside through a crude peek hole.
Beside a small rear door Theodore waited impatiently, a look
of thunderous unapproachability upon his face.

"What is this thing?" Linnea asked, eyeing the warped roof.

"Get in!" He grabbed her arm and pushed her inside, then
followed, closing the door. The interior was warm and dark. A
fire gleamed through the minute cracks of the tiniest round iron
stove she'd ever seen. It was no bigger than a cream can, but
more than ample to heat the small space. A thin ray of daylight
threaded in through the peek hole up front. She felt the floor
rock as Theodore made his way past her, advising, "There's
no seats, so you'd best stand up here by me and hang on."

Before she could follow orders, he slapped the reins and
nearly set her on her backside. Rocking, she grappled forward and grabbed the edge of the peek hole, through which
the horses' rumps were visible.

"What about Kristian?"

"He's doing the chores. I'll bring him later."

"But you always do the chores before breakfast."

"Had to put this thing together before breakfast," he stated in his grumpiest voice.

Immediately her temper sizzled. "You didn't *have* to do anything, Theodore. I could have walked!"

Staring through the peek hole, he retorted, "Ha."

"I didn't ask to be treated like some . . . some hothouse pansy!"

"You got any idea what wind like that does to bare skin when the temperature's thirty-eight below?"

"I could have covered my face with a scarf."

In the dim square of light that fell on his face, she watched him roll his eyes her way. He gave a deprecating chuckle, then glanced away again.

"I'm *sorry* I put you out," she said sarcastically. "Next time, before you build a wagon for me, you might ask me first if I need a ride."

"I didn't *build* a wagon for you," he returned in a tone that matched her own. "It breaks down and stores in the lean-to. All I had to do was stand it on the bobsled runners and hook it together."

She was getting angrier by the moment at his high-handedness and the insulting tone of his voice.

"Theodore, I don't know what in the world's the matter with you lately, but you're acting like some . . . some bear with a thorn in his paw!"

He threw her a withering glance but said nothing.

"Well, what did I do?" she demanded angrily, rocking with the motion of the vehicle, trying not to bump his arm.

His jaw bulged. He glared straight head. Finally he bit out, "Nothin'! You didn't do nothin'!"

They pulled into the schoolyard and she leaped out into the slicing wind, anxious to be away from him. But, to her surprise, he followed, grasping her elbow so hard she winced as they trudged through thigh-deep drifts. The wind was so ferocious it threatened to pluck off her scarf. Theodore held his hat on with his free hand. The edges of their footprints began blurring even before they reached the steps, which were buried beneath a drift so deep they had to search for footholds as they climbed.

She stumbled once and he mercilessly yanked her to her feet. The door was totally blocked by a wall of white. After attempting to open it and failing, Theodore plowed his way back down the steps toward the wagon. In a moment he returned with a shovel.

"I can do it!" she shouted as he came back to her. "Give it to me!"

She reached for the shovel handle. One of her mittens closed around it beside his worn leather glove. She pulled. He tugged. They glared at each other stubbornly. The wind flickered his hat brim and sent her scarf tails whipping like a flag. The tip of her nose was wet. The tops of his ears were red.

Wordlessly he wrenched the shovel from her grasp, then ground through his teeth, "Just get out of my way." He shouldered her rudely aside and rammed the shovel in the snowdrift with uncontrolled vehemence.

"Theodore, I said I can do it!"

It took no more than twelve flying shovelfuls to free the door. He jerked it open, grabbed her elbow, and thrust her inside.

"I will shovel the goddamn snow!" he bellowed, then slammed the door in her face.

She stared at it while tears scalded her eyes, then gave it a vicious kick. Angrily she swung inside to get the coal hod. But when she marched out with it he yanked it from her hand, jammed his shovel in a drift, did an about-face, and without a word trudged around the corner of the building through knee-deep snow. She was standing rigidly with her back to the door when he clumped inside and cracked the pail down beside her with a force that shook the windows. Behind her his boots thudded like hammer blows, then both doors slammed.

She built the fire with enough banging and clanging to shake the teeth loose in his head—she hoped! When it was lit she tightened the ends of her scarf so hard it nearly choked her. She had just opened the cloakroom door and was heading for the water pail when he barged in from outside, with the same intent. Sour-faced, she watched him grab it and head outside. She slammed her door before he could slam his.

He was back in minutes. With her back to the door, arms crossed tightly, she stood by the stove and listened to him transfer the water to the crock in the corner. Next came the clap of the wooden cover, then he returned the pail to the cloakroom.

The inner door slammed.

Was he in or out?

She glared at the stovepipe for two full minutes, wondering. Nothing but silence. Curiosity finally got the best of her and she peeked over one shoulder. There he stood, hands on hips, glaring at her from under the brim of his Stetson.

She snapped around to the stove again.

"Well, are you going to tell me about him or not?" came his belligerent voice.

"Tell you about whom?" she retorted stubbornly.

"Whom?" He laughed derisively and his boots clunked slowly across the floor. He stopped no more than a foot behind her. "Adrian what's-his-name, that's who!"

"Mitchell. His name is Adrian Mitchell."

"I really don't give a damn what his name is. Are you going to tell me or not?"

"I told you, he works at my father's store," she spit.

"I'll bet," he returned sardonically.

She spun around. "Well, he does!"

His eyes were shadowed by the brim of his hat, but even so she could make out the anger gleaming in their depths. His jacket collar was turned up around his ears, his boots planted wide. "Another one for your collection?" he accused.

"And what do you care?" she retorted, making fists inside her mittens.

"Is he?" Theodore spit back, making fists inside his gloves.

"It's none of your business. How dare you question me about my personal life. All you are is my landlord!"

"What did you do, go out riding in *automobiles* with him?" Theodore sneered.

"Yes, as a matter of fact, I did. And I had fun, too. And he took me to a party, and ice-skating, and we danced and drank champagne punch, and he came to my house for supper. And you know what else he did, Theodore?" She thrust her nose closer, taunting him with bright, snapping eyes. "He kissed me. Is that what you want to know? Is it?"

She thrust even closer and squared her jaw while Theodore's face burned pepper-red between cold, mottled white spots.

"You're pushin' your luck, missy," he threatened in a low, gravelly voice.

She backed off and gave a derisive sniff. "Oh, don't make me laugh, Theodore. It would take a railroad locomotive to push you. You're scared of your own shadow." He took one threatening step forward, but she held her ground, blue eyes gone black with challenge. "Aren't you?"

They faced off, each looking for a weakness in the other, finding none. Finally Theodore demanded, "How old is he?"

"Twenty, twenty-one maybe. Now run, Theodore, run like you always do!"

He glared at her, the muscles in his neck so tense a pain shot up the back of his head. Then Theodore, who rarely cursed, growled his second curse of the day.

"Damn you." He jerked her forward by both elbows, dropping his mouth over hers in a savage kiss. Immediately her mouth opened, and she struggled as if to call out, but he ruthlessly held her, feeling her arms tensed to fight. Beneath his mouth she made a muffled sound as if trying to speak, but he refused to free her lips and let her rail at him again. His tongue thrust between her teeth and hers met it, full force. Only then did he realize she was struggling not to get away from him but to get *to* him. He eased his grasp on her elbows and immediately she flung her arms around his neck. Up on tiptoe she went, moving close, clinging. His arms circled her back, pulling her flush against him, the bulk of their woolen clothing forming a barrier.

He lifted his head abruptly, forcing her away from him, breathing hard. Her eyes were like chips of coal to which a match had been touched. They burned bright and intensely into his face.

"Teddy, Teddy, why do you fight it?" Her breath came in quick, driving beats.

He closed his eyes to get control, pressing her away by the arms. "Because I'm old enough to be your father. Don't you understand that?"

"I understand that you only use it as an excuse."

"Stop it!" he shot back, opening his eyes to reveal a tortured expression. "And think about what you're saying, what we're doing! You're eighteen years—"

"Closer to nineteen."

"All right, so you'll be nineteen next month. And I'll be thirty-five two months after that. What difference does it make? There'll still be sixteen years between us."

"I don't care," she insisted.

"Your pa would care." Immediately he saw that he'd touched a vulnerable spot. "Your pa, who probably has a young fellow named Adrian all picked out for you and already working in his store, isn't that right?"

"Adrian wrote to me. I didn't write to him."

"But you kissed him and did all those things with him and I'm jealous and I got no right to be, don't you see? You should be with young people like him, not with old bucks like me."

"You're not an old buck, you're way more fun to be around than he is, and when he kisses me nothing happens like when you—"

"Shh!" He covered her mouth with one gloved finger, the anger falling away as fast as it had come.

For a long moment their eyes locked, then she freed her lips from his hand and whispered, "But it's true."

"You live in my house. Don't you understand what people would say, what they might think?"

"That you love me?" she questioned softly. "Would that be so terrible?"

"Linnea, don't," he uttered, still pressing her away.

"Oh, Teddy, I . . . I love you so much I do crazy things," she admitted plaintively. "I kiss blackboards and windows and pillows because you won't kiss me."

Though he tried to steel himself against her, her ingenuousness made his mouth flicker in a sad smile. Trouble was, what he liked most about her were the very things that made her too young for him. No other girl he'd ever known had been so natural and unspoiled. He let his eyes drift to her hairline, the red plaid scarf tied severely around her face. Her sincere eyes. Her sweet mouth.

Much more softly she said, "I do love you, Teddy."

Lord, lord, girl, don't do this to me.

But when she raised her eyes to his once more, he gave up and drew her into his arms, gently this time. He closed his eyes and nestled her beneath his chin with one gloved hand holding the back of her head. "Don't," he requested in a dry, scratchy voice. She felt him swallow against the top of her head. "Don't try to grow up too fast and waste these precious years on me. Be young and foolish. Kiss blackboards and windows and talk to people who aren't there."

Chagrined, she burrowed deeper beneath his chin. "You guessed, didn't you?"

"That you talk to people who aren't there? Yes, after the day I surprised you at the blackboard here. And one other time I heard you upstairs, talking to your friend Lawrence. Are you ready to tell me who he is yet?"

He leaned back, the better to see her. She hung her head sheepishly. One leather-covered finger tipped her chin up until she couldn't avoid meeting his eyes. A blush appeared on the crests of her cheeks and she blinked wide. "He's nobody," she admitted, "I made him up."

Theodore scowled. "Made him up?"

"He's just a figment of my imagination. Somebody to take the place of the friend I didn't have when I first came out here. Actually, I invented him when I was about thirteen or so, when I first noticed the difference between boys and girls. He and I . . . well, I could just talk to him, that's all. Like I never could to a real boy." She dropped her chin and studied a pocket flap on Theodore's jacket.

He studied her nose, her eyebrows, the sweep of lashes dropped docilely over her pretty blue eyes. Her lips were delicate and slightly puffed, and he wanted worse than anything to kiss them and teach them the hundreds of ways of kissing back.

"What am I going to do with you, little one?" he questioned softly.

She looked up and told him, "Marry me."

"I can't. No matter how I'd like to, I can't. It wouldn't be fair to you."

Why should it be unfair of him to do something that would make her the happiest woman in the world?

"Fair? To me?"

"Linnea, think. Think about twenty years from now when you'd still be young . . . I'd be past middle age."

"Oh, Teddy, you have an obsession with years. You're forever counting them. But don't you see it's more important to count happiness? Why, even in twenty years we could have more happiness than some people have in fifty. Please . . . "

Her eyes were so sincere and her mouth trembled as she stood a heartbeat away. When her gaze dropped to his lips his pulse beat thudded out a warning, but he found it impossible to move as she slowly lifted on tiptoe, raised her slightly parted lips to his, then held both sides of his face between her sleek mink mittens. "Please . . . " she murmured, tipping her head and softly plucking at his mouth, then slipping her hands around his neck and pressing herself against him. "Please . . ."

He steeled himself to resist, but her tongue glided over his lips, then shyly probed inside, over his teeth, and the sensitive skin of his inner lips. With a throaty sound he gathered her close, slanted his head and joined her fully. Their tongues met in a silken encounter and their bodies strained together. Their hearts seemed to collide, breast to breast, and arousal took them by storm.

He tasted faintly of morning coffee and smelled of winter air. The interior of his mouth was hot, moist, and more tempting than anything she had ever imagined. None of the kisses she'd experienced had ever moved her as this one did. She thought she would simply die if it couldn't be hers forever.

But suddenly he pulled back and jerked her arms from around his neck. The scarf had fallen back and lay in soft folds about her collar. Her eyes were wide and pleading, her lips parted, exuding small, panting breaths. His voice shook and his breath was driven.

"I have to go."

"But what about us?"

"The answer is still no."

She swallowed the lump in her throat and said shakily, "Then I'll have to go, too. I can't stay in that house with you any longer. Not the way I feel."

He'd known it would come down to this, but he hadn't expected it to hurt quite this much.

"No. I promise I wouldn't—"

She touched his lips to silence him. "I can't make the same promise, Teddy . . . " she whispered.

Everything in him seemed to hurt. Everything in him wanted. He wanted Linnea, but so much more—the rich, full life she could bring. He'd never known he could hurt so bad, want so bad.

"I'll be back for you at five o'clock and we'll talk about it then. You're not to start out for home, is that understood?"

"Yes," she whispered.

"When you need more coal, send Kristian out for it. Promise?" When she didn't respond he shook her a little, demanding softly, "Promise?"

"I promise."

"Fix your hair. I think I've messed it in the back." The words were gravelly as he stepped back, steadying her by her arms.

"I will," she replied woodenly.

Then he dropped his hands and left without looking back.

19

BECAUSE THE WEATHER was so frigid, all the fathers delivered and picked up their children that day. Linnea left a note for Teddy on the schoolhouse door and rode home with Trigg and Bent. She took one look at Clara and the tears she'd held at bay since morning came gushing with a vengeance. A moment later she was in Clara's consoling arms.

"Why, Linnea, what is it?"

"Oh, Clara," she wailed, clinging.

Clara telegraphed a silent message to Trigg and he disappeared with Bent, who stared in astonishment as his teacher broke into sobs.

"Shh . . . shh . . . it can't be as bad as all that. Is it something with Allen again?"

Linnea withdrew, sobbing, searching out a hanky. "It's Th . . . Theodore."

"Ah, brother Theodore. What's he done this time?"

"Oh, C . . . Clara, it's j . . . just awful."

Clara drew back to see Linnea's face. "What's awful? I can't help you if you won't tell me."

"I l . . . love him."

The older woman controlled a smile. "That's awful?"

"He loves m . . . me too and he w . . . won't m . . . marry me."

341

Clara hugged Linnea again as a new rash of weeping wilted her. She rubbed her shuddering back and turned her toward the table. "You mean you asked him?"

Linnea nodded wretchedly and let herself be lowered to a chair. Clara couldn't help smiling. Poor Teddy, didn't he ever get the chance to do the proposing himself?

"You did, huh? Well, that took some courage. So exactly what did he say?"

"He th . . . thinks I'm too young f . . . for him, and he s . . . says he d . . . doesn't want any more b . . . babies and oh, Clara, wh . . . what am I g . . . going to do?" She laid her head on the table and let the misery flow.

Babies? thought Clara. They've already talked about having babies? Poor Teddy was already fated to Linnea and didn't know it.

"Cry it out, and when you've dried up a little we'll talk it all over."

That's exactly what they did. Linnea unburdened herself, relating all her feelings, all the complications Theodore insisted on throwing in their way. Clara listened, and sympathized, and soothed. And when the story was out and all that remained of Linnea's tears was the puffiness in her eyelids, the younger woman said, "Clara, I have to ask you something. It's awfully presumptuous of me, but you're the only one I can think of to ask."

"What is it? You can ask me anything, you know that."

"Could I come and stay here with you and Trigg? I just can't live there anymore, and the school board will pay you, and I don't eat much. I thought maybe with the baby coming I could help you with things around the house. And it'd only be till spring. I . . . well, I doubt that I'd be coming back in the fall."

It took Clara only a few moments' consideration to decide.

"Of course you can." She cupped Linnea's tear-shined cheek. "And I'll be only too happy for the help. I'm already so enormous it's an effort just to wobble around. Now . . . " She boosted herself to her feet and spoke brusquely. "You'll stay for supper, then Trigg can take you to Ma's to get your things. How does that sound?"

When Linnea and Trigg walked into Nissa's house a short

time later, the atmosphere was funereal. The three members of Linnea's "family" all stood back, uncertain, unhappy, not knowing what to say while she explained that Clara needed her during this last part of her pregnancy, so Trigg was taking her back there.

"Tonight?" Nissa asked.

"Yes, as soon as I get my things together."

"A little sudden, ain't it?"

Linnea knew Theodore didn't believe her story, and it was questionable whether Nissa did, but all she wanted was to gather her things and escape as quickly as possible. She avoided Theodore's eyes, but sensed his stunned disbelief as he hovered in the background, staring at her, saying nothing. Kristian kept glancing at Nissa as if expecting her to stop Linnea, while Nissa put on her prune face and tried to decide if she should feel hurt or not.

There wasn't a lot for Linnea to pack—she hadn't much more than she'd come with, except a pair of mink mittens, a carved cat, a crocheted shawl, and a leather-bound volume of Tennyson. She forced herself not to dwell on them as she stuffed them into her valise.

When she came back down she wasn't sure she could manage the good-bye that was necessary. The tears were so close to the surface that the inside of her nose stung, and the clot of emotion in her throat made speaking an effort. But she did her best job of acting ever, pasting a bright smile on her face and injecting an excited bounce into her footstep.

The hug she gave Nissa was fleeting. "One less to cook for," she chirped.

The finger she pointed at Kristian's nose was playful. "Now see to it you do homework even when I'm not here at the table in the evenings."

The handshake she gave Theodore was convincing. "You'll do wonderfully with your reading, I know you will. Kristian can help you with it. Well, Trigg, all set."

She whirled out with all the apparent eagerness of a child approaching a candy store, but when she was gone the three remaining Westgaards looked at each other and didn't know what to say. Nissa finally broke the silence.

"Well, what do you know about this, Teddy?"

He swallowed and turned away. "Nothin'."

"Kristian?"

"Nothing."

"Well, that child had been cryin', and cryin' hard. She didn't fool me one bit. Tomorrow I intend to march over there and find out what's goin' on."

"Leave it, Ma."

"Leave it?"

"She wants to go there and live, let her. Like she said, it's one less mouth to feed."

But nothing was good without her. It was as it had been when she'd gone home for Christmas, only worse, because this time she wasn't coming back. Mealtime was a sullen ordeal. Nobody talked. They all stared at their plates and wondered why the food didn't taste good. They caught each other glancing at Linnea's empty chair and tried to pretend they hadn't been. John was back—his cold was better—but though he'd come out of his shell since Linnea had come into their lives, now that she was gone, he was more indrawn than ever. He shuffled in with his head down and shuffled out the same way. Though Kristian saw her at school every day, he came and went without a word about how she was. How is she doing, Theodore wanted to ask. Does she seem happy? What was she wearing? It took an effort to get up mornings and pretend the day had some meaning. Evenings were torture. Nobody brought out a book, nobody brought out a slate. Trigg took her to school these cold days; his rig passed regularly, morning and afternoon. But he had the warming house on, and if she was in it, she couldn't be seen. Theodore found himself hovering around the outbuildings at those times of day, straining for a glimpse of the vehicle that carried her.

At night he tossed in bed restlessly, pondering his future. Kristian was already seventeen. Ma was seventy. They wouldn't be around forever. And when they weren't, what then? Then there'd be him and John. Two old men batching it in their lonely prairie farmhouses, talking mostly to the animals, waving to wagons that passed on the road, hoping one of them would turn in and bring company.

He thought about Linnea, up there at Clara's, wondered how

she was getting on, and if she missed him. Lord, she was strong, that girl. He'd never thought she'd up and leave like she did. He reckoned she was happy up there, with the kids always making some kind of excitement—she sure loved kids, no doubt about it. Loved Clara, too, and the two of them got along like peas in a pod. He supposed when the new baby came Linnea would be in her glory being around it.

He thought about babies. Girl like that deserved babies, but a man his age had no business having 'em. Still, he wondered what they'd look like, his and Linnea's. Blond, probably, and robust and full of energy like her.

He saw her at church on Sunday and got all goggle-eyed and tight-chested. But she looked happy as a lark, wearing a great big smile and her bird-wing hat. She said, "Oh, hi, Teddy. Where's Nissa?" Then she was gone before he could get his tongue unglued. After Sunday dinner he sneaked into his room and combed his hair, figuring they'd be here any time; Clara and Trigg always came to Ma's on Sunday. But they didn't come.

By late afternoon, when they hadn't shown up, he hid his slate under his jacket and went down to the tack room to see if a little schoolwork would relieve his wretchedness. But he wasted a good half hour staring at the saddle on the sawhorse, and another staring at the name he'd written on the slate. Linnea. Linnea. Linnea. Lord God almighty, what should he do? He hurt. Hurt. Love wasn't supposed to hurt like this. He wrenched himself to his feet and tried cleaning the tool bench, but it was already in perfect order. He reared back and threw a hoof trimmer so hard it knocked over three cans and sent horseshoe nails skittering to the floor. Then with a violent curse he swung, picked up the slate, and stormed from the room.

Nissa and Kristian were both in the kitchen when he came back in. They watched him but said nothing. He went to his bedroom, reappeared momentarily with his suspenders and underwear top turned down, filled the basin, washed, shaved for the second time that day, patted bay rum on his face, macassared his hair, combed it meticulously, disappeared once more, and returned shortly wearing his Sunday suit and a clean white shirt with a brand-new collar. He looked neither at his son nor mother but pulled on his coat, picked up the slate and speller, and announced, "I'm going up to Clara's, see if I can get on with my reading lessons."

When the door slammed behind him Kristian stared at it, speechless. Nissa's knitting needles didn't miss a beat as she studied her grandson over the rim of her spectacles.

"I could've given him a reading lesson," Kristian declared belligerently.

"Yup." *Clickety-snickety* went the knitting needles. Kristian's eyes swerved to Nissa's.

"Then why'd he have to go up to Clara's?"

She dropped her eyes to the stitches, though she could form them blindfolded. " 'Pears to me your pa's gone courtin'," she replied with a satisfied air.

At Clara's, Linnea was preparing Monday's lessons at the kitchen table, where the whole family sat eating popcorn. A sound filtered through the wall. "Somebody's coming." Trigg got up and squinted through the window into the dark. "Looks like Teddy."

Linnea's hand stopped halfway to her mouth and her heart jumped into double-time. She scarcely had time to adjust to the announcement before the door was opening and there stood Theodore, turned out as if it were his burial day. He glanced at everybody in the room except Linnea.

"Howdy, Clara, Trigg, kids. Thought you'd come up't the house today. Decided to ride down and see if everything's okay."

"Everything's fine. Come on in."

"Cold out there."

Linnea felt a blush rise.

"Uncle Teddy! Uncle Teddy! We got popcorn!" Little Christine barreled against him, reaching up. He set her on his arm and chucked her under the chin, smiling. Finally he met Linnea's eyes above the child's blond head. His smile dissolved and he gave a silent nod. She dropped her attention to her schoolwork.

"Pull up a chair," Trigg invited, and stuck one between himself and Bent.

"What did you bring?" Bent inquired.

Theodore joined them at the table, with Christine on his

knee. "My slate and speller." He laid them on the table. "I'm learning how to read."

"You *are?* Gosh, but you're awful old to—"

"Bent!" his parents scolded simultaneously.

The little boy glanced from one parent to the other, wondering what he'd done wrong. "Well, he *iii*s."

Linnea wanted to crawl beneath the table.

"A person's never too old to learn," Theodore told the eight-year-old. "What do you think, Miss Brandonberg?"

She met his eyes and not one blessed word came to her mind.

"If you can spare the time, I'd like to go on with the reading lessons."

Reading lessons? Dressed like that he came claiming he wanted reading lessons? How could she possibly concentrate on teaching him when her blood had set up such a singing in her head?

"I . . . well . . . sure, why not?"

He smiled and nodded and reached for some popcorn, and one of the children said something that diverted his attention. Linnea felt Clara's inquisitive scrutiny and wrote at the top of a paper, "Don't leave!" Silently she flashed it toward Clara, praying she'd heed the message. It would have looked utterly conspicuous for Clara and Trigg to disappear suddenly; the kitchen was the warmest room in the house, the gathering place on cold evenings like this. The front room was rarely used in winter.

Thankfully, Clara took Linnea's plea to heart. When the popcorn was gone, everyone shifted places so Linnea and Teddy could sit side by side, but everybody stayed. The children found a ball of yarn and played on the floor with Patches, their pet cat. Clara stitched on a baby quilt. Trigg read a *Farm Journal.* Linnea and Teddy tried to concentrate on a lesson that meant not a whit to either one of them. Though their elbows rested on the table, they made certain not to touch. When their knees bumped once beneath the table, they sat up straighter in their chairs. Though they studied each other's hands, they never looked directly at each other. They had been working for nearly two hours when Teddy silently pushed the slate across the table to her. On it were written three words.

Please come home.

A heart-burst of reaction flooded Linnea's body. Love, pain, renunciation. She glanced up sharply, but Trigg and Clara were occupied. Teddy studied her; she felt his eyes like a longing caress on her cheek. His knuckles were white as the chalk he gripped. It would be so easy to say yes, knowing how he felt about her. But he wasn't offering anything permanent, only a temporary solution to their misery.

She reached for the chalk, slipping it from his fingers and watching as he forcibly relaxed them. She wrote only two words—I can't—and for the first time that night, met his gaze directly.

Oh, Teddy, I love you. But I'll have it all or nothing.

She saw that he understood clearly. She saw how fast he was breathing. She saw him fight with himself. And everything in her rushed outward toward him in a silent plea.

But he closed his speller, set it atop the slate, and pushed his chair back. "Well, it's late, I'd best be going." He stretched to his feet and reached for his coat. "Can I come again tomorrow?"

"Why sure," Trigg answered.

"Linnea?"

She couldn't quite find the strength to say no. "If you'd like."

He nodded solemnly and said good night.

He came the next night, but not in his Sunday best. He wore a gray plaid flannel shirt with the sleeves rolled to the elbow and the throat open, revealing the sleeves and placket of the ever-present winter underwear. He looked utterly masculine. Linnea wore her hair caught up in a ribbon, flowing down her back. In her navy and white middy dress she looked utterly young.

She gave him a story to read and he settled down to do so, slunk low in his chair with his temple propped on two fingertips. She looked up once to find that over the top of the book he was studying her breasts, which rested over her crossed wrists on the edge of the table. Her face turned red, she sat back, and his eyes returned to the book.

The following night she told him to write a sentence using the word blue and he wrote, Linnea has beautifull blue eyes.

In a snap, Linnea's beautiful blue eyes met Theodore's beautiful brown ones. Her face became a blushing red rose and Teddy smiled. Flustered, she took refuge in grabbing the slate and correcting his spelling. Unperturbed, he erased the whole thing, applied the chalk again and wrote, You look pretty when you blush.

He came six nights and still she refused to return home. They sat at the table as usual, Clara and Trigg with them, and Theodore covertly studied Linnea. She corrected papers while he was supposed to be reading, but it was impossible. She had done something different with her hair tonight, gathered it up in a loose puff with a tiny pug knot in the back, like an egg in a fat nest. At her temples tendrils trailed and she caught one around her finger, winding and rewinding it abstractedly. Suddenly she giggled at something on the paper. "You have to see this." She angled it so they all could see. "It's a spelling test I gave today. This word is supposed to be sheet."

S-h-i-t, it said.

They all laughed and settled back. Theodore watched her giggles subside and her head bend over her work again. In time she finished and smacked the pile of papers straight, looked up, and caught him admiring her.

"Did you finish reading your assignment?"

He cleared his throat. "Ahh . . . no, not quite."

"Theodore!" she scolded, "you can read faster than that."

"Some nights."

"Well, you can finish it at home. It's time for a couple new words." She pulled out the slate and they began working, elbows and heads close. She smelled like almonds again. It created havoc with his concentration. He remembered dancing with her, smelling that almond flavor up close. He remembered kissing her, and how she had made him feel. Young. Alive. Bursting. Just looking at her brought it all back again, made his blood surge and his heart knock. He reached for the slate as if he had no choice in the matter, and though he felt fearful and even a little timid, he had to ask. He just had to. It was pure hell without her.

Can I pick you up for the dance tomorrow? he wrote.

This time she expressed no surprise. No blush lit her cheek. No excitement kindled her eyes. Only a sad resignation as their gazes met and she slowly shook her head.

He felt a brief flare of anger: what was she trying to do to him? But he knew, and he knew she was stubborn enough, strong enough to hold fast in her resolution to live the remainder of the year at Clara's. And next fall she wouldn't be back. He saw it all in her sad eyes as they confronted him, and suddenly his life stretched out before him like a bleak, eternal purgatory. He knew full well what he must do to turn that purgatory to heaven. He knew what she was waiting for.

He felt as if he were strangling. As if the walls of his chest would collapse at any moment. As if his heart would club its way out of his body—the hard ache beneath his ribs, the sweating palms and shaky hands. But he took the chalk anyway and wrote what all the common sense of the universe could not keep him from writing.

Then will you merry me?

There wasn't a sound in the room as he turned the slate her way and waited. The muscles in his belly jumped.

When she read it the shock passed over her face. Her lips dropped open and she took a sharp breath. Her eyes widened upon him and they stared at each other, breathing as if they'd just come up for the third time. Their faces were suffused with color and neither of them seemed capable of movement. At last she reached an unsteady hand for the chalk . . . and for once she didn't correct his spelling.

Yes, she wrote. Then the blackboard was jerked from her hand and clapped upside down on the table. In one swift, impatient leap Theodore was on his feet, reaching for his jacket, carefully refraining from looking at her.

"There's northern lights tonight. Linnea and I are going out and see 'em."

It seemed to take a year instead of a minute for them to button into their outerwear and close the door behind them. And the only lights they saw were those exploding behind their closed eyes as he swung her recklessly into his arms and crushed his mouth to hers. They kissed with a wild insatiability, until everything in the world seemed attainable, and life ran rampant in their veins. They freed their mouths, clutching each other till their muscles quivered, murmuring half-sentences in desperate haste.

"Nothing was good without . . . "

"I've been miserable . . . "

"Will you really . . . "

"Yes . . . yes . . . "

"I tried not to . . . "

"I didn't know how to get you to . . . "

"Oh God, God, I love you . . . "

"I love you so much I . . . "

They kissed again, unable to climb into each other's skins as they wanted to, striving nonetheless. They ran their hands over everything allowable and as close to the unallowable as they dared. They pulled back, giddy in the unaccustomed release brought by agreement. They kissed again, still astounded, then paused to find equilibrium.

She rested her forehead against his chin. "Remind me to teach you how to spell *marry.*"

"Don't I know how?"

She pivoted her forehead against his chin: "No."

He chuckled. "Seems like it didn't make any difference."

She smiled and rubbed up and down his sides with both hands. "M-a-r-r-y spells will you marry me. M-e-r-r-y spells will you happy me."

"Ah, little one." He smiled and pulled her closer. "Don't you know that when you're my wife you'll do both?"

She had not known a heart could smile.

They kissed again, less hurried now—the initial rush was sated; they could explore at leisure. She caught his neck, drew his head down, tasting his warm, wet mouth with her own, savoring every texture, experimenting with seduction. His head moved in lazy circles, his hands kneaded her ribs. Impatience became a thing to be reckoned with and he forced himself to back off. "I said I was bringing you out here to look at the northern lights. Maybe we should take a look anyway."

"Bad idea," she murmured, crowding, kissing his neck.

He chuckled low. She felt it against her lips. "Such an unappreciative girl. Nature putting on a show like that and she doesn't even care."

"Nature's putting on another show right here and I'm trying to show you exactly how much I care."

But Theodore was noble, not heroic. He swung her around

in his arms and planted her back against his chest, circling her
from behind.

"Look."

She looked. And was awed.

The indigo sky to the north radiated an unearthly glow,
shifting fingers of pinkish light that reached and receded in
ever-changing patterns. The aurora borealis spread like the
earth's halo lit from below, reflecting from the white-mantled
land. At times not only the sky, but the earth itself seemed to
radiate, creating a night vista much as if the earth's fiery core
were glowing up through a vast opaque window. For as far
as the eye could see the land lay sleeping, swaddled in snow.
Flat, endless space, leading away to forever, like the rest of
their lives together.

"Oh, Teddy," she sighed and tilted her head back against
his shoulder. "We're going to be so happy together."

"I think we already are." He rocked them gently while they
watched the sky brighten and dim, by turns.

"And we'll live to tell the story of this night to our grandchildren. I'm just sure of it."

He kissed the crest of her cheek, envisioning it.

She covered his arms with hers. "Do you think our horses
are out there somewhere?"

"Somewhere."

"Do you think they're warm and full?"

"Mmm-hmm."

"Just like us."

That's what he loved about her: she never took joy for
granted.

"Just like us."

"Some of the best moments we've shared have been like
this, just looking at nothing . . . and everything. Oh, look!"
The lights shifted, like fresh milk spilling upward. "They're
beautiful!"

"The only place they're brighter is in Norway," Theodore
told her.   ·

"Norway. Mmm . . . I'd like to go there sometime."

"The land of the midnight sun, Ma calls it. When she and
Pa first came here they thought they'd never get used to this
prairie. No fjords, no trees, no water to speak of, no moun-

tains. The only thing that was the same was 'the lights.' She said when they got to missing the old country so much they couldn't stand it, they used to stand just like we are now, and it got them through."

Somehow Theodore's hand had come to rest on Linnea's breast. It seemed right and good so she held his wrist to keep it there.

"I've missed Nissa this past week," she said.

"Then come home with me. Tonight."

They both realized where his hand was and he moved it. She turned to face him.

"Do you think that's wise?"

"With her and Kristian right there all the time?" He pressed her collar up, leaving his hands circling her neck. "Please, Linnea. I want you back there, and we'll be married as soon as Martin can heat up the church. A week. Two weeks at the most."

She wanted very badly to give in. She'd enjoyed her stay with Clara, but it wasn't home. And it was farther to school, and Trigg had put himself out to get her there these cold mornings. And she'd missed Theodore with an ache so fierce it was frightening. She raised up on tiptoe and hugged him, sudden and hard.

"Yes, I'll come. But they'll be the longest two weeks of our lives."

He crushed her to his sturdy chest and lowered his face to her almond-scented neck and thought that if he had no more than two score years with her he'd be grateful.

He singled out Kristian at the dance the following night. "I need to talk to you, son. Think we could go outside a minute?"

Kristian seemed to measure his father a moment before replying, "Sure."

They went out where the air was brittle and the moon no bigger than a fingernail paring. The surface of the snow crunched beneath their feet and they ambled with no apparent destination, until they found themselves near the clustered wagons. The horses stood asleep with hoarfrost trimming their coarse nose hairs. Unconsciously the two men gravitated toward their own Cub and Toots and stood before their great heads, silent for some time. Down in the barn the music stopped, and the only sound was that of the horses breathing like enormous bellows.

"No lights tonight," Theodore observed at length.

"Nope."

"Lots of 'em last night."

"Oh?"

"Yeah, Linnea and me we ... " Theodore trailed off and started again. "Son, remember the day you and me we went to Zahl for coal?"

"I remember." Kristian knew already; it wasn't often Theodore called him son, and when he did it was something serious.

"Well, you told me that day how you felt about Linnea, and I want you to know I didn't take it lightly."

It was the second time he'd referred to her as Linnea when he'd never used her given name before.

"You're gonna marry her, aren't you?"

Theodore's heavy hand fell to Kristian's shoulder. "I am, but I got to know how you feel about it."

There was disappointment, but nothing like Kristian had expected. He'd had time to absorb the idea since Nissa's startling deduction.

"When?"

"Week from today if we can arrange it, two weeks if we can't."

"Wow, that's fast."

"Son, it rankled, knowing how you felt about her. I didn't set out to fall in love with her, you got to know that—I mean, after all, there's sixteen years difference between us—but it didn't seem to matter in how we felt. Guess we don't have much choice about who we fall in love with. When it happens it happens, but when it did I had plenty of guilt pangs since you'd set your cap for her first."

Kristian knew what he must say.

"Aw, she just thinks of me as a kid. I can see that now."

"It might surprise you to know that's not true. We've talked about you, and she—"

"You mean she knew how I felt about her?" Kristian's head

came up in consternation. "You told her?"

"I didn't have to tell her. What you have to understand is that a woman can tell a thing like that without being told. She could see how you felt and she was scared it'd make for problems in the family." Theodore put his palm beneath Toots's nose, feeling the white puffs of breath push against his glove. "Will it?"

They wouldn't have any problems from Kristian no matter how tough it was for him to get used to her being his father's wife. "Naw. It was probably just puppy love anyway, like Ray says." Kristian strove to lighten the mood. "But I won't have to call her Mother, will I?"

Theodore laughed. "I hardly think so. She'll still be your friend. Why don't you call her Linnea?"

Kristian peered at his father. "Would you mind?"

Theodore was the one who'd come out here to ask that question. It struck him how lucky he was to have a son like Kristian, and he turned to do something he rarely did; he took Kristian in his arms and pressed him close for a minute.

"You'd do well, son, to try to get a boy like you someday. They don't come much better."

"Oh, Pa." Kristian's arms tightened against Theodore's back.

Behind them Cub set up a gentle snoring, and from the barn came the dim sound of a concertina starting another song. In another part of the world soldiers fought for peace, but here, where a father and son pressed heart to heart, peace had already spread its blessing.

20

THEODORE AND LINNEA were married on the first Saturday of February in the little country church where Theodore and most of the wedding guests had been baptized. Its pure white spire, like an inverted lily, was set off majestically against the sky's blue breast. The one-note chime of the bell reverberated for miles on the crisp, clean air. In the graveled patch before the building the hitching rails were crowded, but the curious horses turned their blinders toward the automobiles that arrived with sound unlike any whinny they'd ever heard and left a tracery of scent definitely not resembling any leavings of their kind.

Across the delphinium sky a raucous flock of blackbirds sent forth their incessant noise, while from a field of untaken corn came the tuneless roup of pheasants. A freshly fallen snow lay upon the shorn wheat fields like a fine ermine cape, and the sun poured into the modest prairie church through the row of unadorned arched windows, as if to add an omen of joyful promise to the vows about to the exchanged.

Almost all the people who mattered most to Theodore and Linnea were present in the congregation. The horse-less carriages belonged to Superintendent Dahl and Selmer Brandonberg, who along with his wife and daughters had arrived early that morning. All the students from P.S. 28 were there, and all of Theodore's family except Clara and Trigg—

she'd had a baby girl two days earlier and was still confined
to bed. Kristian was Theodore's attendant; Carrie, Linnea's.

The bride wore a simple dress of soft oyster-white wool,
brought by her mother from the city. Its hobble skirt was
shaped like an unopened tulip bud, no wider at the hem than a
ten-gallon barrel. Her matching wide-brimmed hat was wrapped
with a frothy nest of white net that made it seem as if a covey
of industrious spiders were artfully spinning homes about her
head. On her feet were delicate satin pumps with high heels
that brought her eyes to a level with Theodore's lips and elic-
ited sighs of envy from all of her female students.

To Theodore, Linnea had never looked prettier.

The groom wore a crisp new suit of charcoal woolen wor-
sted, white shirt, black tie, and a fresh haircut that accentuated
his one lop ear and made his neck look like a whooping crane's.
His hair was severely slicked back, revealing the remnants of
his summer tan that ended an inch above his eyebrows.

To Linnea, Theodore had never looked handsomer.

"Dearly beloved . . . "

Standing before Reverend Severt, the groom was stiff, the
bride eager. Speaking their vows, he was sober, she smiling.
Bestowing the gold ring, his fingers shook while hers remained
steady. When they were pronounced man and wife Theodore
emitted a shaky sigh while Linnea beamed. When Reverend
Severt said, "You may kiss the bride," he blushed and she
licked her lips.

His kiss was brief and self-conscious, with their wedding
guests looking on. He leaned from the waist, making certain
to touch nothing but her lips while she rested a hand on his
sleeve and lifted her face to him as naturally as a sunflower
lifts its petals to the sun. Her eyelids drifted closed but his
remained open.

In the carriage on the way to the schoolhouse, with her
father's and Superintendent Dahl's automobiles spluttering
along behind them, he sat stiff as an oak bole while
she contentedly pressed her breast and cheek against his
arm.

At the schoolhouse, throughout a dinner provided by all the
church women, he was stiff and formal while conversing with
her parents, acting as if he were scared to death to touch their

daughter in front of them. When the dancing started he waltzed mechanically with Linnea, making certain their bodies stayed a respectable distance apart.

The most romantic thing he said all day was when Selmer and Judith congratulated them. "I'll take very good care of her. You don't have to worry about that, sir."

But at the dubious expression on her father's face and the crestfallen one on her mother's, Linnea could see they were not reassured.

She herself was rather amused by Theodore's uncharacteristic nervousness. There were times when she looked up and caught him studying her across the room, and to her delight, *he'd* be the one to blush. She watched him drinking beer and was fully aware of his taking care not to drink too much. And when she danced with Lars, or Ulmer, or John, she knew his eyes followed admiringly. But he was careful not to get caught at it.

Now they stood in the dusk of late afternoon with her father's car chugging off down the road and the new snow shimmering in the brilliant glow of a tangerine sunset. From inside the school building it sounded as if the fun were just beginning. Theodore buried his hands in his pockets as he looked at his wife. "Well . . . " He cleared his throat and glanced at the building. "Should we go back in?"

The last thing in the world she wanted to do was go back in to mingle and dance like a pair of wooden Indians. They were husband and wife now. She wanted them to be alone . . . and close.

"For how long?"

"Well . . . I mean, do you want to dance?"

"Not really, Theodore. Do you?" she inquired, gazing up fetchingly.

"I . . . well . . . " He shrugged, glanced at the schoolhouse door again, tugged out his watch, and snapped it open. "It's only a little after five," he noted nervously, then put the watch away.

Her eyes followed as it flashed in the waning daylight and disappeared inside the pocket of a tapered vest that had captivated her all day long, clinging to his ribs and pointing to his stomach.

"And people would think it was strange if we left at such an odd time of the day?"

Her bold conjecture corrupted his calm. He swallowed hard and stared at her, wondering exactly what people *would* say if they left now.

"Wouldn't they?" he choked out.

Poor Teddy, suffering with buck fever on his wedding night. She could see she'd have to be the one to get things started.

"We could tell them we're going to stop by Clara and Trigg's, like we promised."

"But we already did that on the way to the church."

She stepped close and rested a hand on his breast. "I want to go home, Teddy," she requested softly.

"Oh, well then, of course. If you're tired, we'll leave right away."

"I'm not tired. I just want to go home. Don't you want to?"

At her request Theodore's skin grew damp in selective spots. Lord, where did she get the calm? His stomach felt as if it held a hundred fists that clenched tighter every time he thought about the night ahead.

"Well, I . . . yes." He worked a finger inside his celluloid collar and stretched his neck. "It would feel good to get this thing off."

She raised up on tiptoe, balanced eight fingertips against his chest, and kissed him lightly. "Then let's go," she whispered. She heard the sharp hiss of indrawn breath as his palms dropped over her upper arms. He cast a cautious glance at the schoolhouse door and dropped a light kiss on her forehead.

"We'll have to say our good-byes."

"Let's say them then."

He turned her by an elbow and they moved around a horse and buggy and up the steps.

Kristian was having a wonderful time. He'd had a couple of beers, and danced with all the girls. It was plain as the pug nose on Carrie Brandonberg's face that she liked him. A lot. But every time he danced with her, Patricia Lommen's eyes followed every move they made. A song ended and he sought her out, teasing, "Next one's yours, Patricia, if you want it."

"Think you're special, don't you, Westgaard? Like you're the only boy in the place I'd care to waltz with."

"Well, ain't I?"

"Hmph!" She turned her nose in the air and tried to whip away, but he swung her into his arms without asking permission, and in seconds they were cozying up in a waltz. The longer they danced, the closer they got. Her breasts brushed his suit coat and one thing led to another, and somehow, by some magic, she was pressed against him. He thought nothing had ever felt so good in his entire life.

"You sure smell good, Patricia," he said against her ear.

"I borrowed my mother's violet water."

Her cheek rested on his jaw and the warmth of their skins seemed to mingle.

"Well, I sure like it."

"Smells like you got into your pa's bay rum, too."

They backed up and looked into each other's eyes and laughed and laughed. And both fell silent at once. And felt a wondrous tug in their vitals, and moved close again, learning what it feels like when two bodies brush.

When the song ended he held her hand. His heart slammed with the uncertainty of all first times. "It's kinda warm in here. Want to go cool off in the cloakroom for a while?"

She nodded and led the way. They had the chilly room to themselves, but moved to a far corner. From behind, he watched as she fluffed the hair up off her neck.

"Hoo! It *was* warm in there."

"You might get chilled. You want me to get your coat?"

She swung to face him. "No. This feels good."

"Hey, you're a good dancer, you know that?"

"Not as good as you, though."

"Yes, you are."

"No, I'm not, but I have better grammar. At least I don't say ain't."

"I don't say ain't anymore."

"You just did. When I was teasing you about being the only boy in the place I wanted to waltz with."

"I did?"

They laughed and fell silent, trying to think of something else to say.

YEARS

"Last time we were in the cloakroom alone you gave me the scarf you made for me for Christmas. I felt bad cause I didn't have anything to give you back."

She shrugged and toyed with the sleeve of somebody's jacket hanging beside them. "I didn't want anything back."

She had the prettiest eyes he'd ever seen, and when she looked away shyly, as she was doing now, he wanted to raise her chin and say, "Don't look away from me." But he was scared to death to touch her.

Suddenly she looked smack at him. "My mother says—" Their gazes locked and nothing more came out. Her lips dropped open and his eyes fell to them—pretty, bowed lips; just looking at them made his heart churn like a steam engine gone berserk.

"What does your mother say?" he whispered in a reedy voice.

"What?" she whispered back.

They stared at each other as if for the first time and felt the thrum of fear and expectation beat through their inexperienced bodies. He leaned to touch her lips with his—a kiss as simple and uncomplicated as youth. But when he backed up he saw she was as breathless and blushing as he. He kissed her a second time and timidly rested his hands on her waist to pull her closer. She came without compunction, hooking her hands lightly on his shoulders. When the second kiss ended they backed off and smiled at each other. Then his eyes swerved to the corner and hers dropped to his chest while they both wondered how many kisses were allowable the first time. But in seconds their gazes were drawn together again. There was scarcely a moment's hesitation before her arms lifted and his circled, and they were as close as when they'd been dancing, with their lips sealed tightly.

The outside door opened and he leaped back, blushing furiously but gripping her hand without realizing it.

It was his father and Linnea.

As the newlyweds passed into the shadowed cloakroom they looked up in surprise as two startled figures untwined from an embrace.

"Kristian . . ." Linnea said. "Oh, and Patricia. Hello."

"Hello," they replied in unison.

Linnea felt Theodore halt at her shoulder, staring at his son, obviously perplexed about how to handle such a situation. She spoke into the breach with a naturalness that eased the guilt from Patricia's face and made her stop trying to free her hand from Kristian's nervous grip.

"Your father and I are going home now. Are you staying for the rest of the dance?"

Patricia lifted hopeful eyes to Kristian. The message in them could be read even across the dim confines of the cloakroom. The young man met her gaze, looked back at the pair who'd interrupted, and answered, "For a while, anyway. Then I'll be taking Patricia home. I thought I'd take the wagon, if that's all right with you, Pa."

"That's . . . that's fine. Well, you be careful then, and we'll see you in the morning."

Kristian nodded.

"Well, excuse us while we go in and say our good-byes," Linnea put in.

Kristian nodded once more.

When the farewells were said and they left, the cloakroom was empty. The familiar green wagon was absent from the schoolyard. Searching for it, Theodore frowned.

"Now where do you suppose they've went to?"

"They've *gone* to Patricia's house, in all likelihood. Wouldn't you have when you were their age and the place was deserted while the folks were at a wedding dance?"

He glanced up the road to the east. Standing beside their own black carriage she looked up at the freshly cut hair above his coat collar, his wide shoulders, and his distracted eyes. *The time has come, Theodore, for them and for us. Don't fight it.* Possessively, she slipped a hand under his arm and asked in a quiet tone, "Wouldn't you, *now* when the place is deserted and we have it all to ourselves?" Nissa had gone back to Clara's right after the church service and would be there for at least a week.

He looked down at her, and from the expression on his face she knew Kristian and Patricia had fled his mind.

She made the short ride home beside a stiff, formal stranger, who dropped her at the door and left her to worry while he drove down toward the barn to see to the horse and buggy.

The kitchen was cold. She lit a lamp then sat on a hard chair at the table. Her clothes and personal items were still in her old bedroom upstairs. When would they be moved down? And who would move them?

The door opened and Theodore stepped inside, bringing a current of chill night air that made the lantern flame twist and flicker. He stood looking around the room as if it belonged to someone else. His eyes moved back to Linnea with her high net-swathed hat still on her head, her coat still buttoned, and her gloved hands folded in her lap.

"You're cold. I'll get a fire going."

She sensed his great relief at having something to do as he made the stove clatter and chime. In no time at all he clapped the lid over the fire, and the room fell silent.

Linnea rose from her chair and Theodore wiped his palms on his thighs as she came to stand near him at the stove.

"Well . . . " he said with an uncertain smile.

She wondered if she'd have to be the one to initiate every move throughout this night. What a disappointing thought. She'd imagined that a man who'd been married before would be very adept at this. Instead, Theodore flinched each time she drew near, and his eyes wandered from hers whenever she tried to catch his gaze.

Turning aside, she held out her hands toward the thin warmth from the fire. He studied the back of her hat, the froth of ivory net with its tiny slubs like morning dew caught in a spiderweb, the fine separations in her hair where built-in combs clung to hold the flowery concoction on her head. She dropped her chin and his glance was drawn to the proper little crescent hairstyle beneath the hat brim, the shallow well at her nape where several loose hairs caught on her wool collar. He let his eyes rove from her narrow shoulders to her hips to the hem of her coat, and he was clutched by an ache of arousal so fierce he rammed his hands beneath his armpits to keep from shocking her with what he wanted to do at this ungodly hour of the day. And in the kitchen yet.

"Well, everyone seemed to be having a good time at the dance," she said, though the dance was the furthest thing from her mind.

"Do you want your coat off now?" he asked at the same moment.

"Oh, yes, I guess so." She tugged the new gray gloves from her fingers while he stood watching over her shoulder. She tucked them into her coat pocket, then unbuttoned the garment. He peeled it from her shoulders and stood uncertainly, wondering what to do with it. She had always kept it in her bedroom upstairs.

She glanced over her shoulder and their gazes collided for an electrified second. "Well, I reckon I'll hang this in my room now."

He turned into the front parlor and she listened to his footsteps snapping across the linoleum.

In the semi-dark he hung her coat on a hook, then stood for a moment clinging to the hook with both hands, recalling how carefully he'd dust-mopped the floor in here, and changed the bedding, and put the room in perfect order. Probably not as clean as Ma would have done, but the best he could do. He heaved a deep breath and headed back for the kitchen.

At the sound of his returning footsteps Linnea snatched up the teakettle and began industriously filling it from the water pail.

From the doorway he watched her move across the room with tiny, careful steps in the skirt too narrow to allow proper movement. Such foolishness. Last year bird wings, this year narrow skirts that seemed like shackles. He supposed he'd be paying for many feminine geegaws in his life. But he didn't mind. He wanted to do so much for her . . . so much. And besides, there was something about the skirt and the way it revealed her ankles that turned a man's head clean around.

"What's that called then, that skirt?"

"A hobble."

"It's a mite skinny, isn't it?" He watched from behind as she set the kettle on the stove, then swung around brightly.

"Mother says they're all the rage. A Harvard professor said narrower hems would save on wool for uniforms . . . so this is . . . the . . . "

Looking at him, her words trailed away. He stood staring at her, tallying the hours till their normal bedtime. God in heaven, some nights when they were studying they hadn't gone to bed till nearly eleven o'clock. That was a good five hours and more!

"Are you hungry?" she asked, as if suddenly inspired.

"No." He tapped his vest buttons for effect. "I ate plenty at the school." Guiltily, he remembered his manners. "Oh, are you?"

"No, not a bit." She glanced around as if searching for something. "Well . . . " Now he had her doing it! An hour ago she'd been totally confident. Now his jitters were rubbing off on her. "My things are all upstairs yet. Should I . . . I mean . . . "

"Oh, I'll get them. Might as well bring them down to my room, too."

He practically leaped to the spare lantern in his eagerness to get out of the room. When she heard his footsteps halt above her she smiled, covered her mouth with one hand, and shook her head at the floor. Then she followed him up the stairs to find him standing in her doorway, rattled and uncertain.

"Excuse me, Theodore." He jumped aside to let her pass, then watched her move to the dresser, open drawers, and select things, piling them on her arm—everything white, some with wisps of eyelet and blue ribbon. From the dresser top she took a brass-handled brush, a comb, a hairpin holder, and a heart-shaped bottle of toilet water; from a hook behind the door, her blue chenille robe. Then, on last thought, she returned to the dresser for a small rock.

Joining him, she said brightly, "There. I guess that's everything I need. The rest can wait till tomorrow."

"What's that?" He pointed to her hand.

She opened her palm and they both looked down. "It's an agate I found on the road last fall. It has a stripe of brown the exact color of your eyes."

She looked into them and he was caught off guard, awed afresh by the fact that she was really his and that as long ago as last fall she'd been interested in the color of his eyes. But he stepped back as she moved through the door and down the steps, with the light from his lantern gilding the top of her hat. At his bedroom doorway she stopped politely and let him lead the way inside and set the lantern on the dresser.

Her eyes followed hesitantly; but the picture of Melinda was gone. Theodore opened a dresser drawer, then straightened to face her, eager to please. "You can put your things in here. I cleaned it out and threw some old things away to make room."

"Thank you, Theodore." She placed her collection in the drawer beside a stack of blue cambric work shirts and a pair of elastic sleeve holders he never used. His blood pounded, having her so close. It had been so long since he'd watched a woman do such things: smooth the clothes, shut the drawer, align her brush and comb on the dresser scarf, place the rock and the hairpin dish and the bottle of toilet water beside two spare celluloid collars, his own hairbrush and . . . and a handful of *rivets?*

His hand lashed out and scooped them up. "I was fixin' a harness yesterday," he explained sheepishly and dropped them into a drawer, then slammed it guiltily behind him.

With a tilting smile she stepped over and opened the drawer again, nudging him out of the way. She dug in the corner beneath a pile of winter underwear and found the metal pieces, and dropped them where they'd been before, on top of the dresser.

"This is still your room. If we're to share it, you may leave your rivets exactly where you did before you married me."

Had she recited a flowery poem, he could not have loved her more at that moment. He wondered again what time it was and if she'd think him perverted if he leaned over and kissed her and carried her to the bed as he wanted to, ignoring the fact that the rest of the world was either doing their milking or eating their supper right now. Or dancing at his wedding dance without him. What in God's name were they doing talking about rivets? How did a man lead up to the suggestion that his wife get ready for bed at five forty-five in the afternoon?

She looked around the room, all guileless and innocent, her top-heavy hat making her neck appear very fragile. The bodice of her dress disappeared beneath a form-fitting jacket with a high neck and tiny looped buttons running waist to throat. Lord, let it be a whole dress under there, he thought, as he suggested, "You might like to take your jacket and hat off and get more comfortable, so I'll leave you alone for a few minutes."

She'd had dreams of how this night should be. They had not included a painfully shy husband. She remembered things

Clara had told her, and she greedily wanted it all. In a soft, quavering voice, she ventured, "I thought that was the husband's job."

Theodore's eyes shifted to the clock that stood on the bedside stand ticking, ticking, ticking into the sudden silence, the hour hand nearly touching six. He looked back into his wife's eyes. "Did you?"

She nodded twice, so slightly he had to watch closely to catch it. Her eyes were wide and lustrous in the lamplight as she stood with one hand resting on the edge of the dresser.

He took one step and her lips parted. He took a second and she swallowed. He took a third and her head tilted up, her eyes dark now, lifting to his from underneath the hat brim. They stood close, rapt, watching each other breathe. He kissed her once, very lightly, much more lightly than he wanted, then turned her around by the shoulders. In the mirror she saw only the top half of his face above the beehive of netting.

His blunt fingertips searched out the teardrop pearl and withdrew a nine-inch hatpin. He clamped it in his teeth and gently freed the combs behind her ears. As he lifted the hat free, one comb caught a blond strand and pulled it free. She reached up nervously to brush it back while he anchored the pin in the hat and set it down before her.

Their eyes met in the mirror, so dark neither appeared to have color beyond the sparkle of anticipation. The wisp of loose hair trailed free behind her ear. He stood so close his breath sent it waving like a strand of wheat in a summer breeze. He touched it, lifting and clumsily tucking it back in, then watched it drift stubbornly down her thin, sculptured neck. She waited breathlessly, willing him to go on. As if he divined her thoughts, his unaccustomed fingers probed the secrets of her chignon, finding celluloid pins hidden within, freeing them one by one until the mass of gold drooped, then tumbled under its own weight to lay in a furl on her shoulders. He combed it with callused fingers. Its fine texture caught on his horny skin. When had he last smelled a woman's hair? He bent and buried his face in the fragrant mass, and drew a prolonged breath. In the mirror she watched his face disappear then reappear as he straightened.

When their eyes met, a thousand pulsebeats seemed to fight for space in his throat. She had taken up the perfume bottle. Holding his gaze in the mirror, she slowly uncapped it, tipped it against a fingertip, then brushed the scent beneath her uptilted jaw. Once, twice, until lily of the valley had turned the room to a bower. She pushed back a cuff, exposing the delicate blue-veined skin of one wrist, scented it, then the other, and silently recapped the bottle, all the while holding him prisoner with her sapphire eyes.

Where had a girl her age learned to do a thing like that? All day long, each time he'd thought of this hour, his imagination had stalled at the thought of her inexperience. But her invitation was unmistakable.

He pressed her arms, pivoted her like a ballerina in a music box, then studied her shadowed eyes momentarily before reaching for the button at her throat. It was a quarter the size of his thumbnail, caught in a delicate loop that thwarted his fumbling fingers twice before he discovered how to manage it. Then slowly, slowly he worked his way down thirteen of the same.

Beneath the jacket her bodice fit taut over breasts that lifted and fell to the rapid beat of her breathing. He lifted his eyes to her delicate mouth, the lips parted and waiting.

How incredible—they were man and wife.

He bent to touch her mouth with his own, the shadow of her hair eclipsing his face as he cupped her jaws and kissed her with a first tender consideration—soft, plucking, plural kisses while the sleek warmth of his inner lips joined hers. She swayed toward him, her fingertips touching his lapels.

When at length he lifted his head, they were both breathing harder, their hearts dancing a rondo as they gazed into each other's eyes.

Wordlessly he removed her jacket, folded it, and laid it on the dresser.

She reached for his tie and collar button, determined to do her share.

Tick, tick, tick came from the bedside.

"It's only six o'clock," he reminded her in a strange, forced voice.

Her fingers fell still at his throat. Her clear, guileless eyes lifted and met his squarely.

"Is there a right and a wrong time?"

He'd never pondered the question before. In his whole life he'd never done anything like this except at bedtime, in the sheath of late hours and darkness. With something akin to surprise he realized he'd come here prepared to be the teacher, only to find himself being taught.

"No, I guess not," he replied, and his heart thrust hard as she proceeded, removing his tie, opening his collar, and freeing the top three shirt buttons until the vest stopped her progress. Glistening dark hair sprang into view, and she pressed her lips into the cleft, something she'd long imagined doing.

A ragged breath fanned the top of her hair and his arms came around her.

"Your jacket," she interrupted, and he pulled back and let her take it from him to hang on a wall hook beside her coat. Next, she freed his vest buttons, then took his watch in her hand and looked up at him.

"Let's never watch clocks, Teddy," she requested softly, then laid it on the dresser.

When she turned he was waiting to haul her near, slanting his mouth over hers with lips open, tongue searching out the treasures of her willing mouth. She pressed close, lifting, nestling. His arms swept her up commandingly and took her against muscle and sinew she'd touched too few times—ah, far too few.

The kiss twisted between them with wondrous urgency, his tongue slewing the interior of her mouth, hers probing in a wild, loving quest. She spread her fingers wide over the warm satin back of his vest, inquisitive to know each taut inch of him. His chest heaved against her breasts, making them yearn for more.

He ripped his mouth from hers, labored breath pouring on her ear. "Oh, Linnea . . . "

She backed away only far enough to search his eyes. "What's wrong, Teddy? All day long you've been acting as if you're scared to death of me."

"I am." He chuckled ruefully—a forced, pained sound in the lamplit room, then he scraped the hair back from her temples and held her head in two broad palms. "You're so young. It keeps coming back to me, no matter how I try to put it from my mind."

"I'm not. I'm a woman, and I'm ready for this. You have a fixation with time—clocks, years. What do they matter when there's love? Please . . . please . . . " She dropped a nosegay of quick kisses on his chin, his cheek, his mouth. "Please . . . count the love, not the years. I'm your wife now. Don't make me wonder any longer."

One quick, unresolved kiss, then he drew back to search her dress for closures. Without a word she presented her back, lifting her hair aside while he released buttons to her spine. Inside she wore a sleeveless white cotton garment that disappeared into her petticoats. He watched, fascinated, as she unbuttoned the waistband of those petticoats, then shimmied the dress down her arms and let both drop over her slim hips.

When she turned to face him he saw her undergarment fully. It covered her from shoulder to mid-thigh, where it was banded with elastic on both legs. The waist was secured by a thin white cord tied in front. The scoop-necked bodice held another row of buttons—closed—revealing little more than the shadows at her collarbone.

His ma wore undershirts and snuggies, and in winter, long underwear. He'd never seen anything like the white bit his wife had on. Filmy stockings disappeared inside the pantaloonlike legs, and her calves were slender and shapely as she stood before him in the gleaming satin shoes that arched her foot daintily.

When his eyes rose from them to her face, both Theodore and Linnea were flushed and breathless.

A self-conscious smile winged past her lips and disappeared. His vest took a sudden ride down his arms and landed on the floor behind him, revealing crisp black suspenders that dented the shoulders of his starched shirt. He hooked them with his thumbs and sent them drooping, then yanked his shirttails out of his trousers and reached for her hand, holding it loosely while his eyes wandered to her breasts and he unconsciously freed his last few shirt buttons.

It was a glorious sight, watching him undress. Watching the play of shrugging shoulder muscles, and suspenders falling, and a sea of wrinkles appearing on a shirt bottom, and wrists twisting while cuffs were freed.

Then the shirt lay on the floor and Linnea couldn't withhold an exclamation of appreciation.

"Oh, Theodore . . . " she breathed on a falling note. "Look at youuu . . . " Impulsively she reached out four fingertips and tested the dark hair that branched across his warm chest, then followed it halfway down his belly before realizing where she was heading. Quickly she retracted the curious hand and clasped it with the other. Her wide eyes flashed up. He captured her hand and placed it on the spot it had abandoned.

It played over him, tantalized.

How hard, how silky, how masculine. How wondrously different from herself he was. While she explored the hollow of his throat, the backs of his knuckles stroked her collarbone, then brushed down her front buttons.

She forgot how to breathe.

His hand moved back up and gently cupped a breast.

Her eyes dropped closed and she stood shadow still, steeped in sensation. Goose bumps climbed her arms, her belly, rippled the breast he gently kneaded. It hardened for him and changed shape beneath his palm. His tongue touched her lower lip, traced a wet, circular path, bringing him back to the point of origin, which he bit and sucked into his mouth, massaging it with only the tip of his tongue until she wriggled slightly and shivered. Up stole her hands to his chest, his neck, his hair, fingers spreading wide within it, caressing his skull as she pulled his head down to receive a bride's kiss.

Her tongue danced lustily within his mouth. Her body strained high, pulsing against him until he took both breasts and felt her driving the handfuls of flesh into his clasp. Around her back he reached, hands skimming down her buttocks, gripping hard to lift her high against him. Rhythm began, a sweet slow lolling that rocked them one against the other.

He set a river flowing in her body, flooding its banks. The sensation was so sudden it took the starch from her knees. As she drooped, their mouths parted with a soft succulent sound, and for a moment he bore her weight with a knee, until, astride, she knew a momentary relief from the pressures building within. The knee let her back to the floor, then slipped away.

His hands played over her spine. Their tongues and lips were joined when he first touched bare skin on her backside. His head jerked up in surprise.

"What is this thing?"

Arms looped around his neck, she tilted her head back, somewhat surprised, too. Truly, she thought he'd have known.

"A teddy."

"A what?" He backed away and looked down, holding her loosely by the waist.

"A teddy. The kind that's not named after Mr. Roosevelt."

He chuckled and gave it a second look.

"Mmm . . . a teddy, huh?" Kissing her again he buried his hand inside an open porthole that seemed to extend from the back of her waist to eternity. He soothed her curved flesh while wondering exactly how far the access extended, moved to explore her stomach, and sure enough, the open placket ran from belly to backside, under her legs.

But as his explorations continued, the construction of her garments ceased to matter. His fingers found their way inside the white cotton welt and flattened over her warm stomach to ride lower, lower, finally touching her intimately. At his entry she jumped once, then relaxed against the strong arm banding her waist. Worlds of wonder opened up in her mind's eye, worlds no amount of imagination had prepared her for. Colors danced behind her closed lids, from pastoral to passionate. She swayed and rocked against him, flowing into primal rhythm.

His touch went deeper, infusing her with delight in her own flesh.

"Oh, Teddy . . . Teddy . . ." she murmured, awash with desire.

He left her to move toward the lantern, and she called softly, "No!" He paused, turning. "Please . . . I've never . . . I mean . . ." Her cheeks pinkened and she looked down at her hands, then resolutely at him. "I want to see you."

His heart drummed heavily at her request. He had not thought of women that way—a new lesson for Theodore Westgaard.

Leaving the lantern glowing softly, he drew her to the side of the bed and leaned down to loosen his shoestrings. She followed suit, slipping the satin shoes from her heels and setting them neatly side by side. He reached beneath his trouser legs to

peel off his stockings, and again she followed his lead, rolling
her elastic garters to her ankles and taking the opaque stockings with them. He stretched to his feet, unbuttoned and doffed
his trousers, but her eyes remained downcast as she realized he
was standing before her naked.

"Linnea . . . "

She raised her eyes in an evasive sweep until they locked
with his. The only sound in the room was the tick of the clock
and the thunder of their hearts in their ears. He reached out a
hand, palm up. She placed hers in it and he drew her to her
feet and dispensed with the teddy without further delay.

Before she had time to grow self-conscious he swept her to
the bed, dropping beside her in a full-length embrace. With
their mouths joined, he rolled her to her back, finding her naked
breast first with his hand, then with his tongue, murmuring
low in his throat as it pearled up in nature's reach for more.
He laved it, leaving it wet for the stroke of his thumb. He
smiled down at it, then rubbed his soft, upturned lips over its
ascended tip with infinite gentleness before turning his attention to its twin.

She twisted languorously, murmuring his name, lifting in
invitation, threading his hair with her fingers. His wet tongue
felt silken and profoundly powerful as he suckled, released,
suckled again, drawing sensation from deep in her belly. She
cried out, one ecstatic hosanna, as he tugged gently with his
teeth. She lolled, immersed in pleasure, stretching her arms
over her head until her belly went hollow and he stroked it
with his hand, then gave it a lingering kiss before crushing
her tightly, taking her on a rolling journey across the bed. She
landed on top and shinnied down for more of his mouth. Her
hair caught between them; he flicked it aside and kissed her
almost roughly. She clung, returning stroke for stroke.

After long minutes she lifted her face.

He held the hair back from her temples with both hands,
eyes glittering up at her with dark, intense passion. "Linnea, I
love you. I used to lay here alone and think of this. So many
nights, when you were upstairs, over my head. But you're better than you were in my wishes."

I love you . . .

I love you . . .

I love you . . .

Some of the words were his, some hers, indistinguishable one from the other as they sated themselves upon kisses until kisses would no longer suffice.

He rolled her to her back, leaning above her, studying her eyes while their hearts pounded with one accord. A brief kiss on her parted lips, a briefer one on her breast, a hand on her stomach, an intense flame leaping from his gaze to hers while he reached low, low . . .

He touched her with care, tutored her limbs to widen beneath his caress, her flesh to blossom to his exploration. And when she was lithe and lissome and fervid, he captured her hand and curled it inside his own, then placed it on his distended flesh and taught her some things a woman has to know.

He closed his eyes and groaned softly while his flesh slipped through her hand. His head dropped back, while she wondered at her power to bring such abandon to a man so strong and indomitable. When he trembled and his breathing grew ragged, there awaited that greatest pleasure of all. He hovered above her and his voice came shaken at her ear. "If anything hurts, tell me and I'll stop. Now easy . . . easy . . . "

His entry was slow, sacred. His elbows trembled near her shoulders while he waited. She drew him deep.

"Lin, ahh, Lin . . . " came his utterance as she lifted to impale herself.

Nature had planned nothing in vain; sword to sheath, key to lock—they fit with an arcane exquisiteness. He found her no girl, but all the woman he'd ever want. She taught him a new youth, a boundless thing of the heart rather than the calendar. Lying beneath the sinuous motion of his driving hips she followed his wordless commands and lifted in accommodation. She came to know the touch of his breath moving her hair and warming her neck; he the gentle grip of those strands as they coiled against his damp forehead. Together they discovered a timeless lovers' language fashioned of murmurs and rustles and sighs. She learned his capacity for gentleness; he her capacity for strength. Together they learned when to reverse roles. He found a joy in making her arch and gasp, she an equal joy in his shuddering call of release. She discovered that twice was possible for a man; he that thrice was not enough for some women.

And the keen, seeping pleasure to be found in the after minutes. Ahh, those weak, wilted stretches of time when their sapped bodies could do no more or no less than tangle together in sated exhaustion.

And years mattered little. All that mattered was that they were man and wife, consummate, that it was their wedding night and through it they gave each other the ultimate recompense for all of life's tribulations . . . again . . . and again . . . and again . . .

21

IT WAS A winter of great change, that winter of 1918. The changes happened not only within the Westgaard family, but within their newest member, and throughout the world at large. In her blissful, newly married state it would have been easy for Linnea to forget that American doughboys were going to France to make the world safe for democracy and to bask instead in the happiness that glowed within her heart. But the example set by her own family made her realize she, too, had an obligation, perhaps an even greater one in her position as a teacher. Linnea talked Superintendent Dahl into allowing the school to subscribe to the newspaper, and with the children she followed the events in Europe in an effort to understand.

The cry to defeat fascism was everywhere, but while in late January it was announced that the first U.S. troops were occupying front-line trenches, stateside military camps were still bulging with restless soldiers forced to drill in civilian clothes with broomsticks instead of rifles. Democratic fervor alone would not win the war. It would take supplies, and supplies took raw materials, and raw materials were limited. The War Board was formed to determine production priorities, and America cheerfully tightened up, cut back, and sang rousing patriotic songs. New factories sprang up overnight, turning out overcoats, shoes, rifles, gas masks, blankets, trucks, and locomotives, while all businesses not engaged in war contracts closed on Mondays. A ban was put on Sunday automobile driving. People were encouraged to use more sweaters and less coal, eat more bran and less wheat, more spinach and less meat, and adopt the "gospel of the clean plate." But above all, Americans were asked to give.

What it gave most of was its men. A half million of them reached France by the spring of 1918, and one of the volunteers was Bill Westgaard. The church had a special service for him on the Saturday before he left, and from that day on a service flag bearing a single blue star hung in the nave, raising countless prayers that there never come a time when a gold star be sewn in its place. Shortly thereafter, Judith wrote with the news that Adrian Mitchell had received a draft notice and was already gone.

Bill and Adrian may have been rejected suitors, but it mattered little to Linnea. The war had touched her personally now, and she felt a zeal to do her part in whatever way possible.

There were countless things the children could do to help with the war effort; all they needed was organization. Noon knitting became the favorite pastime. Linnea herself sought Nissa's help in learning how, and each mother was asked to teach her daughters. At school a chart was posted, with a star for each stocking or muffler completed. To Linnea's amazement, Kristian and Ray showed up one day, each with a ball of yarn and a pair of needles. It caused a great deal of laughter when the boys awkwardly took up the craft, but soon they had every boy in the schoolhouse joining them. With the exception of Allen Severt, who adamantly called knitting "sissy stuff" and became an outcast because of his attitude.

But all the others were willing and eager to help with all of Linnea's plans. Patricia Lommen came up with the idea of piecing a quilt and everybody enthusiastically agreed to bring scraps of cloth from home. As the children watched it take shape, plans were begun for an auction sale at which to sell it, proceeds to be donated to the Red Cross. Word of the auction spread and the cloakroom began filling with a motley collection of donations, including several prime muskrat skins from Ray and Kristian. Libby Severt, who showed a promising talent in art, made two large posters advertising the event: one was hung in the church, the other in the Alamo General Store and Post Office. A farmer from a neighboring township volunteered a player piano and even offered to deliver it. From then until the day of the auction, the schoolhouse rang with music.

It was Nissa who suggested a cakewalk to go along with the auction, and softhearted Frances who read in the newspaper about clothing drives for refugees and shyly suggested taking up a collection for that cause along with all the rest.

The big day was dubbed "War Day," and as it approached excitement ran high and auction items overflowed into the main schoolroom. An auctioneer from Wildrose volunteered his services and old man Tveit brought an unexpected wagon of coal to put up for auction. By the time the day was over, P.S. 28 had earned $768.34 for the noble cause.

Theodore watched Linnea bloom throughout that winter. She took up her war project with characteristic enthusiasm and carried it to completion only to immediately begin another: this time a book drive for soldiers overseas. It was as successful as the auction sale had been. After the book drive came the making of scrapbooks for soldiers lying in European hospitals and the formation of a Junior League to sell liberty bonds. And when the state school board officially announced that the study of the German language was being dropped from all curricula, she stood up in church one Sunday and requested that in accordance with the current administration's fervor for Americanization, all table prayers be said in English instead of Norwegian. How could anyone refuse a woman who'd almost single-handedly raised $768 in the name of life, liberty, and the pursuit of happiness?

And if Linnea brought a fervid enthusiasm to her organizational abilities, she brought no less to her marriage. She turned nineteen in late February and was fond of whispering into Theodore's ear as she lay atop him in bed at night that she was learning more during her nineteenth year than in all the years of her life. And it was much more fun.

She was an ardent, uninhibited lover, insistent on "trying" things even Theodore had never tried before.

"How come you know about that?" he asked one night when the quilts were thrown back and the lantern was burning, as usual.

"Clara told me."

"Clara!"

"Shh!" She covered his lips and giggled.

He lowered his voice to a whisper. "You mean my little sister, Clara?"

"Your little sister Clara is a woman, in case you hadn't noticed, and she and Trigg have a wonderful time in bed. But if Clara ever finds out I told you, she'll kill me."

"Hmm ... I'll have to remember to thank Clara next time I see her."

She socked him a good one. "Teddy, don't you dare!" He caught her wrists and flung her beneath him and bit her bottom lip.

"You wanna talk about it all night or you wanna try it, Mrs. Westgaard?"

Within minutes they were trying it.

Another time, after they'd made love, Linnea lay in the crook of Theodore's shoulder, thinking of how she used to wonder what lovemaking would be like.

She chuckled and admitted, "I used to think you'd squash me like a bug if we ever made love together."

A rumble of laughter sounded beneath her ear. "Oh? So you used to think about it?"

"Sometimes."

"How much?"

"Oh, I don't know."

"Come on ... how much?"

"Oh, all right. A lot."

"When?"

"What do you mean, when?"

"I mean, how long before we were married?"

"Mmm ... at least four years."

"Four—aw, you didn't even know me then."

"Yes I did. But your name at that time was Lawrence."

"Lawrence!"

"Oh, lay back down and don't get all huffed up. I had to name you *some*thing, since I didn't know who you were yet."

A powerful arm looped her neck in a lazy headlock. "Girl, you're a little bit crazy, you know that?"

"I know."

He chuckled again. "So tell me what you used to imagine."

"Oh . . . at first I used to imagine how it was to kiss a boy—I mean a man. I've kissed an awful lot of strange things in my day. Tables, icy windows, pillows—pillows work really well, actually, if you haven't got the real thing. Then there are blackboards, the back of your own hand, plates, doors—"

"Plates?"

"Well, sometimes when I'd be doing the dishes I'd imagine I'd just finished having supper with a man and he was helping me do the cleanup afterward. I mean, you look in this nice clean plate and there's this person looking back at you, and you close your eyes and pretend and . . . well, you've got to use your imagination, Theodore."

"Not anymore, I don't," he countered, and rolled her onto his belly to end the night as they ended each.

She was more than he'd ever hoped for. She was bright, happy, spontaneous. She made each day a joyous sharing, a cause for celebration, a span of hours so piercingly rich and full he wondered how he'd ever survived those solitary years without her. He took her to school each morning, and from the moment he kissed her good-bye beside the warming stove, he counted the hours till he could go back and collect her. He never knew what she'd come up with next. She saw things from a refreshingly youthful perspective that often made him laugh, and always made him happy she was as young as she was.

One particularly frigid morning as they stood beside the stove waiting for the building to warm up, the school mouse slipped out of hiding and cowered by the mop board.

"Didn't you ever catch that pest?"

"I never tried. I didn't have the heart to kill the poor little thing, so I've been feeding him cheese instead. He's my friend."

"Feeding him! Linnea, mice are—"

"Shh! He's cold . . . see? Be very still and watch."

They stood silently, unmoving, until the mouse timidly scuttled closer, drawn by the heat, and stood on the opposite side of the stove on his hind legs, warming his front feet as if they were human hands.

Theodore had never seen anything like it in his life.

"Do you two do this often?" Theodore asked, and at the sound of his voice the creature retreated, stopped, and turned a bright-pink eye on them.

"There's enough death—don't you think—that we don't have to cause any more."

He wondered if it were possible to love any stronger than he did at that moment. Life had never been more perfect.

But one day in late March Kristian shattered that perfection.

He'd been down along the creek bottom with Ray, hauling in their traps for the season, and at supper that night, Theodore could tell there was something on the boy's mind.

"Something bothering you, Kristian?" he asked.

Kristian looked up and shrugged.

"What is it?"

"You're not gonna like it."

"There's lots of things I don't like. That don't change 'em."

"I've been talking with Ray about it for a long time, and I'm not sure if he's decided yet, but I have."

"Decided what?"

Kristian set his fork down. "I wanna enlist in the army."

Eyelids could have been heard blinking in the room. All eating stopped.

"You want to *what?*" Theodore repeated menacingly.

"I've been thinking about it for a long time. I want to do my part in the war, too."

"Are you crazy? You're only seventeen years old!"

"I'm old enough to shoot a gun. That's all that counts."

"You're a wheat farmer. The draft board ain't gonna get you. You're exempt from the draft—have you forgotten that?"

"Pa, you aren't listening."

Theodore jumped to his feet. "Oh, I'm listening, all right, but what I'm hearing don't make a lick of sense." Linnea had never seen Teddy so angry. He pointed a finger at Kristian's nose and shouted, "You think all that's going on over there is them doughboys still pointing brooms at each other, well you're wrong, sonny! They're getting shot and killed!"

"I want to drive airplanes. I want to *see* 'em!"

"Airplanes!" Theodore drove his hands into his hair, twisted away in exasperation, then rounded on Kristian again. "What you'll drive is a pair of horses and a plow, because I won't let you go."

"Maybe I want to do more with my life than drive horses and a plow. Maybe I want to see more than horses' rumps and smell more than horse droppings. If I enlist, I can do that."

"What you'll see over there is the inside of a trench, and what you'll smell is mustard gas. Is that what you want, boy?"

Linnea touched Theodore's arm. "Teddy—"

He shrugged it off violently. "Keep out of this! This is between me and my boy! I said, is that what you want?"

"You can't stop me, Pa. All I have to do is wait till school's done and walk down that road, and you won't know where to find me. All I have to do is tell 'em I'm eighteen and they'll take me."

"Now I raised a liar, too, as well as a fool."

"I wouldn't have to be one if you'd give your okay."

"Never! Not so long as I draw breath."

Kristian showed profound control as he said quietly, "I'm sorry you feel that way, Pa, but I'm going just the same."

From that day forward the tension in the house was palpable. It extended into Theodore and Linnea's bedroom, too, for that night was the first since they'd been married that they didn't make love. When she touched his shoulder, he said gruffly, "Let me be. I'm not in the mood tonight."

Abashed that he'd turn away her offer of comfort when he most needed it, she rolled to her side of the bed and swallowed the tears thickening her throat.

At school, too, Linnea's placid days seemed to be over. As if the sap were rising in him as well as in every cottonwood on the prairie, Allen Severt started acting up again. He put pollywogs in the water crock, a piece of raw meat behind the books in the bookshelf, and syrup on Frances's desk seat. There were times when Linnea wanted to bash his head against the wall. Then one day he went too far and she did.

He was walking past her at the four-o'clock bell when he nonchalantly plucked her watch out and let it retract with a snap against her breast. Before her shock had fully registered, she grabbed two fistfuls of his hair and cracked his skull against the cloakroom wall.

"Don't you ever do that again!" she hissed, an inch from his nose, pulling his hair so hard it lifted the corners of his eyes. "Is that understood, *Mis*ter Severt?"

Allen was so stunned he didn't move a muscle.

The young children looked on saucer-eyed, and Frances Westgaard snickered softly.

"You're hurtin' me," Allen ground out through clenched teeth.

"I'll do worse than that if you continue with this sort of behavior. I'll have you expelled from school."

With his eyes slanted back, Allen looked more malevolent than ever. She could sense the vindictiveness in those cold, pale eyes, something worse than heartlessness. It was a cruelty with which she simply did not know how to deal. And now she had embarrassed him in front of the other children for the second time. She could sense his vengefulness growing, and her hands shook as she released his head.

"Children, you are excused," she said to the others, her voice far from calm. Allen shrugged away from the wall and shouldered her roughly aside on his way to the door. "Not you, Allen. I want to talk to you. . . . Allen, come back here!"

But he swung around at the bottom of the steps and pierced her with a venomous glare. "I'm gonna make you sorry, teacher," he vowed, low enough that only she could hear, then turned and marched away without a backward look.

She stared after him, realizing only after it was over how weak-kneed she was. She sank onto a cloakroom bench, hugging her shaky stomach. Well, he's backed you into a corner again, so what are you going to do, sit here quaking like a pup with the palsy or march down to his house and tell them what a devil they have on their hands?

She marched down to his house to tell them what a devil they had on their hands. Unfortunately, Martin wasn't home at the time, and his wife's response was "I'll speak to Allen about it." It was said dryly, condescendingly, with one eyebrow raised. Her lips were compressed into a superior moue as she held the door open for Linnea's exit.

I'm sure you'll speak to Allen, thought Linnea, while her own hope of having Allen dressed down on the spot went unsatisfied.

She walked home feeling more frustrated than ever and utterly ineffectual.

Two days later she found her mouse dead in a baited trap.

She told Theodore about it and he wanted to march right down to Severt's house himself and put a couple more dents in the kid's skull, but she said she could handle it, and he said are you sure, and she said yes, and something good came of it anyway, because they made love again as they used to, and afterward she begged him to talk to Kristian about going to war, only this time without anger. And he agreed to try.

But the attempt failed. The two of them talked down in the barn the next day, but Theodore's fear for his son's life manifested itself in anger once again, and the session ended with the two of them shouting and Kristian marching out and heading down the road without telling anybody where he was going.

He went to Patricia's house because lately it felt better to be with her than with anybody else he knew.

"Hi," he said when she answered the door.

"Oh . . . hi!" Her eyes brightened and a flush beautified her face.

"You busy?"

"No, just knitting. Come in!"

"I was wondering if you could come out instead. I mean, well . . . I'd like to talk to you. Alone someplace."

"Sure. Just let me get my coat. Ma?" she yelled. "I'm going for a walk with Kristian!" A moment later she appeared in a brown wool coat with a tan scarf looped over her head, its tails hanging over her shoulders. They both stuffed their hands into their pockets as they headed down the prairie road. Beside it the snow was already pithy and showed deep ruts. The north-westerlies had a milder breath—soon the snowdrops would blossom in the ditches. The days were growing longer and the late afternoon sun was warm on their faces.

He needed to talk, but not now. What he needed now was to simply walk along beside Patricia with their elbows softly bumping. She took her hand out of her near coat pocket and he followed suit. Their knuckles brushed ... once ... and again ... and he took her hand. She squeezed his tightly and looked up at him with something more than a smile: a look of growing awareness and trust. She tipped her head against his shoulder for two steps, then they walked again without saying a word.

Not until they'd turned and were heading back did he speak.

"You ever get sick of looking at the same old road, the same old fields?"

"Sometimes."

"You ever wonder what it's like beyond Dickinson?"

"I've been beyond Dickinson. It looks just like it does around here."

"No, I mean *way* beyond Dickinson. Where there's mountains. And the ocean. Don't you wonder what they look like?"

"Sometimes. But even if I saw them, I'm sure I'd come back here."

"How can you be sure?"

"Because you're here," she answered guilelessly, looking up at him.

He stopped. Her blue eyes were clear and certain, her mouth somber. The tan scarf had fallen back and the March wind ruffled her hair. In his broad hand, hers felt fragile. He suffered a moment of doubt about the wisdom of going to war.

"Patricia, I . . . " He swallowed and wasn't certain how to put his feelings into words.

"I know," she replied to the unspoken. "I feel the same way."

He leaned down and kissed her. She went up on tiptoe and lifted her mouth, resting her hands against his chest. It was a chaste kiss, as kisses went, but it filled their hearts with the essence of first love, while all around them the land readied for spring, for that season of bursting renewal.

In time they moved on, back through her yard, but loath to part yet.

"Want to go in the corncrib?" she asked. "We could shell some corn for the chickens."

He smiled and she led the way to the far side of the farm-yard, pulled a corncob from the hasp on a rough wooden door, and he followed her into semi-privacy. Inside the sun angled through the slatted walls against the steep hill of hard yellow ears. At the base of the corn sat a crude wooden box with a hand sheller attached, and beside it a seat made of nothing more than an old chopping block. Kristian sat down and fed an ear into the hopper and began turning the hand crank. Patricia leveled off the corn and sat down cross-legged on the lumpy ears, watching. It was warm in the corncrib, protected from the wind as it was, with the sun radiating off the wall of gold behind them. She flung off her scarf and unbuttoned her coat. He finished the first ear and she handed him another as the naked cob fell free. He watched the ear rotating as the teeth of the grind wheel gripped it; she watched his shoulders flexing as he cranked the wide flywheel. When the ear was only half clean, he dropped the handle and swung to face her. They hadn't come to the corncrib to shell corn, and they both knew it.

"What would your ma say if she knew we were out here?"

"She probably does. We walked right past the house."

"Oh." He wished she were closer, but felt uneasy about moving over beside her when they sat in a building where anybody could see right through the walls.

Their mutual hesitation hung heavy between them for a moment, then she laughed and plucked up a piece of dry, brown corn silk. "Let's see what you'd look like in a moustache." The corncobs rolled as she moved to kneel before him and fit the tuft of corn silk beneath his nose and lips.

It tickled and he jerked back, rubbing a finger across his nostrils.

She laughed and pulled him forward by the front panel of his jacket. "Here, don't be so twitchy. I want to see."

He submitted, letting her hold the corn silk in place again and study him assiduously.

"Well, how do I look?"

"Gorgeous."

The sun threw bars of light and shadow across her face as she knelt between his knees, and the wind whistled softly through the slatted walls.

"So what do you think, should I grow one?" He hardly realized what he was saying; his thoughts were on her and how pretty she looked with her lips the color of sunset and her long-lashed eyes intent upon him.

"I don't know. I think I should kiss you first and then decide."

"So kiss me."

She did, with her finger and the corn silk in the way, both of them giggling and the fine brown strands tickling terribly. Until she came up against his open legs and they pulled back, staring into each other's eyes.

"Oh, Kristian . . . " she murmured just as he, too, murmured her name. Then no excuse was needed. The corn silk fell to his jacket collar as she flung her arms around him and they kissed fully, pressed as close as gravity would allow, with her stomach cradled by his warmest parts and their arms clinging tenaciously. He tightened his thighs against her hips and callowly explored her lips with his tongue. It took some coaxing before she realized what was expected of her and allowed her lips to slacken, and his tongue to probe inside.

The warm, sleek contact rocked them both, and when the kiss ended, they backed off to stare at each other, still somewhat overcome by discovery.

"I think of you all the time," she whispered.

He straightened a strand of her auburn hair that had caught on her forehead. "I think of you, too. But I need to talk to you about something, and when we start kissing I forget all about talking."

"Talk about what?"

"Me and my pa had a dilly of a fight—two of 'em, actually."

"About what?"

He swiveled around and started shelling corn again. Above the loud metallic grinding and the sound of the kernels falling she thought she heard him say "I want to enlist." But that was silly. Who'd *want* to go to war?

"What?"

This time he turned so she saw his lips move. "I want to enlist," he said louder, still cranking.

She put her hand on his and forced him to stop. "Enlist? You mean go fight?"

He nodded. "As soon as I graduate in the spring."

"But Kristian—"

"I suppose you're going to argue with me just like my pa did."

Crestfallen, she gulped and stared at him, then sat back and folded her hands between her thighs. "Why?"

"I want to fly airplanes and . . . and I want to see more of this world than Alamo, North Dakota! Oh, damn, I don't know." When he would have leaped to his feet she grasped his knees and made him stay.

"Couldn't you do that without becoming a soldier?"

"I don't know. My pa says I'm a wheat farmer and I guess I'm afraid that if I don't go now I probably will end up being a wheat farmer all of my life, and maybe I could be something more. But when I try to reason with my pa about it, he just gets mad and shouts."

"Because he's scared, Kristian, don't you see?"

"I know he is—so am I. But does he have to shout at me? Couldn't we just talk about it?"

She didn't know how to answer. She herself had had bouts with her own parents recently that seemed to flare out of nowhere.

"I think it's part of growing up, fighting with your parents."

She was so calm, so reasonable. And looking at her made him waver in his convictions.

"What would you think if I went?"

She studied him intently for a moment, and answered softly, "I'd wait for you. I'd wait for as long as it would take."

"Would you?"

She nodded solemnly. "Because I think I love you, Kristian."

He'd thought the same thing about her more than once lately, but hearing her say the words was like a blow to his senses. In a flash his hands were on her arms, drawing her up into his embrace again. "But we shouldn't say it," he said against her neck. "Not now, when I'm planning to leave. It'll make everything too hard."

She clung, pressing her breasts firmly against him. "Oh, Kristian . . . you might get killed." Her words were muffled by his coat collar before he forced her head around and their mouths joined. As they strained against each other, his trembling, uncertain hand slid inside her warm coat, glided over her back, her side, and finally sought her breast. Her breathing stopped and her mouth hovered close without meeting his.

"It's a sin," she whispered, her breath warm against his damp lips.

"So is war," he whispered in reply.

But she stopped his hand anyway and drew it to her lips and kissed his knuckles.

"Then stay," she pleaded.

But he knew as he kissed her one last time and backed away that she was part of what would keep him here his entire life if he didn't leave in June.

22

SPRING CAME TO the prairie like a young girl preparing for her first dance, taking her time primping and preening. She bathed in gentle rains, emerging snowless and fresh. She dried with warm breezes, stretching beneath the benign sun, letting the wind comb her grassy hair until it lifted and flowed. Upon her breast she touched a lingering scent of earth and sun and life renewed. She put on a gay bonnet, trimmed of crocus and snowdrop and scoria lily, fluffed her red-willow petticoat, then tripped a trial dance step upon the stirring April breeze.

The animals returned as if on cue. The "flickertails"—striped gophers—perching beside their fresh-dug holes then chasing each other in playful caprice. The prairie dogs, barking and churring to their mates at twilight. The sharp-tailed grouse, drumming like thunder in lowland thickets. Mallards and honkers, heading north. And last but not least, the horses, heading home.

They came with the instinct of those who know their purpose, appearing one evening at the fence in the low pasture, whinnying to get in, to be harnessed, to turn the soil once again. All shaggy and thick, they stood in wait, as if the sharpening of plowshares had carried their tune across the prairies and beckoned them home. They were all there—Clippa, Fly, Chief, and the rest—two mares, Nelly and Lady, thick with foals.

They all walked down together to greet them, and Linnea observed the reunion with a renewed sense of appreciation for a farmer and his horses. Nose to nose, breath to breath, they communicated—beast and man happy to be together again. Teddy and Kristian scratched the horses' broad foreheads, walked in full circles around them, clapped their shoulders, checked their hooves. Linnea watched Teddy rub one big hand under Lady's belly, recollecting his voice raging, "I've had my family and he's damn near a full-grown man." What would he say when she told him, if what she suspected was true? She had missed one menstrual period and was waiting until she'd missed a second before giving him the news. They hadn't talked about babies again, but if it was true and she was expecting, surely he'd be overjoyed, as she was.

April moved on and the plowing began in earnest, but the older boys were present at roll call each day. Linnea wasn't certain whether it was due more to the fact that the schoolmarm was now Teddy Westgaard's wife or to the fact that he and Kristian still weren't talking.

In the fourth week of April Theodore turned thirty-five. He and Linnea were preparing for bed that night when she slipped her arms around him and kissed his chin. "You've been a little out of sorts today. Is anything wrong?"

He rested his hands on her shoulders and looked down into her inquiring eyes. "On the day I turn a year older? Do you have to ask?"

"I have a birthday gift for you that I think will cheer you up."

He grinned crookedly, held her by both earlobes, and teasingly wobbled her head from side to side. "You cheer me up. Just having you here at night cheers me up. What do I want with gifts?"

"Oh, but this gift is special."

"So are you," he said softly, releasing her ears and kissing her lingeringly on the mouth. When the kiss ended she looked up into his earth-brown eyes and kept her stomach pressed close against him.

"We're going to have a baby, Teddy."

She felt the change immediately: he tensed and leaned back. "A b . . ."

She nodded. "I think I'm about two months along."

"A baby!" His surprise turned to outright displeasure and he pushed away. "Are you sure?"

Her heart thudded heavily. "I thought you'd be pleased."

"Pleased! I told you a long time ago I didn't want any more babies! I'm too old!"

"Oh, Teddy, you aren't. It's just a notion in your head."

"Don't tell me I'm not! I'm old enough to have one of my own going off to get himself killed in a war and you expect me to be happy about having another one so I can go through this agony again?"

She was so hurt she didn't know what to say. The disappointment was too intense to bring tears. She stood stiffly, wondering how to handle the huge lump of distress that seemed to lodge in her womb beside their growing fetus. All the excitement she'd felt dissolved and left only disillusionment.

"And besides," he went on peevishly, "you and I have barely had any time alone together. Three months—not even three months and you're pregnant already." Turning away, he cursed softly under his breath, folded himself on the edge of the bed, and held his head.

"Well, what did you expect to happen when we practically never miss a night?"

His head came up sharply, jutting. "Don't throw that up to me now, at this late date," he snapped. "You and your 'let's try this and let's try that,'" he finished on a mordant note.

Her hurt intensified. She pressed her stomach. "Teddy, this is your child I'm carrying. How can you not want it?"

He jumped to his feet in frustration. "I don't know. I just don't, that's all. I want things to go on like they were. You and me, and Kristian back in the fields where he belongs, and no more of this talk of war and . . . and . . . oh, goddammit all!" he cried and pounded from the room.

She was left behind to stare at the door, to press her hands to her stomach and wonder how someone who loved her so deeply could still hurt her equally as deeply. How could he have said such things about their lovemaking, as if he'd never felt the same wondrous compulsions she had?

She put on her nightgown and crept into bed, lying like a plank with the covers tightly under her arms, staring at the ceiling. Thinking. Sorrowing. Waiting. Odd, how tears didn't seem to accompany the most grievous hurts in life. She lay dry-eyed and stricken and praying that when he came back in he'd gather her into his arms and say he was sorry—he'd been unreasonable and he wanted their baby after all.

But he didn't. Instead, he blew out the lantern, undressed in the dark, got in beside her, and turned away. She felt his continued reproof as palpably as if he'd struck her.

The following day she walked to school alone. They hadn't spoken a word during breakfast and it was almost a relief to escape the tension.

It was Arbor Day; she and the children spent it doing the traditional outside cleanup. They had all brought rakes and put them to use tidying up from one end of the yard to the other. While the older boys painted the outhouses, the girls washed windows. It was a sunny day, so warm that some of the children had removed their shoes and stockings to go barefoot. When the yard work was all done they would go down to the creek bottom and select one sapling to dig up and transplant in the schoolyard.

They piled all the yard clippings on a sandy spot in the ditch and set them afire. Linnea was tending the blaze when she looked up to find Theodore and John passing by in a buckboard. Her heart skittered.

John waved and called, "Hello!"

"Hello!" She waved back. "Where you going?"

"To town."

"What for?"

"Get a share welded and buy supplies!"

"Have fun!"

She waved effusively. John waved back and smiled. Theodore gave a wan greeting with one palm, and she watched them move on down the road.

They finished the yard work by twelve-thirty, doused the embers with water, and headed for the lowlands with their lunch pails. Roseanne and Jeannette skipped along holding hands, singing, "Merrily in the Month of May." Allen Severt found a baby bullsnake and tormented the girls with it. Patricia Lommen walked beside Kristian, their arms touching.

They found a sunny glade beside Little Muddy and flopped in the grass to eat a leisurely lunch. Some of the children tried to wade, but the creek was still icy. They turned instead to exploring, searching for duck nests along the banks, probing into· anthills, examining the locomotion of a pair of green inchworms.

Finally Linnea checked her watch and decided they must find their tree if they were to make it back in time to replant it. They chose a straight, vigorous-looking sapling with bright silver bark and fat pistachio-colored buds. The older boys dug it up and put it in a pail to carry back.

They made a fetching sight, trooping over the prairie in a straggly line, the younger children skipping, chasing gophers, the older ones taking turns carrying the tree. They were crossing the stretch of wheat field just northeast of the school, the bell tower already in sight, when a frigid current of air riffled across the plain and a huge flock of blackbirds lifted, squawking raucously. The smaller children shivered; Roseanne pulled up her skirt and used it for a cape.

Ahead of Linnea, Libby halted in her tracks, pointed to the west, and said, "What's that?"

They all stopped to stare. A solid mass of white was rapidly moving toward them.

"I don't know," an awed voice answered. "Mrs. Westgaard, what is it?"

Grasshoppers? Linnea stiffened in alarm. She'd heard of grasshoppers coming in legion to devastate everything they touched. But it was too early for grasshoppers. Dust? Dust, too, could suddenly darken the sky out here. But dust was brown, not white. They all stood in fascination, waiting, as the wall of white moved toward them. Seconds before it struck, someone uttered, "Snow . . . "

Snow? Never had Linnea seen snow like this. It smote them like a thousand fists, instantly sealing them in a colorless void, bringing with it a wicked wind that tugged at the roots of her hair and pressed her clothing flat.

Two children screamed, unexpectedly cut off from the sight of all around them. Linnea stumbled over a warm body and knocked it off its feet, raising a cry of alarm. Dear God, she couldn't see five feet in front of her! She set the child on his feet and groped for his hand.

"Children, grab hands!" she shouted. "Quickly! Here, Tony, take my hand," she ordered the boy behind her. "Everyone back toward my voice and hold onto the person next to you. We'll all run together!" She had the presence of mind to take a hasty roll call before they moved. "Roseanne, are you here? Sonny? Bent?" She called all fourteen names.

Everyone accounted for, they followed the wheat rows, the small children crying now in their bare feet. Within minutes there were no wheat rows to follow, and she prayed they were heading in the right direction. All sense of perspective was lost in the white maelstrom, but they clung together in a ragged, terrified line and fought their way through it. These were not the usual fat, saturated snowflakes of late spring, the kind that land with a splat and disappear instantly. These were hard and dry, a mid-winter type of storm wrapped in a front of frighteningly frigid air.

They had no idea they were near the schoolyard until Norna ran headlong into one of the cottonwoods of the windbreak. She bounced off the tree and sat down hard, howling, taking two others down with her.

"Come on, Norna." Raymond was there to pick her up and carry her, while Linnea, Kristian, Patricia, and Paul herded the remaining youngsters blindly across the yard. How incredible to think they'd been blithely raking it only hours before.

There was no question of finding shoes that had been left on the grass. They were already buried. The shivering picnic party straggled up the steps, the barefoot ones stubbing toes and crying.

Inside, they stood in a trembling cluster, catching their breath. Roseanne plopped down, whimpering, to check a bruised toe. Linnea took a nose count, found all present and accounted for, and immediately started issuing orders.

"Kristian, are you good for one more trip outside?"

"Yes, ma'am."

"You get the coal." He was heading for the coal shed before she got the words out of her mouth.

"And Raymond, you get water."

He was right on Kristian's heels, grabbing the water bucket on his way out.

"Raymond, wait!" she shouted after him. In blizzards like this men were known to get lost between the house and barn, heading out to do the evening chores. "Kristian can follow the edge of the building, you can't. Climb the ladder and untie the bell rope."

"Yes, ma'am." Without hesitation, Raymond made for the cloakroom.

"Paul, you go with him and hold the end of the rope while he goes to the pump. Those of you with bare feet, take off your petticoats and dry them. Girls, share your petticoats with the boys. Don't worry about keeping them clean. Your mothers can wash them when you get home. And I know your toes are freezing, but as soon as Kristian has a fire going they'll be warm as toast again. How many of you have any lunch left in your pails?" Six hands went up.

A tiny voice quaked, "I lotht my lunth pail. Mama will thpank me."

"No she won't, Roseanne. I promise I'll explain to her that it wasn't your fault."

Roseanne began to wail nonetheless, requiring soothing before she'd settle down. Patricia and Frances were dispatched to oversee the smaller children and to take their minds off their discomforts.

Kristian returned and built a fire. Allen and Tony were given the job of periodically shoveling the steps to keep the door free.

When at last everyone was settled down as comfortably as possible, Linnea called Kristian aside.

"How much coal do we have?"

"Enough, I think."

"You think?"

It was late April. Who ever would have thought it would become a concern when wildflowers were already blooming on the prairie? Exactly how cold could it get this late in the year? And how long could a blizzard rage when May Day was just round the corner?

Kristian squeezed her arm. "Don't worry about it. This can't keep up for long."

But 1888 was heavy on her mind as Linnea stalwartly went to her table, took out a theme book, and made her first entry, hoping—praying—no one ever need see it: April 27, 1918, 3:40 P.M.—*Caught in a blizzard on our way back from the creek bottom, where we'd gone to dig an Arbor Day tree and have our picnic lunch. The day began with temperatures in the low 70s, so mellow some of the children went barefoot cleaning the schoolyard in the morning.*

Suddenly Linnea's pen stopped and her head snapped up.

Theodore and John!

She stared at the windows, which looked like they'd been painted white and listened to the wind howling down the stovepipe and rattling shingles.

With her heart in her throat, Linnea swung a glance at Kristian. He was hunkering close to the stove with the other children, all of them talking in low voices. She got to her feet, feeling fear for the first time since the blizzard had struck. She moved to the window, touched its ledge, and stared at the white fury that beat against the panes. Already triangular drifts webbed the corners, but beyond all was an impenetrable mystery. Forcing a calm voice, Linnea turned.

"Excuse me, Kristian. Could you come here a moment?"

He glanced over his shoulder, rose, and crossed the room to her.

"Yes, ma'am?"

She tried to sound nonchalant. "Kristian, while we were still cleaning the yard did you see your father and John pass by on their way home from town?"

He glanced at the window, then back at her. His hands came slowly out of his back pockets and concern sharpened his features.

"No."

She affected an even lighter tone. "Well, chances are they're still in town, probably at the blacksmith shop all snug and cozy around the forge."

"Yeah . . . " Kristian replied absently, glancing back to the window. "Yeah, sure."

She forced herself to wait a full five minutes after Kristian had rejoined the group before moving to the edge of the circle. "Raymond, would you mind climbing back up to the cupola and tying the rope back on the bell again? It occurs to me that on a day like this we may not have been the only ones caught unawares by the blizzard. It might be a good idea to toll the bell at regular intervals."

It was terribly hard to keep her voice steady, her face placid.

"But why you gonna do that?" Roseanne inquired innocently.

Linnea rested a hand on the child's brown hair, looked down into an upturned face whose wide brown eyes were too young to understand the scope of true peril. "If there's anyone out there, the sound might guide them in." Linnea scanned the circle. "I'm asking for volunteers to stay in the cloakroom and ring the bell once every minute or so. You can take turns, two at a time, and we'll leave the cloakroom doors open so it won't be quite so cold in there."

Kristian was on his feet immediately, followed by Patricia whose troubled eyes had been resting on him throughout the exchange.

Skipp Westgaard spoke up next. "Mrs. Westgaard, don't you think our pas will drive to school to get us?"

"I'm afraid not, Skipp. Not until this snow lets up."

"You mean we might have to stay in the schoolhouse overnight?"

"Maybe."

"B . . . but where we gonna sleep?"

Allen Severt answered, "On the floor—where else, dummy?"

"Allen!" Linnea reprimanded sharply.

Allen demanded belligerently, "What I wanna know is what we're gonna eat for supper."

"We'll share whatever is left in the lunch pails, and I—"

"Nobody's gettin' my apple!" he interrupted rudely.

Linnea ignored him and went on. "I have emergency crackers and raisins on hand. There's water to drink and I have a little tea. But we'll worry about that if and when the time comes. For now, why don't you all think up a game to keep yourselves occupied? In case you hadn't guessed, school is over for the day."

That brought a laugh.

Overhead the school bell sounded. Automatically Linnea checked her watch.

She moved back to her desk to make a second entry: 3:55. *We will toll the school bell every five minutes to guide in any ships that might be lost in the night.*

But she couldn't sit at her desk a moment longer. The windows drew her, eerily. She stood staring out at the obscured world, shuddering within. With her back to the room she folded her hands on the sill and twisted her fingers together till the knuckles paled. Her eyelids slid closed, her forehead rested against the cold pane, and her lips began moving in a silent prayer.

The horses had been acting skittish all the way from town. Theodore continuously checked the sky, the horizon, the road behind, the road ahead, wondering at the animals' restlessness. Coyotes, he thought. You always had to be on the lookout for coyotes out here. They spooked the horses. Not that they'd attack, only make the horses bolt. That's why Theodore carried the gun—to scare the varmints off, not to kill them. Coyotes ate too many grain-eating critters to want to see them dead.

Seeing none, his thoughts turned to Linnea. He shouldn't have been so rough on her, but—hang it all!—she didn't understand. She was too young to understand! You raised a boy, pinned your hopes on him, watched him grow, nurtured him, provided love, sustenance, everything, only to find yourself helpless when he took a fool notion into his mind to jeopardize his life.

But he'd been unfair about the other part, too. It rankled, how he'd taken her to task for bringing about the pregnancy as if he'd had no part in it. Displeased with himself, he forced his mind to other things.

The burrowing owls were back, nesting in the abandoned badger holes from last year—a sure sign of spring come for good. The snowshoe rabbits had exchanged their white coats for brown. Ulmer said the trout were already biting down on the Little Muddy. Maybe the three of us, me and Ulmer and John, should try to get down there together one day soon and dip our lines.

"Ulmer says the trout're bitin'."

Beside him, John's eyebrows went up in happy speculation, though he didn't say a word.

"Sounds good, uh?"

"You betcha."

"We get an early start tomorrow and we could have the northeast twenty done by four or so."

They rode along, content, picturing fat, wriggling "rainbows" flopping on the creek bank, then sizzling in Ma's frying pan.

Cub shied.

"Whoooa . . . Easy there, boy." Theodore frowned. "Don't know what's wrong with them today."

"Spring fever, maybe."

Theodore chuckled. "Cub's too old for that anymore."

John noticed it first. "Somethin' up ahead."

Theodore's eyes narrowed. "Looks like snow."

"Naw. Sun's out." John leaned back and gave the blue sky a squint.

"Never saw snow that looked like that. But what else could it be?"

The first bank of chill wind struck them full in the face.

"Might be snow after all."

"That thick? Why, you can't see the road on the other side of it nor nothin' behind it."

They stared, intent now, puzzled. Theodore stated wryly, "Better turn your collar up. Looks like we're about to leave spring behind." Then he calmly rolled his sleeves down and settled his hat more firmly on his head.

When the wall of wind and snow struck, it rocked them backwards on the buckboard seat. The horses danced nervously, rearing in their traces while Theodore stared in disbelief. Why, he couldn't see Cub's and Toots's heads! It was as if somebody had opened a sluice gate that held back the Arctic. Like an avalanche it hit, a flaky torrent mothered by a fearsome wave of cold air that grew colder by the second.

Struggling, Theodore finally got the animals under control. Though they moved forward, he had no idea where to direct them, so he let them have their heads. "You think it's only a snow squall, John?" he shouted.

"Don't know. That air's like ice, ain't it?"

The air *was* ice. It bit their cheeks, pecked at their eyelids, and filtered into their collars.

"What you wanna do, John? Go on?"

"You think Cub and Toots can keep on the road?" John shouted back.

Just then the team answered the question themselves by rearing and whinnying somewhere in the white blanket that kept them from sight.

"Giddap!" But at the slap of the reins the horses only complained and shied sideways.

Cursing under his breath, Theodore handed the lines to his brother. "I'll try leading 'em!" He vaulted over the side, bent into the wind, and groped his way to the horses' heads. But when he grasped Toots's bridle, the team pranced and fought him. Theodore cursed and tugged, but Toots rolled her eyes and planted her forefeet.

Giving up, he made his way back to the wagon again and shouted up at John, "How far you figure we are from Nordquist's place?"

"Thought we passed it already."

"No, it's up ahead."

"You sure?"

"I'm sure."

"We could take Cub and Toots off the wagon and let them lead on. They might get us there."

"But will we see the house when we're in front of it?"

"Don't know. What else we gonna do?"

"We could walk the fence line."

"Don't know if there's any fence along here."

"Hold on. I'll check."

Theodore left the wagon behind, walked at a right angle from it, feeling with his hands. He hadn't gone five steps before he was swallowed up by the snow. He checked both sides of the road. There were no fences on either side. He had to follow the sound of John's voice back to the wagon. Sitting beside John again, he announced, "No fences. Try the horses again."

John shouted, "Here, giddap!" He slapped the reins hard. This time the horses lurched forward valiantly, but in moments they became disoriented and started shying again.

Theodore took the reins and tried coercing them. "Come on, Cub, come on, Toots, old gal, on with y'." But they continued balking.

The temperature seemed to be dropping at a steady, relentless pace. Already Theodore's fingers felt frozen to the lines, and though he'd rolled down his shirt sleeves, they were little protection against Nature's unexpected wrath. The wind keened mercilessly, straight out of the west, smacking their faces to a bright, blotchy red.

Holding his hat on, Theodore took stock of the situation. "Maybe we better wait it out," he decided grimly.

"Wait it out? Where?"

"Under the wagon, like Pa did that time. Remember he told us about it?"

John looked skeptical, but his eyebrows were coated with white. "I ain't much for cramped spaces, Teddy."

Theodore clapped John's knee. "I know. But I think we got to try it. It's gettin' too cold to stay up here in the wind."

John considered a minute, nodded silently. "All right. If you think it's best."

Together they climbed down and released the traces with stiff fingers. They removed the singletree, laid it on the ground, and beside it piled flour, sugar, and seed bags, then did their best to kick away the snow and clear a place for themselves. When they overturned the wagon it landed atop the sacks, braced up far enough that they could shinny underneath the opening. They tied the horses to a wheel and Theodore went down on his knees.

His gun went under first, he next, on his side, shivering, hugging himself, watching John's heavy boots shuffling nervously on the far side of the opening.

"Come on, John. It's better out of the wind." Inside the cavern his words sounded muffled.

John's boots shuffled again, and finally he got down, rolled himself underneath, and lay facing the thin band of brightness with wide, glassy eyes.

Rocks and last year's dried weed stalks gouged into Theodore's ribs. In spite of their efforts to kick the snow away, some remained. It melted through the side of his shirt and clung to his skin in icy patches. Something with prickles scratched through his sleeve and bit the soft underside of his arm.

"Best try to get comfortable." Theodore raised up as best he could, tried to scoop the biggest pebbles and dried plant stalks from under his ribs, then lay down with an elbow folded beneath his ear. Beside him, John didn't move. Theodore touched his arm. "Hey, John, you scared?" John was trembling violently. Theodore made out the stiff shake of John's head in the dim light. "I know you don't like bein' cooped up much, but it probably won't be for long. The snow's bound to let up."

"And what if it don't?"

"Then they'll come and find us."

"Wh . . . what if they don't?"

"They will. Linnea saw us heading for town. And Ma knows we ain't back yet."

"Ma ain't rid a horse in years, and anyway how could she get through if we couldn't?"

"The snow could stop, couldn't it? How much snow you reckon we can have when it's almost May?"

But John only stared at the daylight seeping in beneath the wagon, petrified and shaking.

"Come on. We got to do our best to keep warm. We got to combine what little heat we got." Theodore shinnied over and curled up tightly against John's back, circling him with one arm and holding him close. John's arm came to cover his. The cold fingers closed over the back of Theodore's hand, clenching it.

When John spoke, his voice was high with panic. "Remember when Ma used to make us go down in the 'fraidy hole when there'd be a bad summer storm?"

Theodore remembered only too well. John had always been terrified of the root cellar. He'd cried and begged to be released the whole time they'd waited out the storm. "I remember. But don't think about it. Just look at the light and think about something good. Like harvest time. Why, there's no time prettier than harvest time. Riding the reaper off across the prairie with the sky so blue you'd think you could drink it, and the wheat all gold and shiny."

While Theodore's soothing voice rolled over him, John's unblinking eyes remained fixed on the reassuring crack of light. Occasionally miniature whirlpools of snow puffed in on a backdraft, touching his cheeks, his eyelashes. The wind whistled above, setting one of the wagon wheels turning. It rumbled low, reverberating through the wood over their heads.

After some time, Theodore gently loosened his hand from John's tight grip. "Put your hands between your legs, John. They'll keep warmer there."

"No!" John's fingers clutched like talons. "Teddy, please."

John was bearing the brunt of the cold, lying closer to the opening. But his fear of confinement seemed worse than his fear of freezing, so Theodore assured him, "I'm only going to put my arm over yours, okay?" He lined John's arm with his own and found the back of his hand like ice.

"Snow's a good insulator. Pretty soon we'll probably be snug as a cat in a woodbox."

Reassuring John kept Theodore's own panic at bay. But as soon as he fell silent, it threatened again. Think sensibly. Plan. Plan what? How to keep warm when we're dressed in thin cotton shirts and neither one of us smokes, so we don't even have any matches to burn the wagon if we need to? Even their long winter underwear had been discarded days ago when the weather turned mild. Short of the snow suddenly stopping, there was nothing that could help them. And if it didn't stop . . .

You shouldn't have tied the horses.

Oh, come on, Teddy. One of you panicking is enough. You've only been under here twenty minutes. Takes a little longer than that to freeze to death.

But it already felt like parts of him were frostbitten.

He laid and thought about the horses until he couldn't hold back any longer.

"Listen, John," he said as casually as possible. "I gotta roll out a minute."

"What for?"

Damn you, John, after a lifetime of not asking questions, this is a fine time to start.

"Gotta make yellow snow," he lied. "But you stay here. I think I can roll over you."

Outside, he was alarmed to see how quickly the drift was building up around their makeshift shelter. Already it had stopped the free wheel from turning. He flicked the reins off the wagon wheel, and in spite of the cold, took a moment to affectionately brush each horse's muzzle, whispering into their ears, "You're a good old girl, Toots. . . . You, too, Cub. Remember that." Their rumps were to the wind, head down. Snow glistened in their tangled manes and tails, but they stood patiently, unconcerned about whatever befell.

Just like John's done all his life.

But fatalistic thoughts did no good. Theodore pushed them from his mind and went down on one knee. As his palm pressed a sack of seed corn, he had an inspiration. He leaned low and peered through the opening. "Roll to the back, John. Gonna give us something warmer to lay on." He took a jackknife from his pocket, plunged it into the bag, and tore a long gash. As the corn poured out he scooped it under the wagon with both hands. It was blessedly warm with trapped heat. "Spread it in there, John." He had only three sacks to spare. The others were necessary to hold the wagon up and give them an escape hatch. But when the three bags were distributed, the corn made a more comfortable bed. Huddled again, belly to back, the two men wriggled into it, absorbing its warmth.

They'd been snuggled for some time when John asked, "You didn't go out to pee, did you?"

Startled, Theodore could only lie. "Course I did."

"I think you went out to turn Cub and Toots loose."

Again Theodore thought, *A fine time for you to get wise, big brother.*

"Why don't you close your eyes and try to sleep for a while. It'll make the time go faster."

But time had never moved so slowly. After a while the corn shifted, leaving them lying on pebbles and sticks again. What little warmth they'd absorbed from it ended. The shudders began—first in John and eventually in Theodore. They watched the white of day fade to the purple of evening.

They'd been lying in silence for a long time when John spoke. "Did you and the little missy have a fight, Teddy?"

A knot clogged Theodore's throat. He closed his eyes and tried to gulp it down, refusing to admit why John had brought up such a subject at a time like this.

"Yeah," he managed.

John didn't ask. John would never ask.

"She's pregnant and I . . . well, I got real ugly about it and told her I didn't want any more babies."

"You shouldn't't've did that, Teddy."

"I know."

And if they froze to death under this damn wagon, he'd never have a chance to tell her how sorry he was. Her image as he'd last seen her filled his mind—standing with a rake in one hand, her eyes shaded by the other, the children scattered all around her like a flock of finches, and the white building in the background with its door thrown wide. He recalled the row of cottonwoods coming in green at their tips, the ditch filled with wild crocus, Kristian raking near the edge of the ditch—the two people he loved most in the world, and he'd been ugly to both of them lately. Linnea had waved and called hello, but he'd been stubborn and had scarcely waved back. How he wished now he had. He ached and felt like crying. But if he cried, who'd keep John from giving up?

To make matters worse, John suddenly snapped. He thrust Theodore's arm away and shinnied on his belly toward freedom.

"I can't take it no more. I gotta get out of here for a while."

Theodore grabbed the seat of John's overalls. "No! Come on, John, it's bad under here but it's worse out there. The temperature is dropping and you'll freeze in no time."

"Let me go, Teddy. Just for a minute. I just got to, before night falls and I can't see no more."

"All right. We'll go out together, check the horses and the snow. See if it's lettin' up."

But it wasn't. The horses were almost belly deep and the wagon was a solid hillock now. The only opening was on the leeward side, where the wind had swirled, creating a one-foot crawl space for their use. Standing in it, Theodore hugged himself, watching John stretch and breathe deeply, lifting his face to the sky. Damn fool would have frozen fingers if he didn't tuck his hands beneath his arms.

"Come on, John, we got to go back under. It's too cold out here."

"You go. I'm just gonna stay here a minute."

"Damn it, John, you'll freeze! Now get back under there!"

At the severe tone of the reprimand, John immediately became docile. "A . . . all right. But I got to be closest to the opening again, okay, Teddy?"

His childlike plea made Theodore immediately sorry he'd scolded.

"All right, but hurry. If our hands aren't froze already, they will be soon."

Back in their burrow, John asked, "Can you feel your fingers anymore, Teddy?"

"Don't know for sure, but I'm not gonna think about it."

They fell silent again. Soon the world beyond their shelter grew totally black.

"I think my nose is froze," John mumbled.

"Well, if you'd turn over here and face the inside or let me be on the outside for a while it might thaw. What difference does it make now anyway? It's night outside, just as black out there as it is in here."

All John would say was, "I got to have my air hole at least."

Miraculously, they slept.

Theodore awakened and blinked, disoriented. At his side John was too still. Panic clawed through him. "John, wake up! Wake up!" He shook his brother violently.

"Huh?" John moved slightly. Theodore reached for his face in the blackness. It felt frozen. But maybe what was frozen was his own hand.

"You got to roll over. Come on now, don't argue." This time John submitted. Theodore put both arms around him and held him as if he were a child, willing his own fright to subside. They couldn't die out here this way. They just couldn't. Why, when they left home Ma had had sheets hangin' on the line and bread rising in the oven. By now it would be baked and in the bread box. They were gonna go fishing with Ulmer one day this week. And Kristian was going to be graduating from the eighth grade in four more weeks. What ever would Kristian say if his pa missed the ceremony? And Linnea—oh, his sweet Linnea— she still thought he was mad at her. And she was going to have their baby. He couldn't die without seeing their baby. Lying in the inky blackness beneath an overturned wagon, with his brother shaking in his arms, Theodore found all these thoughts to be valid reasons why the blizzard couldn't win.

His ribs hurt terribly. There was no feeling in his toes, and his head throbbed when he tried to lift it off the corn. In spite of it, he dozed again, but some distracting thought kept him just short of sleeping fully—something he had to tell Linnea when he saw her next time. Something he should have told her last night.

He awakened again. John's breath was steady on his face. He wondered how much time had passed, if it was still the first night. But he felt disoriented and mysteriously weightless. As if his entire body were filled with warm, buoyant air.

He couldn't keep his thoughts clear. Was he close?

No!

He thrust John back.

"Wha . . . "

"Git up, John. Git out of here. We got to move, I think, else more of us is gonna freeze, if it isn't already."

"Not sure I can."

"Try, damn it!"

They rolled out, stumbling. The blizzard was worse than ever. It hit them with the same invincible wall of snow and wind as before. The horses were still there, loyally waiting. They whinnied, shook their heads, tried for a step forward but were thwarted by the drifts beneath their bellies.

The men fought their way to the animals. "Put your hands by Cub's nose. Maybe his breath will warm 'em." Theodore instructed.

They stood at the horses' heads, trying to warm themselves against anything that would provide the slightest bit of heat. But it was hopeless, and Theodore knew it.

In the eastern sky a dim light was beginning to glow through the driving snowfall. By it he tried to check his watch, only to find that his fingers could not handle the delicate catch to open its lid. He returned it to his pocket, held Toots's head, leaning his cheek on her forelock, wondering if a man knew when he'd stretched fate to its limits—the exact hour, the exact minute when destiny needed manipulation if he were to survive.

There was one possible way. But he resisted it, had been resisting it all through the cramped, fearful hours of the long night when he'd lain trying to warm his quivering body against his brother's, knowing that the rifle lay just behind his back. He hugged Cub's face with an apology the beast didn't understand. He pressed his icy lips to the hard bone just above her velvet nose. How many years had he known these horses? All his life. They'd been his father's even before he himself had grown old enough to take up the reins. Behind them he'd learned the terms and tones of authority. To their long, nodding gait he'd learned to control power great enough to kill, should it turn on him. Yet it never did. Cub. Toots. His prized pair. The ones he kept behind, winters. Older than all the others, but with so much heart there were times their understanding seemed almost human. They had, in their years, provided a good life. Could he ask them now to give him life at the cost of their own?

He stepped back, steeling himself, telling himself they were dumb animals, nothing more. "John, get my gun."

"Wh . . . what . . . y . . . you . . . g . . . gonna . . . d . . . do?" John's teeth were rattling like the tail of a snake.

"Just get it."

"N . . . no! I ain't g . . . gonna!" It was the first time in his life John had ever defied his brother.

With a muttered curse, Theodore knelt and fished the gun from beneath the wagon. He'd barely regained his feet when John's hand clamped the barrel and pointed it skyward. They stared into each other's eyes—haunted, both—neither of them feeling the icy black metal in their frozen fingers.

"Teddy, no!"

Theodore cocked the gun. The metallic clack bore the sound of doom.

"No, T . . . Teddy, you c . . . can't!"

"I got to, John."

"N . . . no . . . I'd r-r-rather f . . . freeze t . . . to d . . . death."

"And you will if I don't do it."

"I d . . . don't c . . . care."

"Think of Ma and the others. They care. *I* care, John." They stood a moment longer, gazes locked, while precious seconds ticked away and the blizzard raged on. "Let the gun go. Your fingers're already froze."

As John's hand fell, so did his head. He stood slumped, abject, unaware of the wind howling about his head, throwing fine shards of ice down the back of his collar.

Theodore stood beside Cub, his whole body trembling, jaw clenched so tightly it ached more than any other part of his body. In his throat was a wad of emotion he could neither swallow nor cough up. It lodged there, choking him. I'm sorry, old boy, he wanted to say, but could not. His heart slammed sickeningly as he raised the gun only to find he could not see down the sight. He lifted his cheek from the stalk and backhanded the tears away roughly, then took aim again. When he pulled the trigger he didn't even feel it; his finger was frozen. He fired the second shot rapidly, giving himself no time to think, to see.

Just do it, something said. Do what you got to do and don't think. He opened the pocket knife with his teeth because his fingers couldn't manage it. The blade froze to his tongue and tore off a patch of skin. Again, there was no feeling. He had closed himself off from it, moving with a grim determination that had hardened the planes of his face and turned his eyes flat and expressionless.

He plunged the knife to the hilt, shutting his mind against the gush of scarlet that colored the pristine snow at his knees. He ripped a hole two hands wide and ordered, "Get over here, John!"

When John remained rooted, Theodore lurched to his feet, jerked him around by the shoulder and gritted, "Move!" Ruthlessly, he gave his brother a shove that sent him to his knees. "Get your hands in there. This is no time to be queasy!"

Tears were coursing down John's cheeks as he slipped his hands into the sleek, wet warmth.

Mercilessly, Theodore turned to utilize the warmth of the second animal. While his hands thawed, he forced from his mind all thought of what pressed against his flesh. He thought instead of Linnea, her hair streaming in the wind, her face bright with laughter, the gold watch on her breast, the child in her womb. As the feeling returned to his hands, the pain grew intense. He clenched his teeth and rocked on his knees, swallowing the cry he could not let John hear.

But the worst was yet to come.

When his hands had warmed and he could hold the knife, he knelt beside the warm carcass, closed his eyes, and drew several deep, fortifying breaths, swallowed the gorge in his throat, and ordered John, "Get out your knife and gut 'er."

But even while Theodore set to work on his own grisly task, John knelt motionless, in a stupor. "Do it, John!" Terror, nausea, and pity tugged at Theodore's body while he performed woodenly, forcing the gruesomeness from his mind. Several times he had to struggle to his feet and turn away to breathe untainted air and gather fortitude. And all the while John knelt beside Toots's felled body, rattling now with shock, unable to perform the smallest task.

By the time Theodore finished, he was—unbelievably—sweating. It was arduous labor, the horse's carcass heavy and unwieldy. Much of the job had to be done by feel, leaning low, his cheek laying against the familiar brown hide while he slashed and pulled.

When at last he struggled to his feet, dizzy and weak, he knew John was incapable of helping either of them in any way.

"Get in, John. I'll help you."

Staring, glassy-eyed, John shook his head. Snow had made a fresh drift around his knees. His bloody hands rested motionless on his thighs.

Frantic, close to shock himself, Theodore felt tears of desperation form in his eyes. If they coursed down his face, he couldn't tell, for his cheeks were long since numb. "Goddammit, John, you can't die! I won't let you! Now get in!"

Finally, realizing John was incapable of making decisions, or of moving, Theodore rolled him off his knees and pushed him back, stood over him, and wedged the carcass open. "Double up. You'll fit if you roll up in a tight ball." The strain was immense, lifting the dead weight. Theodore's arms trembled and his knees quaked. If John didn't move soon, it would be too late.

Just when he thought he'd have to let go, John clenched his knees and backed in. A pathetic whimper sounded, but Theodore had no time to waste.

Gutting the second horse was more difficult than the first, for his energy had been sapped. Steel-willed, he struggled on, shutting out the smell and the sight of steam rising from the entrails in the snow and the sound of John's whimpers. Once he had to rest, near exhaustion, hands supporting himself, head drooping. The knife blade broke on a bone and he gave up the fight, unable to labor any longer. Through a dizzy haze, he crawled toward the life-giving warmth, but when he was struggling to get inside, his mind grew lucid for several seconds, and he finally remembered what it was that he had to tell Linnea.

On hands and knees he crawled through the snow, groping for the broken knife, taking it with him as he pulled himself underneath the wagon one last time.

Lying on his back in the murk, he pictured the letters, just as she'd taught them. L is for *lutefisk*. I is for ice. N is for— he couldn't remember what N was for, but he need not know. By now he could spell her name by heart.

"Lin," he carved blindly, "I'm sorry."

His ears buzzed. His head felt ten times its size. Somebody was crawling through the snow on bloody hands. Now why would anybody want to do a thing like that? On leaden limbs he reached his destination, unaware of the miasma or the gore or the fact that he tore his shirt and scraped both his belly and back as he squeezed inside. There, emotionally and physically exhausted, he lost consciousness.

In the school building six miles up the road a child rubbed her tear-filled eyes and wailed, "But I don't *like* raith-inth."

Linnea, her own eyes rimmed with red, forced patience into her voice and soothed Roseanne when all she wanted to do was cry herself. "Just eat them, honey. They're all we have."

When Roseanne toddled away still sniffling over her handful of sticky raisins, Linnea wearily pulled the bell rope again, then clung to it with both hands, eyes closed, forehead resting against the scratchy sisal while the woeful *clong-g-g* resounded like a dirge. Outside the wind picked up the shivering sound and carried it over the white countryside. One minute later it carried another . . . then another . . . and another . . .

23

THE BLIZZARD LASTED twenty-eight hours. In that time, eighteen inches of snow fell. The children were rescued just before dark on the second day by men on snowshoes, pulling toboggans. The first one to reach the school was Lars Westgaard. He rammed his snowshoes into a drift, opened the door and met a circle of relieved faces, three of them—his own children's—tearfully happy.

But as he held Roseanne, clinging to him like a monkey, and petted the heads of Norna and Skipp who hugged close, he met the haunted eyes of Linnea, waiting beside Kristian.

"Theodore and John?" she asked quietly.

He could only shake his head regretfully.

A sick, rolling sensation gripped her stomach and panic girthed her chest. She interlaced her fingers with Kristian's, squeezing hard and meeting his young, worried eyes.

"They're probably sitting at someone's place in town, worrying about us more than we're worrying about them."

Kristian swallowed pronouncedly and muttered, "Yeah . . . probably." But neither of them were convinced.

The other fathers straggled in, stomping off snow, and warmed themselves by the fire. When all had arrived, search plans were made, then the fire was banked and the little schoolhouse closed. Someone had brought a spare toboggan and snowshoes for Linnea. Dressed in someone else's coat, scarf, and mittens, she was pulled home by Kristian.

Already the air was mellowing. In the western sky the red-gold eye of the sun squinted through purple clouds, sending long spans of gilt streaking across the transformed world. The shadows on the downside of the snowdrifts were the same deep purple as the westerly clouds that were already breaking and separating, shedding more sunny shafts and promising a clear day tomorrow.

They made a mournful little caravan, four toboggans pulled by Ulmer, Lars, Trigg, and Kristian, with Raymond walking beside. It had been decided, in the interest of expedience, that the Westgaard children would all be taken to Nissa's, which was closest, so the men could set out immediately on their grim errand. Even on the short walk home they were alert, watchful, each of them carrying a long cane pole, occasionally stopping to pierce a drift in several places. Each time, Linnea watched the latticed tracks of their snowshoes create cross-stitches on the snow, listened to their low, murmuring voices, and dreaded what they might find. She gazed in horrified fascination at the depth to which the cane poles sank and, holding her stomach as if to protect her unborn child from worry, said a silent prayer.

Poor Kristian. She herself was weary beyond anything she'd ever imagined, and he must be, too. Yet he stalwartly moved with his uncles over the suspicious-looking hillocks, watching while the poles disappeared again and again into the snow, leaving it pockmarked. Each time he returned to her toboggan, resignedly picked up the rope, and high-stepped behind the others, the sleds whining a mournful lament against the pristine surface of the snow.

When they reached Nissa's house the men had to shovel a drift from the back door. They worked to the continuous bawling of the cattle who stood near the barn in snowdrifts, with painfully bulging bags, waiting to be milked since last night at this time. But the cattle were ignored in light of the much greater urgency.

It was clear that Nissa hadn't slept at all. It was equally clear that she was one of those who functions well under stress, whose thought processes clarify in direct proportion to the necessity for clear thinking. She had gear all packed: quilts tied into tight bundles like jelly rolls; steaming coffee and soup in fruit jars bound with burlap; sandwiches wrapped in oilcloth; bricks in the oven and hot coals ready to be scooped into tins. Though her face appeared haggard, her movements were brisk and autocratic as she scurried about the kitchen, getting the boys outfitted and prepared to move out again. Recognizing the value of time, they wasted little of it on useless consternation. The only pause came when Kristian and Raymond insisted on going along. The men exchanged glances, but to their credit included them. "You sure?" Ulmer asked.

"My pa is out there," Kristian answered tersely.

"And I go with Kristian," Raymond stated unequivocally.

With Ulmer's nod, it was decided. Within minutes after their arrival, the men were gone again.

Nissa neither fretted nor watched them snowshoe away. Instead, she turned her attention to her grandchildren, for whom she'd prepared a pot of thick chicken noodle soup. There was fresh bread, too, and a batch of fresh-fried *fattigman,* evidence that she'd remained industrious during her worried hours alone.

How Linnea admired the scuttling little hen. No taller than her eight-year-old grandsons, Nissa didn't slow down a bit. She moved like heat lightning, rarely smiling. Yet all seven children instinctively knew she loved them as she tended to their needs and they babbled about their night at the schoolhouse.

Somehow Roseanne's voice could be heard above all the others, shrill and lisping. "And Grandma, gueth what! Aunt Linnea made me eat raith-inth, and I *did* it! I can't wait to tell Mama." Her mobile face suddenly drooped. "But I lotht my lunch pail and Mama'th gonna thpank me for thure."

The jabber continued as soup bowls were emptied and refilled. When the children were stuffed, they seemed to droop in unison, and within minutes were asleep on the two downstairs beds.

The house quieted. From outside came the sound of snow melting off the roof, dripping rhythmically, even though the sun had gone down.

Nissa gripped the tops of both knees as if to navigate herself up from the hard kitchen chair. Her faded skirt drooped between her thighs like a hammock. She looked as if a deep sigh would have done her a world of good, but instead she sounded stern.

"Well, I guess I better try to give them cows some relief."

"I'll help you," Linnea offered.

"Don't think so. Milkin' cows is harder'n it looks."

"Well, I'd like to try, at least."

"Suit yourself." Nissa donned her outerwear without the slightest hint of self-pity. If a thing's got to be done, it's got to be done, her attitude seemed to say. For Linnea there was great reassurance in sticking close to the stubbornly determined little woman.

Dressed in Theodore's and Kristian's outsized overalls, they trudged through the snowdrifts to the barn.

Milking, as Nissa had declared, was "hardn'n it looked." Linnea was a total flop at it. So while Nissa milked, Linnea shoveled a path between the barn and the house. Together they carried the white frothing pails up, cleaned the children's soup bowls, then faced the dismal task of waiting with idle hands.

Nissa filled hers. She found a fresh skein of yarn and sat in the kitchen rocker, winding it into a ball. The rocker creaked in rhythm with her winding. Outside the sky was the color of a grackle's wing. Stars came out, and a moon thin as a scimitar blade. Not a breeze stirred, as if the last twenty-eight hours had never happened.

The rocker creaked on.

Linnea tried knitting, but couldn't seem to keep her hands steady enough to make smooth stitches. She glanced at the woman in the rocker. Nissa's blue-veined hands with their thin, shiny skin worked mechanically, winding the dark-blue yarn. It was the same color as the cap she'd knit for Teddy at Christmas. Was she thinking of that cap now, packed away in mothballs along with all of Theodore's and John's other woolen clothes?

"Nissa?"

The old woman looked over her spectacles, rocking, winding.

"I want you to know, I'm carrying Teddy's baby."

They both knew why Linnea had told her—if Teddy didn't make it, his child would. But Nissa only replied, "Then you oughtn't to have shoveled all that snow."

At that moment Roseanne toddled to the kitchen doorway, rubbing her eyes and her stomach. "Grandma, I got a thtomach ache. I think I ate too much thoop."

The blue yarn lost all importance. "Come, Rosie, come to Grandma." The drowsy-eyed child padded into her grandma's open arms and let herself be gathered onto the warm, cushioned lap and settled beneath a downy chin. The old bones of the rocker creaked quietly into the room.

"Grandma, tell me about when you was a little girl in Norway."

For long minutes only the chair spoke. Then Nissa started recollecting the story that had obviously been told and retold through the years, in terms sometimes strange to Linnea's ears.

"My papa was a crofter, a big strong man with hands as horny as hooves. We lived in a fine little glade. Our house and byre was strung together under a green-turfed roof and sometimes in spring violets blossomed right there on the—"

"I know, Grandma," Rosie interrupted. "Right there on the roof."

"That's right," Nissa continued. "Some wouldn't call it much, but it had a firm floor that was always fresh-washed and Mama made me go out and collect fresh green sprays of juniper to spread on it after she swept. And at our front door was a fjord. . . ." Nissa looked down. "You 'member what a fjord is, don't you?"

"A lake."

"That's right, a lake, and at our back door was the purple mountains. Up a hill toward the woods and marshes was the village of Lindegaard. Sometimes Papa would take us there and we'd dress in dark homespun and the men wore plush hats, and off we'd go, maybe at Whitsuntide when the spinneys on the hills was only just tinged with pale green and the bare fields smelled like manure and the night never got darker than pale blue. And that was because Norway is called . . ." Nissa waited.

"The land of the midnight thun," Roseanne filled in.

"Right again. There were alder trees and birch woods and heather—always heather."

Roseanne looked up and rested a hand on her grandmother's neck. "Tell about the time when Grandpa brought you the heather."

"Oh, that time . . . " The old one chuckled low in her throat. "Well, that was when I was fifteen years old. Your grandpa picked me a bouquet so big a girl couldn't hold it in both arms. He delivered it in the back of a two-wheeled cart behind a jet-black pony—"

"I 'member the pony's name!" put in the eager child.

"What?" Nissa peered down through her oval spectacles.

"El-tha."

"That's right. Else. I'll never forget the sight of your grandpa, leading that little mare up the lane, comin' to call. Course he had to sit politely and visit with my family a long time. And Mama brought out thick curdled cream with grated rusks and sugar on top as if that was all in the world he'd come to do was have sweets with us." Wistfully, Nissa rested her chin on Roseanne's head while the child picked at a button on her grandma's dress.

"He was a fisherman, like his papa. But the fishing off the Lofotons had failed four years running and there was talk of America. Sometimes in the evening when he'd come to call we'd sit in the door yard and talk about it, but, shucks, we never dreamed we'd come here.

"Oh, those evenin's were fine. There'd be black cocks callin' from the bird-cherries, and they'd be in blossom, and when the sun would set behind the snowcapped mountains the cottage windows would blaze like as if they was afire." Nissa rocked gently, a wistful expression on her face. "The woods to the north opened onto a peat bog, and in the spring of the year the air was filled with the smell of peat fires and roasted coffee beans, and always you could smell the sea."

"Tell about the grindstone, Grandma."

Nissa pulled herself from one reverie to another. "There was a grindstone at the back of the byre where my papa sharp—"

"I know, Grandma," the child interrupted again, leaning back to look up at the face above her. "Where your papa tharpened

toolth and the thound wuth like the drone of a hundred beeth—
bth, bth, bth!"

Nissa smiled down indulgently, wrapped her arms more
securely around Roseanne, and went on. "And I had a Lapland
dog . . . " She waited, knowing it was expected.

"Named King," put in Roseanne. "And you had to leave old
King behind when you married Grampa and came on the boat
to America."

"That's right, little one."

The name lit a warm flame in Linnea's heart. Theodore had
called her by it at times, and she knew now from whom he'd
learned it.

Sonny and Norna toddled out from their nests, and the old
woman gathered them 'round, taking sustenance from their
sleepy faces. One by one they all came, beckoned by some
call none could divine—much as the horses had appeared when
the fields needed them—to leave their cozy beds and gather at
their grandmother's feet as she reached into the past for ease.
They surrounded her chair, some sitting on its wooden arms,
some sinking to their knees and resting their cheeks against
her thigh. Nissa's fingers sifted through a head of silken hair.
Watching, listening, Linnea felt a lump form in her throat. She
understood, as she never had before, the why and wherefore
of family, of generation leading to generation, flesh to flesh,
past to future.

Posterity.

She said silently to the child she carried, Listen now, this
is your legacy.

The tale went on, laced with more mysterious words: ban-
nocks and moors and bilberries and brambles.

Much later the lights of bobbing lanterns showed in the east.
Linnea stood at the window with dread thickening her throat.
It buzzed through her veins and popped out in liquid pearls on
her forehead. She stared into the night, loath to tell Nissa they
were coming, giving her time—she was old and had too little
of it left—all the time it was possible to give.

No horses—where were the horses?—but a pair of toboggans with two shadowed forms upon them, and downturned
faces in the light of the gold lamps. Linnea despaired. Oh
God, oh God, not both of them!

Nissa's voice lilted on. "There were fires in the hills on Whitsuntide, and they burned long into the night. . . . "

Was it Linnea's own voice that finally spoke, so quiet, so calm, when it felt as if she herself were dying a little as each second passed?

"They're coming."

Nissa's story stopped. So did the rocker. Gently she pushed the young ones off her lap while her sons and grandsons trudged toward the house with their burdens trailing on the moon-washed snow. A blanket of dread worse than any she'd ever imagined pressed down on Linnea.

She opened the door and Lars came through first, his haunted eyes going directly to the rocking chair.

"Ma . . . " he croaked softly, voice breaking.

Nissa sat forward, pain flickering through her eyes.

"Both of them?" she asked simply.

"No . . . j . . . just John. We got to Teddy in time."

Nissa's softly-fuzzed cheeks collapsed into swags of sorrow. Her cry keened quietly through the room. "Oh no . . . oh, John . . . my son, my son . . . " She wrapped her body with one arm, covered her mouth with a hand, and rocked in short desperate motions. Tears rolled down, catching on the lower rim of her spectacles before finding the valleys of despair in her face and riding them to her chin.

"Ma . . . " Lars managed again and went down on one knee before her. Clinging, they grieved together. Watching, Linnea felt gratitude and grief conflicting within her breast. Teddy was alive . . . but John. Gentle John. Tears streamed from the corners of her eyes and her shoulders shook. The children, silent and uncertain, looked questioningly from their grandma to their teacher. Some of them understood but were hesitant to believe. Some of them still thought the worst hazard of a blizzard was having to eat raisins.

The men came in, carrying the toboggans like litters. They set the quilt-wrapped burdens by the stove and Kristian entered behind them, his face gaunt and pale. His stricken eyes immediately found Linnea's.

"Krist . . . " she tried, but the word tore in half.

He lunged into her arms, closing his eyes and swallowing hard against the tears he could contain no longer.

"Pa's alive," he managed in a guttering whisper.

She could only nod yes against his shoulder, her throat too constricted to speak. Kristian drew himself from her arms and she found Raymond beside them, watching, looking as drawn as all the others. She hugged him hard while across the room Nissa cried softly and Ulmer knelt on the floor beside the toboggans.

"Somebody get the children out of here," he ordered in a quivering voice.

Crushing back the need to see for herself that Teddy was alive, Linnea did what she knew was most needed.

"Come, ch . . . children . . . " She dashed a hand beneath her eyes. "Come w . . . with me upstairs."

They balked, sensing disaster, but she herded them ahead of her, up the squeaking steps into the gloom overhead. "Wait right where you are. I'll get a lamp."

What she saw when she turned back to fetch a lamp made her freeze in her footsteps. Ulmer had rolled back the quilts, revealing Theodore's body coiled into a fetal pose, his hands crossed and clutching his shoulders. His hair was plastered to his head and his clothes pasted to his body with a gruesome mixture of gore and entrails. On his face and hands was a film of liquid that looked like red oil. His eyes were closed and lips open as if in an eternal gasp, yet not a muscle moved. He looked as if he were the dead one.

A cry escaped Linnea's throat.

Ulmer looked up. "Take the children upstairs, Linnea," he ordered sternly.

She stared, horrified, her jaw working, mouth agape. "What—"

"He's alive. We'll take care of him, now get the lantern and go!"

With her stomach lurching she spun from the room.

Upstairs all seven children settled on her old bed, their knees crossed, their eyes wide and frightened. She fought helplessness, tears, and nausea. *Theodore, oh dear God, what happened to you? What did you suffer out there in the wrath of the storm? Something more deadly than the blizzard itself? Something with teeth and jaws?* She tried to recall where his skin was broken, but there'd been so much blood it was impossible to tell from where it had come. Shudders wracked her body as she hunkered on the edge of the mattress and hugged herself, rocking. *What kind of animal stalks humans and attacks in the middle of a blizzard? Please, oh please, somebody, tell me what happened to him. Tell me he'll live.*

What brought her out of her shock was the touch of a small hand on her back and a tiny, frightened voice.

"Aunt Linnea?"

She turned to find Roseanne kneeling behind her. Linnea saw the fear in the wide brown eyes and the downturned mouth, saw it reflected in the circle of faces with their big, wondering eyes and their still poses. She realized they relied upon her to keep their world secure right now.

"Oh, Roseanne, honey." She swept her arms around the child, kissed her cheek, and held her tightly to her breast, suddenly understanding even more fully why Nissa had welcomed having the children near during the last hour of her vigil. "All of you . . . " She opened her arms to include them all, and though they wouldn't all fit, they nestled as close as possible, seeking comfort, too. "I'm so sorry. I've been thinking only of myself. Of course you want to know what happened." Her troubled eyes scanned the circle of faces. "Let's hold hands now, all of us." As they had on Thanksgiving when there'd been so much to be grateful for, they formed a continuous ring of human contact while she told them the truth.

"Your uncle John is dead, and your uncle Teddy is . . . well, he's very . . . ill. They were caught in the blizzard yesterday on their way home from town. Now we'll all have to be very strong and help Grandma Nissa and Kristian and all of your papas and mamas. They'll be v . . . very s . . . sad."

But she could go on no longer. She let the tears roll unheeded down her cheeks, holding two small hands that felt like lifelines. She watched their faces change from fearful to respectful, and understood that most of them were dealing for the first time with death. What came as the greatest surprise was how they dealt with their sorrowing teacher. Their first concern was for her. Seeing her crying and in the throes of near shock frightened them worse than anything so far. In their inexperienced way, they tried to comfort. And during those minutes while they huddled on the bed, the bond of love among them drew even tighter.

Downstairs, Nissa staunchly set aside her grief and attended to the living. She insisted on bathing Teddy herself, washing his hair, while he lay on the toboggan beside the stove. Only after that did she allow his brothers to dress, lift, and carry him to his own freshly made bed. Throughout it all he remained unconscious, sealed in the protective security of natural escape.

It was near dawn when Kristian went upstairs to fetch his young cousins. In Linnea's old room a jumble of sleeping bodies huddled on the bed, leaning, tilting, curled together like a ball of spring angleworms. At their core sat Linnea, with her back to the bedstead, ear to shoulder, limp arms circling Bent and Roseanne, while the other children tangled as close as they could get.

He felt awkward waking her.

"Linnea?" He touched her shoulder.

Her eyelids flickered. Her head lifted. She winced and let her head ease down at an acute angle and slept again.

"Linnea?" He shook her gently.

This time her eyes opened slowly and her head stayed up. Disoriented, she looked into Kristian's eyes. Slowly things began to register—Kristian's hand on her shoulder, the children slumped around her, the pale light of dawn coming in her window.

She jerked to life and tried to get off the bed. "Oh, no, I didn't mean to fall asleep. I should have been down there—"

"It's all right. Grandma took care of everything."

"Kristian," she whispered, "how is he?"

"I don't know. He hasn't moved. They washed him and put him to bed. Now Ulmer and Lars are doing the milking, then they have to go home. Helen and Evie will be worried about the kids." He straightened, then glanced at the sleeping children strewn about her lap.

"I want to go see him."

Kristian sat heavily on the edge of the bed. "He looks bad."

She felt the same hideous fear as last night, but she had to know. "Kristian, what happened to them?"

He sucked in a deep, shaky breath and ran a hand through his hair. When he spoke his voice reflected the horror of the past night. "When the blizzard first hit they must have overturned the wagon and laid underneath it to get out of the wind. When that wouldn't protect them enough they . . . " He swallowed and she reached for his hand, clasped it tightly. "They shot the horses and g . . . gutted them and c . . . crawled inside."

The horror on his face was reflected in hers. "C . . . Cub and Toots?" Theodore's favorites. "Oh no . . . " Her stomach suddenly churned. A myriad of images flashed through her mind—the horses nodding along on their way to town on a mellow Arbor Day morning, the entire herd prancing away to freedom while Cub and Toots trumpeted to them from inside the pasture fence, the countless times she'd seen Theodore rub their noses. Oh, what it must have been like for him to slay the beasts he loved so well, and for Kristian to find them. She pressed the boy's cheek. "Oh, Kristian, how awful for you."

He sat perfectly still, tears coursing slowly down his cheeks, his eyes fixed on a point beyond her shoulder. She stroked the wetness with her thumb. In a choked voice, Kristian went on. "It looked like Uncle John must've b . . . " His Adam's apple bobbed twice. "Been in . . . inside T . . . Toots, but he must not've b . . . been able to st . . . stand it, because we f . . . found him sitting beside her in the snow as if . . . aw, Jesus—" Sobs overwhelmed him and he hunched forward, burying his face in his hands. He sobbed brokenly, shoulders heaving. Linnea was crying, too, as she dislodged herself from the sleeping children and struggled to the edge of the bed. On her knees she circled Kristian from behind, pressing her cheek against his trembling back, holding him tight.

"Shh . . . shh . . . it's all right. . . . "

He found one of her hands, twined his fingers with hers, and pressed it hard against his aching heart. "I can't f . . . forget all that r . . . red snow."

She felt his heart beat heavy beneath her palm. "Kristian . . ." she sympathized, unable to come up with any words of ease. "Kristian . . . " Her tears left dark splotches on the back of his blue shirt. Then neither of them spoke. They let grief have its way, solacing each other.

In time Kristian heaved a long shuddering sigh and Linnea released her hold on him. He blew his nose and she dried her eyes with a sleeve.

"Grandma's with Pa. She could use a breather."

"And you, too. You look like you're ready to tip over."

He managed a weary smile. "Tipping over sounds wonderful."

"Help me wake the children, then you do just that."

The young ones were half-carried, half-nudged downstairs to make the long rides home on toboggans behind their weary, heartsore fathers whose chores today would include making funeral arrangements for their brother as well as seeing after the carcasses of two dead horses and an overturned wagon. The only blessing—and it was an ironic one at best—was how quickly eighteen inches of snow had melted to nine.

The sun yawned awake, strewing the prairie with tardy warmth, painting sky and snow vivid pinks and oranges before stealing higher into a lustrous sky as clear as springwater.

It streamed into the east window of Theodore's room, while in the doorway, Linnea hesitated.

Beside the bed, Nissa slumped on a hard kitchen chair, her chin resting on her chest and her fingers laced loosely over her stomach. Linnea's glance moved to the bed. She stifled a gasp. He looked so haggard, so drawn . . . and undeniably old. The healthy color was gone, replaced by a wan, waxy tone. His eyes, behind closed lids, were surrounded by flesh tinted a faint blue. His cheekbones appeared to have sharpened into hooked blades that seemed as if they might slice through the flesh at any moment. His cheeks were sallow, and upon them shone lighter spots where frostbite had deadened the skin. His beard had grown for—for what?—two, almost three days. It seemed years since she'd waved his wagon off to town from the schoolyard. Studying the whiskered jaw and chin, she grieved afresh for all he'd been through.

Her gaze passed to Nissa. Poor, afflicted mother. How tragic to outlive your own children. Linnea moved into the room to touch the slumped shoulder.

"Nissa."

Her head snapped up. The spectacles had slipped low on her nose.

"He took a turn for the worse?"

"No. He's the same. Why don't you go lie down in your own room and I'll sit watch for a while?"

She flexed her shoulders, wedged her fingertips beneath her glasses, and rubbed her eyes. "Naw . . . I'll be fine."

Linnea could see it would be useless to argue. "Very well, then I'll sit with you."

"I'd welcome the company. Ain't no other chairs in here, you'll have to—"

"This will be fine." Linnea snagged the small creweled footstool and brought it near Nissa's chair. She folded herself on it and drew her ankles in with both hands. The room smelled of camphor and liniment. Outside a rooster crowed and a robin boisterously heralded the morning. Inside, the regular beat of Theodore's breathing was soon joined by the heavier purr of his mother's soft snore.

Linnea glanced up to see the old woman threatening to topple from her chair.

She awakened her again, gently. "Come on, Nissa. You're not doing Teddy any good when you can't keep your own eyes open." She gathered Nissa unresistingly against her side and guided her to the bedroom next door.

"Well . . . all right . . . just for a minute." Nissa dropped to the bed and rolled to her pillow without even bothering to remove her glasses. As Linnea slipped them from her nose, Nissa mumbled, " . . . chicken soup on the stove . . . "

"Shh, dear. I'll see to him. Rest now."

Before leaving the room, Linnea loosened Nissa's shoestrings and slid off the high-topped black shoes, then gently drew a comforter to her shoulders.

Back in their own room she stood beside the bed, studying Theodore's haggard face. The silent cry was gone from his lips. With two fingertips she gently brushed his eyebrows, his temple. She leaned to kiss the corner of his mouth; his skin was cool and dry. She touched a strand of his hair—clean but disheveled, curling slightly at the tips. She watched his chest lift and fall. The blankets covered his ribs. Above was the exposed wool of his exhumed winter underwear, buttoned all the way up to the hollow of his throat where the morning shadows delineated the trip of his pulse. His hands lay atop the coverlets. She took one; it lay lax and unresponsive, its skin callused and hard. She thought of that hand lovingly mending harnesses, soothing the belly of the pregnant mare, turning down Cub's ear as he whispered into it . . . then grasping the haft of a knife and eviscerating his beloved beasts.

Tears burned her eyelids again, and this time when she kissed his temple she lingered, breathing in the scent of his living flesh and hair, feeling his reassuring pulsebeat beneath her lips. Oh, Teddy, Teddy, we came so close to losing you, the baby and me. I was so scared. What would I have done without you?

She stretched out beside him, on top of the covers, pressing her stomach close against his side, wrapping a protective arm around his waist, and for a while she slept, with their baby pressed between them.

His cough awakened her. She sat up, listening for signs of congestion, got off the bed, and pulled the covers up to his ears. On the chair beside the bed, she kept vigil. For the most part he lay quietly, but once he rolled to his side, not with the wild flinging of one experiencing haunted dreams, but with a slow, tired deliberation, as of one too exhausted to move quickly. He spoke not a word, no unconscious outcries prompted by the horror he'd suffered. For now, he seemed at peace.

He awakened near noon, as undramatically as he'd slept. He was flat on his back, hands on his stomach when he opened his eyes and rolled his jaw to the pillow. His pupils and mind tried simultaneously to focus, finally lighting on Linnea. When he spoke his voice sounded like nutshells cracking.

"John?"

Her throat and mouth filled. Her heart wrenched with pity. She'd feared being the one to whom he'd awaken and ask the question, yet perhaps it was best that Nissa and Kristian be spared answering it.

She took his hand. "John didn't make it."

"Tell him to get under the wagon," Theodore said very clearly. Struggling to brace up on both elbows, he ordered in an eerily normal tone, "John, get in," then made as if to get up and see to it.

Linnea sprang to her feet, pushed him back, and struggled to keep her tears hidden.

"Go to sleep . . . please, Teddy . . . shh . . . shh . . . "

He fell back, closed his eyes, and rolled toward the wall, again claimed by the blissful arms of sleep.

He was still dead to the world when Nissa came to spell Linnea. And later in the afternoon, when the men returned to discuss funeral arrangements. Linnea took Nissa's place again and was sitting beside the bed when Lars and Ulmer came to the bedroom door and knocked softly. Lars asked, "How is he?"

"Still sleeping."

The two men came in and quietly stood looking down at their sleeping brother. Ulmer reached to brush the hair from Teddy's forehead, then turned to rest a hand on Linnea's shoulders. "How you doing, young 'un?"

"Me? Oh, I'm fine. Don't waste your worries on me."

"Ma tells us you're in a family way."

"Just barely."

"Barely's enough. You take it easy, okay? We don't want Teddy to wake up to more bad news."

He glanced at Teddy again while Lars leaned over to give Linnea a kiss on the cheek. "That's wonderful, Linnea. Now how about a breath of fresh air?"

She glanced at Theodore. "I'd rather not leave him."

"We went out with a couple horses, cleaned up the mess, tipped over the wagon, and brought it back home. It's sitting down by the windmill. There's something carved in the bed of it we think you should see."

They let her go alone. On the fast-disappearing snow the shadow of the windmill stretched long. She ran through the late afternoon toward the parsley-green wagon with its bright red wheels. The words were easy enough to spot—after all, Theodore kept everything in shipshape, including the thick green paint on the wagon bed. The letters were slightly disconnected, but decipherable just the same.

Lin, I'm sorry.

More tears? How was it possible to feel more pity, more love than she already did? Yet she experienced as real a pain while reading the message as she imagined he had felt writing it. She ran her fingertips over the scarred paint, picturing him lying beneath the overturned wagon carving the words, afraid he'd die without saying them, without seeing his child.

Love welled up, combined with grief, despair, and hope, a mixture of emotions brought about by the random hand of fate choosing one life and sparing another.

That evening, when she was sitting beside Teddy, his eyes opened. She saw immediately he was lucid.

"Linnea," he said croakily, reaching.

She took his hand; his fingers twisted tight and pulled. "Teddy . . . oh, Teddy."

"Come here."

Gingerly, she sat beside him.

"No . . . under."

Sweater, apron, shoes, and all she got beneath the covers where it was warm and he was waiting to roll her tight against his stomach and hold her as if he were shipwrecked and she was a sturdy timber.

"I'm so sorry, Linnea . . . so sorry . . . I didn't think I'd—"

"Shh."

"Let me say it. I've got to."

"But I found the carving on the wagon. I know, love, I know."

"I thought I was going to die and you'd think I didn't want the baby, but when I was laying under that wagon thinking I'd never see you again I . . . I kept thinking that the baby was a godsend, only I'd been too stubborn to recognize it. Oh, Lin, Lin . . . I was such a fool." He could not hold her close enough, nor kiss her hard enough to convey all he felt. But she understood fully as his hand stole down to mold her stomach where his seed grew, healthy and strong.

"And I thought you'd die in the blizzard and I wouldn't get a chance to tell you I knew you hadn't meant it. But you're alive . . . oh, dear Teddy . . ."

"You feel so good, so warm. It was so cold under that wagon. Hold me."

She did, gratefully, until his tremors passed.

In time she whispered, "Teddy, John . . ."

"I know," came his voice, muffled against her chest. "I know."

He shuddered once, convulsively, then his hands clutched her sweater and he pulled her tightly against him while she cradled his head, her lips buried in his hair.

There were no words she could say, so she didn't try. She let him breathe of her warm, live, pregnant body, clutch it, draw from it, until the worst had passed. When he spoke, he spoke for both of them. "If the baby's a boy, we'll name it after him."

A life for a life—somehow they both found ease in the thought.

24

JOHN'S FUNERAL WAS held on May Day, the temperature reaching an unprecedented seventy-nine degrees. There remained no hint that the blizzard had ravaged the countryside save for the casket of the man who'd lost his life in it. Indeed, the wild crocus and buttercups blossomed euphorically. In the cemetery beside the little white country church a myriad of spring flowers was up and radiant beside the headstones—creeping phlox in carpets of purple, peonies in explosions of heliotrope, and bridal wreath in cascades of white.

But what a woeful scene at the graveside. On a day when the children should have been gathering those flowers for May baskets, they stood instead among them in a crooked flank, singing a farewell hymn in clear, piping voices while their teacher directed them with tears in her eyes. The family stood nearby, hemmed in close, their elbows touching.

When the song ended, Linnea took her place by Theodore's shoulder; he was still too depleted to stand through the ceremony, so sat instead on a plain wooden kitchen chair. It looked out of place with its spooled legs buried in the spring grass. It was the kind of chair usually seen with toddlers climbing on its seat, or with a man balancing it on two legs while considering what card to play, or with a work jacket carelessly flung over its back. The sight of it at the graveside brought Linnea's tears up again with new vigor.

But it wasn't really the chair at all. It was Theodore who made her cry, sitting upon it so wan and gaunt, dolefully formal, his legs crossed at neither ankle nor knee. The gentle breeze riffled his pant legs and fingered the hair on his forehead. He still hadn't shed a tear, though she knew his agony was even greater than her own. But all she could do was stand at his side and squeeze his shoulder.

And then there was Nissa, listening to Reverend Severt eulogize her son, breaking down at last and turning against Lars's broad chest for support until from somewhere a second kitchen chair was produced and she was gently lowered onto it.

The faces of John's siblings were vacant, each of them undoubtedly reliving their own private memories of the gentle, unassuming man they had protected all their lives.

The eulogy droned on. Funny, Linnea thought, but it didn't seem to touch on any of the important things: John, self-consciously shuffling his feet while peeking around a cloak-room door with a Christmas tree hidden behind him; John, blushing and stammering as he asked the new schoolmarm to dance; John, winking at his partner just before playing the winning card; John, planting morning glories by his windmill; John, saying, "Teddy, he never gets mad at me, not even when I'm slow. And I'm pretty slow."

Oh, how they'd miss him. How they'd all miss him.

The ceremony ended as Ulmer, Lars, Trigg, and Kristian lowered the coffin into the grave. When a symbolic spadeful of dirt was dropped upon it, Nissa collapsed in a rash of weeping, repeating woefully, "Oh, my son . . . my son . . . " But Theodore sat on as before, as if part of his own life had been snuffed out with John's.

During the hours following the service, while the mourners gathered at the house to share food, Theodore looked haggard and spoke little. When the house emptied at last and the quietude settled too thickly, Nissa sat at the kitchen table, listlessly tapping the oilcloth. Kristian went for a walk up the road with Patricia and Raymond. Linnea hung up wet dishtowels on the clothesline and returned to the tranquil house.

Nissa stared vacantly at the sunset sky, the budding caragana bushes, the windmill softly turning. Linnea stepped behind her chair and leaned to kiss the old woman softly on the neck. She smelled of lye soap and lavender salts. "Can I get you anything?"

Nissa heaved herself from her reverie. "No . . . no, child. Guess I've had about everything a body's got a right to expect."

The tears stung once more. Linnea closed her eyes, leaned back, and held a deep breath. Nissa sighed, squared her shoulders, and asked, "Where's Teddy?"

"I think he slipped away to the barn to be by himself for a while."

"You reckon he's all right out there?"

"I'll go down and check on him if it'll make you feel better."

"He's awful weak yet. Didn't see him eatin' much today either."

"Will you be all right alone for a few minutes?"

Nissa gave a dry laugh. "Y' start alone, y' end alone. Why is it that in between folks think y' always need company?"

"All right. I won't be long."

She knew where he'd be, probably slumped on his chair polishing a harness that didn't need it. But when she came to the door of the tack room she found him instead with idle hands. He sat in the ancient chair, facing the door, with his head tipped back against the edge of the tool bench, eyes closed. On his lap, washing her chest, sat John's cat, Rainbow, with Theodore's hands resting inertly beside her haunches. Though he at first appeared to be asleep, Linnea saw his fingertips move in the soft fur, and from the corner of his eyes, tears seeped. He wept as he'd awakened—quietly, undramatically—letting the tears roll down his face without bothering to wipe them away.

Linnea had never seen Theodore cry before; the sight was devastating.

"Theodore," she said gently, "your mother was worried about you."

His eyes opened, but his head didn't move.

"Tell her I just wanted to be alone."

"Are you all right?"

"Fine."

She studied him, trying to keep her lips from trembling, her eyes from stinging. But he looked so forlorn and alone. "Did Rainbow come down here by herself?"

With an effort he lifted his head to watch his fingers probe the cat's fur, the look on his face so desolate and lifeless it tore at her soul. "No. Kristian went and got her. Figured she'd sit on John's doorstep meowing for food . . . t . . . till . . . " But he never finished. His face suddenly furrowed into lines of grief. A single harsh sob rent the room as he dropped his head and covered his eyes with one hand. Rainbow started and leaped away while Linnea rushed across the concrete floor to squat before him, touching his knees.

"Oh, Teddy . . . " she despaired, "I need so badly to be with you right now. Please don't shut me out."

A strangled cry left his throat as his arms lashed out to take her close. Then she was in his embrace, on his lap, holding him fiercely while his ragged sobs heaved against her breast, and hers upon his hair. Clutching, they rocked. Against her dress he brokenly uttered her name while she clung to him—consoled, consoling.

When the crying subsided, they were left limp, depleted, but feeling better and infinitely closer. A step sounded in the outer barn and though Teddy straightened, Linnea stayed where she was, with her arms around his neck.

Kristian stepped to the doorway, looking lost and lonely himself. "Grandma was worried. She sent me down here after you two."

They'd each had their time alone. Now it was time to draw strength from others. Linnea got to her feet, drew Theodore up, and said, "Come. Nissa needs to be with us now." She looped one arm around his waist, the other around Kristian's, and, followed by John's cat, they walked up past the sighing windmill toward the house.

Life went on. Theodore returned to the fields alone. Nissa started putting in her garden. P.S. 28 had been closed long enough.

How fast the school year was coming to a close. May seemed to pass in a blur. There was the county spelling bee in Williston—won by Paul this year. Then came *Sytende Mai*—the seventeenth of May—the biggest Norwegian holiday of the year, celebrating the day the homeland had adopted its constitution. There were games and a picnic at school, followed by a dance, at which Linnea brought up the subject of Kristian's enlistment.

"He's not a child anymore." They watched Kristian and Patricia dancing, so close a gnat couldn't have come between them. "If he's made his decision, I think you'll have to let him go."

"I know," Theodore said softly, his eyes following the pair. "I know."

And so the end of the school year would bring additional heartache. But, come what may, the days marched on and Linnea felt both the exhilaration inherent with term's end and the sadness of realizing these were her last precious days as a teacher. She had been a good one; she felt no false sense of modesty about it and wished that when fall came she could somehow have both the baby and her old job back. But when she said good-bye to the children on the last day, she'd be bidding farewell to a phase of her life.

Final examinations were held, then it was time for the last-day picnic. The class had voted to hold it down by the creek so they could all swim.

The day turned out ideally—warm and sunny with little wind. Just perfect for a crew of excited children celebrating the end of school. They played games, swam, ate, explored. The boys fished downstream while the girls searched for wildflowers and twined them in each other's French braids.

It was near the end of the afternoon when Norna approached Linnea with a frown, announcing, "I can't find Frances anyplace."

"She's with the others, picking flowers."

"She was, but she isn't anymore."

Linnea glanced upstream. Laughter floated down from the small group of girls who were busily engaged in making clover rings. But Frances wasn't with them.

Automatically, Linnea turned to the one she always seemed to turn to. "Kristian, have you seen Frances?" she called.

Kristian's head came up. He and Patricia were sitting quietly on the creek bank, talking. He glanced around. "No, ma'am."

"Have you, Patricia?"

"No, ma'am."

All four of them looked at the creek. But it wasn't deep enough here for Frances to drown. Quickly Linnea took a nose count. Her heart beat out a warning when she realized Allen Severt, too, was missing.

Frances Westgaard had been in and out of the creek four times that day. She had water in one ear that refused to be shaken out, and a bad case of shivers. Hugging herself, she made her way through the thick underbrush toward the place where the girls had left their clothes.

When she grew up, Frances decided, she was going to be a teacher, just like Aunt Linnea. She'd take her class on picnics like this all the time, at least once every week when the weather was good. And in the winter they'd cook soup, too. And rabbits on Thanksgiving and popcorn whenever the kids said they wanted it.

Her wet bathing drawers felt thick and sticky. They clung like leeches when she tried to pull them down. Hobbling around, she managed to work them to her hips, and finally to her knees, but even hopping one-footed she couldn't get them off completely. Finally she gave up and plopped down on the scratchy grass. Her teeth were chattering, her jaw dancing as she tried to work the clinging drawers over her ankles.

"Hey, Frances, whatcha doin'?" an unctuous voice drawled.

Frances jumped and tried to jerk the drawers back up, but they were rolled up tight as a new rope. "I'm changin' my clothes. You git outa here, Allen!"

Allen stepped out from behind a cottonwood with a smart-aleck expression on his mouth. "Why should I? It's a free country." Allen had had all year long to nurse his rancor for Mrs. Westgaard and Frances. Both of them had caused him embarrassment more times than he cared to count. There was no way for him to get back at his teacher, but he could even the score with this little dummy.

"You better get outa here or I'm gonna tell Aunt Linnea!" Frantically Frances fumbled with the drawers, trying to straighten them out, but Allen advanced and stood over her, pinning the wet garment to the ground between her ankles with his foot. "Oh yeah? What you gonna tell her?"

Allen's eyes raked Frances's bare skin and she shielded her lap with her hands.

"You ain't supposed to be here. This is where the girls change."

But Allen only gave a sinister laugh that struck a bolt of fear through the girl.

"Allen, I don't like you. I'm gonna tell on you!"

"You been tellin' on me all year, gettin' me in trouble all the time. Haven't you, snot?"

"No, I—"

"You have, too, and I'm gonna make you sorry . . . dum-my!"

Before she could wiggle away Allen jumped her. The force of his body knocked her flat. She shrieked out, "I'm gonna tell!" before he clapped a hand across her mouth and slammed her head against the earth. Frances's eyes widened with fear and her mouth opened in a suppressed scream beneath his palm.

"You tell and I'll get you good, Frances!" he threatened in an ugly voice. "You tell and I'll do something worse to you next time. All I wanna do now is look."

Again Frances gave a muffled scream. She thrashed and kicked, but he was older than she and much bigger. "Frances, you shut up! You scream and they'll all come runnin' and I'll tell 'em you pulled your pants down right in front of me. You know what they do to girls who pull their pants down in front of boys?"

Terrified, Frances fell still, her heart hammering pitifully as Allen thrust a knee between her legs, trying to force them apart. But the wet drawers shackled her ankles, aiding her. Nose to nose, they struggled until Allen finally managed to wedge her knees open. Beneath him the frightened face had turned the color of chalk, only the dark, horrified eyes holding any color. Allen's breath came in a hard hiss. He squeezed her face till her cheek sliced against a tooth and she tasted blood. Struck afresh by terror, she squirmed harder. Twisting franti-cally, fighting for breath, Frances felt his weight shift as he yanked her wet shirt up. Behind his hand, she screamed again. His face contorted with ugliness. "You scream and you'll be sorry. Cuz once you do they'll all know you been doing dirty things with me." With the speed of a snake he shifted, got her by the neck, and squeezed, completely subduing her at last. Her fingers uselessly plucked at his stranglehold while he knelt between her legs and braced back.

The next moment he was jerked to his feet like a marionette, then a fist slammed into his face and sent him crashing against the trunk of a cottonwood.

"You filthy rotten son of a bitch!" This time the fist caught him in the solar plexus and doubled him over like a pocket-knife. In a flash he was jerked erect and hammered again. Somebody screamed. Blood flew across the grass. Children came running. Sobs filled the air. Linnea shouted, "Kristian, stop it this moment! Kristian, I said *stop!*"

It ended as abruptly as it had begun.

Allen Severt held his bloody face in both hands and looked up to see Kristian spraddled above him like Zeus outraged. Linnea held a whimpering Frances in her lap. Libby Severt gaped at her brother in horrified disbelief. Raymond stormed onto the scene with fists clenched. "Get away from him, Kristian. It's my turn!"

"Mine, too!" echoed Tony, arriving on his brother's heels. Had the situation not been so grave it might have been humorous to see Tony, bristling mad, clenching his weak fists and squaring his skinny shoulders as if he had the power to do more than swat mosquitoes.

"Boys! That's enough!"

"That puny little bastard ain't gonna forget the day he laid hands on my little sister!" Raymond vowed, being restrained now by Kristian.

Transferring the weeping Frances into Patricia's arms, Linnea leaped to her feet and confronted the three angry boys. "Watch your language in front of the little ones, and don't raise your voice to me!" Her insides trembled and her knees had turned to aspic, but she hid it well. "Allen, get up," she ordered officiously. "You get back to school and wait for me, and so help me God, you'd better be there when I get there! Patricia, help Frances get dried and dressed. Raymond, you may carry your little sister back to school. Kristian, button your shirt and head cross country to our place and get Clippa for Raymond and Frances. The rest of you, change out of your wet things and collect your lunch pails."

Linnea's quick commands subdued them all, but she herself was still in a state of fury thirty minutes later when she marched up the lane to the Severts' front door. She followed Libby inside while Allen whimpered behind them, holding his jaw, blood congealed in one nostril and dried on his fingers.

"Mother?" Libby called, and a moment later Lillian Severt appeared in the far archway.

"Allen!" She scurried across the room. "Oh, dear Lord, what's happened to you?"

"He got precisely what he deserved," Linnea retorted, then went on coldly, "Where is your husband?"

"He's busy right now, in the church."

"Get him."

"But Allen's face—"

"Get him!"

"How dare you—"

"Get him!" Linnea's blast of outrage finally stunned Lillian Severt into compliance. She ran from the room, casting a baleful glance over her shoulder at Allen's bloody nose, while Libby dropped her chin. When Mr. and Mrs. Severt returned, Linnea gave them no chance to coddle their son. She made sure she had him sitting on a straight-backed chair with herself standing over him like a prison guard. His face was swollen, the right eye nearly shut. Lillian moved as if to console him, but Linnea stopped her by ordering, "All right, Allen, talk!"

Allen held his jaw and mumbled, "Can't . . . hurts."

She gave him a nudge that nearly knocked him off the chair. "I said, talk!" He dropped his head onto the table and cradled it in his arms. "Very well, I'll tell them myself." She pierced his parents with a glare. "Your son attacked Frances Westgaard today during the school picnic. He pulled her pants down and—"

"I did not!" howled Allen, coming up straight, but immediately he clutched his jaw and subsided into moans of pain.

"He followed her to the girls' changing spot when nobody else was around and attacked her. Pulled her pants down and threatened to get her again and do worse if she dared tell on him. He had her pinned to the ground by the throat when we found them."

"I don't believe you!" declared Lillian Severt, her eyes huge.

"You didn't believe me the last time I came to you, or the time before that. Not only didn't you believe me, you went so far as to intimate that the fault for Allen's misbehavior should be placed on me. You refused to see that his violations are much more than simple boyish pranks and that steps must be taken to help him. This time, I'm afraid you'll have no choice. The whole school witnessed it. I happened to have all the children out searching for them when it happened. Tell them, Libby."

"I . . . he . . . " Libby's terrified eyes flashed from her brother to her teacher.

"You needn't be afraid, Libby," Linnea said, softening for the first time, but she could see Libby's fear of retribution was greater than her fear of not answering. "You know that to avoid telling the truth is as good as a lie, don't you, Libby?"

"But I'm scared. He'll hurt me if I tell."

Martin finally spoke up. "Hurt you?" He came forward, reaching for Libby's hand.

"He always hurts me if I do anything to make him mad."

His wife began, "Martin, how can you be concerned with her when his nose is bleeding and—"

"Let her talk," Martin demanded, and encouraged his daughter. "Hurt you? How?"

"He pinches me and pulls my hair. And he said he'd kill my cat. He said he'd put k . . . kerosene in her . . . in her . . ." Chagrined, Libby hung her head.

"What a preposterous—"

"Quiet!" Martin roared, spinning toward his wife. "You've had your way with him for as long as you're going to. If I had stepped in years ago, this never would have happened." Gently he turned to Libby. "So it's all true, what Mrs. Westgaard said?"

"Yes!" she cried. "Yes!" Tears poured from her eyes. "He was laying on top of poor Frances and he was choking her and her . . . pants were down and . . . and . . . everybody in the school saw it and then Kristian pulled Allen off and slugged him a good one and Raymond wanted to slug him, too, but Mrs. Westgaard wouldn't let him. But I wish he would've! I wish Raymond would've knocked his teeth clear out . . . because he's . . . he's mean and hateful and he's always teasing people and calling them names when they never did anything to him. He just hurts everybody to be sp . . . spiteful!" When she broke into a rash of weeping and buried herself in her father's arms, Linnea took over.

"Mr. and Mrs. Severt, I'm afraid this time there will be serious repercussions. I'm going to recommend to Superintendent Dahl that Allen be officially expelled from school as of today. And I caution you to see to it that Allen does nothing to hurt Libby because she told the truth."

Mrs. Severt's face had turned ashen, and for the first time ever she had nothing to say in defense of her darling. By the time Linnea left the house, Allen was howling in pain, but getting little sympathy.

She went directly to Ulmer and Helen's to find Frances already tucked into bed, being coddled by all her sisters and brothers. A moment after Linnea arrived, so did Theodore. He stalked into the house scowling, and announced, "Kristian told me. How's the little one?"

So naturally they banded together in times of distress. Without hesitation, without explanation. Seeing Teddy appear with Kristian at his side brought tears at last to Linnea's eyes. She'd been running on adrenaline for well over an hour, but now that Teddy was here and the incident was over, she felt like a piece of old rope.

"You okay?" Teddy asked, turning to her.

She nodded shakily. "Yes."

But he opened his arms anyway, and she went into them like a child to her mother. "I'm so glad you're here," she whispered against his chest. His shirt was stained beneath the arms and he smelled of sweat and horses, but she had never loved him more nor been more grateful for his support.

"This time we're gonna nail that little bastard," he vowed against her hair. He rarely cursed, and never in front of Kristian. Hearing him, she realized the depth of his concern. "I brought the wagon," he added, "figured you could use a ride over to Dahl's."

She looked up at him and smiled tenderly. "If I accept, will you think I'm a hothouse pansy?"

And there before all the others he did something he'd never done before: kissed her full on the lips.

Not only did Raymond and Kristian refuse to be shunted off from underfoot while the incident was discussed, they insisted on coming along to relate the tale as they'd seen it. They were old enough to be in on this and weren't going to budge until they were assured that Allen Severt got his comeuppance.

Though it took the remainder of the day, the outcome was decided before nightfall. Allen Severt was officially expelled from school and would not be allowed at the graduation ceremonies. Whether or not he would be allowed to attend next year would be decided by the school board at its next meeting.

The children tittered about the fact that if Allen were allowed to return, he'd undoubtedly do so not only much mollified, but also much thinner, for Kristian's first punch had broken Allen's jaw, and it would have to be wired shut for six weeks.

The graduation ceremony was held in the schoolyard on the last Friday evening in May. Mourning doves cooed their soothing vespers. The sun slanted down through the ticking leaves of the cottonwoods and dappled the scene with gray and gold. The smell of fecund earth lifted from the adjacent fields where wheat sprouted like a youth's first beard.

The parents came in wagons, bringing kitchen chairs again, setting them in neat rows upon the beaten grass of the schoolyard. The four- and five-year-olds scrambled among the recitation benches up front, pretending they were as old as their sisters and brothers.

Kristian delivered the valedictory speech with all due gravity. He spoke of the war in Europe and the responsibility of the new generation to seek and assure peace for all mankind. When it was over Linnea, with misty eyes, directed the children in "America the Beautiful."

Superintendent Dahl gave his windy oration at the end of which he surprised Linnea by declaring that her leadership had been superlative, her innovations noteworthy, and her personal conduct exemplary. So much so, he continued, that the state board of education had asked him on their behalf to bestow upon her an award for excellence for organizing the first official "Domestics" class in a school of this size in the state; also for her organizational ability on behalf of the war effort, for her cool-headedness during the blizzard, and her foresight in having stocked emergency rations beforehand. Mr. Dahl added with a grin, "In spite of what some of the children might think of raisins as emergency rations." A ripple of laughter passed over the crowd, then he continued, earnestly, "And last but not least, the State Board of Education commends Mrs. Westgaard for accomplishing what no other teacher has done before her. She has persuaded the P.S. 28 parents to agree to extend the school year to a full nine months for both girls *and* boys of all ages."

Linnea felt herself blushing, but hid it as she rose to take the podium herself. Gazing out at the familiar faces, looking back on the rewards and heartbreak of the past nine months, she felt a lump form in her throat. There were few out there whom she couldn't honestly say she loved. Equally as few who didn't love her in return.

"My dear friends," she opened, then paused, glanced over their sunlit faces. "Where should I begin?"

She thanked them for a year of wonderful experiences, for their support, their friendship. She thanked them for opening their homes and hearts to her and for giving her one of their own to be her own. And she announced that though she would gladly have come back next fall to teach another year, she'd be staying home to have a baby. She invited the children to come and visit her during the summer, and admonished them to start victory gardens. In the fall, should the war not have ended, they could work together with their new teacher on an autumn-harvest auction.

Lastly, with a lump in her throat, she asked them all to pray for world peace, and told them Kristian would be leaving the following day for Jefferson Barracks, Missouri, for voluntary enlistment into the army.

She thanked them one last time with tears in her eyes and turned the program back to Superintendent Dahl for the distribution of grade-achievement certificates and eighth-grade diplomas.

Afterward, they had apple cider and cookies, and Linnea found herself hugged by nearly every parent present, and to a number, her students told her they wished she were coming back next year. By the time the benches were carried into the building and stacked up against the side walls, it was dusk.

Kristian had gone off with Patricia, but Nissa and Theodore waited in the wagon.

Standing in the cloakroom doorway and looking at the shadowed room with its desks pushed against the side walls, its flag furled tightly in brown paper, its blackboard washed, and its stovepipe freshly cleaned, Linnea felt as if she were leaving a small part of her heart behind. Ah, the smell of this room. She'd never forget it. A little dusty, a little musty—like sweating heads—and perhaps tinged with the undying after scent of cabbage from their Fridays' soup.

"Ready?" Theodore asked behind her.

"I guess so." But she didn't turn. Her shoulders sagged slightly.

He squeezed them, pulling her back against his chest. "You'll miss it, huh?"

She nodded sadly. "I grew up a lot here."

"So did I."

"Oh, Teddy . . . " She found his hand and pulled it to her lips. The twilight settled upon their shoulders. Outside, the horses waited—Nelly and Fly now. Inside, memory's voices drifted back from yesterday—the children's, John's, Kristian's, the hired hands', their own.

"In six years one of ours will be coming here," he mused. "And we can tell him the stories about when his mother was teacher."

She smiled up at him over her shoulder, then raised up on tiptoe and kissed him.

He rested his hands on her waist. "I know how much you'd like to come back . . . and it's okay. Cause I know you want the baby, too."

"Oh, I love you, Theodore Westgaard." She linked her fingers behind his neck.

"I love you, too, little missy." He kissed the end of her nose. "And Ma's waiting."

With one last look, they closed all four doors and walked arm in arm to the wagon.

It was a breezeless night. The big dipper was pouring light into the northern sky and the moon in three-quarter phase lit the world like a blue flame. The first crickets had arrived and they sawed away dissonantly from the shadows, stopping momentarily at the sound of a horse passing, then tuning up again.

Clippa plodded unhurriedly along the grassy verge between two wheat fields, head down, backside swaying lazily. On her warm, bare hide Kristian rode with the reins loose in his fingers and Patricia's cheek pressed against his back, her hands hugging his belly. They'd been riding that way, aimlessly, for nearly an hour, loath to face the final good-bye.

"I should get you home."

Her arms tightened. "No, not yet."

"It's late."

"Not yet," she whispered fiercely. Beneath her palm she felt his heartbeat, strong and sure. Against her thighs she felt his legs rub with the rhythm of the hoofbeats on the grass.

"We're almost to the creek."

The branch of a black willow touched his face and he bent to avoid it, tilting her with him.

"Stop a minute."

He reined in. Clippa obeyed instantly, her head drooping while the pair on her back sat still, listening. They could hear the purling water some distance off, and the pulsing duet of two bullfrogs. Kristian tipped his head back to look at the stars. It bumped hers and he felt her breath blowing warm through his shirt, heating his shoulder blade. He swallowed and closed his eyes, covering her arms with his own.

"We shouldn't've stopped."

She kissed his shoulder blade once more. "You could die, Kristian."

"I'm not gonna die."

"But you could! You could, and I'd never see you again."

"I don't want to go either."

"Then why are you?"

"I don't know. It's just something in me. But I aim to come back and marry you."

Behind him, he felt her straighten. "Marry me?"

"I've thought about it. Haven't you?"

"Oh, Kristian, you really mean it?"

"Course, I mean it." Her arms snaked around his belt and her breasts warmed his skin through the white cotton shirt. "Does that mean you would?"

"Of course I would. I'd marry you today if you'd let me." Her palms moved to rub the tops of his thighs where his trousers stretched taut over firm, young muscle. Abruptly he swung a leg over Clippa's head and slid off. Looking up, he reminded Patricia, "You aren't done with school yet. Better get that done first, don't you think?"

"I'm fifteen. My grandmother was married a year already by the time she was fifteen." In the moonlight her face was shadowed, but he understood the expression in her eyes even though he couldn't make it out. "Come on, let's walk." He reached for her waist, and she for his shoulders, but when she dropped from the horse their bodies brushed and neither of them moved. The night thrummed around them. Their heartbeats matched its rhythm. Their breaths came quick and heavy.

"Oh, Kristian, I'm going to miss you," she breathed.

"I'll miss you, too."

"Kristian . . . " She lifted to him, looping his neck with her arms, pressing close. When their lips met it was with the singular desperation only farewells can bring. Their bodies were tensile and straining, burgeoning with imminent maturity and the awesome need to lay claim to one another before tomorrow's separation. His arms bound her tightly and his tongue evoked an answer from hers. His hands began traversing her body, dreading the loss of it even before the gain.

He found her breasts—firm, small, upthrust—her curved feminine length against his hard, honed body. He set a rhythm against her and she answered, until they could not have come closer together but tried nonetheless. He went down to his knees, hauling her with him, falling to the thick, dry grass that whispered beneath them as they added a new, pulsing rhythm to those of the summer night around them.

When the rhythmic caress grew reckless, he hauled himself away. "It's wrong."

She brought him back on top of her. "One time . . . just once, in case you never come back."

"It's a sin."

"Against who?"

"Oh God, I don't want to leave you with a baby."

"You won't. Oh, Kristian, Kristian, I love you. I promise I'll wait for you, no matter how long it takes."

"Oh, Patricia . . ." Her body formed a cradle upon which he rocked. Their bodies fit with mysterious conformity unlike any they'd imagined. He rolled aside, touched her here, there, discovering. She was the answer to the myriad questions of his universe. "I love you, too . . . you're all soft . . . and so warm . . ."

She brushed her knuckles across his masculine secrets, discovering, too. "And you're hard and warm . . ."

When they undressed each other it was only by half, and haltingly. When their bodies sought each other it was with the fumbling uncertainty of all first times. But when their flesh linked, so did their souls, bound together in both a promise and prayer for the future.

"I love you, don't forget it," he said later, at her door. She was sobbing too hard to answer, able only to cling. "Tell me once more before I go," he said, wondering why he'd ever been so anxious to grow up when growing up hurt this much, wondering why he'd ever wanted to leave this place when it was all the things he loved.

"I l . . . love y . . . you, K . . . Kristian."

He forced her back, holding her head in both wide palms. "There, now you remember it. And pray for me."

"I w . . . will . . . I p . . . promise."

He kissed her hard, quick, then spun and mounted Clippa before he could change his mind again, sending the mare galloping at breakneck speed through the summer moonlight.

It was just past sunrise. Grandma waited at the door with six blood-sausage sandwiches wrapped in oilcloth.

Kristian looked down as she thrust them into his hands.

"Grandma, I don't need all that."

"You just take 'em," she said sternly, trying to keep her chin from trembling. "Ain't nobody in the army knows how to make blood sausage."

He took them, and the fresh batch of *fattigman,* too.

"Now, git! And hurry and take care of them Jerries so you can git back home where you belong."

Her little gray pug was neatly in place, her glasses hooked behind her ears, her apron clean and starched. He didn't ever remember seeing her any other way, not in all the years they'd lived in the same house. The morning sun lit the hairs on her chin to a soft, gilt fuzz, and reflected from the sparkle she couldn't keep from forming behind her oval spectacles. He scooped her against him so hard her old bones barely stayed intact.

"Good-bye, Grandma. I love you." He'd never said it before, but it suddenly hit Kristian how true it was.

"I love you, too, you durn fool boy. Now git going. Your pa's waiting."

He rode into Alamo on the seat of the double-box wagon, flanked by Theodore and Linnea, holding the sandwiches and cookies on his lap. In town, he studied the buildings as if for the first time. Too quickly they reached the depot. Too quickly the ticket was purchased. Too quickly the train wailed into sight.

It clanged in beside them and they stood in the white puffs of steam, all of them trying valiantly not to cry.

Linnea needlessly adjusted Kristian's collar. "There are more socks in your suitcase than any *two* soldiers could possibly need. And I put in some spare hankies, too."

"Thanks," he said, then their eyes met and the next moment they were hugging hard, parting with a swift kiss. "We love you," she whispered against his jaw. "Keep safe."

"I will. Got to come back and see my little sister or brother."

He turned from her tear-streaked face to Theodore's.

Jesus, Mary . . . Pa was crying.

"Pa . . . "

His face wracked with sorrow, Theodore clutched Kristian to his wide, strong chest. His straw hat fell from his head but nobody noticed. The conductor called, "All aboard," and the father clutched his son's hale body and prayed he'd return the same way. "Keep your head low, boy."

"I will. I'm c . . . comin' back . . . you can c . . . ount on it."

"I love you, son."

"I love you, too."

When Kristian backed away they were both crying. They leaned toward each other one last time . . . straining . . . clasping each other's necks. As adults, they had never kissed; both of them realized they might never get the chance again. It was Theodore who leaned forward, kissing Kristian flush on the lips before the boy spun for the train.

It lumbered into motion, gathering speed, giving them a brief glimpse of Kristian waving from a window before whisking him away. The breath of its passing stirred the June air, lifting dust and Linnea's skirts as the caboose swayed eastward along the track.

She clutched Teddy's arm against the side of her breast, trying to think of something to say.

"We'd best get home. There's wheat to be planted."

The wheat . . . the wheat . . . always the wheat. But now they had a real reason to keep loaves going to Europe.

25

OH, THAT SUMMER, that endless crawling summer while the war in Europe absorbed half a million doughboys and German submarines sank civilian barges and fishing schooners off America's east coast. In the Westgaard living room the newest addition was a gleaming mahogany Truphonics radio around which the family gathered each evening to hear the news from the front, via the scratchy transmissions from Yankton, South Dakota.

Linnea was shocked the day the age limits for the draft were extended to include men eighteen to forty-five. Why, most of the men she knew fell into that age bracket: Lars, Ulmer, Trigg . . . Theodore. Thankfully farmers were exempt, but it struck her that even her own father could be drafted! At church, where the service flag now held an additional blue star, she prayed more intensely, not only for Kristian and Bill, but that her father would not be called up. How would her mother survive if he went to war?

Poor Judith, bless her heart, whose husband had always owned a store with fresh and tinned goods available, had planted a victory garden. But her letters were filled with complaints about it. She hated every moment spent on her knees amid the weeds and cutworms. The cabbages, Judith com-

450

plained, attracted little white butterflies and resembled Swiss cheese. The green beans ripened so fast no mortal could keep up with them, and the tomatoes got blight.

Linnea wrote back and advised her mother to leave the victory gardens to someone else and continue with the other war efforts at which she was so good. Meanwhile, she herself was learning the ins and outs of gardening from Nissa. Together they planted, weeded, picked, and canned. Linnea had never before realized how much work went into a single jar of perfect gold carrots gleaming like coins beneath their zinc lid. As the summer rolled on and Linnea's girth increased, the work became more arduous. Bending grew difficult, and straightening made her dizzy. Being in the sun too long made black dots dance before her eyes. Standing too long made her ankles swell. And she lost both the inclination and agility to make love.

Nighttimes, after listening to the radio and worrying about where and how Kristian was, she could not offer Theodore the consolation to be found in her body. She felt guilty because now, more than ever, he needed the temporary release. He worried about Kristian constantly, especially during his long hours alone, crisscrossing the fields behind the horses. They'd heard from Kristian—he'd completed his basic training and was assigned to the seventh division under Major General William M. Wright and had left for France on August eleventh after only eight weeks of training upon U.S. soil. Even with additional training in France, how could a farm boy who'd had to deal with nothing more belligerent than a shying horse be equipped for combat in so little time?

Then, as the summer drew to a close, news of another threat, more insidious than flamethrowers and mustard gas, made its way across the ocean to worry not only Theodore and Linnea, but all the fathers, mothers, wives, and sweethearts of the men fighting in Europe. This was an enemy who took no sides. It struck American, German, Italian, and Frenchman alike. With absolute impartiality it smote down hero and coward, experienced commander and pea-green recruit, leaving them sneezing and shivering and dying of fever in the trenches on the Marne and at Flanders Field.

The name of the threat was Spanish influenza.

From the time the news of it reached American shores, Theodore's restlessness and concern escalated. He became edgy and untalkative. And when the epidemic itself reached America and started spreading westward through its cities, the news affected everyone.

Meanwhile, Linnea grew enormous and ungainly, and looked in the mirror each day to find herself so unappealing she couldn't blame Teddy for paying her little attention lately. She loved going down to Clara's and holding baby Maren, telling herself *this* was what her payoff would be, and it would be well worth it.

One day, when Maren was asleep in her crib and Clara was rolling out crust for a sugarless apple pie, Linnea sat on a nearby chair like a beached whale. "I feel like a fat old ugly hippopotamus," she wailed.

Clara only laughed. "You're not fat and ugly and you're certainly not old. But if it's any consolation, we all get to feeling like that toward the end."

"You did, too?" Even at full term, Clara had always looked radiantly beautiful to Linnea, and had never seemed to lose her gaiety.

"Of course I did. Trigg just teased me a little more and made me laugh to keep my spirits up."

Linnea's spirits drooped further. "Not Teddy."

"He has been rather grouchy lately, hasn't he?"

"Grouchy—hmph!—there's got to be a worse word for it than that."

"He's got a lot on his mind, that's all. Kristian, and the baby coming, and threshing about to start."

"It's more than that. I mean, in bed at night he hardly even touches me. I know we can't do anything with the baby only six weeks away, but he doesn't even snuggle or . . . or kiss me or . . . well, he acts like he can't st . . . stand me." Linnea put her head down and started to cry, which she'd been doing with some regularity lately.

Clara dropped the rolling pin and wiped her hands on her apron, coming immediately to comfort the younger woman. "It's not you, Linnea. It's just the way men are. If they can't have it all, they don't want any. And they all get ornery without it. Teddy's acting like they all act, so you just get it out of your head that you're fat and ugly."

"B . . . but I am. I w . . . waddle around like a Ch . . . Christmas goose and all I do is bawl all the time, and oh, Clara . . . I don't think h . . . he likes m . . . me anymore!" she sobbed.

Clara rubbed her friend's shaking shoulders. "Now that's silly and you know it. Of course he likes you. Wait till that baby is born and you'll find out."

But before the baby was born someone else came along to lift Teddy's spirits and make him forget his cares temporarily: Isabelle Lawler.

Her cook wagon came rocking into the yard and Linnea's intestines seemed to tighten into knots. Isabelle was the same as ever—large, loud, and lusty. Same pumpkin-colored hair. Same face that looked like a bowl of half-eaten pudding. Same bawdy mule-skinner's voice. The transient cook was the furthest thing from a lady Linnea had ever seen. And even unpregnant, she outweighed Linnea by a good forty pounds. Why then the grin on Theodore's face the moment he saw her? From the time she and the threshing crew arrived, his crankiness mellowed. He smiled more, laughed with the hired hands, and took his meals in the cook wagon, as he had last year. He said the men expected it of him, but Linnea thought he had other reasons.

The night of the first dance, she counted: four times he danced with Isabelle Lawler. Four times! She kept no tally on the other women, so didn't realize he'd danced equally as many times with Clara, and with Nissa, and with plenty of others. She only knew that each time he took the cook onto the floor her own sense of inadequacy redoubled and she felt the embarrassing urge to cry. She was standing on the sidelines watching them when Clara found her.

"Whew! It's warm in here."

"Teddy's plenty warm—I can see that. Seems to be warming up more by the minute," she noted caustically.

Clara glanced at the dancing couple, then back at Linnea. "Isabelle? Oh, honey, don't be silly. He's just dancing with her, that's all."

"This is the fourth time."

"So what? That doesn't mean anything."

"Tell me what he sees in her, will you? Look at her. With those teeth she could eat corn through a picket fence, and that hair looks like somebody set fire to a haystack. But he's smiled more since she got here than he has in the last two months."

"He's always happy during threshing. All the men are."

"Sure. So how many times did Trigg dance with her? Or Lars?"

"Linnea, you're overreacting. Teddy just loves to dance, that's all, and he knows you tire easily now."

Though Clara's observation was meant to console Linnea, it only made her gloomier. "I feel like marching out there and telling that orange-headed tub of lard to find her own damn man and leave mine alone!"

"Well, if it'd make you feel better, why don't you do it?"

Linnea glanced at Clara to find her wearing a gamine grin and couldn't resist grinning back.

"Oh sure, and start everybody for forty miles around talking?"

"She's been coming here for—golly, what is it?—five years? Seven? I don't even remember anymore. Anyway, if there was something between them, don't you think people would have been talking long before this?"

Linnea's ruffled feathers were smoothed momentarily, but later that night, when Theodore flopped into bed beside her, she immediately sensed a difference in him. He rolled to his side facing her and lay a wrist over her hip.

"Come here," he whispered.

"Teddy, we can't—"

"I know," he returned, bracing on an elbow to kiss her, kneading her hip. He'd been drinking beer and the flavor of it lingered on his tongue. He pulled her close. Her distended stomach came up against his, then he found her hand and brought it to his tumescence, sheathing himself with her fingers.

She realized he'd been aroused even before he hit the bed.

Hurt, she whispered, "Who brought this on?"

"What?"

"I said who brought this on—me or Isabelle Lawler?"

His hand paused. Even in the dark she sensed him bristling. "Isabelle Lawler? Now what's that supposed to mean?"

"You've been bundling up on your own side of the bed for weeks, and now after dancing with her all night long you come to me hard as a fresh-dug rutabaga and expect me to take care of it for you? How dare you, Theodore Westgaard!"

She thrust his flesh away as if it were distasteful and flopped onto her back. He, too, rolled to his back angrily.

"Isabelle Lawler hasn't got a thing to do with this."

"Oh, hasn't she?"

"Come on, Linnea, all I did was dance with her."

"Four times. Four times, Theodore!"

He plumped his pillow and flounced over, presenting his spine. "Pregnant women," he mumbled disgustedly.

She grabbed his arm and tried to yank him onto his back again with little success. "Don't you 'pregnant woman' me, Teddy, not after you made me this way! And not after you've been walking around here smiling all week like some . . . some Hindu who just got his thirteenth wife!"

"Thirteenth . . ." Head off the pillow, he looked back over his shoulder, shrugged his arm free, then settled down with his back to her again. "Go to sleep, Linnea. You've got no reason to be jealous. You're just not feeling yourself these days."

This time she punched him on the arm. "Don't you go—"

"Ow!"

"—playing possum with me, Theodore Westgaard. Roll over here, because we're going to have this out! Now, don't tell me there's nothing between you and Isabelle Lawler, because I don't believe it!"

He folded his hands beneath his head, glared at the ceiling in the dark, and said nothing.

"Now tell me!" she insisted, sitting up beside him.

"Tell you what?"

"What there is between you and that woman."

"I told you, there's nothing."

"But there was, wasn't there?"

"Linnea, you're imagining things."

"Don't treat me like a child!"

"Then don't act like one! I said there's nothing and I meant it."

"I can see the way she likes to hang around you. And you're the only one she never cusses with. And tonight before the dance you . . . you put on bay rum and you were humming."

"I put on bay rum before every dance."

Did he? She'd never watched him get ready for a dance before. She flounced onto her back and tucked the bedclothes beneath her arms. Picking at a knot of yarn on the quilt, staring at the moonlight on the opposite wall, she steeled herself to accept whatever he might say. Her voice became softer.

"You can tell me, Teddy, and I promise I won't get mad. I'm your wife. I've got a right to know."

"Linnea, why do you keep on this way?"

"Because, you know you were the first one for me."

"You already know there was Melinda."

"That's different. She was your wife."

He pondered silently for some time before going on. "And suppose it was true. Suppose there was a whole string of other women. What good would it do for you to know it now?"

She turned her head to face him and spoke sincerely. "There shouldn't be secrets between husbands and wives."

"Everybody's got a right to their own secrets."

She was hurt at the thought that there were things he didn't share with her. She shared everything with him.

"What was there between you and Isabelle?" she prodded.

"Linnea, drop it."

"I can't. I wish I could, but I can't."

He lay silently a long time, ran a hand through his hair, and wedged it behind his neck, emitting a long sigh.

"All right. Every year at threshing time I saw Isabelle in her wagon, after bedtime."

The jealousy Linnea had felt before became pallid beside this gargantuan lump in her chest. "You were . . . lovers?"

He drew a deep breath, let it out slowly, and closed his eyes. "Yes."

Now that the truth was out, she wished she'd let sleeping dogs lie, but some perverse instinct forced her to ask further questions. "This year?"

"No, what do you think—"

"Last year then?"

A long silence, then, "Yes."

Rage burned through her. "But that was after you met me!"

"Yes." He braced up on one elbow, looking down into her face. "And we couldn't look at each other without snapping. And I thought you were too young for me, and that it was indecent to have stirrings about my son's school teacher. And I thought you couldn't stand my guts, Linnea."

He tried to touch her but she jerked away. "Oh, how could you!"

Typical woman, he thought, says she won't get mad, then bristles like a hedgehog. "It's been fifteen years since Melinda ran away. Did you think there'd be nobody in all that time?"

"But she's . . . she's fat and . . . and uncouth and—"

"You don't know anything about her, so don't go casting stones," he returned tightly.

"But how could you bring her back here this year and parade her under my nose."

"Parade her! I'm not parading her!"

"And what *else* are you doing right under my nose?"

"If you're insinuating—"

"Coming to bed hornier than a two-peckered goat when you and I haven't been able to make love for nearly a month. What am I supposed to think?"

"If you'd stop acting like a child, you'd realize that no man can go fifteen years without something . . . someone."

"Child! Now I'm a child!"

"Well, you act like one!"

"So go to Isabelle." Tossing the covers back, Linnea leaped from the bed. "With her build and her language, nobody'd ever mistake her for a child, would they?"

He sat straight up, jabbing a finger at the spot she'd left. "I don't want Isabelle, now will you get back in this bed?"

"I wouldn't get back in that bed if my clothes were on fire and it was made of water!"

"Lower your voice. Ma's not deaf, you know."

"And you wouldn't want her to know about your little peccadilloes, would you?" she returned sarcastically.

He didn't know what "peccadilloes" meant and it made him

all the angrier. He braced his elbows on his updrawn knees and ran both hands through his hair. "I should've known better than to tell you. I should've known you couldn't handle it. You're just too damn young to understand that everything in life isn't black and white. Isabelle and I weren't hurting anybody. She was alone. I was alone. We gave each other what we needed. Can you understand that?"

"I want that woman out of here tomorrow, do you hear?"

"And who's gonna feed the threshers? You, when you're eight months pregnant and can hardly make it to the end of a dance?"

"I don't care who does it, but it better not be Isabelle Lawler!"

"Linnea, come back here—where you going?"

At the door she paused only long enough to fling back, "I'm going to my old room!"

"You are not! You're my wife and you'll sleep in my bed!"

"You can expect me back in it when Isabelle Lawler disappears!"

When she was gone he sat staring at the black hole of the doorway, wondering how any woman could be so perverse. First she says she won't get mad, then she yells loud enough to wake the dead—much less, Ma—and marches off as if she expects him to go whimpering after her and apologize. Well, she'd wait till hell froze over cause he didn't have anything to apologize for! Last year had nothing to do with this year, and this year all he'd done with Isabelle was dance. And how could she think he'd be so faithless as to take Isabelle to bed just because he had to do without from his pregnant wife for a couple months?

Cut to the quick, Theodore lay on his back and stewed.

Just who did she think she was, that little snip, to dictate orders? Isabelle was a damn fine cook, and without her they'd be in a pretty pickle. She'd cook till the end of the threshing season, and if Linnea didn't like it, she could go right on bunking upstairs! He'd sleep better with her up there anyway; all she did all night long was make trips to the commode and wake him up.

Lord God . . . pregnant women, he thought again, flopping

onto his side. Well, never again! He was too old to be going through this. This one baby and that was it . . . the end! And he hoped to high heaven when she had it she'd get over this testiness and life would get back to normal.

In the morning Nissa didn't say a word, though she most certainly must've heard the ruckus through the wall last night, and she knew Linnea had slept upstairs.

The three convened in the kitchen for breakfast.

"Fine mornin'," Nissa offered to no one in particular.

Nobody said a word.

"Ain't it?" she snapped, eyeing Linnea over the tops of her glasses.

"Yes . . . yes, it's a fine morning."

Theodore crossed the room with the milk pails, eyeing his wife silently.

"Need me a couple more pieces o' coal for the fire. Reckon I'll go out and get 'em, get me a sniff of this morning air."

When the old woman was gone, taking the half-full coal hod with her, he studied Linnea a little closer. He could tell she'd been crying last night. "Mornin'," he said.

"Morning." She refused to look at him.

"How'd you sleep?"

"Like a baby."

"Good. Me, too." It was a lie; he'd slept hardly at all without her beside him. His palms were damp. He wiped one on his thigh, intending to reach out and touch her arm, but before he could she spun away—"Excuse me. I have to comb my hair"—and flounced into the bedroom without once glancing his way.

All right, you stubborn little cuss, have it your way. It'll get colder than an eskimo's outhouse in that room before long and you'll come back wanting to snuggle. Meantime, the cook stays!

And she did.

Isabelle stayed through the entire week while Linnea refused to look at or speak to Theodore, unless he spoke to her first. By Saturday night the tension in the house was horrendous. Nissa was the only one getting a decent night's sleep. The other two managed only enough to get by, and the strain was showing in their faces.

There was a barn dance at their place Saturday night, and Teddy and Linnea spent the first hour laughing and dancing with everybody in the place but each other. Teddy slugged down two beers, eyeing her over the beer glass most of the time, thinking how pretty she looked pregnant. Some women got dowdy and washed-out looking when they were carrying babies. Not his wife. She glowed like someone had lit a candle inside her cheeks. He screwed up his courage to cross the hayloft and ask her to dance, and after several minutes, made his move. Before he reached her, his palms were sweating again.

With feigned jocularity, he paused beside her, hooked his thumbs in his waistband and raised one eyebrow. "So what do you say, you wanna dance?"

She flicked him a glance of unadulterated feline haughtiness, shifted it pointedly to Isabelle Lawler, and replied, "No, thank you." Then, with a slight lift of her nose, she turned away.

So he danced with Isabelle. And one hell of a lot more than four times!

Linnea tried not to watch them. But Teddy was the best darn dancer in the county, and every corpuscle in her body was bulging with jealousy. Thankfully, Nissa offered an escape.

"Think I overdid it with the homemade wine," she said. "Either that or the spinning or both, but I feel a little dizzy. Would you walk me to the house, Linnea?"

Naturally, Linnea complied. Halfway there, Nissa took up reminiscing in an offhand manner, "I 'member once when my man brung home this new rag rug. I says to him, what you wanna go buy a rug for when I can make 'em myself? What you wanna waste your money on a thing like that for? He smiles and says he thought it'd be nice one time, me not having to make a rug, but just flop it down on the floor already warped, woofed, and tied. But me, I got mad at him cause one o' the boys—I can't remember which one—was near out of his shoes. Should've got new boots for the boy, I says, instead of throwin' your money away on rag rugs. He said there was a widow woman with two young ones peddling her rugs in town

that day and he thought it'd help her out if he bought that rug."
Nissa sniffed once. "Me, well, I asks, what you doin' talkin'
to widow women, and he says I might be his wife, but that
don't give me the right to tell him who he can and can't talk
to. So I asks who this widow woman was, and he tells me,
and I recall these several times we was all at a barn-raising
together and how he'd talked and laughed with her some, and
my hackles got up and before you know it I asks how she's
gettin' on without her husband, and where she's livin' now.
And, by Jove, if he can't answer every one of my questions.
And pretty soon I'm telling him I don't want his blame rag
rug, not if he got it from her! As I recall, we didn't speak
to one another for over a week that time. Rag rug laid on the
floor and I refused to put a foot onto it, and he refused to pick
it up and take it away.

"Then one day I went to town and happened to run into her
on the street. She'd got tuberculosis and coughed all the time
and was nothin' but a bag of bones, and when she saw me
she says how grateful she was that my man bought that rug
from her, and how one of her little ones had needed a pair of
boots so bad, and when she sold that rug, she'd been able to
buy 'em."

Linnea and Nissa had reached the back door by this time,
but the older woman stood on the steps a moment, looking up
at the stars. "Learned a thing or two that time. Learned that a
man's heart can get broke if he's accused when he ain't guilty.
Learned that some men got hearts o' gold, and gold, it don't
tarnish. But gold . . . well, it's soft. It dents easy. Woman's got
to be careful not to put too many dents in a heart like that."
Nissa chortled softly to herself, turned toward the door, and
opened it but hesitated a moment before stepping inside. "As
I recall, the night I finally told him I was sorry, he laid me
down on that rag rug on the floor and put a couple rug burns
on m' hind quarters . . . hmm . . . still got that old rug around
here someplace. In a trunk, I think, with my wedding dress
and a watch fob I braided for him out of my own hair when I
was sixteen years old." She shook her head, touched her brow.
"Land, lookin' up like that makes a person dizzier than ever."

Without glancing back, she continued into the house. "Well, good night, child."

Linnea was left with a lump in her throat and a thick feeling in her chest. She glanced toward the barn. The apricot lanternlight shone dimly through the windows. The distant strains of concertina and fiddle music drifted dimly through the night. Go to him, it seemed to say.

She glanced in the opposite direction. Nestled beside the caragana hedge the bulky form of the cook wagon hovered like a threatening shadow. The moon, like a half-slice of shaved cheese, threw its light across the yard while the night breeze played the dried seedpods of the caragana bushes like tiny drums. But it's he who should be apologizing, they seemed to say. He's the one who's dancing with somebody else.

Dully, she went inside and climbed the stairs to her old room once more, then lay beneath the covers, cold and lonely.

Each night she'd expected Theodore to come to her. She'd lain and imagined him opening the door silently, standing in the shadows and looking at her sleeping form, then kneeling beside the bed to awaken her, press his face to her neck, her breast, her stomach, and say, "I'm sorry, Lin, please come back."

But this was the eighth day and still he had not come. And he was down in the barn jigging with another woman while his pregnant wife lay in tears. Why, Teddy, why?

She was determined to stay awake until the dance ended and the wagons pulled out of the yard, then watch through the window to see if he came straight to the house. But in the end she fell asleep and heard nothing.

In the morning she awakened as if touched, her eyelids parting like two halves of a sliced melon. Something was wrong. She listened. No sound. Not so much as a tinkle of silverware or the crackle of an expanding stovepipe. Stretching an arm she found her watch on the table. Why wasn't Nissa up at seven-fifteen? Church would begin in less than two hours.

She heard footsteps on the stairs just as her heels touched the floor. Without wasting time on a wrapper she flung the door wide and met Theodore on the landing, his eyes dark with worry, hair tousled from sleep.

"What's wrong?"

"It's Ma. She's sick."

"Sick? You mean from blackberry wine?" Even as she spoke, Linnea was following Theodore down the stairs in her bare feet.

"I don't think so. It's chills and congestion."

"Chills and congestion?" Linnea's skin prickled as she rushed to keep up with Theodore. At the bottom of the steps she grabbed the shoulder of his underwear, swinging him to an abrupt half. "Bad congestion?"

His eyes and cheeks appeared gaunt with concern.

"I think so."

"Is it . . . " After one false start she managed to get the dread word past her lips. " . . . the influenza?"

He found her hand, clutched it hard. "Let's hope not."

But that hope was dashed when the doctor was summoned from town. When he left, a yellow and black quarantine sign was tacked on the back door, and Theodore and Linnea were given instructions that neither of them was to enter Nissa's room without a mask tied over both nose and mouth. The two stared at each other in disbelief. The influenza struck soldiers in the trenches and people in crowded cities, not North Dakota farmers with an endless supply of pure air to breathe. And certainly not old bumblebees like Nissa Westgaard who buzzed between one task and the next so fast it seemed no germ could catch up with her. Not Nissa, who only last night had been tippling wine and dancing the two-step with her boys. Not Nissa, who rarely even contracted a common cold.

But they were wrong.

Before the day was over Nissa's respiratory system was already filling with fluids. Her breathing became strident and chills wracked her body, unmitigated by the quinine water they periodically forced her to drink. Theodore and Linnea watched helplessly as her condition worsened with fearful rapidity. They sponged and fed her, kept her propped up with pillows, and took turns sitting watch. But by the end of the first day it seemed they were fighting a losing battle. They sat at the kitchen table, disconsolately staring at the servings of soup neither of them felt like eating, their hands idle beside their bowls.

Their worried gazes locked and their own differences seemed inconsequential. He covered her hand on the red and white checked oilcloth.

"So fast," he said throatily.

She turned her hand over and their fingers interlocked. "I know."

"And there's nothing we can do."

"We can keep sponging her and feeding her the quinine. Maybe during the night she'll take a turn for the better." But they both suspected it was wishful thinking. The influenza preyed first upon the very old, the very weak, and the very young. Few of them who contracted it survived.

Theodore stared at their joined hands, rubbing his thumb over Linnea's. "I wish I could get you out of here where you'd be safe."

"I'm fine. I don't even have a sniffle."

"But the baby . . . "

"The baby's fine, too. Now you mustn't worry about us."

"You've put in a long day. I want you to rest."

"But so have you."

"I'm not the pregnant one, now will you do as I say?"

"The dishes . . . "

"Leave 'em. I can see you're ready to tip off that chair. Now, come on." He tugged her hand, led her to their bedroom, turned the bed down, sat her on the edge of it, then knelt to remove her shoes. His tender consideration wrenched her heart, and as she looked down at the top of his head it seemed she could scarcely contain her love and concern for him. He had suffered the loss of a beloved brother; his son was off fighting a war; must he now watch his mother die, too?

When her second shoe was off, Theodore held her foot, caressing it while raising his eyes to hers.

"Linnea, about Isabelle—"

She silenced his lips with a loving touch. "It doesn't matter. I was stupid and childish and jealous, but you've got enough on your mind without worrying about that now."

"But I . . . "

"We'll talk about it later . . . after Nissa gets well."

He tucked her in lovingly, securing the quilts beneath her

chin, then sitting beside her on the edge of the bed. With hands braced on either side of her head, he leaned above her, studying her face as if in it he found the strength he needed.

"I want to kiss you so bad." But he couldn't; not while there was influenza in the house. He could only look at her and rue the past week of idiocy that had kept them alienated, that had made him do foolish things to hurt her when she was the last person in the world he wanted to hurt.

"I know. I want to kiss you, too."

"I love you so much."

"I love you, too, and it feels so good to be back in our bed again."

He smiled, wishing he could crawl in beside her and snuggle tight behind her with his hand cradling their moving child. But Ma was in the next room and she'd been untended long enough.

"Sleep now."

"Wake me up if there's any change."

He nodded, rested a palm on her stomach, turned off the lantern, and left.

Nissa's lungs filled with fluid and she died on the third day. Before the undertaker's wagon could come to bear her body away, Linnea's worst fears were realized: Teddy was stricken with the dread virus. She was left alone to nurse him, to mourn, and to worry, locked in a house with nobody to spell her bedside vigils or comfort her in her grief. Already depleted from three days of little sleep and weighted by despair, she was near exhaustion when a loud banging sounded on the door and Isabelle Lawler's voice came through. "Mrs. Westgaard, I'm comin' in!"

Linnea called, "But you can't, we're under quarantine."

The door burst open and the redhead pushed inside. "Makes no difference to a tough old buffalo like me. Now you need help and I'm the one's gonna give it to you. Lawsy, child, you look like that undertaker should've toted you off, too. You had any sleep? You eat?"

"I . . ."

The brazen woman didn't give Linnea time to answer. "Set down there. How's Ted?"

"He's . . . his breathing isn't too bad yet."

"Good. I can poke quinine down him just as easy as you can, but you got his young one to take care of and if I let somethin' happen to it or to you, I'm afraid I'd lose my cookin' job around here, years to come, so step back, chittlin'." While she spoke, Isabelle shrugged out of a heavy, masculine jacket. Linnea got up as if to take it.

"Set down, I said! You need a good meal under your belt and I'm just the one to see it gets there. I'm the best durn cook this side of the Black Hills, so don't give me no sass, sister. You just tell me what needs doin' for him, and how often, and if you're worried about me seein' him in his altogether, well, I seen him that way before, and you know it, so I ain't gonna blush like no schoolgirl and cover my eyes. And if you're thinkin' I got designs on your man, well, you can put that out of your head, too. What was between us is finished. He ain't the least bit interested in no loud, sassy moose like me, so where's the quinine and what would you like to eat?"

Thus the audacious Isabelle dug in for the duration.

She was nothing short of a heaven-sent blessing to Linnea. She mothered and pampered her with continued bumptiousness, and took her turns seeing after Theodore's needs with equal brashness. She was the most flagrantly bold woman Linnea had ever met, but her very outspokenness often made Linnea laugh, and kept her spirits up. Isabelle blew through the house like a hurricane, her rusty hair ever standing on end, her mannish voice loud even when she whispered. Linnea was utterly grateful to have her there. It was as if she forced the fates to accept her zest for life and to transfer a good bit of it to the ailing Theodore.

When he was at his worst, the two women sat together at his bedside, and oddly enough, Linnea felt totally comfortable, even knowing that in her own way, Isabelle loved Theodore. His breathing was labored and his skin bright with fever.

"Damn man ain't gonna die," Isabelle announced, "cause I ain't gonna let him. He's got you and the young one to see after and he won't be shirking his duty."

"I wish I could be as sure as you."

Another woman would have reached out a comforting hand. Not Isabelle. Her chin only jutted more stubbornly.

"A man as happy as he is about that baby and his new wife's got a lot o' reason to fight."

"He . . . he told you he was happy?"

"Told me everything. Told me about your fight, told me the reason you were sleepin' in the spare room. He was heartsick."

Linnea dropped her gaze to her lap. "I didn't think he'd tell you all that."

Isabelle spread her knees wide, leaned forward, and rested her elbows on them. "We could usually talk, Ted and I."

Linnea didn't know what to say. She found herself no longer able to harbor jealousy.

Isabelle went on, her eyes on Theodore while she leaned forward in her masculine pose. "It's nothin' you need to worry about, what me and Ted did together. You're young yet, you got things to learn about human urges. They just got to be satisfied, that's all. Why, shoot, he never loved me—the word never come up once." She sat back, reached in her pocket for cigarette makings, and started rolling herself a smoke. "But he's a kind man, a damn kind man. Don't think I don't know it . . . I mean, a woman like me, why . . . " Her words trailed away and she gave a single self-deprecating sniff, studying the cigarette as she sealed the seam, then stroked it smooth. She reached in her apron pocket and found a match, set it aflame with the flick of a blunt thumbnail, and sent fragrant smoke into the room. She leaned back, rested her crossed feet on the edge of the mattress, and puffed away silently, squinting through the smoke. After some time she said, "You're a damned lucky woman."

Linnea turned to study Isabelle. Her apron was filthy. Her stomach looked more pregnant than Linnea's. She held the cigarette between thumb and forefinger like a man would, and her chair was tilted back on two legs. But in the corner of her left eye Linnea thought she detected the glint of a single tear.

Impulsively, she reached and lay a hand on Isabelle's arm. The redhead looked down at it, sniffed again, clamped the cigarette between her teeth, patted the hand twice, then reached for the cigarette again.

"You'll be back next year, won't you?" the younger woman asked.

"Damn tootin'. I'll be dyin' to git a gander at Ted's young 'un."

On the seventh day they knew that Theodore would live.

26

THE VERY OLD, the very weak, the very young. Indeed, the Spanish influenza preyed first upon these, and it chose from the Westgaard family one of each. Of the very old it took Nissa. Of the very weak, Tony. And of the very young, Roseanne. Nissa died never knowing her grandchildren, too, had fallen ill.

It was a mercurial disease, indiscriminately ravaging home after home on the Dakota prairie, while leaving others totally untouched. There seemed no rhyme nor reason as to whom it took, whom it left. Its very unpredictability made it the more deadly. But as if Providence had better things in mind for Theodore and Linnea Westgaard, Theodore pulled through with nothing longer lasting than a ten-pound weight loss, and Linnea was untouched.

On the morning Theodore awakened clear-eyed and clear-headed, she was there alone beside the bed, asleep in a chair, looking as if she'd fought the war single-handedly. He opened his eyes and saw her—slumped, breathing evenly, hands folded over her high-mounded stomach. Linnea, he tried to say, but his mouth was so dry. He touched his forehead; it felt scaly. He touched his hair; it felt oily. He touched his cheek; it felt raspy. He wondered what day it was. Ma was dead, wasn't she? Oh, and Kristian—was there any news of him? And what about the wheat . . . the milking . . . Linnea . . .

He rolled to one side and touched her knee. Her eyes flew open.

"Teddy! You're awake!" She tested his forehead then gripped his hand. "You made it."

"Ma . . . " he croaked.

"They buried her over a week ago." She brought a cup to his lips and he drank gratefully, then fell back weakly.

"What day is it?"

"Thursday. You've been sick for two weeks."

Two weeks. He'd lain here two weeks while she looked after him. She and Isabelle. He had a vague recollection of Isabelle tending him, too, but how could that be?

"Are you all right?"

"Me, oh I'm fine. I've come through unscathed. Now no more questions until I get you something to eat and you feel stronger."

She would brook no more talking until she'd brought him strong beef broth and, after he'd drunk it, washed his face and helped him shave. She herself had found time to change her dress and comb her hair, but even so, he could see on her face the effects of her long vigil. When she was bustling about, cleaning up the room, he made her sit down beside the bed and rest for a minute.

"Your eyes look like bruises."

"I lost a little sleep, that's all. But I had good help." She glanced at her lap and toyed with the edge of her apron.

"Isabelle?" he asked.

"Yes. Do you remember?"

"Some."

"She refused to obey the quarantine sign. She came in and stayed for nine days and took care of both of us."

"And she didn't get it either?"

Linnea shook her head. "She's some woman, Teddy." Her voice softened as her gaze met her husband's. "She loves you very much, you know."

"Aww . . . "

"She does. She risked her own life to come in here and take care of you, and of me because she knew it would hurt you if anything happened to either me or the baby. We owe her a lot."

He didn't know what to say. "Where is she now?"

"Out in the cook wagon, sleeping."

"What about the wheat?"

"The wheat is all done. The threshing crew kept right on working."

"And the milking?"

"They took care of that, too. Now you're not to worry about a thing. Cope says he'll stay on until you're strong enough to take over again."

"Has there been any news from Kristian?"

"A letter came two days ago and Orlin read it from the end of the driveway." Orlin was their mail carrier. "Kristian said he hadn't seen the front yet, and he was just fine."

"How long ago did he write the letter?"

"More than three weeks."

Three weeks, they both thought. So many shells were fired in three weeks. She wished there were a way to reassure Theodore, but what could she say? He looked gaunt and pale and inutterably sapped. She hated to be the one to add new lines of despair to his face, but there was no escaping it. She leaned both elbows on the bed, took his hand in both of hers, turning the loose-fitting wedding ring around and around his finger.

"Teddy, there's more bad news, I'm afraid. The influenza . . . " How difficult it was to say the words. She saw the faces of those blessed children she'd come to love so much. Such innocents, taken before their time.

"Who?" Theodore asked simply.

"Roseanne and Tony."

His hand gripped hers and his eyes closed. "Oh, dear God."

There was nothing she could say. She herself ached, remembering Roseanne's lisp, Tony's thin shoulders.

Still with his eyes closed, Theodore drew Linnea down atop the coverlets. She lay beside him and he held her, drew strength from her.

"But they were so young. They hadn't even lived yet," he railed uselessly.

"I know . . . I know."

"And Ma . . . " Linnea felt him swallow against the crown of her head. "She was such a good woman. And sometimes, when she'd . . . when she'd get bossy and order me around I'd wish to myself that she wasn't here. But I never meant I w . . . wanted her to die."

"You mustn't feel guilty about thoughts that were only human. You were good to her, Teddy, you gave her a home. She knew you loved her."

"But she was such a good old soul."

So were they all, Linnea thought, holding him close. John, Nissa, the children. They'd lost so many . . . so many. *Lord, keep Kristian safe.*

"Oh, Teddy," she whispered against his chest, "I thought I was going to lose you, too."

He swallowed thickly. "And I thought the same thing about you and the baby. At times I'd wish I could die real quick, before you got it, too. Then other times, I'd come to and see you sitting there beside the bed and know I just had to live."

His heartbeat drummed steadily beneath her ear while she spoke a silent prayer of thanks that he'd been spared. Between them pressed the bulk of their thriving, unborn child and an old quilt that had been pieced and tied by Nissa's hands years and years ago. She who had passed on. He who was yet to come. A new life to replace an old.

"It's as if we and our baby were spared to carry on. To take the place of those who are gone," she told him.

And carry on is what they did, like many others who'd suffered losses. The epidemic ran its course. The quarantine signs disappeared one by one, and the Westgaards bid goodbye to Isabelle Lawler, waving her away while she bellowed that she'd be back next year to see the young 'un. Still, there were the dead to mourn, the living to console. The Lutheran church had a new minister now that the Severts had moved away. Reverend Helgeson held one bitterly sad memorial service for the seven members of his congregation who had died and been buried while their families were not allowed at the gravesides, and together they prayed for peace and gave thanks that the service stars on the church flag yet remained blue. The bereaved drew strength from above and lifted their eyes toward tomorrow.

There came a day in November when Theodore was outside beneath a chilly overcast sky, ballasting the foundation of the house with hay. It was a typical late-autumn day, dreary, with a bite to the wind. The leaves of the cottonwoods had long since fallen. The wind lifted topsoil and sent it against the legs of Theodore's overalls as he wielded the pitchfork, time and again. The job would normally have been done much earlier, but had been delayed this year due to his illness. But his strength had returned, and Cope had gone back home to Minnesota.

From overhead came the rusty carping of a tardy flock of Canadian honkers headed south. Theodore paused and glanced up, watching the birds fly in majestic formation. Kristian hadn't got to fly those airplanes like he'd wanted to. But he'd ridden in one, his last letter said. Theodore smiled, thinking of it. His boy riding up there as high as those geese. What was this world coming to? There was talk about those airplanes being the up-and-coming thing, and that when and if this war ever ended, they'd be used for something better than killing people.

Was Kristian still alive? He had to be. And when he came home Theodore wondered how he'd like to be set up in a business of his own, transporting goods by airplane maybe, like folks said was going to be the coming way. What the hell, he was a rich man. The war had forced wheat up to the landmark price of $2.15 a bushel. It had never seemed right, getting rich off the war, but as long as he was, he might as well share some of that wealth with his son who'd gone to fight it. Heck, Kristian didn't want to be no wheat farmer, and if that boy would just make it home, Theodore promised himself he'd never try to force him again, after all, it wasn't—

"Teddy! Teddy!" Linnea came flying out of the house, leaving the door open wide behind her. "Teddy, the war's over!"

"What!"

The pitchfork went clunking to the ground as she came barreling into his arms, shouting and crying all at once. "It's over! The news just came on the radio! The armistice was signed at five o'clock this morning!"

"It's over? It's really over?"

"Yes! Yes! Yes!" she rejoiced.

He spun her off her feet. "It's over! It's over!" They couldn't quit saying it. They danced around the yard and tripped on the pitchfork. Beside them Nelly and Fly stood before a wagon-load of hay and turned curious heads to watch their antics. Nelly whickered, and Linnea flew out of Theodore's arms and kissed the horse on her nose. When she'd likewise kissed Fly, Theodore swooped her into his arms again and lifted her toward the wagon seat.

"We got to be with the others."

They were scarcely out of their driveway before the school bell began clanging in the east. They had not traveled one mile before it was joined by the church bell from the west. They met Ulmer and Helen on the road halfway to Lars's house and got down from the wagons to hug and kiss and listen to the bells resounding from both directions. While they were celebrating in the middle of the gravel road, Clara and Trigg appeared, with baby Maren swaddled warm but howling loudly, upset by all the unusual commotion. On their heels came others, including Lars and Evie, and old man Tveit, who was out delivering a load of coal.

"Everyone'll gather at the school," Ulmer predicted. "Let's go!"

And sure enough, by the time they got there, the building was already filling. The bell kept pealing. The crowd kept growing. The new teacher, Mr. Thorson, announced that classes were dismissed for the day. The children stood on their desk seats and clapped. Reverend Helgeson arrived and led them all in a prayer of thanksgiving, and the celebration continued on into the late afternoon.

By the time the rejoicing band broke up, the snow that had been threatening all day had begun in earnest. They drove their wagons home through the wind-driven flakes, carefree in spite of them, their joy undaunted by the prospect of a winter storm. The wheat was in. The world was at peace. There was much to be grateful for.

Linnea awakened with her first pain at one o'clock that morning. She wasn't certain what it was, so waited for another, which was some time in coming. She didn't wake Theodore until an hour had passed and she was certain.

"Teddy?" She shook him gently.

"Hmm?" He rolled over and braced on an elbow. "Something wrong?"

"I think my pains have started."

Immediately he was awake, straining toward her, reaching for her stomach. "But it's a month early."

"I know. I must have done too much dancing and shook things loose."

"How close together are they?"

"Fifteen minutes."

"Fifteen . . ." He was out of bed in a flash, reaching for his trousers. "I got to get to town and get the doc."

"No!"

"But you said it's—"

"No! Look out the window. I won't have you going out in that!"

From within the dark room it was easy to see how bright it was outside. The snow, still swirling, had whitened everything and gathered in the corners of the window ledges in thick white triangles.

"But, Linnea—"

"No. After John, no! This baby's gonna know his father!"

"But it's not a blizzard. It's just a regular snowfall."

She struggled from the bed and caught his arm as he reached for his shirt.

"Teddy, we can do it ourselves."

His muscles tensed beneath her hand. "Are you crazy? I've never delivered a baby."

"You've delivered horses, haven't you? It can't be too much different."

"Linnea, I'm wasting time."

"You're not going!" She clung to him tenaciously, pulling him back when he would have leaned for his boots. But suddenly she gasped. "Oh . . . Teddy . . . oh!"

"What is it?"

Terrified, he lit the lantern and turned to find her standing in the middle of the floor with her feet widespread, staring down.

"Something's coming out already. Oh, please don't leave me."

He gaped at the puddle between her feet, frantically wondering what to do. With Melinda it had taken hours . . . and Ma had been here to see to things.

"Your water broke. That means it . . . it won't be long."

"Wh . . . what should I do?" shē asked, as if there were anything she could control.

In three steps he'd swept her off her feet and deposited her on the bed again. "Rest between pains, don't fight them when they come. I've got to light a fire and get some rope."

"Rope! Oh, Teddy, please don't go to town. We—"

"I'm not." He pressed her back, took a moment to soothe her, brushing her hair back from her forehead, kissing her wild eyes closed. "The rope's for you to hang onto. I'll be right back, all right? And I promise I won't go to town. But I have to go out to the barn. Just stay here and do like I said when the pains come."

She nodded in the brisk way of one too afraid to argue. "Hurry," she whispered.

He hurried. But—blast his hide!—why hadn't he got things ready before? He'd thought he had another whole month, and even then, the doctor usually brought leather stirrups and sterilized instruments. He never thought he'd have to cut ropes and boil scissors. Damn these Dakota winters! What in tarnation would he do if complications set in?

The snow bit into his cheeks as he made his way back from the barn with the cleanest length of rope he could find. Linnea seemed frantic by the time he reached the bedroom.

"They're coming f . . . faster, Teddy, and I . . . I got the bed all wet."

"Shh, love, don't worry. The bedding can be washed."

In between pains he lit a fire, sterilized scissors, found string, and a clean blanket for the baby, and a washbasin and towel for its first bath. He lifted Linnea from the bed and lined it with a rubber sheet, then padded it with a soft, folded flannel blanket over which he stretched a new, clean sheet. He was holding her in his arms, transferring her back to the bed when she was hit by the most intense pain yet. She gasped and stiffened, and he held her, felt her body tense, her fingers dig into his shoulder through the worst of it. When it was over, her eyes opened and he kissed the corner of one. "Next time a war ends, not so much dancing, all right, Mrs. Westgaard?"

She gave him a quavering smile, but sighed and seemed to wilt as he laid her down again.

"I want a clean gown," she said when her breath evened. "But what does it matter?"

"Our child will not be born while his mother wears a soiled nightgown. Now get me a clean gown, Theodore."

When she called him Theodore in that tone of voice, he knew he'd best not cross her. He flew to the dresser, wondering where the sudden show of spunk came from when a moment ago she'd been submerged in pain. Women, he thought. What did men really know about them after all?

The old gown was off, but the new one still rolled in his hands when the next pain struck. She fell back and arched, and he saw her stomach change shape with the contraction, saw her knees go up and her body lift of its own accord. Sweat broke out across his chest. Low across his belly he thought he felt the same pain she'd experienced. His hands shook when he helped her don the clean, white nightgown and folded it back at the waist.

He'd never tied knots so fast in his life. He slashed the rope into two three-foot lengths, secured each to the metal footboard of the bed, then fashioned the opposite ends into loops through which Linnea's legs could slip. The last knot wasn't quite finished when she gasped his name, reaching with both hands. She gripped his hands so hard he felt bruised, and drew on him with a force that made both their arms quiver. Sweet Jesus, those ropes would cut right through her flesh!

When the contraction ended, they were both panting.

He rushed to the kitchen and found two thick towels to pad the ropes for her legs. He moved the bedside table and kerosene lantern toward the foot of the bed where it shone on her exposed body. Gently, he lifted her feet and placed them through the ropes, then carefully slid them up behind her knees. The lanternlight threw a golden tint upon her white thighs. For the first time it struck him fully how vulnerable a woman is during childbirth.

Her bleary eyes opened. "Don't be scared, Teddy," she whispered. "There's nothing to be scared of." There remained no trace of the fear he'd sensed in her earlier. She was calm, prepared, confident in his ability to play the part of midwife. He moved to her side and bent over her, loving her more than ever before.

"I'm not scared." It was the first time he'd ever lied to her. Looking down into her flushed face he would gladly have taken her place if only he could. He stretched her arms over her head and gently placed her hands around the metal rods above her. "Now save your energy." He covered her fingers with his own. "Don't talk. Scream if you want, but don't talk."

"But talking takes my mind off the p—"

She grimaced and sucked in a deep breath. Heart pounding, he rushed to the opposite end of the bed, feeling uncertain and clumsy and even more frightened than when he and John had been trapped in the blizzard.

Her muscles strained. The ropes stretched taut. The iron bed rails chimed and bent inward. She growled deep and long while a trickle of pink flowed from her body. He stared at it, horrified at being responsible for bringing her to this travail, vowing, Never again. Never again.

Teeth clenched, he whispered, "Come on . . . come on . . ." as if the child could hear.

When Linnea's pain eased, Theodore's shirt was damp beneath the arms. She rested and he wiped her brow.

"How you doing?" he asked softly.

She nodded, eyes closed. "Tell me when—" she began, but this time the pain brought her hips higher off the bed than before. He watched the trickle of pink grow brighter and thought, oh God, she's dying. Don't let her die. Not her too! He was wracked by the need to do something for her, anything whatever to help. He placed his hands beneath her and helped her lift when lifting seemed what Nature intended.

"Come on, get out here," he muttered. "Scream, Lin, scream if you want to!"

But when a cap of blond appeared, he was the one who yelped, "I see the head!" Excitement rushed through his body. "Push . . . once more . . . come on, Lin . . . one more big one . . . "

With the next contraction the child came into his big callused hands in a squirming, slithering, slippery mass of warmth. At the sound of the child's lusty yowling, Theodore smiled as wide as a man can smile. He wanted to tell Linnea what it was, but couldn't see through his tears. He shrugged and cleared his eyes against his shoulders.

"It's a boy!" he rejoiced, and laid the wriggling bundle on Linnea's stomach.

"A boy," she repeated.

"With a little pink acorn." She chuckled tiredly and managed to lift her head. But it fell back weakly and her fingertips searched for the child's head.

By some miracle, Theodore had grown as calm as the eye of a tornado. It seemed he'd never in his life been so efficient as he tied the two pieces of string around the umbilical cord and severed it.

"There. He's on his own now."

Linnea laughed, but he could tell she was crying. He lifted the infant and stuck a finger into his mouth, to clear it of mucous.

"He's sucking already," he told Linnea, thrilled at the feel of the delicate tongue drawing on his little finger.

"Does he have all his fingers and toes?" she asked.

"Every one of 'em, but they're no bigger'n a sparrow's bones."

"Hurry, Teddy," she said weakly.

Forcing the afterbirth from her body hurt him as much as it hurt her, he was sure. Her stomach was soft and pliable as he pressed upon it with both palms. Once more he promised himself never to put her through this again. If they could take turns, he'd go through it. But not her. Not his precious Linnea.

It was the first time he'd ever given a baby a bath. Mercy, how could a human being be so tiny yet so perfect? Fingernails and eyelids so fragile he could see right through them. Legs so spindly he was afraid to straighten them out to dry behind the tiny knees. Eyelashes so fine they were scarcely visible.

He wrapped his son in a clean flannel blanket and placed him in Linnea's arms.

"Here he is, love. He's a tiny one."

"John," she cooed softly, in welcome. "Why, hello there, John."

Theodore smiled at the sight of her lips on the baby's downy head.

"He even looks a little like our John, doesn't he?"

He didn't of course. He had the look of all newborn babies: wrinkled, red, and pinched.

But Linnea agreed, anyway. "He does."

"And I think I see a little of Ma around his mouth."

His mouth was nothing whatever like Nissa's, but again Linnea agreed.

Theodore settled beside her, the two of them gazing at the miracle their love had created. Born into a family who had lost so many, he embodied the hope of new life. Born to a man who'd thought himself too old, he would bring renewed youth. Born to a woman who thought herself too young, he would bring about a glowing maturity. Conceived in a time of war, he brought with him a sense of peace.

Theodore nudged the baby's hand with his little finger and thrilled when his son's tiny fist closed around it.

"I wish they could see him," he said.

Linnea touched Theodore's hand, so big and powerful compared to the baby's fragile grasp. She looked up into his eyes.

"I think they do, Teddy," she whispered.

"And Kristian," Theodore said, hopefully. "Kristian's gonna love him, isn't he?"

Linnea nodded, her eyes locked with Theodore's, suddenly knowing in her heart that what they said was true. "Kristian's going to love him."

He kissed her temple, his lips lingering.

"I love you."

She smiled and knew a deep sense of fulfillment. "I love you, too. Always."

They listened to the prairie wind worrying the windows. And the sound of their son, suckling nothing. John's cat slipped around the doorway and stood looking curiously at the three. With a soft, throaty sound, it leaped to the foot of the bed, circled twice, and settled down to sleep on Nissa's old quilt.

The cantankerous wheat farmer who'd greeted the new schoolmarm at the station so gruffly the first time she'd appeared sat with his arm cradling her head. He wondered if it was possible to make her understand how much he loved her.

"I lied before. I *was* scared," he confessed.

"I could tell."

"Seeing you like that, in so much pain—" He kissed her forehead. "It was awful. I'll never put you through that again."

"Yes, you will."

"No, I won't."

"I think you will."

"Never. So help me God, never. I love you too much . . . "

She chuckled and brushed her fingers over the fine hair on John's head. "I want a girl next time, and we'll name her Rosie."

"A girl . . . but—"

"Shh. Come. Lie down with us." With the baby in the crook of her elbow, she moved over and made room for him. He stretched out on top of the quilt and rolled to his side, folding an elbow beneath his ear and stretching a protective arm across the baby to Linnea's hip.

Outside, somewhere on the prairie, the horses ran free. And Russian thistles rolled before the wind. And upon the derrick of a windmill the dry, tan husks of last summer's morning glories still clung while the blades rapped softly above. But inside, a man and wife lay close, watching their son sleep, thinking of their tomorrows and the blessings to be reaped, the life to be lived to its fullest . . . the minutes, the days, the years.